DATE			

JUN   1995

BAKER & TAYLOR

S0-AIF-002

GRAILS

Visitations of the Night

Edited by Richard Gilliam,
Martin H. Greenberg, and
Edward E. Kramer

A ROC BOOK

ROC
Published by the Penguin Group
Penguin Books USA Inc., 375 Hudson Street, New York, New York 10014, U.S.A.
Penguin Books Ltd, 27 Wrights Lane, London W8 5TZ, England
Penguin Books Australia Ltd, Ringwood, Victoria, Australia
Penguin Books Canada Ltd, 10 Alcorn Avenue,
Toronto, Ontario, Canada M4V 3B2
Penguin Books (N.Z.) Ltd, 182-190 Wairau Road,
Auckland 10, New Zealand

Penguin Books Ltd, Registered Offices: Harmondsworth, Middlesex, England

Published by Roc, an imprint of Dutton Signet, a division of Penguin Books USA Inc.
Portions of this book first appeared as *Grails: Quests, Visitations and Other Occurrences,* published in a limited edition by Unnameable Press.

First Roc Printing, August, 1994

10 9 8 7 6 5 4 3 2 1

(The following page constitutes a continuation of this copyright page.)

LIBRARY OF CONGRESS CATALOGING IN PUBLICATION DATA:
Grails : visitations of the night / edited by Richard Gilliam, Martin H. Greenberg, and
  Edward E. Kramer.
    p.   cm.
  ISBN 0-451-45304-2
  1. Grail—Romances—Adaptations. 2. Fantastic fiction, American. 3. Quests—
  Fiction. I. Gilliam, Richard. II. Greenberg, Martin Harry. III. Kramer, Edward E.
  PS509.G68G74 1994
  813'.0876608—dc20   93-43764
                                                                          CIP

Printed in the United States of America

This book is dedicated to Fritz Leiber,
whose literary works have inspired us all.

The editors would like to thank Susan Barrows,
Paul Cashman, Robert A. Costner, Pamela Lloyd, Susan Phillips,
Ellenina Riley, Jame A. Riley, Elizabeth A. Saunders,
Lamar Waldron, and Caran Wilbanks for their assistance
in preparing the manuscripts for this tome.

Contents

—— ✠ ——

An Introduction

———— ✠ ————

Brian M. Thomsen

My first exposure to the Grail myths came from a comic book.

Having been a fan of the *Prince Valiant* comic strip in the Sunday funnies, and the Walt Disney feature *The Sword in the Stone,* I quickly became acquisitive of all things Arthurian, die-cast metal knights, castle play sets, and such. Since kindergarten age is a bit too young for the T. H. White or Pyle (let alone Malory and Geoffrey of Monmouth), I quickly settled for a somewhat less demanding format, namely the Classics Illustrated comic book of *The Knights of the Round Table.* See Arthur pull the sword out of the stone, see the knight in red fight the knight in black, see old man Merlin. It was all there in words (in white balloons) and pictures. As much of the story as any kid could want.

One of the images that still stands out in my mind featured three knights kneeling in front of an altar that resembled a mini Saint Patrick's cathedral, while two angels joined them in prayer floating in midair (they were depicted in outline only with light blue shading, which I later learned meant, in comic lingo, that they were invisible). Suspended in midair between the angels and the knights was a punch bowl-like object (shaded in blue like the angels) with a cross engraved on its base. Whether the illustrator knew it or not, he had managed to capture several aspects of the mystery surrounding that object known as the Holy Grail.

- Was it an actual object (physical) or just a symbol (invisible)?

- Was it a cup/chalice or a dish/bowl?
- Were its origins Christian or some other?

Of course, not even I was precocious enough to raise these questions at that tender age. Yet this scene from a no longer available comic book captures the essence of the Grail legend as perceived by most Arthurian fans.

The Holy Grail, as succinctly put by *The Oxford Companion to English Literature* (5th edition), was a symbol of perfection sought by the Knights of the Round Table. As the tales were related by Thomas Malory in their most popular form in the fifteenth century, the Grail became more specifically identified as the cup/chalice used by Christ at the Last Supper, in which Joseph of Arimathea later caught his blood at the Crucifixion, thus symbolizing the transubstantiation believed to take place during the Christian sacrament of the Holy Eucharist. Though all of the knights go forth from Camelot in search of this holy cup, only four achieve the personal knowledge that their quest was not in vain. The Grail is tracked to the castle Corbenic, where three of the knights are invited into a chapel and are allowed to look upon the cup. It transforms into a vision of Christ, who administers the sacrament of Eucharist to them. The purest of the three, Galahad (believed to be the illegitimate son of Lancelot), is immediately consumed in rapture and dies in ecstasy supposedly ascending into heaven. Perceval survives, leaves the chapel, and enters a monastery where he dies two months later (possibly having repented of his mortal sins enough to join Galahad in heaven). Bors, the third, also survives, remains a pure and holy man for the rest of his life, but also returns to Camelot, to tell the fates of Galahad and Perceval so that others may learn from the successful outcome of their quest. The fourth knight who completes the quest is Lancelot, who had already undergone penance of both a physical and spiritual manner en route to the chapel. Though his ordeal has indeed distinguished him as one of the purest of the knights, he is nonetheless barred from entering the chapel and actually looking upon the Grail due to his adulterous love toward Queen Guinevere. Like Moses before him, he is denied entrance to the promised land, though allowed to witness proof of its existence. Lancelot, too, returns to Camelot, and life goes on as before. Case closed ... well, not quite.

Though Malory's version makes for good storytelling it also raises several questions. What happened to the Grail after the quest? Why didn't anyone go after it before then? How did all of these knights become so, how shall I say, Christian, given their less than churchly backgrounds? Malory obviously distilled preexistent myths and legends in his version in such a way that it struck a common chord with the people of his time; R. S. Loomis backs this up, noting that despite the long history of the Grail, the principal versions of the legend were written within a period of fifty years, which includes such seminal texts as those by Chertien de Troyes (1180), von Eschenbach (1205), and Gerbert (1230). But, what were his (and the others') sources? Moreover, does the Holy Grail merely act as the chalice used for a commemorative celebration of the sacrament of Holy Eucharist, or does it possess restorative power of immortality on either the earthbound plane (as in *Indiana Jones and the Last Crusade*) or on the symbolic celestial plane. The "simple story" thus leads to even more complex questions.

Baigent, Leigh, and Lincoln in their marvelous work of nonfiction *Holy Blood, Holy Grail* sum up the problem in the question—"Why should something of such intense relevance and immediacy to Christendom remain buried for as long as it apparently did?" It is perhaps not a coincidence that it resurfaced in "folklore" at the height of the Crusades, which they further describe as "when the Frankish kingdom of Jerusalem was in its full glory, when the Templars were on the apex of their power, when the Cathar heresy was gaining a momentum that threatened to displace the creed and canon of Rome itself."

Their research led them back to the seasonal pagan rituals of rebirth, as connected to the timings of the planting and harvesting. This subject of rebirth and fertility is further played out in the *Maginogion,* a compilation of Welsh legends, which preceded the Grail Renaissance ever so slightly. These mythos included a mysterious cauldron of rebirth in which dead warriors, thrown in at nightfall, are resurrected the following morning in a mild variation of the Norse afterlife myth of Valhalla. Baigent further noted that "this cauldron is often associated with a giant hero name Brana . . . (who) also possessed a platter, and whatever food one wished thereon was instantly obtained—a property also sometimes ascribed to the Grail."

It would thus appear that the Grail Renaissance (pertaining to the Christian tradition) was a direct result of the incorporation of popular pagan ritual and myth, with the mythic Arthurian historical tradition, and the Christian symbolism to co-opt the symbol to further the cause of Rome's crusades and holy wars. That, of course, led to an all-encompassing legend with many contradictions in an effort to bring it all under one universal church. It has even been suggested that the very name of the Holy Grail is derived from the Latin *San Grael,* which loosely translated means sacred dish/bowl. A simple error (intentional or otherwise) by some scribe often resulted in it being written as *Sang real*, whose translation is royal blood, thus leaving yet another avenue available to be co-opted by the papal politicians of Rome. In simplistic terms, if the sacred cup/dish really existed as an object/relic in the physical world, it was Christendom's heaven-directed duty to protect it and restore it to the rightful hands as part of the crusading forces of the holy land. In terms of political history, the Holy Grail seems to emerge as a medieval equivalent of Sam Houston's "Remember the Alamo," FDR's Pearl Harbor speech, and the justifications of Reagan and Bush administrations for their military raids on Grenada, Panama, the Persian Gulf, and the Central American drug lords. Thus the final result of this co-option of Christian legend/religion, pagan fertility/horn-of-plenty symbolism, and Celtic tales with origins in the Irish, transmitted through the Welsh and Breton, is, indeed, an amalgam that was so eloquently described by T. S. Eliot in his masterwork "The Wasteland" as a "heap of broken images" to be used as a rally cry for the Crusades.

Yet, despite the confusion of its origins or the practical rationale behind its popularization, we are left with the thematic concept from which the most popular of all fantasy subgenres has come to fruition—The Quest.

Drawing from the basics of Malory and his predecessors, we

have seen such Arthurian masterworks as "The Idylls of the King" by Tennyson, the numerous versions of *Parzival,* and such (not to forget such memorable cinematic works as John Boorman's *Excalibur*), numerous satiric twists on the tradition as in Thomas Berger's *Arthur Rex,* Mark Twain's *A Connecticut Yankee in King Arthur's Court,* and, of course, *Monty Python and the Holy Grail,* and even in scenarios set in the future as in DC Comic's *Camelot 3000* (which pioneered the maxiseries/graphic novel form in the United States). This is not to say that all works dealing with the mythos are successful and grand because many are most definitely not (some even deserve the label of "boring"), and yet such fertile ground continues to yield such rich harvests as *The Mists of Avalon* in literature, Rick Wakeman's *Myths and Legends of King Arthur and His Knights of the Round Table* in music, and Terry Gilliam's *The Fisher King* on the screen.

For those whose tastes don't run to the Arthurian, the Grail quest manifests itself in more subtle ways. Perhaps in Luke Skywalker's pursuit of the Force as a Jedi Knight, Dorothy's quest for home in *The Wizard of Oz,* or in any fancy-named talisman that is the evening's goal for a friendly role-playing game scenario. Almost any substitute will do. Preparation, quest, discovery. A simple formula.

A Grail.

A plate.

A dish.

The Holy Chalice.

Or a simple goal.

The choice is yours.

And the tradition is grand.

Exalted Hearts

—— ✠ ——

Tanith Lee

I found the Grail. It was in a tower of gold, beyond a wall of bone . . . as they said. They do not lie. And the Cup itself? Yes, a single tear, now like blood and now like emerald and now like the sky of night with all the stars inside it.

But first, I must say how my search began.

It was a summer day, when the hermit came out of the eastern mountains, down to the plain, to the castle of the King. The hermit was an old man, clothed in abject rags, but round his head, the hair of which was like a tangled lion's mane, a faint light shone that could not be denied.

He struck his staff upon the painted floor, and silence sank on the great hall. We looked at him, astonished. For though we were young and he so old, yet he seemed stronger and more bright. And though the King was there, yet the hermit seemed more of a King than he.

"In the west," the hermit said, "a Cup stands on an altar in a golden tower. You know of it. From its brim the lips of God have tasted."

Then the silence tingled. The King sat with the wine bowl raised in his grip, waiting. And I, who sat at his right hand, stared at the hermit, wondering at him.

"Know now," he said, this old and shining and curiously horrible man, "the fabric of the worlds has parted. It may be possible for one to go in and find the Cup. To take it and bring it away, that ever after it will exalt the hearts of men. Who then will dare it?"

Up from their chairs the knights leapt, bold and loud. "I! I will dare!"

A challenge in the hall of our King was never to be avoided. It was our honour. And I rose with the rest, but more quietly. I could not have said why.

"And will you go too, my friend and brother?" asked the King softly.

"In your place, my liege," I said. "For seeing you are the King, you may not."

"Ah, but how I wish it otherwise," he said. His head bowed as if the jewelled crown bore him under like a cross.

Inside three days, vast preparations had been made. Not all the King's knights were permitted to depart. Only the chaste, those who had never known a woman, those abstemious in food and wine, those who were valorous, their swords sharpened and their muscles hard. And of that number I was. Yes, even to chastity, for though I had been betrothed, she and I were true. Our lips and hands had touched, and no more than that.

I went to her in the sunset of the third day. The rosy glow hung low upon the orchard, and she walked there in her pale summer gown, her gold hair flowing like a stream of light off from her fair face, round her shoulders, to her narrow waist. If I had not done more than touch her mouth or fingers, that too was my strength, for she was beautiful.

"My love. I must be gone with the dawn."

"I know it."

"And I must ask you, will you wait for me? This road may be long, arduous and cruel."

"Yes, I will wait, my knight. My soul is in your heart."

"And mine in yours," I said.

She wept, and her tears were sweet to me, for by her pain I saw her love—God knew, I had had no other proof.

I gave her a ring of gold set with a square blue gem. It lay on her white hand like a flower.

"I will return to you, and you will be my wife."

"I know it, too."

We kissed and parted, and the sun went down.

At sunrise thirty-one knights of the King's court rode out of his castle on the plain, and turned their horses' heads towards the west that was yet dark and closed with night.

The land went up and down, ran out in bridges over the shallow rivers of the summer, and into the gorges that had been greater rivers in the time before man. The hills came, and the woods, and one by one the days and nights fled over us like clouds and were gone. And one by one we separated from each other. What a company we had been, the young men in their burnished mail, the pennons of scarlet and yellow and mauve fluttering behind like tongues of flame, the glinting swords and faces of clear eyes. We went away by our differing paths, into the west, and were gone from each other, and from the country of our King. And I from her, and all that I knew on earth.

Tales are told of such a quest, of the adventures that attend it and the perils that hunt it down. But there were no mighty deeds or terrors that befell me, though of others I heard things now and then, and some I learned met their deaths along the way. It is a fact I was challenged at this and that place, fought knights mounted and on foot, brought them low, and made on. In certain areas, as a representative of a king, I settled disputes. I saved from burning women that some fools had judged witches, or saw men hanged who had preyed upon their fellows.

I slept by night in ruined chapels, under tall hills, beneath the eaves of forests; or else in byres, in rich lords' halls. And now and then I was tempted by women in coarse and dirty smocks, or fine silk. But I turned from them. There was only one woman I had wanted, and I had never taken her. They were easy enough to resist.

When winter came, I kept on. Through the huge drifts of snow, over the frozen lakes that were like roads of glass. The woods were bones and crows beat in their rib cages like black hearts. More than one winter came and went, as had more than one summer. They were all alike, as the villages were like each other: the squat churches, and the carven halls.

I understood the way. It was only to go on. For if the fabric of existence had been allowed to part, and two worlds touched, Heaven and earth, a breach might be made anywhere, as God willed it. Only to the west we must progress, onward, onward, as the sun did every day. The west which, at sunset, stained itself with blood and with the green of emerald, and in which the stars came out at last.

It might be I should not find my goal.

So much too I comprehended.

I was humble, patient. Yet, was I not sure? As if I rode upon the wings of some elemental thing, the horse still under me, I felt myself borne forward, to meet a sorcerer's lodestone.

And the land flowed by, the hills and high mountains, and sometimes the sea, glimpsed white-blue in the cold, and purple-green in the months of the sun. There were cities, also, with strange clockworks, and walls fenced up with towers. And at these I glanced, thinking of the walls of bone, and the tower of gold, where it stood upon the altar—the Grail.

By night I dreamed of it. I dreamed I came and put my hand upon it. Sometimes it burned and again it might be icy. Or it changed to water and slipped away, or into a snake and wrapped about my arm and stared into my eyes. But I knew I would see it. And in the days I dreamed of it too, more and more, and it seemed to me that the more often the Grail was there before my inner vision, the more certain I should be to come to it. As if—God forgive my blasphemy—I gradually and carefully fashioned it myself, out of the air.

Then there was an Easter-tide, and when I beheld the children playing in the house, I thought of sons and daughters. And that night I dreamed, in the soft bed, of the children a young knight should have with his young wife. The boys were valiant and the girls were lovely. But at midnight I woke, as if to the tolling of a bell.

I rose then, and clad myself, and left the house. I rode away along the rim of a wide hill.

At length the moon swam up, and by her virgin's lamp, I saw below a desolate and barren valley. Nothing grew there, not a tree nor a bush, and perhaps not a blade of grass. The rocks thrust out of the parched soil and cast down their shadows from the silver light. I stared at this place, and dismounted. I sat beneath a crippled thorn, my sword across my knees. There was no sound beyond the purr of the wind. The night was chill, and open as a door to other things.

Nearby the horse chewed at the turf on the hillside. He was not the beast I had known before, and I looked at him in a curious surprise, for in that moment I had forgotten. My body ached, and my eyes scorched. I wanted to rest, and yet a cool excitement played in me. Eventually I slept.

And when I woke, the moon was down, but I did not need her light. There in the valley, which was bare as a desert, something blazed now. I knew at once. The white wall that encircled it, and inside the single slender tower, like a golden needle with, high in its topmost point, a window like a fiery star.

I went down into the waste, and crossed it stiffly, sword drawn, yet nothing came at me, to hinder or harm. It required an age to go over the space and yet it was quickly done. The awful gate arose, but without a challenge or a cry, it drew back its two stern leaves.

Into the court I stepped, and up the straight white stair, and so into the golden tower.

What wonders did I see? I saw none. No angels and no demons, nothing. It was as if they had gone away in pity, to let me pass in peace. The inner stair was crystal, and this I climbed haltingly, shivering, and reaching the golden door, I stretched out with the hilt of my sword to knock. And the door opened, and there the chamber was, all sunned with radiance as of a thousand candles, though none burned there.

On a slab of stone draped in snow white, it stood. Yes, a single tear, now like blood and now like emerald and now like the starry night.

I hesitated a while, and then I went to it, and lifted it from the altar without a qualm. No lightning struck, no peal of thunder dashed from Heaven. I wrapped the Grail, the desire of all men, inside my worn cloak, and carried it away.

On the hill I glanced back, and saw the tower of gold was gone. The valley was verdant and simple, with sheep grazing under the trees. Through two worlds I had passed, and the Cup with me. It was done.

It was a slow, sore journey home, and I had been so long on my road, I had mislaid the way. But, I was a traveller now, and it was all one to me. Did I yearn for the known land, the castle on the plain, the gardens and the court? They were dreams, I yearned for them. But idly. I had grown used to loss.

When I reached my King's country, I noticed a difference. The people were poor and slovenly, resentful and unkind. Several great houses had tumbled, while from others I was sent off by dogs.

I rode down to the castle of my King in a deepening twilight, and even so, beheld few lamps alight, and all the garden plots were run to seed, like the fields I had ridden through. Above, the banners blew, blots on the dusk.

They were courteous, seeing my colours, and let me in. An ancient servant took me to the hall, and I entered there.

Around the tables were many empty seats, each with a folded pennant over it. In their chairs sat the remaining knights, and none of them I knew, not one, for they were ancient men all, sunk in at cheek and chest like rotted trees. And on his gilded throne a king still was, but he too was old and white-haired, and he toyed with a little wooden doll and giggled, so the servant must go to him and entreat him to look up at me.

"What do you want, you ancient knight?" the old King asked of me.

"Liege, I have searched these many, many years, and brought home to you the Cup of Love. The Grail."

Then they murmured, and even into his muddy eyes there swelled a sort of gleam. But it faded.

"Well, show me then."

So I showed the Grail.

For a moment, there in that ill-lit, cobweb hall, it shone and flamed, blood emerald starry-dark. But then it dimmed, and was only a thing of jewels and shape; yet this I set before the King.

He reached out and, from the sacred brim, he gave his doll an imaginary drink.

Later, I sought my lady in the broken gardens, and under the apple trees which had died, she met me. She gazed at me askance, finding how I had aged, so lank and lean and grey. She too was wizened and her beauty was all gone, like her golden hair, but on her withered hand the blue ring still perched, a drop of summer water on a dying leaf.

"I have been a long while," I said.

"I know it."

"But I will wed you now."

"No," she said, "we will not marry. For my dreams of children are all dead, and besides I should not please you."

Then I bowed my head and tears fell from my eyes, into the grass and thistles, as her tears had fallen at our former parting. But she was old and half blind, and did not see them.

During the days which followed, the King's antique cranky men decreed that a magical cup must be hidden in a golden casket, inside a tower of stone, and this sealed with iron and bronze, and a great wall built up, guarded by mastiffs. This, to keep all safe. Therefore barely any remember now that such a treasure is with us, and only a handful know that it was I who strove, and completed the quest. I do not have a care for that, or for anything.

In this way I sought and found the Grail, which exalts the hearts of men.

One Paris Night

——— ✠ ———

Karl Edward Wagner

"I can't understand how you came to be shot *there.*"

Adrian Becker was in a foul mood. He paced about the rubble of the shelled cathedral. In the distance they could hear the Prussian shells hammering Paris.

"What's so odd about being shot in a sporting house?" Sir Stanley examined the dressing.

"I meant being shot in the arse!" Becker had performed the attendant surgery and applied the dressing himself. While he had some medical education, he had gained extensive practical experience while riding with Quantrill during the recent American Civil War.

"I imagine it was the first target the Communard saw," Sir Stanley argued. "You saw how they burst in upon us. Paris is in chaos. There is no respect for any institution."

"You should have guarded your backside." Becker retained the Prussian zeal for order, despite the fact his former fellow uhlan lancers would now shoot him on sight.

"Well, it was her backside I had in mind just then, old man," Sir Stanley pointed out. He had found most of a cigar in his coat, and he lit it from their lamp. Despite the risk, Becker had demanded proper light to dress the bullet wound. "Furthermore, one doesn't expect a husband or angry suitor to make an outraged entrance into a whore's bedroom."

"Why then did he shoot you?"

"He shouted that I had devoured his sister." Sir Stanley sucked on the bedraggled cigar.

"He said what?"

"Well, my French isn't all that good, and he was in a state. But I believe that that was what he said, before I shot him dead."

Becker observed Sir Stanley with suspicion. "Well. Had you?"

Sir Stanley was affronted. "Well, certainly not. It's the Parisians who have resorted to cannibalism during the siege, not us. P'raps I didn't fully understand him. You should understand: One instant I was furiously at work on Mimi or whatever her name was; the next, a crazy Frenchman kicks in the door and begins shooting his revolver at me. Yes, and another thing I recall. He called me Bertrand."

"So, then. A quarrel of some sort. The wrong room. The wrong man. Now we are caught between the Communards and the Prussians. This is not good."

Colonel Adrian Becker, late of the Army of the Confederacy under General Quantrill, had found it expedient to leave the Confederate States of America shortly after the truce was declared in 1868. Born during the tumult of an emerging Germany to a Bavarian countess and a Prussian officer, Becker had returned to his fatherland to join a Prussian uhlan regiment. His experience had taught him the suicidal futility of cavalry charges against Gatling guns—in this case, mitrailleuses. As the siege of Paris reached its inevitable bloody conclusion this May of 1870, Becker looted the regimental treasury while the rest were looting Paris.

In the process Becker had freed Sir Stanley Sutton, supposedly of the something Lancers and a British observer. While none of the above credentials could stand the test of evidence, it was proved that Sutton was a spy of some sort, and he was awaiting the firing squad when Becker killed his guards. Becker had known him as British liaison to Quantrill's Army of the West near the close of that war. Becker also knew him as a ready adventurer and an expert killer, and Becker needed help robbing the regimental treasury.

A stray shell—French or Prussian, Becker never decided—had blasted their wagon and its concealed treasure. With whatever gold they had earlier pocketed, the two had crept into the wreckage of

Paris. In civilian clothes and with enough gold to buy anything they couldn't steal, or bribe anyone they couldn't kill, Becker reckoned they could blend into the chaos of looting and destruction until time to slip away to England. Becker had seen towns sacked from Lawrence to the burning of Washington, and he knew how to blend.

Then a crazy Frenchman had shot Sir Stanley in the arse while they were enjoying themselves in a sporting house. Sutton couldn't sit a horse or walk a dozen steps. Becker was a ruthless killer, but he wouldn't leave a comrade. They needed a carriage or wagon, and instead they were hiding out in a shelled-out cathedral in a Paris that was in its death throes.

Becker wondered which side would try to kill them first. He wasn't even sure how many sides there now were, at work at the slaughter. The cathedral was ringed with the bodies of priests and nuns shot down by the Communards before the shells had struck.

"What's that howling?" Becker peered through the ruins of an eleventh-century window.

"That's a dog, Adrian." Becker had given Sutton a bottle of brandy he'd found in the rubble. Sutton was killing his pain with liberal swallows.

"No. It's a wolf." Becker had lived in the Harz Mountains as a child.

"Wolf or dog, it's more likely to be the wind. The Communards have eaten even the zoo animals. Have you priced rat meat?"

"And I say that it is a wolf. I know that sound."

Adrian Becker was in his late twenties, but years of war on two continents had aged him, as surely as the saber cut that faintly scarred his left forehead. He was tall—just over six feet—and had the broad-shouldered, hard-muscled swagger of a cavalryman. His face was handsome enough to the ladies, although just now his blond hair and goatee were unkempt. His eyes were of a blue-grey shade, and their full stare was unnerving. He had been trained in martial skills since a child in 1848, after his parents had fled the failed revolution. Sutton had seen Becker draw, but he could never see the movement of his left hand between the instant of deciding to kill and the impact of his bullets.

"Why did he call you Bertrand?" Becker had drawn one of his pair of .36 Colt Navy revolvers and was wishing for a Henry rifle.

"Who knows? All cats are grey in the dark."

Sutton had readjusted his clothing and was feeling quite a bit better, thanks mostly to the brandy. At least he'd had the presence of mind to snatch up his clothing as they'd fled. While the wound had bled profusely, his trousers, clutched under one arm, had been spared. The cathedral had been close by, and, with Becker supporting him, they had reached its cover just as the shelling resumed. Sutton doubted anyone would have pursued them in the ensuing chaos.

Sir Stanley Sutton, as he styled himself, was half a foot shorter than Becker and rather leaner. He had a polished military bearing that came of being drummed out of several crack regiments, and an easy aristocratic air that came of being born into a noble house whose name he had agreed never to disgrace by claiming it as his own. He had wavy brown hair, a bristling beard, innocent hazel eyes, and a brooding romantic face that the ladies would swoon for. His skill with pistol and sword had kept him alive thus far in his twenty-some years, although luck had helped a great deal. Which was why, instead of having faced a firing squad, Sir Stanley Sutton was merely holed up in the rubble of a Paris cathedral with Colonel Adrian Becker, a bullet hole in his bum, shells falling all about, with the certainty that either side would happily shoot down the both of them.

Becker fired his pistol twice. Sutton drew his Adams double-action revolver and strained to see what his friend was shooting at. Knowing Becker, it was either dead or dying.

"Where are they?" Sutton whispered, seeing nothing.

"There was something by the break in the wall there," Becker said. "I could not have missed. The full moon backlighted him."

"How many?"

"Just the one, I think. He did not fall."

"Use my fifty-four bore," Sutton suggested, holding out his Adams revolver. "More stopping power."

"Same bullet as the American .44 calibre," Becker said. "I think the .36 ball is more accurate."

"All right then, Adrian. Where's your Communard?"

"I'll just go finish him."

Becker stepped carefully over the rubble, pistol cocked, and leaving Sutton a line of fire. There had been something wrong with that silhouette. The man had crouched like an ape, then had sprung away when shot, as though he were unhit. Becker was certain of his aim.

A shell screamed through the night. Becker flung himself head-long beneath a pew. The cathedral foundations shook, hunks of debris pelted through the breached wall, dust and slabs of plaster scattered across the pew. Almost deafened by the near hit, Becker barely heard the scream of the next shell in time to burrow deeper beneath the pew. This shell struck cleanly through the Norman Gothic arches and exploded somewhere about the altar.

Large things fell upon Becker's scant shelter. One of them wore many petticoats and smelled of gardenia perfume.

Becker wiped away dust and petticoats from his face, still holding his pistol which he had somehow managed not to fire. The next shell struck some distance away. Stunned by the concussion, Becker became vaguely aware that he was being held by an equally dazed woman who had parted from her outer dress at some point. She was a lovely mass of lace and stockings and corset, and she was clinging to him fiercely. For an instant, Becker wondered whether she might be an angel, dragging him to Heaven. However, this seemed an unlikely destination for him, and no angel would wear a whore's perfume. Besides, he recognized the face beneath the grit and tousled black hair.

"Jacqueline?"

"Oh, Adrian!" She clung to him with far more ardor than she had shown him earlier that night. "It is horrible out there! I followed you when you two fled. There was much blood!"

Becker lowered the hammer on his Colt. He struggled upward, dragging both of them to their feet. His ears rang, and his head throbbed. From the shudders beneath his feet, he sensed that the shelling was moving away—for now.

"You should have taken refuge in the cellars." Becker was trying to ascertain Sir Stanley's earthly presence. The lantern had somehow remained intact and alight. Something was stirring amidst the debris.

"Bertrand was hiding there!" Jacqueline hissed.

"Lucky for him," Becker said. He led Jacqueline over to where Sutton was cursing, and he pulled away some wainscoting that had probably been in place for five centuries until a minute ago. The Englishman was unhappy but unhurt. He thanked Becker with scant courtesy, then favored Jacqueline with a begrimed smile.

Jacqueline pressed back against Becker. "It is not Bertrand! But with his beard he *looks* like Bertrand!"

"*Sehr Gut,*" said Becker, still stunned and struggling with his English. "At least we have one thing here tonight settled. This Bertrand. Who is he that someone shoots my friend by mistake?"

Jacqueline's eyes widened. "Bertrand is a . . . *loup-garou!*"

"I . . . I believe she means werewolf," Sir Stanley supplied.

"Is there any of that brandy left?" Becker asked.

Sir Stanley surrendered the bottle. "This is a lot of rot."

Becker took a swallow, handed the bottle to Jacqueline. "I told you I heard a wolf. I was a child in the Harz Mountains. I do not miss when I shoot a man."

Jacqueline coughed a bit after her liberal swallow. Sir Stanley gallantly arose and presented her with his coat. Becker was mumbling to himself in German, watching the openings in the walls.

Finally he said: "Yes. I know what a werewolf is."

"Come on, old man!" Sutton suspected shell-shock. "This *is* the nineteenth century, after all."

"Adrian is correct!" Jacqueline interceded. "I have seen this thing! He killed Yvonne! Bit her through the throat! Chewed her flesh horribly! He was Bertrand when he entered her room, but when we broke down the door, it was a wolf that leapt from her window!"

"A wolf escaped from the zoo," Sir Stanley explained. "It was famished and lucky not to have been eaten itself by the Communards." He put his arm around Jacqueline, purely to reassure her.

"How did you find us?" Becker asked suddenly. He was recovering from the shell blast.

"I saw in which direction you had fled. Then I followed the trail of blood. The moon is quite bright."

From outside the cathedral echoed a long bestial howl. A shell hit in the near distance, muffling the cry.

Becker searched his pockets. "Who has silver?" He found a few gold coins and some copper.

"Afraid I'd paid Mimi in advance," Sutton apologized.

Jacqueline had obviously fled in haste. "A cross?" Becker asked her. "Some rings?" But she only shook her head and pressed closer to Sir Stanley.

"We must have silver to kill the werewolf." Becker looked all about. "Perhaps a crucifix from the altar?"

"You won't find as much as a biscuit," Sutton said. "This cathedral was thoroughly looted while the Communards were at work butchering everyone from Mother Superior to altar boy."

Becker peered through the broken wall carefully. "Well, we'll have to look for silver. I can't say how long Bertrand will be content with the nun."

"What?" Sir Stanley joined him at the breach.

The full moon glared down upon the churchyard beyond. Tombstones and funeral monuments shone white and shattered like a scatter of broken teeth. The corpses of the executed clergy lay in windows. Something was moving upon the body of one nun.

Sutton's first thought was of a man in a fur coat. Then he saw that, while it was male, it wasn't a man. It was a man-shaped creature, covered in dark fur. Its face was the muzzle of a beast. The nun's habit had been ripped apart, her legs outflung. As the creature hunched obscenely between her thighs, its wolfish muzzle gnawed at her dead breasts.

Sutton turned away, stunned for once in his checkered career.

"It is Bertrand," Jacqueline said.

"Don't look!" Sir Stanley pulled her away.

"She is a whore in a city gone mad," said Becker. "What now can shock her? But why has nothing been done to destroy this Bertrand?"

"We only recently suspected." Jacqueline was in a near faint.

"With all this killing, the riots . . . How easy to hide his crimes amongst so many!"

"Shoot the thing, man!" Sutton relinquished the collapsing girl and drew his revolver.

"It will only return his attention to us." Becker pushed away the other man's gun. "We must have silver."

"And if we can't find silver?"

"Then we must hope that he will be content amidst the dead until daylight. Unfortunately the werewolf prefers the blood and flesh of the living, and you, my friend, have left a recent blood trail. I think that very soon he will come for us, and you are unable to run."

"Then I say give him a belly full of lead right now!"

"Sir Stanley, I tell you that I shot him. As you can see, there was no effect. Watch him now, while I search for silver."

"And what if he moves toward us?"

"Then you must shoot him and pray that I am wrong."

"What about fire?" Sutton wondered, watching the necrophilic feast with growing horror.

"Well, first you catch and skin him," Becker suggested. "I'll get a fire started to roast him over."

"Firebrands!" Jacqueline said. "Wild beasts fear fire."

"Werewolves are only part beast." Becker picked up the lamp. "And they move very fast."

Jacqueline gathered up her petticoats to follow him across the rubble. "You seem to be very well informed of the *loup-garou*. Have you bagged very many?"

"One is sufficient," said Becker, and she thought she saw him shiver. It was probably only the difficulty of walking over the rubble-strewn floor, as they approached the ruined altar.

Becker held high the lamp. "Look for a crucifix, a chalice, silver plate, anything the looters missed."

The shell had blasted the altar into hopeless debris, piercing the cathedral floor and disgorging the crypts beneath. The bones of crusaders and bishops were heaped together in shattered and moldering piles, like the wreckage of unstrung and rotted puppets. Broken swords and rusted armor lay amidst desiccated flesh and tatters of worm-eaten finery. The smell was of dust and mold—the stench barely noticeable against the greater stench of smoke, burnt powder and recent death that pervaded Paris this night.

"I can't bear this." Jacqueline shuddered and covered her face with her hands.

"Then hold this lamp." Becker thrust the lantern toward her, waited until she had it in her grasp, then carefully clambered down through the rubble into the exposed crypt. He had seen far worse too many times before, and the moldering skeletal remains of the centuries-dead held neither terror nor awe, so long as they didn't move.

"Here! Shine the light here, Jacqueline!"

The wreckage from the shelling made it impossible to be certain of anything—everywhere bones and fragments of rusted armor and rotted vestments—but Becker judged the crypts dated from the Crusades. There was a black chalice lying intact amidst the rubble, evidently dislodged from the crypt by the explosion. Becker recognized age-blackened silver, and he snatched it from the debris.

A skeletal hand clutched at its stem, refusing to relinquish its grasp. Becker swore as the chalice was pulled away from his fist. Drawing his bowie knife, he hacked frenziedly at the leathery knots of desiccated flesh and bone, prying the dead fingers one by one from their grip. Steel prevailed, and in a moment he was scrambling out of the crypt, carrying his prize.

"Now we must have a fire. Gather some of this wood, please. We must hurry, Jacqueline!"

"The beast has moved away into the shadow," Sir Stanley warned, as Becker busied himself with his kit. "I can't spot him!"

"Keep looking!" For his pistols, Becker carried percussion caps, a flask of black powder, a tin of grease, wadding, spare balls, a capping tool, and a bullet mold. While Jacqueline made a fire from the smashed woodwork, Becker quickly removed powder and ball from the cylinder of one Colt Navy revolver.

With his bowie knife he hacked the ancient silver chalice into chunks. Becker was pleased to see that it was indeed of silver, a plain chalice, obviously quite old. Becker had no time to appreciate its antiquity.

By the time the fire was going well, he had recovered a rusted scrap of a crusader's helmet from the crypt—sound enough to serve as a melting pot. Becker dropped in the mutilated chalice and waited for the silver to melt.

A wolf's howl reminded him of the need of urgency.

"Can you see him?" Becker fanned the coals.

"The clouds are across the moon," Sutton told him. "I can't see anything."

"Jacqueline." Becker pointed to some smashed paneling. "Make firebrands!"

"But can these kill the beast?"

"They might discourage him from further courses of his dinner."

Becker blew on the coals. Silver melted at almost three times the melting point of lead, but the fragments of the chalice were at last beginning to slump and mingle together. Looking about, he found sections of a medieval tapestry crushed beneath the rubble. Quickly he hacked away pieces with his knife to make padding for his hands.

Positioning his bullet mold, Becker clumsily gripped the glowing fragment of helmet, removed it from the fire and poured— trying not to spill much of the molten silver. Replacing the makeshift pot, he flicked the spilled pools of silver back into it, waiting for the mold to cool.

"Any sign of the beast?" Becker opened the mold. Three glinting balls of silver shook out.

"The moon is clear, but I can see nothing," Sutton called back.

"Perhaps Bertrand has eaten his fill," Jacqueline said.

"While the moon is full, nothing can sate his bloodlust." Becker poured again into the mold, then trimmed the flashing from the three .36 calibre bullets, cursing as the hot metal burnt his fingers. They must cool a bit more, or he'd risk their igniting the powder as he charged his pistol. Becker poured a little of the brandy over the hot balls. He opened the bullet mold and cracked loose another three bullets. There remained a good quantity of silver, but time was the essential matter now.

Becker now had six silver bullets. He decided to risk the first three and began to load his revolver, hoping that the wadding would protect the black powder from the hot metal.

The werewolf's growl was like that a mastiff might roar out, if he were the size of a bull.

Sir Stanley yelled out and fired pointblank, as the beast suddenly burst through a shattered window. The remnants of medieval glass tore at its hairy flesh, inflicting as little harm as did Sir Stanley's bullets.

It reared there for a moment amidst the debris, snarling at them—its wolfish muzzle showing carrion-smeared fangs. It was like a great hairy ape with a wolf's head—and yet, there was a red glow of depraved humanity in its eyes. It regarded its three victims, taking in their positions as a diner selects a slice of meat from a buffet, then rushed for Sir Stanley.

The heavy .44 calibre slugs from Sutton's Adams revolver staggered the creature momentarily, but they had no further effect. Unable to run, Sutton swore and flung the useless weapon at the charging beast.

Jacqueline ran toward him with a pair of firebrands.

Becker charged the chambers with powder and rammed home the silver bullets. He had learned well to reload quickly while riding with Quantrill, and the percussion caps were already in place on the revolver's cylinder.

Jacqueline threw herself between the werewolf and Sir Stanley—thrusting the blazing firebrands into its face.

Roaring more in rage than fear, the werewolf reeled back for an instant, striking away the firebrands with one taloned paw. Jacqueline spun away, just avoiding its claws. Sutton shoved her clear. The werewolf reached out for him.

"Bertrand!" Becker shouted.

As the creature turned at his shout, Adrian Becker shot him three times through the heart. There had not been time to load the other chambers. It wasn't necessary.

Putrid smoke boiled forth from the werewolf's chest as the silver bullets tore into him. Flame gushed from the wounds, suddenly setting his entire mass of flesh on fire. Bertrand howled hideously—his bestial roar rising into a human scream. Staggering backward, the creature lurched across the ruined cathedral, crimson flames eating through its flesh. Blackened bones were already poking forth from charred skin as it pitched backward like an obscene sacrifice into the crypt.

Becker and the others gazed down upon the creature. In a short time there was little more than ashes.

"I told you we must have silver," Becker said.

By daylight the shelling had stopped, and most of the fighting had moved to another quarter of Paris. Sir Stanley was still weak from loss of blood, but he insisted that he could walk with assistance. Becker thought they had best press on, before either the French or the Prussians restored order here.

As they passed through the churchyard, they met an aged priest. The tears on his face testified to his feelings upon viewing this scene of massacre and ruin. Nonetheless, he greeted them— then gazed curiously at Jacqueline's petticoats, exposed beneath Sutton's coat.

Sir Stanley noticed his look. Always the gentleman: "She was attacked by the Communards, Father. We were able to drive them away in time to spare her, and sought refuge here. As for me, my wound is nothing."

"Bless you, my children. Such bravery is rare in these terrible days." The old priest gestured toward the massacred victims, then wiped away tears.

"God has gathered these in. Stones may be restored. But here in the crypts of this ancient cathedral is said to be hidden the Holy Grail—the very cup from which Our Lord drank before his betrayal—a silver chalice won by the blood of the crusaders and kept here in secret throughout the centuries."

His age-worn face implored them. "Will you not help me search this ruin for it? Those who guarded its secret are all slain. Perhaps its power could bring an end to all this senseless slaughter."

Adrian Becker exchanged glances with Sir Stanley Sutton.

"Yes," said Becker. "To some of it, certainly."

Dogs Questing

———— ✠ ————

John Gregory Betancourt

By the time the last of the knights had padded in for evening conclave, a great central fire already burned bright and hot. A stag hung over the flames, and grease dripped onto the embers, sizzling and hissing away to nothing. The scent of roasting meat filled the air.

Jerek, the greatest warhound from Farthest Brittany, carved the meat himself that night, and between lapping ale and eating venison, the knights had their usual wild time.

At last, as talk wound down and the fire died to embers, a wise old bard rose, stretched, and moved forward with deliberate solemnity. All grew silent with respect.

"This is the time," the bard said slowly, "to hear the tale of Uthor's Sin and how we came to our great quest."

As all the knights settled into their usual places, the bard hunkered down and sketched a circle in the earth with one sharp nail.

"In the beginning there was only Man . . ."

In the beginning there was only Man (the bard said), and Man's dogs. Man owned home, and food, and fire. Peaceful days running the fields and flushing game for Man's pleasure, and dreamful nights on the hearth with bellies full and the snap-crackle warmth of fire at your back: this was a dog's life, and it was good.

Season blended into season, year following year, each moment a joy of motion and freedom. Then one day Uthor, who is also called Uthor the First, and sometimes Uthor the Snake, looked at

Man and said to himself, "My eyes are sharper than Man's eyes. My nose is keener than Man's nose. My claws are sharper than Man's claws. Why then must I serve him.?"

Uthor did not go into the fields with the other dogs the next morning. Instead, Uthor lay under bushes and peered out snakelike, watching Man as Man went about his duties. Thus Uthor learned the secret way in which Man created fire.

That night Uthor showed the other dogs the trick of fire, too. The young dogs marveled at his daring. The older ones shook their heads sadly.

At last the oldest and wisest dog came forward and said: "This is not our way, Uthor. You will anger Man, and we will all be punished. No more shall you steal from our master."

Uthor was filled with shame. The next day he went with the other dogs to the fields, and there they played in the sun and grass until Man summoned them back to his house for dinner.

So it went for several weeks. Yet a fierce urge to know all that Man knew continued to grow in Uthor, until he could no longer contain himself. Once more he strayed from the fields to spy on Man. Once more he learned one of Man's great secrets: how to make the winds blow at his command. Then remembering the words of the oldest and wisest dog, Uthor did not share his learning with the other dogs.

Over the following months Uthor managed to steal all of Man's secrets. Uthor practiced until he too could pull water from the depths of the Earth, and make the grass grow tall, and cause the sun to rise and set.

When he had learned all he thought there was to learn, Uthor went into the private chamber of Man, where dogs are forbidden, and rose up on his hind legs to look Man in the eye. Uthor said: "I know all that you know."

Man smiled and said, "What do you know, little dog?"

Uthor replied: "Dogs are Man's equal, and you keep us in slavery only to serve you." Then Uthor showed Man that he too could make fire, and bring water to the earth, and cause the sun to rise and set just as Man could.

If Man grew angry or afraid, he did not show it. Man merely

rose, patted Uthor upon the head, scratched once behind Uthor's ears, and gave a soft sigh. Throwing open the doors and windows of his house to all the beasts, Man strode from his ancient home and started down the long pebble path. At the gates of his land, Man paused to gaze around one last time. There were tears in his eyes.

"I guess you truly have no need for me," Man said. Then Man strode out into the world without a backward glance.

Uthor watched all this from a window in Man's house, alone for the first time, and very afraid. Uthor had not expected Man to leave. In his pride, he expected Man to embrace him, so that they could live together as equals.

When the other dogs returned from the fields that night, they found Uthor hiding under Man's bed. Of Man, there was no sign. The dogs dragged Uthor out and made him tell what had happened.

When Uthor finished his story, the other dogs gave howls of dismay and fell on Uthor in a great savage pack, ripping open Uthor's throat and laying bare Uthor's flesh to the bone. Perhaps they thought Man would forgive them if they punished Uthor. Perhaps the anger and fear and loneliness of that moment drove them mad for a time. Whatever, despite their howls and pleadings, despite their pitiful whimpers into the dark and empty night, and despite even Uthor's murder: none of it brought Man back.

Thus did Uthor, first and least of all dogs, die.

Thus was Man lost to the wilderness.

Thus do all dogs even now roam the world, in search of Man, in search of a home, in search of all that they have lost.

When the bard finished his tale, the knights all laid their heads upon their paws, sighed a sad sigh, and felt the pack's emptiness rise around them like a thing alive. They felt Uthor's sin in their hearts and their bones.

To a one, all vowed to continue the quest until Man was found and returned to his place. Then the fields would bloom again, and the breezes blow, and the sun rise up to drive darkness from the land in a frenzy of light.

Only with Man, they knew, would they be whole once more.

Sanctuary

—✠—

Lois Tilton

There were strange ships on the northern horizon.

Brother Caedwall stood up slowly from the worn boulder at the cliffside and strained to see through his faded blue eyes. Years ago they had begun to fail him, until he could no longer sit in the scriptorium to illuminate the pages with elaborate capitals in gold and bright-colored inks. But he could still make out shapes in the distance, as well as any man half his age.

Below him the gray-green sea surged, exploding into foam against the foot of the cliffs. The spray was cool and tasted of salt. Seabirds cried overhead—terns, gulls, gannets. There was no other sound. The monastery was isolated here, a place for prayer, study and meditation, a tranquil retreat from the world.

But approaching now—yes, they were ships. Long, swift-looking craft with powerful oars flashing as they drove through the waves. Brother Caedwall could just make out the square sails and high, curved prows, carved into the shape of fantastic beasts. A serpent. A dragon.

A fiery dragon, flying . . .

The old monk closed his eyes, remembering.

He had been young, a boy newly come to the monastery, a holy place whose former abbot Aidan was already revered as a saint. Where the old lay brother named Gunnar, who had certainly once been a slave, lay dying in his bed.

It was young Brother Caedwall's task to sit by Gunnar's side, to see to his needs, to spoon broth into his toothless mouth and pray for the salvation of his soul.

But the old man was restless and ill at ease. He tossed his head and knocked the spoon away, spilling the broth. He called constantly for *the cup, the cup,* but would not drink when Caedwall held it to his lips.

Weakly, the gnarled, age-spotted hand grasped his, clutched it desperately. "The cup," he wheezed. "In . . . chest, under . . . bed."

Caedwall knelt and reached beneath the pallet where Gunnar lay. He pulled out a wooden casket and handed it to the old man, helping him lift open the lid when his strength failed him.

Inside was an irregularly shaped object, wrapped in coarse cloth. Caedwall unwrapped it slowly, wondering, then stared in astonished disbelief.

It was a cup of pure untarnished silver with a wide, shallow bowl decorated in a raised design of a vine, heavy with grapes. Pearls studded its rim. Caedwall could tell that it was very, very old. He handed it to the old man, who pressed his lips to the rim and wept out loud, tears running down the wrinkles of his face.

At last Gunnar sighed, and Caedwall could see that his breathing was greatly eased. The boy crossed himself and prayed in awe, certain that he had witnessed a miracle.

"Brother, how did you come by such a treasure? It should be on the altar of a cathedral! Why do you keep it hidden?" he asked finally.

Gunnar stared down at the cup, caressing it. He took a breath, still more easily now. Finally he said slowly, "I was a thrall . . ."

I was a thrall, a slave in Geataland, in Scania. Not much older than you, lad, with an iron collar round my neck. My master was a eorl, a hard man. And a hard hand he had. The beatings I got, the bruises everywhere—a hard life, it was. Hard crusts to eat, hard cold bed on the floor, nothing but work and a beating at the end of it.

My master had a helmet—gift of the king, made by Weyland himself, it was. All covered with gold, plates of gold with a boar-design. I was set to polish it one day, and a rivet was loose, a plate of gold broke off. All I could think was how he would beat me this time.

So I ran. Daft, I was. Run from a beating, aye, but where can a thrall run to? Iron collar on my neck. No place to hide.

Far out on the headland there was a heap of stone, an old deserted watchtower. I stumbled on a path leading down to the foot. Old, overgrown, it was. I thought, here they won't follow me. Here my master will never find me, never lay his hand on me.

I climbed down, the trail all broken under my feet. At the bottom there was the entrance to a cave, hidden by a heap of boulders at the very foot of the cliff, all wet from the sea spray. I got to my knees, crawled inside. Looking for shelter, looking for a place to hide, that was all. It was dark, there in the entrance. But soon enough I could stand and see—there was light coming in from above, a crack in the rock—and I saw . . .

The king in his armor, dead and gone to bones! He was all in ring-mail, he was, with a helm on his head and his sword across his knees. I thought to run, I was so afraid, seeing him sitting there, like a hero out of the old heathen tales. We were all heathen in that land, in those days.

But then I saw what it was he warded. Treasure! Such a treasure as even the king's storehouse never saw. All around him, ring-mail and swords, helmets and spears. Arm rings and neck rings, all gold. Plate and cups, a king's treasure, it had to be. And closest to him, at his right hand, a silver cup set with pearls. Aye, this very one.

I could be a free man, I thought, with just a part of it. Enough food for once, and a warm cloak and no more beatings, that's all I wanted. I never meant any harm.

But I was afraid, with the dead king sitting there guarding his gold, holding his sword. I thought he would turn his head and see me there, and rise up, all bones that he was, with his sword in his hand.

But then I wondered, how long he must have been there, all alone. The others, who wore that armor, those rings—how long had they left him there to guard the hoard? And never come back. How long ago?

Where did it come from, all that gold?

The dead king, he didn't need it anymore. The others, all dead, all gone. No one left to wear the armor, all going to rust. No one to be glad of those rings. No one but me. Just one ring, I thought. One cup. Enough to take the iron off my neck, make me free.

But there was something else in the cave, something back in the dark. I saw it just when I took the first step closer to the treasure. Saw it move. Huge, it was. A firedrake, a wyrm, all covered with scales. Claws like black iron. I felt the hot stink of its breath, and I knew—this was no man's treasure, it was a dragon's hoard!

I ran from the cave, only snatching up the closest thing I could reach, the silver cup that sat at the king's right hand. And I ran.

No place to go but back, up the path to the clifftop. Shaking, I was, from fear. I could almost feel the dragon's hot breath on my backside. And suddenly my master's hall looked like a safe place, back behind those thick-timbered walls.

So I went back, back with the cup to face the eorl. And he only hit me once before I could show it to him, beg him to take it, beg him to forgive me. He took the cup, he saw the pearls, the way it was carved. So he held back his hand, and I was glad enough, not to have a beating that day.

But the dragon, when it woke and found its treasure plundered, the man-scent in the cave, its wrath burned hot. When night came, it crawled from the rock, it spread its wings and flew across the land, burning, destroying.

Flame, its breath was. It spewed out and lit the roof-thatch, and the houses burned, even the thickest timbers. Even the great hall of the king was burned to ashes. The flames of the wyrm's vengeance spread as far as you could see.

Then all the people in the land went to the king. He was an old, old man, but his heart was strong. He asked all men who knew what had roused the monster's wrath.

My master's hall was burned, but in the ashes he found the silver cup I had brought him, whole and unharmed. Then he beat me, and he never held back his hand until I told of the dragon and its hoard below the rock. I never meant any harm, but now the land was in flames.

They made me lead them to the place, the dragon's lair. Limping, I was, from my bruises, and afraid, but I had to show them the headland, and the path leading down to the hidden entrance where the treasure lay, and the wyrm that warded it. My doing, that had brought on the dragon's wrath and laid the king's land waste. I'd rather have taken a dozen more beatings than go back to that place, but I had no choice.

Then they all forgot me as the king declared, "I've fought worse monsters when I was young and I'll face this one alone. I'll have his treasure or he'll have my life!"

Oh, he was a true hero, that old king!

And down the path he went, all alone, while the eorls who came with him hid in fear of the dragon's flame. Only one stayed to give him aid—not my master, not that brave man. It was a fearsome battle, the drake's flame against the hero's iron blade. In the end they both lay dead.

Then the people came down, and they brought out the treasure hoard, all the gold. I could see the greed in their eyes.

But the one hero, the warrior who had stayed with his king, cursed all those cowards who had fled and hid. "Let the king be buried in honor," he said, "and all this gold with him, every plate and cup, every ring and coat of ring-mail. He gave you gifts, and you deserted him. No one should rejoice in it now that he lies dead."

The people heard his words, and they brought all the treasure to the funeral pyre, heaped it all up to burn. But I was afraid, for this was a heathen land, and it was the custom there to have a blood-sacrifice at the funeral of a king. Who else would they choose to sacrifice but the thrall who had brought down all this sorrow on them?

So I ran, taking only the silver cup from all the hoard, the one part of the treasure I could call mine. I didn't want to die, that was all. They would've cut my throat and laid me there at the king's feet, with his dog and his horse. That was the heathen way, in those days.

I ran to the enemies of the Geats, and aye, they were glad to hear the old king was finally dead. They cut the iron off my neck and set me free. It was all I'd ever wanted, my freedom and my life.

But I could never stop thinking of the noble old king, killed because of what I had done, taking the dragon's treasure, the one cup. All of them killed, when the firedrake burned their roofs over their heads. My doing, it was.

And that other king, so long dead, who guarded the hoard. What had he waited for, so long, with his sword all ready? Who did he mean to find that treasure, that gold, the cup at his right hand? Not me, I knew that much. I was never meant to be the one.

It gnawed at me, knowing what I'd done, taking that cup. All the deaths that followed. The old songs say sometimes that such gold is cursed, like Andvari's hoard. Did I bring down a curse on that whole kingdom?

I could have lived rich, selling it, that cup. But I kept it with me from one place to the next. From one land to another I went, restless, always searching for—I don't know what.

I came to this land, finally, where I heard the bishop preach, the saint. "Come to me all ye who are burdened," he said, and that was me, burdened all those years with what I'd done, burdened with the cup I still carried. So I came with Bishop Aidan here to the monastery, and here I've stayed, ever since.

"But . . ." Young Brother Caedwall was speechless. Saint Aidan, the bishop who had founded the monastery, had been dead for almost a hundred years! And Gunnar had heard him preach! "It's a miracle!" he finally managed to say, crossing himself reverently.

Gunnar stroked the rim of the silver cup with a shaking hand. "Aye, it may be. All I wanted . . . to be free. Never meant any harm. But I wasn't . . . wasn't the one meant to have it, no.

"My burden . . ."

The old man emitted a broken sigh. His eyelids fluttered closed. His breathing paused, and Caedwall held his own breath, but after a moment Gunnar's feeble respiration began again.

Caedwall gently lifted the silver cup from his slackening grip. He ran his fingers across the raised design, the inset pearls on the rim. He tried to imagine the dead king in his armor, the flaming dragon, the heroic battle, the gold-heaped funeral pyre. But such things belonged to the old, the heathen past. England was a Christian land now.

At last he wrapped the cup again in its cloth and placed it back in the coffer beneath the old man's bed.

Now Brother Caedwall was an old man himself, and his eyes could no longer make out the words on the pages of his beloved books. He leaned on his stick, watching the approach of the strange ships, their dragon-prows so fearsome. With their square sails billowing like wings, they almost seemed to be flying across the sea, like the drake old Gunnar had seen so long ago in heathen times, in a heathen land.

But Gunnar's tale was now told, and his bones rested in peace beneath a plain stone cross in the monastery's graveyard, and the silver cup had long since been placed on the high altar, one of the church's most precious relics. What better place for it than here on the inviolate holy island of Lindisfarne, so far removed from the greed and strife of the world.

Brother Caedwall glanced at the sun. The bell for Nones would be ringing soon. He would just have time to go to the church to pray.

The Unholy

———— ✠ ————

Doug Murray

Giles groaned as one of the hooded men tightened the ropes holding his hands. Why are they doing this? he thought, fighting the strain. He turned his head as far as it would go, desperate to know what was happening behind him, but he couldn't see far enough—the ropes were too tight, the altar stone too big and flat.

He was in the center of a double circle, the outer ring made up of ancient stones, silent and stained, the inner one . . .

The inner ring was alive! A wall of hooded, swaying humanity, moving to the strains of barbaric music that seemingly flowed from the stones themselves. Giles fought to comprehend the dance, tried to make some sense out of the cacophony around him.

Then, suddenly, it all stopped. The circle froze into silent motionlessness.

Giles dropped his head to the stone, sweating. It's over! he thought. Then he caught a hint of movement—the hooded figures were moving toward him, closing in. His mind raced. They're going to kill me! He closed his teeth over his lip, I mustn't cry out, mustn't beg for mercy. Giles tried to relax on his stony bed, tried to straighten his body, preparing for death. I must die proudly—like a Knight!

He heard a noise close at his side—and the fear came flooding back—he strained to see, head rolling as far as it would go, finding . . .

A lone woman, beautiful, unhooded. She climbed beside him, her bright blue eyes staring hungrily at Giles's bound and helpless body. He gasped at that look, vows forgotten, and watched helplessly as her long fingers began to remove garments, first her hood, then the long robe under it, then filmy undergarments . . .

Giles's mind raced. Is this a sin? Should I look away? Close my eyes? What would Lancelot do . . .

The woman was totally naked now. She crawled onto the stone altar between Giles's staked-out feet, creeping slowly toward his unprotected groin while he watched, unable to do more. Sinuously, her hand reached out . . .

"Mother of God!" Giles breathed as the hand gently closed and began to slowly stroke his manhood. Up and down, down and up . . .

The music began again, louder now—wilder. The surrounding figures doffed their long robes, and Giles found himself surrounded by a score of naked men and women, all capering around his sweating body.

Giles closed his eyes, mouthing prayer after silent prayer for the strength to resist this odd torture, but God did not answer, and the woman's hands continued to move, stroking, caressing, commanding . . .

Then, suddenly, it stopped. Giles, panting, forced his eyes open. What happened? Why did she . . . He searched for the woman, and quickly found her, still between this legs, but kneeling up now, her attention to his side. She was unwrapping an object one of the dancers was holding, an object that gleamed in the torchlight. Giles watched dumbly, unable to tear his eyes away as a sheen of silver appeared, then, oddly, a flash of red. He tried to lean forward, curious, and as the last silken wrapping came off, the bound young man found himself looking at a gleaming death's head—a human skull!

No ordinary skull, though—completely covered with silver, this one was, the metal inset with ruby eyes and emerald teeth. Giles stared, his mind racing. Why would anyone go to so much trouble on a skull? It was insane! It was . . .

Then he saw the eyes begin to glow, softly red at first, then brighter, stronger. The dancers leaped madly and Giles found himself bathed in blood-red light as the eyes turned in his direction. He started to quiver then, on the edge of panic.

The woman saw Giles's unrest and smiled a hard smile. She moved the skull closer to his cringing body, laughing, then closed her hand around his member.

Giles's head went back as the stroking and caressing began again. He gasped, straining for control as she speeded up the tempo, adding tongue and lips to the attack. He knew that he should hold out, knew that he should never succumb to this spawn of Satan. But . . . God! He was only human! He fought with every fiber of his being, trying to break the bonds, trying to douse the fire burning through his body! But it was no use, he felt himself begin to spasm and screamed out his anguish just as . . .

He woke up sweating, his body spasming helplessly. Damn! What a dream! He leaped to his feet, hugging the sodden blanket to his loins as he sprinted to the bathing house. If he could only get himself and his blanket washed off before the other squires saw him. He looked around—none of them were stirring, perhaps he could make it. Then he tripped over a practice gauntlet, falling with a clatter. Oh, well . . .

Far above Giles, in the castle tower, an important meeting continued:

"I tell you, Lance, we've got to do something! And quickly!"

Lancelot du Lac leaned back in his couch, smiling ruefully at his oldest friend. "You've been saying that all night, Arthur. But what can we do that we haven't tried already?" He held out his cup for the serving wench to fill. Better'n the old days. He thought. Then we had to fetch for ourselves. "We've already gotten every would-be noble to send us their kids for 'training'—sounds better than demanding hostages like the Romans, right?" Arthur nodded absently. "And we've sent all the troublemakers to the Marches to fight the Kelts—you know what that means." Arthur nodded again. "What more can we do?"

Arthur sighed, pulling his robe more tightly around him as he drained his cup. He looked out the window, noting reddening sky

to the east. Dawn already? He sighed again, Gwen will be very unhappy. He shook his head. "Damn it, Lance, if I had an answer, I
wouldn't be talking with you!" He stood up, stretching. "The men
are bored! There's nobody left to fight, and we can't do what the
Romans did . . ." He turned toward Lancelot. "You know what
would happen if we put our warriors to building roads or cisterns."

Lance tipped a libation out of his freshly filled cup and took a
sip, nodding. "Aye! We wouldna last the day!"

"So it's got to be something else—something that looks
important—now, perhaps the Druids . . ."

Lance walked to the window, staring unseeingly at the dawn.
"No. The villagers wouldn't put up with that. They're thick as
thieves with the holly-waving bastards." He turned back toward
Arthur. "How about Mordred? He's always making some kind of
trouble with that witchy mother of his . . ."

Arthur's eyes clouded in pain as he took another sip of wine
and shook his head. "No. Mordred has been quiet for the last few
months; our spies tell us that he's *not* building up an army—why
tempt the fates? We need something else, something . . ."

"Holy?"

Both men whirled toward the door, Lance's hand spouting a
long-bladed dagger. "Who dares?!"

The newcomer smiled. "Come now! Is that any way to talk
to . . ."

"Merlin!" Arthur rushed to the man's side. "We thought you
were still out of the country!"

The blue-clad mage smiled gently at his protégé. "It seems I
am back just in time. Have I heard correctly? Is the Table Round
in some difficulty?"

Lance sprawled back into his couch, the knife gone from sight.
"Aye. The men tire of peace. They want blood and battle."

Arthur nodded his head. "And glory—that most of all!"

Merlin motioned to the serving girl, who hurried to him with a
fresh cup, shivering slightly as his hand brushed hers. He stared at
the cup for a moment, then nodded.

"Send them on a Quest. A search for the most mysterious relic
in Christendom." He raised his cup high and, before their eyes, it

changed, became golden and glittering, a white light spilling from its mouth. "Send them after the Cup of Christ." He smiled. "Have them find the Holy Grail!"

Giles stood outside the door of the squire's aged confessor, Friar Thomas, hands feeling for the bruises on his face. I cannot blame the other lads for what they did this morning, he thought. What worries me is that they might be right in what they say. He ran his hand over his straight nose, stroked his still hairless lip. I've always known that I was somebody's bastard—but is it possible that I am unholy—a child of the Devil?

He shook his head violently. No! The King would know if I was evil! He would never . . .

The door in front of him began to open. Giles took a deep breath as he worked to order his thoughts. Still, dreams of naked women and jeweled skulls! The young man stepped forward, toward the beckoning priest. They cannot be normal! Perhaps the others are right. Perhaps I have been touched by the enemy.

"Friar Thomas"—Giles dropped his head—"I have a problem . . ."

"Damn the boy!" A fist drove into the waters of the fountain, shattering the shimmering image of Giles. "If that priest recognizes the spell . . ."

"Calm yourself, Mordred!" A more feminine figure gestured calm. "He's a simple Friar—he'll think it was some lascivious dream. The boy'll be set to saying a few dozen 'Pater Nosters' and that will be the end of it."

Mordred whirled around, his cape causing the candles that surrounded the two to gutter, black, oily wax dripping to the table. "And what will we do? Sit here and let Arthur's men find the Grail? Settle down to husbandry here at the far end of nowhere!"

Morganna smiled. "Of course not. We'll try again. Perhaps another dream-sending . . ."

"With you fumbling for his seed again?" Mordred sneered. "And you old enough to be his mother!"

"Not his mother," Morganna's smile widened, tiny points on

her teeth appearing—like those on a cat who has just spied a mouse. "His aunt, perhaps . . ."

"Do you really think . . ."

Morganna whirled on her son. "I know! Just as I know that with the use of his seed, blood, and skin, I can craft a spell that will put you on the throne you want so badly!"

Morganna flowed to the window, "We will send another vision to him—and then when we have what we want from his loins . . ."

Mordred smiled a hard smile. "I will take the rest!"

Giles groaned as the ropes tightened on his arms. He looked up, trying to catch a glimpse of who was pulling on them, but he could not move his head far enough. He gave up, turning from side to side instead, trying to get an idea where he was, and who had captured him.

He saw a ring of stones, huge sarsens, twenty or thirty feet high, all surrounding a second, smaller ring of . . . my God, was this some trick of Satan?!

Giles blinked his eyes quickly, trying to assure that there was nothing wrong with them, but no, they were working well enough.

He was surrounded by women, twenty or thirty of them.

And every one of them naked as the day she was born.

Giles swallowed hard, trying to fill his mind with the prayers that Friar Thomas had given him, trying to close his eyes to the flesh being paraded before his gaze.

To no avail. Somewhere behind him, music began. Pagan melodies, born of bagpipe and drum, surrounded him, pouring into his skin, awakening atavistic memories and primitive cravings.

Giles began to sweat.

Movement started. One by one, the women around him began to dance—a strange dance, one that seemed to involve all the most secret parts of their bodies whirling and writhing and swaying before his imprisoned eyes. The women smiled at him, displaying their white flesh, offering themselves to him if he would just reach out . . .

Closer they came, nearer and nearer, until they were brushing against him as they danced past, touching his hair, his face, his chest. Their long unbound hair floated around him, caressing his body, touching his every part. Desperately he began to pray aloud, trying to drown out the music, blot out the sight.

Then she was there. The same woman who had haunted his previous dream. Tall, with long golden hair that shimmered around her body, hiding nothing, but suggesting much. She smiled at Giles, long white teeth gleaming in the torchlight, and then she crawled beside him, hair brushing his chest, hands moving along his thighs, touching, stroking, caressing . . .

He shivered, trying desperately to pull his arms free, trying to do something, anything to avoid the explosion building up within his loins, an eruption he sensed would bring an end to everything he knew.

He began to pray aloud, screaming the words as loud as he could to the world at large. He heard the woman laugh, low and throaty, her hands moving faster, maddeningly . . .

He screamed the prayer again, trying to beat down the eruption that was wracking his body . . .

"And that's how they found him, sire." Friar Thomas bowed his head. "Screaming prayers at the top of his lungs, blankets sodden and dripping . . ."

Lance stirred, waving for the serving girl at the edge of the table to fill his wine cup. "And what would you have us do about it, Priest? Is it not normal for young men to have night visitations?"

The priest reddened still more, squirming, "Aye, but not like these! The stone circle alone . . ."

Lance straightened up, wine slopping over the side of his cup. "Dreams, Priest! We cannot spend our time worrying about dreams!"

The little priest reddened still more, but shook his head decisively. "These are no dreams! They are something more, something . . . evil! I feel it!"

"Thank you." Arthur spoke before Lancelot could continue the argument. "We will . . . look into this." Friar Thomas sputtered his thanks and hurried away, relieved to have done his duty with the King and his ill-tempered Frankish friend.

"Damn it, Arthur . . . ," Lance began as the door closed.

Arthur motioned him to silence. "Wait!" He gestured the serving girl to him. "Melinda, call Merlin to us—I think this warrants his notice."

Lance bounded to his feet as the girl hurried out, adding more spilled wine to the puddle in front of him. "Are you mad! Calling the mage about some junior squire's wet dreams . . . !"

Arthur shook his own head, "It's more than that, old friend." He took a sip from his own cup. "Much more."

"He must go with our Knights, Arthur." Merlin gaze was imperious as he sipped at his wine. "It is the only way we can save him."

"You're as crazy as Arthur!" Lance was astonished. "Are you trying to start a war? That's what there'll be, make no mistake, if we try to send a junior squire out on this quest—a war with our own men!"

Merlin took another sip of his drink, as, under the table, his left hand began a slow series of movements, fingers aimed toward the serving maid standing in the corner. "Then don't send a junior squire—send a Knight!"

Arthur stirred at that, his own wine cup untouched. "Make the boy a Knight? But he hasn't finished his training, taken the tests . . ."

Merlin's hand completed its pass, and, as the mage watched with a quiet smile on his face, the laces of the serving girl's bodice began to move, slowly pulling themselves out of their eyelets and stays. "So? Those tests are mandated by the King and his Master at Arms—and you are they, are you not?"

The loose lace ends grew longer and longer, the bodice slipped lower and lower, showing more and more creamy flesh. "Besides, you know who this boy is—and how important he could be to all of us."

Arthur took a big gulp of his wine. "Aye, but still . . ."

Lance threw his cup into the fireplace, the fire flashing blue where wine dregs spattered. "So we just tap the boy with Arthur's sword, ignoring all the rules, insulting the senior squires and Knights who spent years at their training! I won't be a part of this! I won't . . ."

Merlin sighed, his hands moving in an intricate pattern. "Lance!" Shards of pottery rose from the fire, reassembling themselves into a cup. "I tell you, it is vital that this boy be saved." The cup floated across the room, stopping in front of the serving maid who had finally noticed the draft and was busily trying to retie all her bodice laces—she froze in mid-movement as the pitcher she was bracing under one arm rose into the air, tipping to fill the cup.

Lancelot sighed. "I know all about your powers . . ."

Merlin's fingers moved again, the brimming cup floated toward the table, braking to a halt directly over Lance's head. "So you think! But I tell you that Morganna is nearly as powerful as am I—and will be far more so if she gets what she wants from that boy."

Merlin rose from his seat, left hand still pointing at the cup, right reaching out to calm the agitated serving girl. "You must send the boy out on this quest." He stopped at the door, fingers still pointed toward the cup. "It's the only way."

Merlin let the door close behind him, then, with a smile, he snapped his fingers.

On the other side of the door, he heard the cup shatter—and Lance's howl of outrage.

Merlin smiled and led the serving girl down the corridor toward the squire's quarters. It was time to talk to the boy.

"So that's the story, lad!" Merlin sat across from Giles, hands playing with a gold coin. "They're going to keep sending those damned dreams to you—and if they get what they want . . ."

Giles fidgeted on his own bed. He didn't dare look the mage in the eye—Friar Thomas had warned him that such men could steal your very soul were you not careful—still, with a half-dressed serving wench smiling on his other side . . .

"But M'lord! What am I to do?"

Merlin smiled, and sat up straighter, reaching into the pockets of his robes for a small vial and a tiny wand. "Just sit tight, my lad, and let me concentrate for a second."

Giles dared a look at the sorcerer, seeing the man's long blue robe and gray beard, then he hurriedly returned his gaze to the wall as the Mage's wise brown eyes turned his way. "Just a second now . . ." The older man tinkered with the vial, odd metallic sounds coming from it, as if it were filled with stones or tiny coins. Merlin waved his wand . . .

What is he doing? Giles began to worry, eyes held away from the girl and the magician. Is he going to unman me? Set some unholy spell that will . . . suddenly, Merlin's hand appeared directly in front of his face, impossible to ignore.

"Swallow this—quickly, now!"

Giles took the little round item from the mage's hand and swallowed, his tongue gave him a fleeting impression of something hard and metallic. He swallowed again.

"Good," the mage boomed. "Now, a couple of wards and we should be done." Giles winced as the mage began a strange chant in a language that the boy had never heard before. What will I tell Friar Thomas?

Merlin finished chanting, then smiled mischeviously. "There! Now, let's just try a little test . . ."

The mage's left hand lifted, fingers gesturing toward the serving girl who stood smiling to one side of the bed—a smile that vanished as she felt the laces at her chest again begin to move.

"Merlin! Do you have to—"

"Quiet, girl." Merlin smiled, calming her in an instant. "It's only in the nature of an experiment."

The girl stood there, afraid to move as the magician's hands continued to move down—and her bodice followed them. "Now, boy, look here . . ."

Giles blushed, his eyes opening wide at the sight. What would Friar Thomas think of this! His eyes widened as he noticed the rapid spread of goose pimples on the pale flesh. So sensitive! I never thought . . . Then he realized that something was wrong.

He looked down, "Hey!" He was suddenly terrified. He'd heard tales of Southern lands, where men were rendered into great fat sexless things . . .

"Come, come boy! Don't look down now—let your eyes feast on one of nature's true wonders!"

Giles eyes went back to the girl, widening still further as more and more of her was revealed. Amazing! What would the other squires think . . . Then he realized that he felt nothing more than admiration. Surely there was something seriously wrong. He looked down then, hand moving toward his oddly quiescent middle . . .

"Good!" Merlin exclaimed, giving the girl a quick pat and indicating that she should do up her blouse. "Very good! They won't be able to get at you that way! Now, if Arthur and Lance just do what I told them . . ."

Giles was nonplussed, still staring down at his oddly-numb privates. "You told the King to do something?"

Merlin got to his feet, putting his arm around the girl and guiding her toward the door. "Aye, boy, it's in his hands now—and yours." He laughed and opened the door. "Now, my dear, there are some things that I want in my hands!"

"Damn the man!" Mordred woke with a start, shocked to find his mother standing in front of him, naked, with the skull-chalice in her hand, glowing red eyes staring at him, green teeth grinning mockingly. "Merlin has gotten to the boy! We can no longer reach him through his dreams!"

Mordred rubbed sleep from his eyes, nodding toward the thing in her hand. "Not even with the help of that monstrosity?"

Morganna glanced at the silver skull filling her hand. "If it were fully activated . . . ," she said, "but as it is now, no, it cannot help me."

"What do we do?" Mordred rose from his bed, pulling on a robe and tossing a fur to his mother. "Do we give up?"

"Never!" She pulled the cover around her, letting it settle over her shoulders as she held the skull before her face. "We must master the power of this vessel! If we do, we shall be invincible!

"Until they find the Holy Grail . . ."

Morganna leaped to her feet, the fur falling off, leaving her naked before his gaze again. "Aye! We'll have to get the boy out of the castle, take him prisoner ..."

"What have I been saying all along?"

"We'll bring him to the circle bodily!" Morganna began to pace the room. "Despite Merlin's spells, I shall have his seed!" Her hands closed. "Then, with he and the chalice mated, we take the blood and skin ..."

Mordred smiled. "And with it, England!"

Lancelot threw himself into his seat, the wood creaking dangerously. "And what, master magician, is this 'Unholy Grail' you're so worried about?"

Merlin, sitting comfortably in front of a small table loaded with wine, water, and salt, made a final pass over a little silver dish, mumbling a last few phrases under his breath. "Let me show you ..."

Directly in front of the magician, the air shimmered for a moment, shadows from nowhere playing over his calm face, then solidifying into images. A shining death's head appeared, floating in front of the mage—ruby eyes staring directly into those of the suddenly uncomfortable Lancelot.

"It started as a simple clay cup," Merlin explained. "The one from which Judas Iscariot drank at the Last Supper." He took a sip of wine. "Later, he used the same vessel to hold his thirty pieces of silver."

"A Devil's Grail," Arthur mused quietly.

Merlin nodded toward the King. "Exactly so! When God caused Christ's Cup to become a talisman of power for good, Satan, aided by natural law, was able to create a vessel of his own."

Lancelot motioned angrily toward the vision in front of him. "This?"

"Aye!" Merlin sipped a little more wine. "As the Holy Grail passed from hero to hero, this Unholy cup has moved alongside it, negating its powers."

"But the skull, the jewels ..." Lancelot shook his head, unable to take it all in.

"Added by an Arab mage, one Abdul Hazalred." Merlin gestured at the image before him, causing the skull-face to lighten, fade, showing the plain clay cup beneath. "He knew that the skull of Judas held great magical powers, so he bound the cup within, scheming that the addition would allow him to overwhelm the holder of the Holy Grail."

"But he failed," Arthur added helpfully.

"Barely." Merlin refilled his cup. "And in that magical battle, both Grails—and both protectors—disappeared."

"And are still missing," whispered Lance.

"Until now."

Lancelot surged angrily to his feet. "And just how do we know that?!"

"Because Giles saw this Grail during the first of his dreams."

Lancelot whirled on the magician. "You mean we're going through all this because some bastard whelp . . ."

Merlin gestured, and the skull lifted, the eyes boring into Lancelot's. "The boy may be a bastard." He intoned. "But if Morganna were to obtain his seed, blood, and skin, she would gain ultimate power over Britain."

Lance pulled his gaze away from the ruby eyes of the skull. "Ultimate power! From some boy! But why . . . ?"

Arthur took a deep breath. "Because Giles Dougal is my son."

Morganna rose in her stirrups, peering at the little campsite ahead. "All right, Mordred, there they are. All you have to do is get the boy and bring him to me—alive and unharmed—remember that, if you spill his blood . . ."

Mordred worked at his right gauntlet, pushing down at the webbing between the fingers, insuring a tight fit and a good grip. He nodded as he hefted his mace, checking it for rust or denting. "We've gone over this a thousand times—I promise I won't hurt a hair on his head." He raised his eyes, looking at her smile. "Why are you so worried about the little bastard?"

Morganna laughed. "Because he *is* a bastard—that's what makes him so important to us."

Mordred looked confused. "I don't understand . . ."

"He's Arthur's bastard, you idiot!"

"Arthur? But he and Guinevere . . ."

"Are frauds!" Morganna sighed as she shifted her weight in the saddle. "Oh, he loves the useless trull—but she's barren—and if he can't get an heir on her . . ."

Mordred's eyes lit up. "I would be the next King . . ."

"Which is the last thing they want." Morganna nodded toward the campsite ahead. "And so Arthur and his bitch wife hatched a plan. For a time, they visited Guinevere's cousin, Susanne, in the north country."

"And Arthur and this Susanne . . ."

"Produced Giles Dougal." Morganna pointed at the little camp.

"Even the boy doesn't know the truth—he thinks himself the son of some raiding Norseman."

"And Merlin and Lancelot?"

"The mage knows—he had a hand in all this. As for the Saintly Frank," Morganna said, laughing, "would you tell him you were contemplating fornication?"

"God, no!" Mordred thought for a second. "I still don't see how all of this helps us."

Morganna shook her head sadly, then hefted the Grail, morning sunlight glinting off the polished silver dome. "The Grail gives special powers through the suffering of its victims—and the blood of the victim determines the degree of power."

"And as Giles is the son of the King . . ."

"His blood will give us power over the whole land! Of course, we must spill that blood after the proper ceremonies. First we must marry him to the Grail with seed and skin." She fixed her son with a hard eye. "And that's why you must be very careful—for if his blood were to be spilled prematurely . . ."

"I understand."

"See that you do!" Morganna held the Grail between both her hands now, staring at it as she mustered all her powers of concentration. "Bring the boy to me, and then wait at our keep."

Mordred pulled the visor of his helm down. "Whatever you say, Mother dearest."

Morganna lifted the Grail, sunlight glinting off the skull's ruby eyes, bathing her with blood-red light. Smiling, she began to chant. "Ave Satannum . . ."

Giles Dougal—Sir Giles now, rubbed his hands to drive the chill of the night out of them. He looked around his meager camp, the tent where he had spent the night dwarfed by that of his companions, Sir James and Sir Garreth.

The other men weren't moving yet—not surprising considering the amount of wine they had consumed at dinner. How can any man drink that much? Giles wondered. And on a holy Quest?

Ah, well, he thought. It's not my place to gainsay such men— I'll just be sure not to make such mistakes myself! Giles turned to watch the squires working around the camp, their eyes never seeming to meet his: They're jealous! He realized. I've been pushed above them—and they don't understand why. He nodded to himself. I'd better go and talk to them . . .

Suddenly, a noise from outside grabbed at his attention. A horse? He looked toward the place their own horses were staked out, counting quickly to ensure that one had not pulled free in the night. No. They're all there.

Giles peered toward the trail far away, trying to see who was coming. It was hard. The morning damp had raised fog, and the smoke of the camp—wait! There they were, now who . . .

"Oh my God!

Giles ran to the tent to alert the others, yelling to the squires to bring armour and weapons.

Although he didn't know what good they would do.

Two hundred yards away, Morganna smiled. This was going to be even easier than she had thought. There were only two Knights with the boy—and a mere handful of squires and men-at-arms. Such were no match for her army. She laughed aloud, holding the Unholy Grail at arm's length, studying the trail of viscous fluid that led from it to the struggling mass ahead of her—she couldn't lose now!

Inside the beleaguered camp, Mordred heard his mother's laugh—all was well. His mace thundered out, connecting with the helmet of Sir James, knocking the older man to the ground. Mordred smiled, bringing the weapon up again. God, I love this! The mace came thundering down, forcing blood and brains out of the shattered helmet before him. I live for this!

Ten feet away, Giles was fighting his own battle—an odd battle against foes who seemed unwilling to strike at him. When the camp was first attacked, Giles had whitened at the terrible aspect of the warriors who faced them. Tall they were, six feet or more, and naked, their bodies ghastly white save where they were covered by some dark blue dye. Each of them seemed possessed of some great wound, a suppurating sore on chest or back that oozed a greenish ichor that trailed behind like the spoor of some unholy snail.

Giles battled the creatures with every ounce of strength he possessed—and found himself able to strike at will! His sword severed a leg here, thrust through a chest there.

And slowed the creatures not a whit.

Giles fought like a madman, cutting around him with power he did not realize he possessed—and still the things kept advancing! He saw Sir Garreth fall, saw Sir James die under the mace of a mad giant, and all the while, he was forced farther and farther back, the wall of flesh forcing him away from the camp, away from the continuing battle.

Finally, surrounded and overwhelmed, he found himself drowning in undead flesh, covered with green slime. He opened his mouth to scream—and found his throat instantly filled. Silenced, he could only watch as the ichor crawled up his face, over his nose, his eyes . . .

His world went green—then black.

Giles awoke to a sickeningly familiar sight. He was bound, hand and foot, to a great stone altar in the center of a circle of stones, the whole scene lit by hundreds of flickering candles placed everywhere.

He struggled with his bonds for a moment, needing to find out if this were real or just another dream. The ropes were real enough, made of some odd, silky material, too smooth to cut into his wrists, but much too strong to break ...

Music started, jarring Giles. He looked around, unsurprised to find himself surrounded by naked women, all dancing in some complicated pattern around the rock altar.

Around him.

Then she appeared. Exactly as he had seen her so many times—naked, her long hair alternately covering and revealing the lush body beneath. She danced wildly around the altar, right hand weaving around and over him, stroking here, caressing there.

In her other hand, she held a horrifying death's head of silver, ruby eyes flashing in the flickering light. Giles shivered as those eyes seemed to look into his own. Evil! he thought. That thing is *evil*!

The woman's dance became wilder, more explicit. She stroked her own breasts, ran hands over her own thighs, then she crawled to the altar, her hands reaching for his unmoving member as her red mouth closed over it.

He felt nothing but revulsion.

She stopped for a moment, then held the chalice up, beginning a drone in some unknown tongue. All around her, the other women dropped to their knees, adding their voice to hers.

The chant swelled as the dance started again, the music slower now, sinuous. Bodies swayed slowly, hair swinging from side to side, hands touching buttocks, thighs, breasts ...

The light of the candles changed, from a flickering yellow to hard, bright white. The music changed as well, speeding up, becoming fiercer, more orgiastic. Giles began to sweat. He felt his heart speed up, thumping in time to the music. Above him, the woman's hands moved even more quickly, more urgently—he gasped as he felt his flesh respond. He looked to the heavens, praying desperately for strength—and suddenly found himself eye to eye with crimson horror. The skull-cup was *floating* above him, red eyes glaring hellishly down at Giles, willing him to do what it wanted, demanding, forcing ...

Deep inside, Giles knew that if he surrendered, he and thousands, perhaps millions, of others would die. He fought on, the chalice hanging above him, its crimson stare cutting deep into his soul . . .

Giles began to shake from the strain, the muscles in his thighs straining, cramping. He hugged the pain to him, nurtured it, tried to enlarge it, force it to overpower the other sensations coursing through him—but it was not enough. His body began to jump, mindlessly, as Giles narrowed his entire consciousness down to one spark, one block to what was about to happen.

He was too late.

Morganna smiled, renewing her dance—in triumph now. She knew he was about to surrender, she knew she was seconds from victory, seconds from ultimate power.

Then the shouting started.

Morganna turned just as the first men came thundering through the stone circle, swords slicing through the few guards that she had set. So! Merlin pays me a call! She thought, grabbing the chalice and focusing her will on it. He and his friends will pay for that! She tightened her concentration, muttering a new spell. The Grail flared bright as the sun for an instant, then dulled as its ruby eyes clouded over. Moisture appeared in its sockets—unholy tears of gray-green ichor. They lengthened, dropped to the ground, puddled, pooled—then began to grow into the semblance of men . . .

Morganna smiled as her dread army reappeared, their undead bodies tethered to her and the Grail by slimy umbilici. She saw the Knights hesitate for a moment, horrified at what they saw, then, as she laughed, her creations began their attack, dragging screaming men from their saddles, tearing helmeted heads from armoured bodies, maiming, killing . . .

Giles stared wildly as Morganna began to once again work on his helpless body. He had been so sure that Lancelot and Merlin would rescue him, but now . . .

He had to do something!

Giles tried again to burst his bonds—and this time felt something different. He looked up, fighting the position he had been placed in, and stared in wonder at the knots on his hands as they began to undo themselves.

He began to hope, but then, Morganna renewed her efforts. He moaned as he felt his loins tighten, knowing that he had just seconds before the sorceress would get what she wanted.

Merlin made one last move with his fingers, then flickered both hands apart, completing the spell. He had done all he could, it was up to Lancelot and the boy now.

Morganna cried out in triumph as the boy spasmed, quickly moving to catch his seed in the mouth of the Grail. I've done it! She thought. I've wed him to the Grail! Now all I need do is add the skin and blood . . . She pulled her knife out, moving its edge to the boy's helpless thigh.

As Giles lay in despair, he felt the last knot slip away from his hands. He knew he must move now—and whatever he did, it must work first try. He knew that this woman had power enough to destroy him with a look, he had to surprise her . . .

He gathered himself—and made his move. He reached up, grabbed her long hair, and pulled as hard as he could. If he could just dash her head against the hard stone of the altar . . .

Morganna was shocked by the unexpected attack—she didn't know where it came from, and was hard put to hold onto the Grail. Her concentration slipped, and all around her, white figures slumped to the earth, melting into piles of green ichor as they fell. She screamed then, as she felt the pain of the Grail's anger—then she fought back, scratching, kicking, doing anything to get her head free. She clawed out with her right hand—letting the Grail drop free . . .

Giles's breath roared out of him as Morganna's kick landed squarely in his groin. He doubled over, losing his grip on her. Her nails clawed deeply into his chest, blood welling out. I've failed! He thought. Failed . . .

* * *

Morganna's head snapped free, the hand holding her hair dropping away. She looked for her attacker, eyes sparking—and saw Giles doubled over in front of her. Morganna's brow furrowed for an instant, how had he gotten his hands free?—then she heard a whisper of sound behind her. She turned just as Lancelot's sword finished its arc.

Giles woke slowly. He'd had some sort of dream, something with naked women and silver skulls and bright red lights . . .

He opened his eyes and found himself face-to-face with Merlin. It hadn't been a dream, then.

"So, Sir Giles, you've finally decided to rejoin us."

Giles's eyes drifted nervously away from the mage—until they touched the hideous sight next to him. He pulled away, gasping.

"Yes, she is quite a sight, isn't she." Merlin worked the bonds free from Giles's feet. "Still, she would have done worse to you."

"Is she dead?" Giles was having problems looking at the woman's face, the jaw near severed by the force of Lancelot's blow.

Lancelot reined to a halt next to them. "No, she lives."

Giles goggled. "You mean . . ."

Merlin nodded. "Aye, that wound looks mortal enough, but to a mage of her powers . . ."

"What are we going to do about her?"

Lancelot shrugged. "Nothing."

"But . . .?"

"Lancelot's right," Merlin added, reaching for something behind Giles's head. "We don't make war on women. If she has the power to heal herself, she will. If she does not . . ." The magician shrugged again.

Giles shivered. *She would have gladly killed me—and yet, the rules of Chivalry . . .*

Giles rose shakily, pulling on a robe that Lancelot handed him. "Don't worry about her, lad." The big Knight nodded toward the ruin. "She wouldn't have thought twice about leaving you to die."

Giles nodded uneasily. "I suppose you're right." He tore his eyes away from the unconscious Morganna and turned toward Merlin. "So what do we do now?"

"We go home, boy, but first"—Merlin was pointing at something that Giles had done his best to ignore. "Pick it up, boy. It's yours to deal with now."

Giles stalled for a second, carefully tying his robe, then steeled himself and reached out to touch the silvery skull in front of him. "Mine?"

"She mated you with it." Merlin gestured a horse toward him. "It's yours to command."

"Do I have to keep it?" Giles stared at the thing, remembering its power. "Couldn't I just give it to you?"

Merlin smiled, grabbing the bridle of the horse as it reached him. "You could, but it's a very powerful magical item—are you sure you want someone like me to have it?"

Giles stared at the sorcerer for a moment. I like him, he thought, but can I trust *any* mage with this much power? Power even *he* doesn't seem to want. He glanced at Lancelot, whose courage had saved them all, and suddenly realized what he must do.

Giles nodded. "You're right." He took the reins Merlin handed to him, pulling the horse closer as he climbed down off the altar stone. "I'll give it to the perfect protector—the bravest, noblest man in Christendom."

Merlin's face froze. "You don't mean . . ."

Giles nodded, sure of himself now. "Aye! Lancelot! Take this unholy thing! Keep it safe until Merlin finds a way to destroy it."

Lancelot was silent for an instant, eyes studying Giles. Perhaps I've misjudged the boy, he thought. Then he took the skull from the offering hands. There *is* something of his father in him. "As you say, Sir Giles. Now, shall we leave this unholy place?"

As the boy climbed onto his horse, Lance looked at the thing in his hands. It's beautiful! And so warm! Perhaps Merlin is wrong about its nature, perhaps . . .

Lance felt eyes on him and turned to find the mage staring worriedly. "It's all right, Master Magician." He stuffed the skull into his saddlebags. "I won't use the thing against you."

Merlin nodded then, a sad look in his eyes. "As you say, Master Warrior. As you say."

Merlin was happy to see the King waiting on the walls to greet the little party as they returned. Now, if he could only get Arthur to take the Grail from Lancelot, put it somewhere for safekeeping . . .

But there was much to do first, and Merlin had to wait until after the celebratory dinner to talk to Arthur.

By then it was too late.

Over the meal, the story of the battle of the Unholy Grail was told. When Lance finished the tale, Arthur asked him to take the Devil's Cup out to show it to the company. The big Frank unwrapped the skull carefully, still nervous as the polished silver touched his hand. "Here it is, sire. And believe me, it is the foulest thing I have ever touched."

Gwen reached forward, her finger almost touching it, and, for the first time, Lance realized how beautiful she was. And how blind he had been.

Merlin saw the two exchange glances, and took a long sip of his wine. The Unholy Grail dirties whatever it touches, he thought ruefully. Even Lancelot . . . He sighed. Maybe I should take the skull and . . . No—that would break the balance. I'll have to wait until our Knights find the Cup of Christ, then . . .

Beyond the muttering wizard, King Arthur tried to find the strength to talk to his unknowing son while his best friend fell madly in love with his wife.

And all the while, the eyes of the Unholy Grail glowed redly in the waning light.

Tacachale

—— ✠ ——

Owl Goingback

"Cursed bugs!" Fernando de Carmona muttered, slapping at the mosquito buzzing his head. Though they had left the humid swamps far to the south, now traveling through relatively dry pine forests, there was no escaping the swarms of insects that dogged their trail, driving the men and horses to near madness and making each day as miserable as the last. Barely twenty years earlier, Juan Ponce de León had christened the new land *"La tierra de la Pascua Florida"*—the land of the flowery feast. He should have named it the land of the hungry bugs.

At the thought of Ponce de León, Fernando smiled and touched his left breast. Hidden beneath his armor and sweat-soaked uniform lay the leather-clad diary of the late explorer.

"Ah, my dear Juan," Fernando said aloud, remembering the former governor of Puerto Rico, and the man he had served under as a captain in 1521. Had the old fool listened to his advice and concentrated his search further inland, instead of sticking to the coastline, he might have discovered the Fountain of Eternal Youth. But he had not listened. And instead of life immortal, Ponce de León's only reward was death by a native arrow.

And now, nearly ten years later, it was Fernando who led the quest for the fabled waters of eternal life. But where Ponce de León had failed, Fernando was determined to succeed. He would find the Fountain of Youth, slipping the bonds of age that cloaked his body as easily as a fine woman sheds a dress. And he alone would enjoy the blessings of King Charles I and the fame and fortune that comes from such a discovery.

Fernando turned and looked behind him. Three hundred soldiers—one hundred on horseback, two hundred on foot—accompanied him. They waited silently for his orders, their faces grim, their posture erect. The Timucua village of Ocali had been found deserted. Such actions could only be expected. Bare flesh and wooden arrows were no match against armored men on horseback and swords of the finest Toledo steel. Perhaps the Timucua had heard of the expedition of Pánfilo de Narváez two years earlier. Narváez, who cut the nose off of the Tocobago chief Hirrihigua, then fed the chief's mother to the dogs, had cut a swath through the interior, like a sword through a pregnant woman's belly. The natives still trembled when they heard Narváez's name. Fernando believed they would soon tremble at his name too, for he also believed it was better to conquer and enslave than to negotiate.

Ordering the men to begin setting up camp, Fernando returned his attention to Ocali. A moderate-sized village, it consisted of thirty or so thatched wooden cabins encircling a public square, much like the courtyards of Seville. On the east side of the square, an earthen mound rose fifteen feet above the ground. Upon this sat a large cabin, probably belonging to the village chief. On the opposite end of the square sat a similar mound with an equally large building. The carving of an owl on the front of the building identified it as a charnel house.

Fernando had seen the inside of a native charnel house only once, but once was enough. In it the corpses were laid out in simple wooden boxes resting on the ground, covered only with loose timbers held down by stones. Wild animals had broken into several of the boxes, scattering the rotting remains of corpses about the premises. The stench had been stifling.

"Adelantado! Adelantado!"

Fernando turned to see three of his soldiers coming across the square, herding an Indian man and woman before them. The soldiers shoved their captives roughly to the ground. "My, my. What do we have here?" Fernando asked, stroking his pointed beard.

"We found them hiding in the storage house," answered one of the soldiers.

"Is that so?" He leaned forward in his saddle to get a better look.

The man was naked except for a covering about his loins. He looked to be in his mid-forties, maybe a little older. Like most savages, he was in excellent physical condition. Bracelets of copper encircled his wrists. Black hair hung to his shoulders.

The woman was a miserable old bag of bones, with not enough meat on her to feed the dogs. Her skin was like wrinkled leather, her hair stringy and grey. She wore a white dress of animal skins, unlike the skimpy garments favored by so many of the Timucua women.

"Stand up," Fernando ordered. He was surprised when the woman stood at once. He raised his eyebrows. "How is it you speak Spanish?"

"You are not the first white man to visit our village," she answered, her voice like dry leaves rustling in the wind. "Others have been here before you."

Others? Fernando wondered. He thought his expedition the first to reach this far north. "And what did these others want?"

"The same as all white men: gold and slaves. There is no gold here."

Fernando laughed. "I am not interested in gold or slaves, old woman. It is a treasure far greater that I seek. I search for the sacred waters that heal all afflictions. The Fountain of Youth."

A look of fear flashed across her face. She recovered quickly, but Fernando had shocked her.

She knows something.

"What is your name, woman?"

"I am called Tacachale."

Tacachale. It meant to light a new fire—kindling a flame to remove or prevent some impurity. Fernando had heard the ritual was an important part of their heathen religion. Maybe it wasn't a name, but a title. A priestess?

"And who is he?" Fernando asked, nodding toward the man.

"His name is Yustega. He is the chief."

Fernando smiled. He found it amusing that the half-naked man standing before him could hold a position of power and leadership. He made a great show of bowing to the chief. Several of his officers laughed.

"I am indeed honored to meet you, your majesty. How grand it must be to be a chief of an empty village. But tell me, where are your people? Your warriors?"

Tacachale answered for him. "They heard of your coming and ran away."

He turned and looked at the distant tree line. An Indian warrior was a skilled fighter, a treacherous foe, who would remain in hiding, watching, waiting for opportunity to attack. Fernando was not worried, however. His men were well trained. Turning, he nodded to the three soldiers guarding the prisoners. "Kill them, and then burn their village."

The soldiers drew their swords and stepped forward. Tacachale shrank back in fear. The chief jumped between her and the soldiers.

Fernando raised his right hand. "Wait."

The soldiers halted. The Indians looked at him. Fernando straightened up. He chose his words carefully, looking into the old woman's eyes. He spoke.

"I will spare your lives if you take me to the Fountain of Eternal Youth."

Again a look of fear crossed Tacachale's face.

By God, she knows where it is! I'm certain of it.

Tacachale turned and spoke rapidly to the chief. Yustega shook his head and answered back, his voice sharp with anger. Suddenly, he pulled a stone knife from the waistband of his loincloth and lunged at the soldier closest to him, driving the knife deep into the soldier's throat. Tacachale turned and raced toward the forest.

The soldier fell to the ground, a shower of blood spraying from the wound. Before Yustega could extract the knife, or make good his escape, the other two soldiers stepped forward and ran their swords through him.

Several crossbows fired. Fernando looked quickly away from the dying chief and saw Tacachale running toward the forest. Arrows flew all around her.

"Don't shoot, you idiots! I want her alive!"

Tacachale fled toward the forest, seeking safety among the trees. A soldier stepped out from behind a building, blocking her path, his arms spread wide to catch her. But Tacachale dodged around him with all the grace of a deer in flight.

"Stop her! Do not let her escape!" yelled Fernando, the flush of anger burning his face. He spurred his horse forward, determined to stop her himself if need be. "You'll not escape me, witch!"

He was almost upon her, but already she'd reached the tree line. Ducking low to avoid being knocked from his mount by a low-hanging branch, he drove his horse into the forest. He could see Tacachale just ahead of him. The old woman moved with speed surprising for her age, weaving between the trees and bushes like a frightened rabbit. From behind came the shouts of Fernando's men and sounds of pursuit, but those sounds quickly faded as the forest closed about him.

Fernando knew he was exposing himself to immense danger by chasing after the woman alone. The forest was alive with bloodthirsty Indians. Still, he was determined not to lose his quarry. He'd come too far, faced too many hardships, to give up so easily. He was certain Tacachale held knowledge about the Fountain of Youth. Perhaps she knew the location of the fabled water. He would find out. The touch of a heated blade could make even the most stubborn talk.

A fleeting glimpse of white up ahead let him know that he was still hot on Tacachale's trail. But the distance between them had widened. Instead of giving him the advantage of greater speed, his horse was slowing him down, forcing him to look for wider gaps in the foliage to squeeze through. Soon he would lose sight of her and all would be lost.

Deciding what must be done, he quickly dismounted, tied his horse to a tree, and continued on foot. It didn't take Fernando long to realize that, even on foot, he was hard-pressed to keep up. The forest seemed to be opposing him, deliberately trying to hamper his efforts. Roots and vines snatched at his feet, tripping him. Branches raked painfully across his face. In a matter of minutes, he was drenched in sweat and panting from the exertion. Still, he plodded on.

It was nearly sunset when Fernando emerged from the forest onto a wide field of tall grasses and weeds. The field was empty, no sign of the woman called Tacachale. Nor had there been so much as a glimpse of her in the past hour or so.

I've lost her.

With a sigh of despair, he slumped wearily to the ground. He had lost the woman. He'd also probably lost his only chance of finding the Fountain of Youth. Removing his helmet, he wiped a hand across his sweaty forehead and looked around. Worse yet, there was a very good chance that he, himself, was now lost. In his haste to capture the woman, he'd failed to pay attention to his surroundings. In such a vast and untamed wilderness, he might never find his way back.

Leaning back on his hands, he watched the sky change into various shades of reds and golds. The sunset was lovely, but it did little to dispel the despair in his heart.

"Why, God? Why? To bring me so close to finding what I seek, and then to fail. Why?"

Perhaps he expected a reply—some mighty voice to come booming forth from the heavens with a solution to his dilemma. No such voice was heard. His question remained unanswered.

With weariness heavy upon his shoulders, Fernando de Carmona stood up, placed his helmet back upon his head, and turned to start his trek back through the forest. Suddenly, from behind him came the flapping of a multitude of wings. He turned quickly, expecting to see a large flock of birds, but the field remained as empty as when he first laid eyes upon it.

But Fernando wasn't imagining it. He heard wings. Thousands of wings. And he heard the cries of birds, too! Herons, gulls, ducks, and countless other water fowl.

"What, in the name of God?"

Maybe the birds were hidden in the field. Perhaps they were beneath the weeds and could not be seen. But Fernando did not believe that. The cries were too many, the beating of wings too numerous, for him not to see at least one bird. No, there was something else at work here. Something strange.

The sun continued to set, bringing forth the beginning of night. As the temperature cooled, a mist gathered over the field, quickly spreading like fog rolling in with the ocean tide. The wind picked up from the west, carrying with it the faint, yet distinct, smell of water.

As Fernando witnessed the day change into night, watching the spreading of the mist, something truly incredible happened. He suddenly found that he was no longer standing at the edge of a field. Instead, he stood at the shore of a vast lake, a lake covered with thousands of water fowl.

"Madre de Dios," he said, crossing himself and turning to flee for his life. He stopped, remembering that one of the Calusa Indians they had tortured had said something about a lake—a lake that could only be seen at sunset, and then only by the pure of heart. In the middle of the lake there was supposed to be an island. What was on the island the Calusa knew not, for none had ever gone there. But a magical lake could only guard something of an even greater magic.

The Fountain of Youth.

Fernando turned back around and studied the lake. Though the lake's surface was shrouded in mist, he could make out a dark smudge in the distance, near its center.

An island. The story is true.

Turning to his right, he began to jog along the coastline, searching for a way around, or across, the lake. He'd only gone twenty paces when he found what he was looking for.

The canoe was made from a log, its sides blackened with fire and polished smooth, its middle hollowed out. It was much smaller than those used by the savages living along the east coast. Nor was it a double-hulled vessel as the Calusa sometimes constructed for ocean use. Lying in the bottom was a wooden, leaf-shaped paddle.

Next to the canoe, Fernando spotted drag marks in the mud, indicating that there had once been a second canoe. There were footprints beside the drag marks, the small, bare footprints of a woman.

"Tacachale," he whispered, his voice barely a hiss. Fernando raised his head, looking across the lake to the distant island.

So, the woman has sought to use trickery to escape me. But God, in his infinite wisdom, knows that my heart is pure and has allowed me to see the lake. And before this night is through, I am certain he will show me the Fountain of Youth.

Freeing the canoe from the mud, he pushed off from shore, jumped in, and began paddling. The mist closed about him as he glided out into the water, making visibility difficult. He would have to paddle slowly and carefully, taking care not to miss the island.

As he crossed the lake, Fernando was surrounded by the cries of countless water fowl. Despite the ruckus, the birds seemed not to be disturbed by his intrusion into their domain. In fact, they barely bothered to move out of his way, remaining close enough that he could reach out and touch them. Which he did . . .

Reaching his right hand out, Fernando attempted to stroke the breast of a grey heron that brushed the side of his canoe. But instead of feathers, his fingers grasped only air as his hand passed completely through the bird.

With a cry of terror, he snatched his hand back as though burned. His sudden motion rocked the canoe, nearly capsizing the tiny vessel.

What manner of madness is this? Birds that can be seen but not touched? But if the birds are not real, then . . .

Fernando slowly leaned forward and reached down to touch the water, but his hand remained dry. No cool water splashed against his fingertips. Like the birds, the water could be seen but not felt. It was as though the tiny canoe rode upon clouds.

Clutching the sides of the canoe tightly, Fernando took deep breaths to calm his racing heart and regain his composure. The thought of falling into the water terrified him. After all, what would happen to him if he fell into a lake of dreams?

His muscles tight with fear, Fernando continued his journey. He paddled for what seemed a great length of time, certain that he had missed the island and was only traveling in circles. He was about to give up when suddenly his canoe ran aground.

Fernando quickly leaped from the canoe, happy to have solid

ground again underfoot. He nearly cried out when he spotted the other canoe no more than twenty feet away and knew that he had landed on the island.

God has guided me safely across the waters.

Fernando checked the other canoe. It was empty. Footprints led to a path that cut through the forest. With no other trail to choose from, he began. After about sixty paces he saw the distinct glow of a fire flickering through the trees ahead of him. He drew his sword and advanced.

Reaching the edge of a small clearing, he discovered that the glow was not that of a campfire. On the contrary, it was caused by thirty or forty brightly burning torches. The torches were stuck in the ground, placed in a circle around a small pool of water. The dark surface of the pool reflected the torchlight like the twinkling of stars.

Fernando would have stepped into the clearing had it been deserted, but it was not. The old woman he had chased for so many miles stood with her back to him, her head back and her hands raised to the night sky. She spoke, but he could not understand her words. Undoubtedly, she was offering up prayers to some heathen god of hers. He crouched lower as she turned to her right, her profile coming into view.

As he watched, Tacachale knelt before the pool and drank of the dark water.

The transformation happened so quickly it took his breath away. No sooner had the wrinkled old woman drunk of the water than she began to change.

Raven color exploded from her scalp, driving the grey from her tangled locks. Her hair, once dull and limp, became luxurious with youth.

Her gnarled hands straightened, the veins sinking back beneath the surface, the wrinkled skin pulling tight. Flesh that hung limp from her arms pulled closer to the bone and tightened with the presence of new, youthful muscles. Her body straightened and grew taller; her legs became long and lean.

The saggy flesh on her chin and neck pulled taut, like leather drying under a summer sun. The wrinkles marring her face disappeared so fast Fernando could scarce believe they had been there at all. Her eyes, once pale and lifeless, darkened and burned with the intensity of a woman who could set men's souls on fire.

Excitement leaped into Fernando's heart. At long last he'd found the fabled Fountain of Youth. He cried out in happiness. Tacachale heard the sound and spun around. Seeing him, her face went livid with rage. Fernando cared not what the woman thought of him. Stepping from his place of concealment, he marched into the clearing boldly. Tacachale moved to block him, but he cuffed her hard across the side of the head, knocking her aside. "As God is my witness," he shouted, "I lay discovery to this Eternal Fountain of Youth and claim it in the name of King Charles I and the country of Spain."

He stopped at the edge of the pool. Staring into it, its dark surface reflecting the glow of torches, he was overcome with the feeling that he was looking up and not down, gazing into the depths of a starry night, looking deep into the heavens. The sensation made him dizzy.

Fernando glanced to his left. Tacachale stood and glared at him, but made no further attempt to stop him. With a quick prayer of thanks, he sheathed his sword, kneeled, and dipped a cupped hand into the water.

The water was as sweet as the finest wine he'd ever tasted and as cold as a winter morning. Fernando drank deeply, experiencing a sensation of strength and power surge through him. Only after he had drunk his fill did he stand back up. Wiping a hand across his mouth, he turned and regarded Tacachale.

The woman watched him with obvious contempt, her dark eyes mirroring the anger in her soul. As Fernando looked at Tacachale, he became aware that he no longer hated her. On the contrary, he suddenly found her quite attractive, even desirable, in a savage sort of way. He studied the way her firm breasts stretched tight the thin fabric of her dress, and how the torchlight glistened off her muscular legs and black hair. Though her mouth was tight, her lips were full and would be soft to the touch, as would other parts of her anatomy.

Fernando smiled as a warm, glowing sensation started in his

loins. It had been many a year since he felt such unharnessed virility. The woman had given him quite a chase. Would she be so energetic in bed?

The glow within him intensified, spread into his stomach, shot through his veins. His feet, hands, and face began to tingle.

He took a step toward the Indian woman, intending to claim his prize. The glow became hotter, bordering on the uncomfortable. Pain flashed along the nerves in his legs and back.

He stopped suddenly, biting down on his lower lip to keep from crying out. It felt as though a heated sword had been thrust deep into his stomach. Fiery pain shot through his limbs.

What's wrong? What's happening?

His fingers trembling, Fernando held his hands before his face. The veins in the back of his hands were moving and quivering, twitching about like a nest of snakes beneath his skin. He felt the veins in his arms and legs doing the same thing. Lowering his hands, he looked at the woman.

Tacachale's face was no longer etched with hatred; her features had softened. Turning her head to one side, she spit a mouthful of water upon the ground. She looked back at Fernando and smiled.

She didn't drink from the pool. No. It can't be. You saw her. Yes, but she didn't swallow. She tricked you. The water is poisoned.

Fernando drew his sword. "You witch. You have poisoned me."

Tacachale shook her head. "I have poisoned no one. You have found what you seek. This is the water you call the Fountain of Youth."

"You lie!" He took another step toward her.

She backed up and shook her head. "I too drank from the pool. Was I not old when first you saw me? Now I am young."

Fernando stopped. "But how? Why?" The burning sensation inside him was unbearable. It was all he could do to hold back a scream. He detected an odor about him like that of burning hair and was certain that the hairs inside his nose had begun to smolder.

"Like everything that you see, this pool was placed here by the Creator. But its use is not for everyone. It is only for those who are pure of spirit and heart. You call yourselves Christians and claim to be pure of heart, but your spirits are filled with greed."

She circled around to the opposite side of the pool, bending over to pick up something lying in the shadows. Torchlight twinkled off of metal as she carried it back around. It was a helmet. A Spanish helmet.

"You are not the first white man to discover this secret place. Others have come before you. Their greed led them to drink from the Fountain of Eternal Life."

"Eternal life!" Fernando shouted. "I'm burning up inside. I'm dying. Help me."

Tacachale shook her head sadly. "My people cannot understand why the white man is afraid of dying. Is your fear so great that you would turn your back on the reward the Great Spirit offers you in the next life—the reward you call heaven—choosing instead to live forever?"

The backs of Fernando's hands were beginning to burn. Tiny spirals of white smoke drifted up from his skin. Larger spirals escaped from around the edges of his armor. His tongue was swollen and it felt as though his eyes were about to ignite in flame.

Tacachale set the helmet down and walked over to a small pile of dried branches. She picked one up and returned to stand before Fernando.

"Your greed has denied you the chance to ever die and enter heaven. Had you taken but one sip from the pool, as I did, you would have become young again and stayed that way for many years. But you drank deeply."

Fernando's armor began to sizzle and pop. His beard and hair smoldered.

Tacachale stepped closer. "While all men grow old and die, only the earth and sky last forever. And now, you too will be part of that sky. Like those who came before you, your soul will be an eternal flame for all to see. It will be a guiding light, a star in the night sky."

"Noooo . . ." He screamed. The flame that burned within him exploded into brilliance, bursting through to the surface. His clothes and hair ignited.

Fernando's flesh burned, turned black, and floated away from his bones as tiny flakes of ash. The metal of his armor liquified and ran to the ground.

Tacachale stepped forward, touching the end of the branch to the flame that consumed Fernando, lighting the torch. She stepped quickly back as what was left of the Spaniard collapsed to the ground. The fire was hot, leaving nothing behind as it burned. Not even bones.

Holding the torch before her, she circled the pool to the far side, placing it in line with the others. The light of the torch reflected in the dark water. As it did, a new star appeared in the sky above. A tiny white star, far away, but beautiful to look at all the same—a star that was once Fernando de Carmona. Tacachale, whose name meant "to light a new fire," looked up at the star and smiled.

Castle of Maidens

———————— ✠ ————————

Richard Lee Byers

The hall was built of white, blue-veined marble. The ancient Athenians had raised it as a temple, and idols of Zeus, Hera, and their kindred, more lifelike than any sculptor carves today, still smiled enigmatically from niches in the wall. The conquering Turks warmed the pale, cold splendor of the place with a riot of color. Persian carpets lay strewn about the floor. Banners, seized from the Bulgars and Servians, depended from the ceiling, and even the humblest slaves wore silk and cloth-of-gold. The Janizaries were particularly magnificent, their cloak pins and the hilts of their scimitars glittering with jewels.

Feeling beggarly in my worn, travel-stained surcoat, my mail leggings clinking and my empty scabbard swinging at my side, I approached the dais and salaamed. Beside me, my commander did the same. A eunuch with a reedy voice announced us: "Bernardino Colleoni, Bishop of Padua, legate from His Holiness Urban VII, and Captain Martin Rivers, knight banneret."

It took an effort not to scowl. Captain of nothing, I thought.

The herald hadn't recited a tithe of Bernardino's titles. Not a promising sign. And he kept us bent over half a minute, which didn't augur any better. Finally, after my back had begun to ache and I'd had ample time to reflect on how undignified I must look with my arse hoisted in the air, he bade us, "Rise," and we straightened up to petition the man on the throne.

I'd heard that Ibrahim, formerly Pasha of Attica, self-proclaimed Sultan since he'd rebelled against the Great Turk, was a notable archer and wrestler. But the gray-bearded fellow before us looked soft, with a double chin and a fat belly. The crooked scar on his forehead, relic of a fall from a horse three years before, shone white as lightning in his olive skin. To my surprise, he smelled of spirits, for all that the corpses of men and women gibbeted for defying their monarch's prohibition on strong drink hung in chains throughout the city. "You come with little pomp," he said petulantly, reminding me of a child whining that he doesn't like his dinner. "Does your master think me of little account?"

Bernardino's long-lashed eyes widened in mock surprise. "Of course not, Your Majesty! His Holiness considers you one of the most august sovereigns in the world. Rest assured, our retinue, laden with tokens of his esteem, will arrive directly." As always, he lied well. I almost believed him myself. "But we came ahead, because our mission is urgent. Is it true you hold," his mellifluous voice dropped unctuously, "the Grail?"

Ibrahim smirked as if Bernardino had said something funny. "Yes. I believe I have it around here somewhere. A Jew, a finder and seller of antiquities, turned it up in Cyprus, then traded it to ransom his wife and daughter." He giggled, and I understood that he hadn't honored his part of the bargain. Then his eyes narrowed. "But how did you know?"

To the left of the throne stood an obese Nubian, the spray of dyed ostrich plumes rising from his turban and the gems flashing in his talismanic rings mute testimony that, in this court established in imitation of the Great Turk's, the chief black eunuch was not only butler of the harem and royal sorcerer but the third-ranking officer in the state. Making sure I didn't so much as glance at him, hoping I was a convincing liar myself, I said, "His Holiness keeps spies in Avignon."

Bernardino spread his arms. It was the gesture of a polished rhetorician, and I was unpleasantly reminded of his final oration to his troops. Still, I was glad of the facility with which he changed the subject. "I beg Your Majesty," he said. "Since you don't follow our faith, the Grail can mean little to you. But to us, there's no more sacred object on earth, and thus it belongs in the custody of the Pontiff. Please, let us take it to Rome. Every Christian in the world will praise your name."

Ibrahim tittered. "Even those who follow Clement?"

Bernardino's wide mouth tightened. "Clement is the Anti-Pope," he said. "It would be a travesty—"

The sultan snapped his fingers. A servant scurried forward, knelt, and proffered a golden goblet. As he took it, Ibrahim said, "Clement's emissaries came in great state. They gave me coffers of jewels and tuns of wine."

"So will we," I said, "but we also offer something more: alliance. Neither Orhan nor the Sicilians recognize your claim to this kingdom." Ibrahim pouted. Courtiers stiffened. Suddenly I regretted taking this tack, but having begun, there was naught to do but press on. "Soon, one or both will invade, and Attica can't muster enough men-at-arms to repel either by itself. But with the Papal States . . ."

Ibrahim threw his cup at me. I could have dodged, but it seemed more politic to let it ring against my breastplate. Throughout the chamber, people cowered. Only the Janizaries remained unperturbed.

"Liar!" the sultan screamed, spittle spraying from his lips. "I am the greatest warrior who ever lived! The shades of Alexander and Saladin anointed me! I don't need anyone's help! Let every host on earth come against me! I'll build cities with their bones!"

"Forgive me, Your Majesty," I faltered. "Obviously, I expressed myself badly. I know you're a superb knight, and I didn't mean to imply that you *require* anyone's aid. You might find it *advantageous.*"

Ibrahim turned to the functionary who'd conducted us into his presence. "Get these pigs away from me!" he cried. "And keep them away till I send for them again."

Bernardino's nostrils flared. He was the son of a count, and I daresay that no one, even the irascible and unreasonable Urban, had ever used him with such discourtesy. Still, whatever he wanted to say, he was prudent enough to swallow it. We bowed and withdrew.

The building housing Ibrahim's hall was only one of a complex of ancient temples. After the dukes of Athens claimed the place for their citadel, each modified, extended, and connected the existing structures in accordance with his own idiosyncratic architectural vision. Thus, as the varlet led us to our quarters, we traversed a mazelike warren of corridors, courtyards, and covered walkways, our path rendered even more circuitous by the necessity of circumventing the harem. As we walked, I noticed how many of Ibrahim's household labored under marks of his displeasure. A gardener burdened with an iron collar and deadweight. A groom with a St. Elmo's belt scraping his waist. A little boy in a mute's bridle scrubbing floors. I shivered. Clearly, the sultan was no respecter of embassies, and it was sheer luck that he hadn't ordered me fitted with some similar device.

When we reached our suite, Bernardino beckoned and led me onto the balcony. Below us, down the mountainside, lay vineyards and olive orchards, then the city, then the dazzling blue harbor, full of fishing boats, where our sole surviving galley waited. But I knew he hadn't summoned me out to admire the view. If we talked in the open air, Ibrahim's spies were unlikely to overhear us.

Bernardino glared at me. "What in God's name possessed you in there?" he demanded. "You told me you'd done this kind of thing before." I experienced an almost overwhelming desire to hurl him over the balustrade.

I wish I could report that I loathed him because he was a pitiful excuse for a priest who'd never set foot in most of his benefices and was ignorant of every sacrament but simony. Or because I'd watched him sack convents, rape nuns, and butcher folk who'd surrendered after he'd pledged them safe conduct. But although I deplored his transgressions, as I'd casually regretted the excesses of many a companion and commander, I see now that my animus was almost entirely personal.

Ever since I was knighted, I'd fancied myself another Knollys. I'd spent years as a rutter, making a name and hoarding plunder, hoping to found a mercenary company of my own. And finally I managed it, though it took every penny I had. Now, less than a year later, my force was gone, and, I feared, my martial reputation with it. Unwilling to blame myself, though I could have left the

Pope's employ at any time, I blamed the lackluster soldier Urban had set above me.

Still, he remained my master, and my comrade in a desperate charade, so I did my best to mask my ire. "We agreed we'd offer him an alliance."

"We didn't agree to insult him."

I struggled to keep my voice low. "What I said wasn't insulting, he just took it that way. In case you didn't notice, he's off his head."

"Clearly, you lack the acuity for this, so from now on, keep your mouth shut. I'll handle everything myself."

My fists clenched. "The way you handled the defenses at Brindisi?"

For a second I thought he was going to throw himself at me. Then a footfall sounded behind us.

We whirled. In the doorway stood Ahmed, the Nubian I'd striven not to incriminate during our audience with the sultan, his smooth face black as ink in the afternoon sunlight. He was puffing from his trek across the palace, and I smelled sweat through the reek of his perfume. "My lords," he squealed, "compose yourselves! What will people think of you and your holy master if they look up here and see you grappling like baboons?"

Bernardino sucked in a deep breath. "You're right, of course," he growled. "I spoke unfairly, Martin. Pray forgive me." I nodded curtly. At that moment, it was the most gracious response I could manage. He turned back to Ahmed. "Though I doubt it matters how we conduct ourselves. The sultan would deny us the Grail in any case."

Ahmed nodded. His ostrich feathers bobbed and the fat under his jaw jiggled. "I fear you're right. For some reason, he doted on Cardinal de Foix. He means to give him the Grail as soon as he returns with more French gold. And once Ibrahim makes a decision, no matter how feckless, it's virtually impossible to change his mind."

I said, "Clement's bounty can't possibly compare with Urban's. When our train arrives . . ."

The eunuch grimaced. "Have done. There are no treasure ships following you, because the Pope knows nothing of your mission. If he did, he would have sent someone other than men who forfeited his trust when they lost his army. Which is why I dispatched my messenger to that wretched little garrison where Urban banished you instead of Rome."

Bernardino goggled. I said, "I don't understand. When you penned your letter, the army was intact."

Ahmed's fleshy lips quirked into a smile. "But its annihilation was written in the stars."

Somewhat recovered from his astonishment, Bernardino asked, "But why did you want false embassies instead of legitimate ones?"

"Because I was sure that even the most eloquent legate would prove incapable of persuading Ibrahim to send the Grail to Rome. But I hoped that bold men-at-arms, desperate to regain their master's favor, might dare to steal it. If I'd proposed something so seemingly harebrained in a letter, I doubt you would have come. So I lured you by writing that even though the sultan had commenced secret negotiations with Clement, I thought he might still treat with Urban's embassies if they materialized on his doorstep, for which deception I apologize."

Bernardino's mouth hung open. Perhaps mine did too. "Surely the Grail's well guarded," he said at last.

"It would be if a pious sovereign held it," Ahmed said bitterly. "Devout Mussulmans respect Jesus as a teacher even if they don't revere Him as the Savior. But it amuses Ibrahim to employ the vessel in his debauches. And most nights, after he casts it aside, it simply lies on the harem floor till morning."

"That means it is well guarded," I said. Once past my initial amazement, I'd begun, reflexively, almost despite myself, to consider the theft as a tactical problem. "Since no one's allowed in that part of the palace save the sultan, the odalisques, and the black eunuchs. Are you planning to sneak it out?"

Ahmed shook his head. "Ibrahim is likely to call for me at any hour of the day or night. And, in truth, I simply lack the courage. But I can slip you in and out, then out the postern. You can flee down the mountain, board your ship, and sail before anyone realizes aught's amiss."

Frowning suspiciously, Bernardino asked the question I was about to pose. "I understand why a minister might summon foreign embassies against his master's wishes, if the act would benefit the kingdom. But why would you help us steal Ibrahim's treasure?"

"Because I was born and baptized a Christian," Ahmed answered, "and I still worship Jesus in my heart. It galls me to see the Grail in Mussulman hands! It belongs in Rome, and if it doesn't go now, before Orhan invades, it'll never get there. It'll rot in a Turkish fortress till the end of time."

"But you risk death," Bernardino said. "Are you truly so devout?"

"Devout and a little vengeful," Ahmed said. "Ibrahim had me cut. And when he discovered I possessed the Sight, he compelled me to study sorcery. How would you feel toward a master who forced you to spend your life urinating through a quill? To traffic with demons and so jeopardize your salvation? Nor was that the end of his abuses. Only a month ago he ordered me bastinadoed, simply because I warned him that his extravagances were draining the treasury. Trust me, my lords, I have ample reason to do him ill. The question is, will you help me?"

Bernardino and I exchanged glances, and I saw we were in accord. "*How* would you slip us into the harem?" I asked.

Ahmed smiled. "With magic. You'll see tonight."

"Can you get word to my squire Geoffrey, so he'll know to be ready to sail?"

"Certainly."

"Then we'll do it," Bernardino said. "What does the Grail look like?"

I sneered. I'd never attended a seminary or university, but simply because I was curious, and read books and listened to scholars when I could, I knew more about sacred matters than he did. "It's made of snow-white metal," I said, "with pearls set about the rim."

Ahmed nodded. "Precisely. Now I must go, before Ibrahim misses me. Look for me after midnight. Fix your couches to look like you're under the covers." He turned and bustled out of the suite.

Bernardino arched an eyebrow. "Well," he said, "an unexpected turn of events. I never dreamed we'd win the Grail so fast."

"We haven't won it yet."

"I know. Still," he looked out to sea, "what do you suppose it's like?"

Surprised at the wistful note in his voice, I said, "Surely Urban's shown you the Tables of the Law and the skulls of Peter and Paul. What are they like?"

"Dirty stone and moldering bone," he said. "Lifeless things that could only move the simple. But do you think the Grail could be different? There are so many stories."

For some reason, I felt a pang of anger. "And this is exactly like the stories, isn't it? Ibrahim's saintly, just like the Fisher King. And look at us, perfect paladins, kissing his arse, pledging him aid against the rightful Christian sovereign of Attica, dissembling, and plotting robbery with a sorcerer. It's a wonder no one's mistaken us for Galahad and Perceval."

Bernardino sighed. "You're right, of course. It's just, well, you understand I didn't enter the Church because I had a calling. Still, I thought that when I celebrated Mass, I'd feel something. But, never mind. I'm going to try to get some sleep." He went inside.

I tried to rest too, but neither of us was particularly successful. As the night wore on, our nerves frayed. When Ahmed scuttled into the suite, he found me drumming my fingers and Bernardino pacing.

The eunuch opened his voluminous robe and brought out our swords and daggers. I winced, because I was afraid the seneschal would notice they were missing. But it was too late to fret about it now.

"Exactly where is the Grail?" Bernardino asked, returning his dagger to its sheath.

"I don't know," Ahmed said. "Wherever Ibrahim dropped it. You'll have to look. But don't worry, you'll be able to move around freely. Now stand still, I'm going to enchant you." Raising his pudgy hands, he started muttering, in a guttural tongue I'd never heard before.

A spicy aroma filled my nostrils. My head swam, my vision blurred, and I had to struggle not to flinch away. When the dizziness abated, a chill spread over my skin like a coating of invisible rime.

"Finished," Ahmed said.

Trying to determine what he'd done, I glanced down at myself. Though I could still feel my gauntlets, my hands looked bare and black.

Bernardino gasped. I turned. To all appearances, the Italian had become a Nubian harem guard, with a round belly, a beardless jaw, and a curved sword sticking through his sash.

"Can we carry our shields?" I asked.

"Yes," Ahmed said, "the illusion covers all, even defects in your speech. Your name is Selim." He turned to Bernardino. "And you, my lord, are Mustafa."

"Where are the real ones?" I asked.

"Drugged," Ahmed replied, "though with luck they'll never realize it. They'll think they simply swilled too much pilfered wine." He crept to the doorway and peeked out. "Come on."

A few minutes' walk brought us in sight of the bare chamber that separated the harem from the rest of the seraglio. Two Janizary halberdiers guarded the near doorway and a pair of black eunuch spearmen stood watch by the far one. "Walk right past them," Ahmed whispered. "When you find the Grail, bring it to your quarters." He gripped our shoulders, then lumbered back the way we'd come.

Even though we could see the illusions veiling our true appearances, it took an effort to advance without hesitation. Beside me, Bernardino trembled, either out of trepidation or because of the coldness that still lay upon our skins.

A scuffing footfall and a kind of snort sounded behind me, where I knew no one had been a moment before. Startled, I almost spun around, an action that might well have aroused the sentinels' suspicion. But I caught myself in time, and when the noises didn't recur, I decided I'd only heard echoes of our own progress.

One of the halberdiers nodded as we passed. I nodded back. Both Nubians smiled, and one wished us a good night. Bernardino replied in kind, and then we entered the harem.

I realized I was holding my breath, and released it. And at that moment, an ironic fancy struck me. Some of the Grail heroes had visited castles full of captive maidens. In one respect, we were like them after all.

Bernardino gazed at the choice of passageways before us. "Which way?" he whispered.

I didn't know any better than he did, but if he wanted me to choose, I would. "This," I said, and led him to the right.

We soon discovered that the harem was both as extensive and as labyrinthine as the rest of the palace, one tiny chamber after another crammed with divans, gilded tapestries, jeweled pipes, flutes, harps, and bird cages hooded for the night. Interspersed with the apartments were sets of baths, steaming *hamams* adjoining cooler *tepidaria*. Most of the lamps had been extinguished and scarcely anyone was up and about, though occasionally we encountered a eunuch sentry on patrol.

Bernardino and I prowled along, peering into doorways. Some of the odalisques slumbered twined together, some smiled into space with opium pills laid out beside them, and a few wept, or writhed in their sleep, their depilated bodies locked inside the same kinds of punishment devices I'd seen employed outside. Eventually we found a fully appointed torture chamber, where skinning cats, skull-splitters, and pincers hung on the walls, the atmosphere smelled of roast flesh, and the remains of a once-beautiful adolescent girl lay burned and broken on the ladder rack.

Sickened, I looked about the room. No Grail. Bernardino gripped my forearm. "What's that?" he said.

"What?" I asked, but as soon as I did, I heard it also—a series of rapid inhalations.

It could have been something innocuous, an odalisque with a cold trying to clear her head. Instinct told me it wasn't. I hastened into the chamber and crouched behind the spiked chair. Bernardino did the same.

Footsteps, soft as the one I'd heard outside the harem, padded up the corridor. Then something snuffled like a hound following a scent. My ears told me it was standing right in the doorway, yet I couldn't see it. The hairs on the back of my neck stood on end.

The phantom sniffed again. Certain that it smelled us and was about to attack, I eased my hand onto the hilt of my sword. Then it stalked on down the passage.

"What was that?" Bernardino quavered.

"I don't know," I said, "but it followed us in past the sentries."

"What? If you knew that, why didn't you say something?"

"Because I thought my ears were playing tricks on me." I nervously tried to loosen my sword in its scabbard. For a moment, it stuck, so I drew it to see why. When I did, Bernardino and I both started in amazement. The blade was red from point to hilt. A coppery stink suffused the air.

I picked up a rusty-stained towel and tried to wipe the weapon clean. Fresh blood oozed out of the steel like sweat seeping from a man's pores.

Bernardino unsheathed his arms. They were gory as well. Then the invisible frost tingled off my skin, and suddenly my companion was a lean Italian again. I hastily checked my own appearance, and saw that it had reverted to normal too.

When I grasped what was happening, I started for the door, promising myself that if I survived, I'd take revenge.

"Wait!" Bernardino wailed. "We can't walk around unmasked!"

"We have to," I replied. "Don't you see? The eunuch conjured a demon to murder Ibrahim, and means for us to take the blame. Ahmed's differences with the sultan are common knowledge, and if his master turned up slain, the Janizaries would ordinarily hold him responsible. But not if they find Christian men-at-arms with bloody swords lurking in the vicinity."

"But we can tell them the truth!"

"Apparently Ahmed is confident that they'll kill us without heeding. Perhaps he cast a spell that will ensure it. Since there's no unguarded way out of there, our only chance is to save Ibrahim, then throw ourselves on his mercy. Now come on!"

We dashed on into the maze. At one point a guard stepped out of a doorway. "The sultan's in danger!" I cried. Snarling, he leveled his tasseled lance. I sprang at him, deflected his point with my shield, and punched him in the jaw. He fell unconscious.

Bernardino and I ran on. Many of the chambers looked alike, and I began to fear that we'd taken a wrong turn and were coursing down corridors we'd traversed before. Then he gasped, "There!"

I peered into the room he was facing. Beyond the threshold, Ibrahim and a doe-eyed Circassian odalisque sprawled on a divan gobbling cakes from a platter. Judging from their nudity, the damp spots on the cushions, and the wet footprints on the floor, they'd recently emerged from the baths behind the doorway in the far wall.

The woman looked up and screamed.

I stepped into the chamber, Bernardino a pace behind me. When I did, I noticed a silver chalice set with pearls lying on its side beneath a table. I should have known, I thought. It makes this whole absurd predicament absolutely perfect.

"Your Majesty," I said, "you're in peril. Ahmed—"

Ibrahim recoiled into a corner, dragging the odalisque with him, interposing her body between us. "Help!" he shrieked. "Assassins! Roman assassins!"

As I opened my mouth to deny it, footsteps pounded up behind me. I wheeled, snatched out my bloody sword, hacked and failed to connect.

The spirit hissed like a colossal serpent. A blow slammed down on my shoulder. It didn't pierce my cuirass, but it staggered me.

I heard the demon scramble to my left, darting around me to reach the sultan. I flung myself back in its path and thrust, missing it again. Its counterstroke whistled at my head and I ducked beneath it.

"Help me!" I shouted, and when Bernardino didn't respond, I shot a glance in his direction. He was gazing in the general direction of the divan and table, his blade still sheathed and an imbecilic simper on his face. Apparently fear of the demon had driven him mad.

Which meant I'd have to fight the thing alone. And I couldn't defeat what I couldn't see.

The devil battered me. Through instinct and luck, I blocked

most of its blows, and my armor turned the rest. When its on-slaught faltered, as every offense must sooner or later, I threw my shield at it, freeing my left hand, sprang backward, tore the oda-lisque out of Ibrahim's arms, punched him, gripped his forearm, and dragged him toward the opening in the back wall.

Though I'd stunned him, he feebly squirmed and pummeled me. I scarcely noticed, because just then the spirit's footsteps rushed at me again. I slashed repeatedly, without pause. Shieldless and encumbered with a captive, I only had one hope of surviving the next several seconds, and that was to lash my sword around so fiercely that it would hold my opponent at bay.

For a few precious moments, the demon hung back. Then it hissed and lunged. Something, a blade or talons, ripped my side.

The wound blazed with pain. Certain I was about to collapse, I reeled, but when I did, I saw how far I'd retreated: the pool was only a few feet away. The realization heartened me, and I managed to throw Ibrahim and myself in.

The hot water seared my face and the gash in my ribs. A cloud of blood, my own and the exudation from my sword, billowed around me. As I floundered to my feet, the demon plunged in after me.

As I'd hoped, its legs poked holes in the water. Now that I could see where it was and read its stance, I might be able to de-stroy it.

I feinted and cut. The demon dodged and riposted. I could tell what it was doing from the way it shifted its feet, and I expected to parry easily. Instead, the force of its swing almost knocked me down. For an instant the world went black.

Shocked, I realized I was nearly spent. If I didn't finish the bat-tle quickly, the spirit would outlast me. Shouting, actually croak-ing, a war cry, I threw my sword at its head to distract it, then dove at it, terrified it would whip its arm in line to impale me. It didn't. I clinched, yanked out my dagger, and ripped at its kidney.

Clawed hands scrabbled at my gorget, then locked around it. I kept stabbing. The steel collar groaned and began to crumple. Then the devil shrieked, released me, and fell back.

It carried my dagger with it, lodged in its body, so I could tell it sank to the bottom. When I was certain it was going to stay there, I blundered to the side of the bath and clung there panting.

Four eunuch warriors burst through the entry to the *tepidarium,* scimitars drawn. Ibrahim pointed at me. "Kill him!" he cried, and they charged.

So much for the gratitude of madmen. Perhaps his wits were so addled that he didn't comprehend that I'd rescued him. I tried to flee, but I was too weak to drag myself out of the water.

Bernardino stepped out of the shadows, his eyes closed like a sleepwalker's, the silver chalice clasped against his heart, and his right hand extended. When Ibrahim saw him, he froze, and the swordsmen stumbled to a halt.

Bernardino kneeled beside the pool and laid his hand on Ibrahim's head. His fingers glowed. The sultan shuddered, and the scar on his brow faded and disappeared. Lines in his face vanished with it, until he almost seemed to be a different man. "Merciful Allah," he whispered, "what have I done?"

Bernardino slumped to the floor, the cup still cradled against his breast. I started to fall backward. I fumbled at the edge of the *hamam,* but my hands were numb and wouldn't grip. Ibrahim caught me and held my head above water, and then I fainted.

A stab of pain awoke me. When I opened my eyes, I was lying on the floor, and a eunuch physician was suturing my wound. Wishing that Bernardino had seen fit to heal me before he swooned, I lifted my head to see what was going on.

Ahmed kneeled at his master's feet. Two Janizaries held him immobile while a third looped a bowstring around his neck.

Strangely, I no longer wished to watch him die. "Don't!" I wheezed.

Ibrahim peered at me quizzically. "Weren't you trying to tell me that Ahmed sent the djinn? He must have, he's the only magician at court."

"He did," I said. "And I don't claim to know why. But if you'd been in his place, and cared aught for the welfare of Attica, what might you have done?"

The sultan scowled, and for a moment I feared I'd offended him. Then he said, "Perhaps you have a point." He turned to the

Janizaries. "Take him to his quarters. Guard him well, but don't mistreat him."

I tumbled into unconsciousness again.

In the week that followed, Ibrahim sent Ahmed into exile, then sailed for Anatolia to beg Orhan's forgiveness. When I felt hale enough to travel, Bernardino and I rode to the harbor. There he, Geoff, and I watched from the dock while our men readied the galley for departure. The air smelled of brine and fish, and gulls wheeled screeching overhead.

Clearly, Bernardino's thoughts were troubled. After a time that seemed quite long, he spoke. "I don't know how to tell you this, but . . ."

"You aren't coming with us," I said.

He blinked. "No. I can't return to the life I led before. How did you know?"

I grinned. "All that prayer and abstinence gave you away. What are you going to do?"

"Wander awhile. It will give me a chance to think. Eventually I might join the Franciscans."

"Take this with you." I handed him the satchel containing the chalice. Geoff gaped, aghast.

The Italian took the bag, then tried to give it back. "This belongs in Rome," he said.

I shook my head. "If Urban got his hands on the Grail, he'd use it to enhance his prestige, and wring money out of his supporters. Coin to hire rutters to slaughter Clement's followers. I think you can put the cup to better use."

After we said our farewells, Bernardino bade the equerry return the palfreys to the palace, then set off on foot. Soon he was out of sight. Geoff and I boarded, and the sailors cast off.

As Athens dwindled behind us, the squire glowered and stamped about the narrow confines of the deck. Finally I took pity on him. "Calm down," I said. "That wasn't the Grail."

He snorted. "Don't even try."

"It wasn't," I insisted. "The Grail isn't silver, it's made of some unearthly stuff Oberon carried out of Paradise. What's more, it isn't a chalice, it's the salver that held the Passover lamb at the Last

Supper. People only think it's a cup because centuries ago, some poet said it was, and since trouveres and minnesingers ape one another, they've been getting it wrong ever since. But plenty of school men know the truth, so I wouldn't care to try to palm a goblet off on Urban, would you?"

Geoff raked his fingers through his straw-colored hair. "If that wasn't the Grail, how did it alter the bishop's character? How did it heal Ibrahim?"

I shrugged. "I wish I knew. There's a mystery in it."

Geoff scowled, pondering. Eventually he sighed and asked, "What's next for us?"

"Ibrahim refilled my purse. Now I have to scour the tarnish off my name. A victory or two should do it. So I'll beg Urban to place me in the vanguard of his remaining forces. And if he won't, I'll seek an employer who will. Who knows, we might find a just cause to fight in. We did once or twice before."

Geoff said, "So long as the pay's good." The sail bellied, and the rowers shipped their oars.

From Camelot to Deadwood

———————————— ✠ ————————————

Gregory Nicoll

Two hours from Finn's Crossing, a Concord stagecoach dubbed the *Pride of New Hampshire* rolled slowly up into the Black Hills, pulled by a lathered team of six. She swayed and jostled her passengers gently, testing the strength of the bullhide thoroughbraces which cushioned their ride against the roughness of the trail. Clouds of white dust swirled in her wake.

Perched up top was the driver, a stout, nearly bald man with a drooping gray moustache. He wore a brown cowhide hat with its brim pinned up in front. Shouting encouragement to the horses, he slapped the reins against their backs as the incline of the road grew steeper. "*H'yah!* Up thar! G'wan!"

Beside the driver sat a small black man with a shotgun across his lap. He squinted against the trail dust, looking warily to either side of the road, his dark-skinned hands never loosening their grip on the polished stock of his weapon.

The bright yellow coach stood out sharply against the forest around it. The trees were tall brown pines, their limbs heavy with green vegetation and fragrant with sap. A jackrabbit bolted from the roadside bushes. Birds called from the high branches, fluttering off when the Concord rumbled past.

Inside the stage, Matthew Brackett swatted idly at a horsefly. He tilted his black top hat to shield his eyes from the sunlight at the edges of the flapping leather curtains. His hat's narrow brim also blocked his view of his two fellow travellers, though Matthew had long ago dismissed them. *A journalist and a missionary—a man of letters and a man of the cloth,* he thought. *And probably both of them Yankees . . .*

Matthew stroked the stiff hairs of his salt-and-peppery beard, and let his thoughts turn to the object of his journey: a dead man lying many miles away, who required the attention of a man graced with Matthew's peculiar skills. The tools and potions he would need rode safely in the black case lashed to the coach roof above. He had carried only enough for one operation, to avoid the additional fee for heavy baggage.

Matthew's mind wandered also to the unusual payment he'd been offered for his work—a new Winchester rifle. He had accepted the offer, but was concerned by the customer's strict deadline. If the stage delivered him to perform his services on time, the Winchester was his. If not, the offer was cancelled. For want of such a fine firearm, he had accepted the gamble.

In the seat opposite Matthew, the missionary whistled nervously. The tune was "Marching Through Georgia."

Matthew's heartbeat quickened. *A Yankee indeed,* he thought.

The missionary cut short his tune. "I say, gentleman," he intoned in the high, nasal voice of a native New Englander.

Matthew turned his head, repositioning his hat. "Yes?"

The missionary was young and soft. A small crucifix hung from a chain around his neck. His clothes were somber, his Wellington boots not yet scarred by use. "I say," he repeated, leaning forward against the jostling and creaking of the coach, "are there highwaymen active in these parts?"

Matthew smiled briefly. "Not many," he answered in his slow, cultured Southern voice. He paused, then added, "Mostly scalphunters."

The missionary recoiled, clutching reflexively at his derby as if to protect his own hair from immediate removal.

Beside him, the journalist let out a boisterous laugh. This man's tone was merry, his voice softened by tobacco. He was roguish and auburn-haired, with a thick black handlebar moustache and a dark slouch hat. A small brown leather notebook lay open in his lap, in which he had periodically jotted observations.

Smiling, the journalist spoke up. "The quaint custom of scalping was *not* originally an Indian tradition." He chuckled. "The French taught it to them—very civilized, very Christian Frenchmen, no doubt. You see, the white man has benevolently removed from the Indian his land, his birthright, and his manhood. In exchange, we gave him whisky, firearms, and Christianity—a bad bargain and an incendiary mixture." He grinned. "Me, I would have left out the Christianity."

Gunfire crashed.

The Concord rocked violently as the bullets hit, scattering splinters of bass-wood and hardened ash. The conductor returned fire, emptying his shotgun in a single volcanic blast. Something heavy tumbled across, then off of, the stagecoach roof.

The *Pride* lost momentum, her driver reining back the frightened team. With wood and leather creaking, the Concord came to a shuddering halt. Matthew lifted aside one of the damask-lined leather window curtains and stared outside.

Four mounted outlaws blocked the route. They were rough men, with clothing as unkempt as bear pelts. Three of them wore filthy scarves to conceal their faces, while the last man's prominent red beard served the same function. They carried Sharps rifles and brandished Remington revolvers.

"All passengers, dismount and give up yer guns," ordered the bearded outlaw gruffly. "Driver, throw down them cases."

Reluctantly, the coachman began to unfasten the cargo and cast it over. Baggage fell to earth with dull slaps.

The journalist pushed open the door and stepped down, gently removing a tiny Smith & Wesson from his duster. He laid the weapon carefully at his feet. Matthew followed, placing his Colt Navy beside it. The missionary offered up no firearm.

"Ain't you got a weapon?" asked one of the masked thieves, who dismounted, pointing his Remington at the man of the cloth.

"My weapon is my faith," said the missionary, producing a Bible from his pocket and placing it near the pistols.

Odd, thought Matthew. *I was certain he had a rifle . . .*

A small masked outlaw darted over and scooped up the revolvers. He ignored the Bible.

The last of the cargo was now on the ground. Appointing one of their number as a guard for the hostages, the others rummaged through the baggage.

The missionary became agitated. He licked his lips and somehow could not keep his gaze on the gun pointed at him.

"Knives!" called out one of the men examining the contents of Matthew's embalmer's case. "I never seen so many queer little knives, an' hooks, an' such!"

"I am an undertaker," said Matthew calmly, "and those are the specialized tools of my trade."

The outlaw let go of them as if he'd touched a heated branding iron. He kicked the case roughly aside and opened another. "What in all creation is *this?*"

The journalist chanced a quick look. "Oh! The device you behold, gentlemen, is the Orphyrreus Compositor," he said, "an invention in which I have invested a considerable sum. It produces typeset text by the use of small levers, one for each character of our alphabet."

"Pshaw!" huffed another bandit. "All the readin' a man needs is the *XXX* on whisky an' gunpowder." He joined the others in opening a large cube-shaped black trunk.

The journalist returned his attention to the pistol pointing at him. "Fortunately there is an *X* among the compositor's levers," he said quietly, "so that it may be used to correspond with men as well-bred as yourselves."

At length a shrill cry went up from the outlaws rifling the cargo. One of them held aloft an enormous silver chalice, its ornate sides crusted with emeralds and pearls.

"Put it down!" called the missionary, his face flushed with anger. He took an abrupt step toward the one with the chalice.

The guard swung his revolver and struck the missionary across the head. The man of God fell to the ground, clutching at his temples and moaning weakly. The guard snorted, disgust evident even through his stained kerchief. He gestured at the other prisoners. "You two, put that feller back in the stage and let 'im sleep it off."

As they hoisted the missionary back into the Concord, Matthew saw a deerhide slipcase partially concealed on the coach's forward seat. A gleaming wooden rifle stock protruded from its end. *I knew it,* he thought as he placed the wounded man there and leaned back out.

The outlaws were already fastening the last of the stolen valuables to their mounts. One freed the coach horses from their traces and strung them together in two groups of three. "We thank ye fer the hosses." The bandit leader chuckled. The outlaws mounted up and rode away toward the north.

Rifle shots thundered from the coach window.

The air filled with white plumes of sulphurous gunsmoke, furious shouts, and the whinnying of terrified horses. Matthew and the journalist ducked behind the hardened hickory spokes of the Concord's wheels as gunfire crashed and splinters fell. They were joined by the stage driver, who leaped down from the roof.

For the first time Matthew noted the absence of the small black guard. He nudged the driver. "Where's our conductor?"

His answer was a single word: "Dead."

When the shooting stopped and hoofbeats receded, the three men crawled from beneath the stage and stood up slowly.

One of the outlaws lay dead. Three coach horses and a Pinto, which apparently belonged to the slain bandit, were grazing by the edge of the woods. Without hesitation the driver produced a rope from beneath the apron on the Concord's rear boot, and set off to recapture the animals.

The coach door swung open and the missionary stepped out. He held a Winchester in his hands, smoke trailing from its barrel. The bruise on his head was big as a goose egg and horribly discolored. He walked over and prodded the dead bandit's limp form with the toe of one Wellington boot. "Vengeance is mine," he announced, "sayeth the Lord."

The journalist stepped up beside him and returned his Bible. "I believe that's in here somewhere," he said thoughtfully. "But damned if I can remember if it comes before or after 'Thou shalt not kill.' "

"Do not make light of this," said the missionary. "That chalice they stole is irreplaceable, one of a kind." Shaking, he sat down on a flat rock. "To *imagine* that the chalice of Joseph of Arimathea could fall to such foul company . . ."

The journalist was intrigued. "That *loving cup*—do you imply that it is the Grail, the one and true Grail?"

The churchman nodded. "Yes, perhaps—or perhaps only a replica to which Joseph gave his blessing. In any case, it was in my family for centuries, and I *must* retrieve it."

The driver returned with all four of the remaining horses secure on a rope. Across one of them he carried his shotgun rider's body, blood glistening from a cavernous wound.

The missionary let out a sob. "The Grail. . . . gone . . ."

"Don't fret, preacher man," the driver said encouragingly. "Them bandits is traders. Just look at this Indian paint-pony they left us. I'd wager a month's pay that they'll swap that cup right away. Most likely, a fortnight from now, some grand chief of the Sioux nation will be sippin' his firewater outa that thing. Maybe the Army can get it back for—"

The missionary's roar startled the others. *"No!* To drink from it would give strength and power! Only a great and worthy man must use it." He looked up at the coachman. "Give me one of those horses. I will pursue the brigands myself."

The driver shook his head. "We'll need all four to pull the *Pride,* and even then it's gonna be slow. Usually use six. Course, we got another problem that's a mite more pressing."

"And what is that?" asked Matthew.

The driver slid his brown hat back and scratched at his hairline. "Well, this stretch of trail up ahead is one of the worst. The Sioux played hell with us here, uh, till we hired Jim. Musta been his black skin that spooked them, I reckon, but they almost never bothered us since he's rode with us."

The writer spoke up. "I have been informed, by learned astronomers back east, that there will be a partial eclipse of the sun late this very afternoon. In fact, I've been struggling with the notion of writing an adventure tale in which this phenomenon has a profound effect on a frontiersman's ability to escape from hostile red men. Perhaps, gentlemen, I now have a rare opportunity to collect, *by actual experience,* the very inspiration I've sought for this story of—"

"Ya mean it's gonna get dark 'fore it's time?" interrupted the driver.

"Precisely," answered the journalist, "and we should be able to travel along the trail unmolested, under cover of this curious oddity in our heavens."

"Day or night," said the driver skeptically, "we're good as scalped without Jim."

"I have a solution to propose," Matthew offered quietly.

Dozens of flies buzzed around the spreading pool of blood.

The chill of the morning gave way to the heat of afternoon as Matthew labored, assisted by the dumbstruck, wide-eyed coachman. The rear boot of the Concord made a barely adequate cooling board for this operation, but it sufficed.

Like the others, the missionary had shucked off his coat in the midday heat and was troubled by insects. He remained at a distance, praying and bemoaning his fate.

The journalist set the Orphyrreus Compositor up on a flat rock, jacked a sheet of stationery into it, and proceeded to test the peculiar machine. Every few seconds one of the tiny levers produced a *snap* as it imprinted a single alphabetic character on the page. He paused frequently to swat the mosquitoes on his bared arms, and to brush curious horseflies from the paper. After more than an hour he rose, lit a pipe, and strolled over to watch the undertaker at his art.

Matthew winced at the pipe smoke but was grateful that it cleared the air of insects.

"Uh, I'm lookin' to retire soon," said the coachman. "Been stashin' my salary. You reckon that Orphelia Compostinator letter-making contraption might be a good investment for me?"

The journalist nodded enthusiastically. "Why, I would be quite delighted to put you in correspondence with the inventors of the, ahem, *Orphyrreus Compositor.*"

* * *

Matthew carefully eased the tip of another long steel needle into the joint of the dead man's knee. "Tell me, sir," he said to the journalist, "are you a veteran of the war?"

The writer smiled. "I was in the Confederate militia."

The undertaker concentrated on the next insertion of the needle. "Me, I was in their infantry, before reassignment to the ambulance corps. I spent the last of the war burying the dead or, in many cases, burying the amputated parts of men who were unfortunate enough to remain living."

"Artillery," the driver volunteered. "Under Beauregard."

The missionary joined them. "I stand before you," he blustered, "a son of Connecticut and a champion of the Gettysburg conflict. Was not one of you also a loyal Union man?"

Ignoring the missionary's indignation, the journalist leaned over to examine Matthew's handiwork. "Excellent job. Jim actually appears to live and draw breath!"

The undertaker shook his head and stood back to admire the fruit of his skills. "This delay has cost me the price of a stage ticket, one full unit of my supplies, *and* a Winchester rifle," he announced. "These expenses I will happily absorb, however, if only to secure the retention of my scalp."

He sighed, then added solemnly, "Our friend Jim is ready."

"And so," said the writer, looking up at the darkening sky, "are the stars."

The inside of the relay station was crowded with soldiers in blue uniforms and gleaming black leather boots. The coachman had drawn a happy cluster of them around him as he awkwardly demonstrated the Orphyrreus Compositor. A fire crackled and spat sparks in the stone hearth. The air in the low-ceiling room was thick with the hovering smoke of cigars and pipes, and the smells of whisky, trail dust, and sage. From outside came the whickering of horses, still confused by the early darkness.

"You sure you don't want that drink?" asked Major Reno.

Matthew shook his head. "I have had one," he said quietly, "and one is enough." He turned his gaze to the gleaming 1873-Model Winchester lying across his lap.

The officer poured himself another glass. "So you embalmed the negro in a *sitting position,* you say?"

The journalist looked up from lighting his pipe. "He certainly did, Major. You should have beheld noble Jim, steadfast and faithful even in death, riding proudly alongside our driver. Why, the pair of them looked calm as two schoolboys adrift on a raft in the Mississippi. A pity that your regiment did not arrive earlier, for you could have attended Jim's interment. That churchman's square portmanteau made an excellent casket for one in Jim's, ahem, unfortunate position, and the preacher gave him a most proper send-off. Why, that man spouted enough hot air in a quarter hour to lift Jim's soul all the way to the Pearly Gates. In fact, we had to bank the preacher's fires so Jim wouldn't overshoot the mark."

The officer waved his gloved hand. "Well, in this new occupation the preacher's selected, he'll have little time for such speech-making."

"What new occupation?" asked Matthew.

The writer leaned forward, discreetly directing his pipe smoke away. "Why, from this evening forward, our missionary will accept his missions only from the United States Army."

"That must be why he made you a gift of his Winchester," added the officer. "Certainly, he wanted to show his gratitude. But such a weapon would be of little use where he's going. The Seventh Cavalry uses only the Springfield carbine."

"So," asked Matthew slowly, stroking his beard, "what prompted the man to make this curious change of career?"

The major smiled. "We identified that paint-horse from the outlaw he killed. Those bandits are well-known to us as traders with the Sioux. When we informed him, your friend determined at once to join us in action—or, as he called it, a 'Holy Crusade'—against their great chiefs."

The journalist coughed on his whisky. "I think perhaps his decision was due more to that bruise on his head."

"Will he be taking orders from you, Major?" asked Matthew.

Reno waved a gloved hand in the air, stirring the cigar smoke. "No. He requested assignment to the troop under one of my fellow officers, whom he apparently remembers from Gettysburg—Lt. Colonel George Armstrong Custer."

Matthew chuckled. "It seems so preposterous—a Connecticut Yankee, seeking the Grail of Arthur in some Sioux Indian chief's court."

The journalist lowered his pipe. "Stated that way, friend," he said thoughtfully, "it seems to me there's quite a story to be written of the tale. A Connecticut Yankee ... in ..."

"Story?" asked the officer. "So, Mr. Clemens, you're a writer, then?"

The journalist nodded. "Yes," he answered, "guilty as charged." He turned to his pencil and began to write.

"And have you authored any book I might know?"

The journalist started to scribble something on his paper and then looked up, his bushy eyebrows converging. "Oh, damn. Now I've transcribed it wrong." He looked over at the officer. "To answer your question, Major Reno, I have a book due in print next year. It will be published under my pen name, *Mark Twain.*" He glanced back down at his page, smiled, and merrily read aloud from it. *"A Connecticut Yankee in King Arthur's Court*—perhaps I can fashion that into an even more splendid story than our own. I believe I've now found exactly what I sought on this journey!"

Several yards away, the Orphyrreus Compositor snapped repeatedly as the coach driver made it hammer out a line of type.

The journalist nodded, indicating the driver. "I believe our coachman has also obtained something he very much wanted."

Matthew nodded. "Yes indeed." He quietly stroked the barrel of his new Winchester. "And so too have I."

The sound of their laughter drifted outside to the darkness of the corral, where it joined the gentle whickering of a fresh team of stage horses. Starlight gleamed off the smooth, curved bass-wood sides of the *Pride of New Hampshire*. The Concord stood strong and ready for the trail.

The seasoned elm shaft of her harness-tongue pointed anxiously to the west.

Under an Appalling Sky

————— ✠ —————

Brad Linaweaver

... speak only of that which one has overcome.
—Friedrich Nietzsche
Human, All Too Human

Against the howling of the wind one angry voice hardly made a difference ... except to a human ear, up close to twisting lips under gray whiskers. Dark clouds made a fist above the heads of the Alberg expedition, huddled together on a rocky crag in the Himalayan mountains. The voice coming out of the bearded face made accusations. The voice found fault. And there was something just a little mad about the voice.

It asked: "If you don't believe in the Grail, why are you here?" As Professor Alberg berated a young SS man, the rest of the expedition fell silent. They had only been kidding the somewhat pompous representative from the Ministry of Culture, but when they heard his stern and angry tone all the years of obeying Hitler spoke to them, and made them stand at attention. Karl was no guiltier of mischief than the rest, but he had been singled out to answer for their high spirits—for nothing more than pretending that any old rock was the object of their quest and they could go home. Karl's comrades knew he wouldn't spread the blame around. He was a good Nazi.

"I meant no disrespect, Herr Doktor Professor," said Karl. "I believe in the Grail."

"Of course you do," said Alberg, voice dripping with sarcasm. "You believed when we were comfortable in the south of France, exploring the Cathar excavations. You believed it less so in Jerusalem, when we started running into trouble. And now that we're going to work hard in a bad climate, well, now you make with the jokes."

Although a little man, the professor's indignation made him seem larger, as though rage could puff him up to the stature he thought his due. He constantly reminded everyone of his personal association with Alfred Rosenberg, for whose outré theories the Fuehrer had established the ministry in the first place. Karl had originally volunteered for the expedition in hope of working directly with the great man who had authored *The Myth of the Twentieth Century*—the first explication of Nazi philosophy placed on the Catholic Index of banned books. But when the mission finally got underway, Rosenberg was too ill to participate. Karl suspected the illness might be Himmler's handiwork, as the ongoing feud between the two men had escalated to the point where anything was possible. All Karl knew was that if Himmler had poisoned Rosenberg, then Himmler was responsible for sticking Karl with this second-rate professor in charge of something terribly important to the future of the Reich. Karl was not the only member of the SS to hate the ostensible leader of the SS!

"Are we going to get back to work or not?" asked Gertrude Feuer, an American/German anthropologist on loan from Harvard as part of a cultural exchange program. Her friends called her Gertie. No one called her Gertie on the expedition.

She was answered by the highest ranking officer, an SS Gruppenfuehrer named Baulmer, selected in part for his lack of imagination. His father had been instrumental in the Night of the Long Knives when the SS slaughtered the leadership of the SA. From this exercise in carnage had come the elder Baulmer's insight into how to make friends and influence people. His son had made him proud. His son knew how to make people calm, especially those who were slated for execution.

The young Baulmer's voice was almost too sweet and reasonable to be heard in the maelstrom: "Please don't concern yourself, Frau Feuer, over matters of policy." He gestured the professor away from the others, exchanging a sympathetic glance with young Karl as he did so. Karl knew everything was going to be all right. Besides, it was something of an honor to be shouted at by Alberg.

The little man was only dangerous when he lowered his voice, which he never did except to conspire against a fellow German.

Since the Third Reich's victory in Europe, and nuclear stalemate with the United States, one might have expected a lessening of paranoia on the part of National Socialism. But one would have reckoned without Hitler, who had recently announced over color television, "While there is one Jew in Europe, we are at risk. While there is one Communist, one Capitalist, one Gypsy, one degenerate race-mixing homosexual, we are at risk." The TV critic who had wondered out loud how a homosexual was in a position to mix races one way or the other had been retired prematurely, without pension, but the general tone was clear. Vigilance was the standard.

Rosenberg's plan to build a Gnostic German Aryan Church received all the funding he could ever want. Both Hitler and Goebbels realized that a de-Judaecized version of Christianity would be easier to sell to the new Europe than Himmler's pipe dream of restoring the Old religion, complete with Odin, Thor and the whole pantheon. The SS had its own country of Burgundy to play around in, but the rest of Europe required careful handling.

If only Christ could be made out to be an Aryan, and St. Paul (Saul) removed from his position of influence, it would be a mortal blow to the last hold of the Jew over the Christian mind! Getting rid of the Old Testament wouldn't be easy, but it might work if the New Church could satisfy the age-old dream of finding the Holy Grail. He Who Held the Grail could change the rules to . . . anything. Lutherans and Catholics would lose their influence in Germany; and the new Christianity would be exactly what Hitler wanted.

As Baumler explained the need for brave German men to let off a little steam with a joke or two, and Professor Alberg fumed but kept silent, Karl studied the faces around him, what he could make out under their scarfs and goggles. He wondered how many of them really believed in the Grail, or had ever decided what the Grail might be. The professor had said it could be one of dozens of things: a stone, a book, or even the traditional chalice. With that sort of flexibility, why not just say anything was the Grail, call it quits and get the hell home? Unfortunately, arbitrary decisions like that could only be made by someone with the right list of university degrees.

Karl noticed that their Tibetan guide was bareheaded; and the man showed no discomfort from the flakes of snow settling on his smooth shaven dome. Karl couldn't help wondering if this fellow was the superman among them. There was no contradiction to National Socialist logic in this. The Indian civilization had been founded by Aryans, after all, and only racial degeneration over the centuries had weakened it. All that had been great in that civilization was preserved among the enlightened few in Tibet. Had not the swastika been chosen by old Haushofer as the party symbol because it was the Tibetan symbol of the sun? Hadn't Hitler brought a small Tibetan colony to Berlin and Munich as far back as 1926, seven years before he achieved power? Once he had the strength of a whole nation behind him, Hitler financed expeditions to find the Grail every year, all to no avail.

The Tibetan guide had a secret name that none of the party knew but for Alberg. (They would have exchanged such information at the Ahnenerbe, the SS occult bureau.) The guide was a high adept who had helped Alberg to convince Rosenberg, and then Hitler himself, that this year would be different. This year they would retrace the route of the previous expeditions; only this time clues would be extracted from earlier sites that would lead to ultimate victory in a new place.

The Tibetan had looked on impassively as Karl and the others made their jokes. Where Hitler was concerned, a promise was as good as a result. Nazis weren't above faking things when politically necessary. How hard could it be to just say any old artifact was the Grail? But as Karl conducted his personal survey of the others, he realized yet again that this was a gathering of true believers. Maybe a few of the SS regulars and he had their doubts, but no one else here had a bit of skepticism. He would do well to reflect on matters of faith if he wished to rise in the ranks.

There was the Parisian, selected for his knowledge on the work and life of Gobineau, the 19th-century French aristocrat who had written the first scientific work (the party insisted it was scientific) on the Aryan race and its role in history. There was the man from

London, an expert on Houston Stewart Chamberlain, the great Englishman who had carried on where Gobineau left off, and who lived to see the full flowering of racial science in the achievements of Alfred Rosenberg. Karl couldn't help but be amused that these two were a little too old, and a little too overweight, for the rigors of this particular mountain. They had both been happier sipping wine over the remains of Gnostic heretics who had been sensible enough to live and die in reasonable climates—Manicheans, Bogomili, Cathars, and anyone else they could dig up.

The other American, besides the woman, seemed a hardy young man named Carter; but his credentials were the most suspect. He had been expelled from Miskatonic University for his doctoral thesis suggesting that the real name of Jehovah was not really Yahweh, but rather something closer to Yog-Sothoth. Every good Nazi who bothered to hold a religious belief denied the possibility that the God of the Old Testament could be the father of Christ; it was par for the course to say that the Jews worshiped the Devil, Jehovah the Demiurge. But Carter based his views on certain obscure occult volumes suggesting a universe so removed from the common imagination that there was no way to make political use of such notions. He had earned his place not for a diploma but on the strength of an admirable degree of anti-Semitism.

Then there were the twins from Sweden. At first, Karl had been unhappy over the presence of women in the group, especially the American whom he found overbearing. But just as the point of the Alberg expedition was to be international, placing the race above nations (while in no way diminishing justifiable German pride), so, too, must both sexes be represented. Goebbels had been pushing for more radical uses of Aryan womanhood (and was disappointed when no practical way was found to drag along Leni Riefenstahl and one of her camera crews). Karl had seen the wisdom of the Goebbels feminist policy the night he got to know the twins better on a bed in a hotel in old Jerusalem. The amount of blond hair, deposited by all three of them, left the wrinkled black sheets looking as if a golden storm had exploded over their damp secrets.

The shortest man on the mountain was from Down Under. One would never guess that he was the foremost authority on the Spear of Longinus since the death of the leading German in the field. The Australian had corresponded directly with Rosenberg over the certainty that the spear acquired along with the Hapsburg treasures had actually pierced the side of Jesus Christ as the savior hung crucified between heaven and earth. The blood of Christ had supposedly fallen into a chalice for which mankind forever searched. The Holy Grail.

Rosenberg convinced Hitler that if the Christ were all God, instead of part man, this would solve the problem of Jewish parentage. It wouldn't matter through what human gate God came into the world. Hitler was partial to the idea that Joseph and Mary weren't really Jews (another simple solution) but didn't really care which theory won. Should Rosenberg be proven correct, the Grail could be in any form, as Christ's blood could have been something quite different from literal blood. Professor Alberg had suggested in his most famous paper on the subject that there might be many other solutions to the Jewish problem; but they all depended on actually finding the Grail.

The last expert in the party was a defrocked Catholic priest who was fighting a one-man campaign against his former church. Himmler was always boasting how the organizational structure of the SS borrowed heavily from the Jesuit order. He loved it whenever he could get his claws into a real apostate. This man, the former Father Tyrell, had gone all the way, even being initiated into the inner circle of Burgundy, the SS nation, and taking the oath affirming a belief that the moon was made of ice.

The remainder of the party was SS soldiery and a few museum officials. Probably not one of them believed the moon was made of ice, Karl reflected. Von Braun promised that the first German rocket to the moon would prove the theory was pure moonshine. For some reason, the occult types didn't seem to care what the technical side of Germany said or did.

While Karl pondered these weighty matters, the Tibetan had been watching the sky. His frosty breath upon the air seemed to mimic the roiling clouds that encircled the mountain. The perfectly shaped head lowered, catching Baulmer's attention as it did so. Professor Alberg and the officer joined their very special guide, and the three men were soon deep in conference. After all this time, Karl still didn't know if the Tibetan spoke German, although it seemed frighteningly possible that the man understood any language he heard.

Alberg's fit of temper was a thing of the past when he addressed them again. "Comrades," he said, "we near the end of our quest. This last stretch will not be easy, but the weather is taking a turn for the worse. We must redouble our efforts." He ignored the groans of those lacking in the virtues of iron discipline. "But when we make camp for the night, it will be in the safety and comfort of a cave." The groans changed to cheers. Alberg let the anarchic behavior go by without a whisper of protest. Maybe he had seen reason. Or maybe he was tired.

Karl enjoyed the skiing that was required. The twins and he were the most accomplished in this regard. They went first, exchanging glances fraught with enough heat to melt all the snow in the world. It was a shame the three of them would have to share the cave with Hitler's field trip tonight. A nice, cozy cave should be used for better things.

He did not enjoy the next part: more climbing. But this was what training was all about. And he imagined that he had more to be happy about than the chubby little Englishman who lost his grip at that crucial moment when he wasn't attached by rope to the rotund little Frenchman, and fell a long, long, long way to his death, screaming all the while in such a frenzy of terror as to gladden the heart of an Irish patriot. They didn't lose anyone else . . . on the climb.

When it was necessary to ask for a volunteer to rappel down an annoying cliff, all eyes turned to Karl before he could even nod assent. He didn't mind. He could already see the cave entrance that was the object of their exertions.

The others had an easier time of it than Karl, but even so he was surprised that the middle-aged members of the party were able to take advantage of what he had prepared for them. After what the Frenchman had seen happen to the Englishman, it was a wonder that he was willing to let his life hang by one thread, or rope in this case; but then, the man had no choice.

Karl was busy enough—being the first inside and soon having his hands full with the Swedish twins who were bringing up his rear—not to immediately notice details about his environment. A gasp from Inga changed all that. The way she was waving around her electric torch put him in mind of the most recent Nuremberg rally that he had been privileged to attend. This was no mere cave but a very long tunnel that seemed to go deep into the heart of the mountain.

By the time everyone had safely arrived, and the professor told them they could remove the outer layers of their protective clothing, Karl was the first to heed the welcome order. He was sweltering. As he began to breathe deeply, he noticed a strange odor, a cold metal smell one might expect to encounter in a factory. And there was a sour taste in his mouth.

Baulmer soon had them working as a unit again. Karl was up in front, along with the brains of the expedition, as they moved forward into the tunnel. Walking slowly, they listened to their own footsteps echoing hollowly against the walls. The professor was uncharacteristically silent. Karl wondered if the death of one of the party had a sobering effect.

The roof of the tunnel did not become lower or higher but maintained the same uncanny distance, about a dozen feet from the floor, as if they were inside a man-made construction of some kind. Suddenly, something scuttled near the American woman, who screamed in a most unprofessional manner.

While the professor lectured her on not making loud noises when inside strange mountains, Karl couldn't help but notice that the creature hurrying off into the darkness was as large his arm, all black and shiny with dozens of squirming legs. It disappeared into a hole in the wall of the tunnel. Much more of this and Karl would seriously reconsider his decision years ago not to work as a farmer for the good of the Volk.

A few more of the cave creatures were moving up ahead, just beyond the range of their lights. Suddenly one of the soldiers bent over and threw up, adding an even more unpleasant odor to the already stifling air. This might have been taken as a bad omen by those without a proper devotion to the cause when the professor instructed them to turn off their lights.

A blue light flickered up ahead. The tunnel made a ninety-degree angle and the light came from the left. Now the Tibetan resumed the authority of guiding them. "Congratulations," he told Professor Alberg in perfect German that all could hear, "you will soon have your heart's desire."

The tunnel reached its end shortly after the turn, but this was no cause for concern. It led them to a huge cavern from which originated the unexpected illumination. "It's some kind of phosphorescence," said Feuer, annoying Alberg who had wanted to say the same thing.

"It covers the walls," added the man from Paris. "I've never seen anything like it."

Karl was more impressed by the sheer size of the cavern than anything else. It put him in mind of a cathedral. Great stalactites provided the Gothic arches. Stalagmites made the pews. A shelf of stone was the perfect altar. And as for priests, the expedition had more than its fair share of interpreters of cosmic truth.

"Look," said the Tibetan, brown hand pointing to a symbol carved in solid rock on the wall nearest them. It was a Hexagon with a claw in the center. Professor Alberg nearly fainted in excitement when he saw it. And then, to Karl's surprise, the newly loquacious guide quoted Goethe's Mephistopheles from Faust: "Everything that exists deserves to perish."

"Oh comrades," cried Alberg, oblivious to his own advice about raising one's voice when tons of mountain hang overhead. He didn't even notice another of the strange cave creatures which had been partly hidden at their feet. As he stepped on the thing, it wriggled and Karl had a clear view of its mouth that was suckers with teeth on the ends.

"We have found evidence of a lost civilization," he continued, noting, for a moment, the monstrosity under his boot. "Why, even this little troglodyte is of an unknown species. Our friends in the most secret of the Tibetan orders have been keeping a few secrets from us." He smiled at the guide. "We of the glorious Third Reich had to win a world before they would reward us with this knowledge."

"What knowledge is that?" asked the American woman. "What has this to do with the Holy Grail?"

Professor Alberg was so excited that he was almost dancing. The raising of his foot gave the creature a chance to slither away. One of the Swedish twins moved close to Karl in a way that made the young man almost grateful to the cave worms, as he was now thinking of them.

"This symbol is known to me," said Alberg. "It is a sign of ancient Atlantis. And we will find the Grail here because the real Christ was Atlantean."

It was Carter's turn to be confused. "But I thought you were of the opinion that the Christ was of completely non-human origin."

"Yes," said Alberg. "Who ever said the denizens of Atlantis were human?"

"But isn't the idea that the Christ is completely spiritual?" asked someone else.

The old irritation was creeping back into Alberg's face, here a twitch, there a discolored patch of flesh. "When will you fools learn to think?" he berated everyone in general. "All that matters is to prove that Christ was no Jew, in any form, at any time. After that, everything else is mere detail!"

"We are grateful for your expertise and close relationship with the Fuehrer," said Baulmer, again the diplomat. "But before we continue with the work, we must rest. We couldn't hope for a better place to make camp than right here."

The guide allowed himself a smile before helping these self-styled rulers of the world to unpack their provisions. Karl hadn't realized how tired he was until he sat down and took a first drink of water from his canteen. His feet felt like swollen bladders, filled with rocks. And there was a pain in his back as deep as the mystery he felt in this place.

As if Alberg had read the young SS soldier's mind, the professor decided to draw him into a discussion where the young Rhinelander could play the part of a representative German citizen. The other experts were every bit as confused as the rank and file, but

Alberg could be counted on to use a strapping young lad as the official dunce-student, so as to lecture everyone else. Top Nazis were incorrigible teachers.

"So, private, er . . . what's your name?"

"Karl, Herr Doktor Professor Alberg."

"Yes, yes. So, Karl, how does proof that Atlantis existed help our cause of the Nordic Christ?"

Karl hated this sort of thing. The part of Nazism that had most appealed to him was the "act, don't think" motto. Many a young man and woman had joined the party because of that promise. They should have known better. National Socialism was as ponderously intellectual as the ideas it had overthrown.

"All the races of the world fall into a natural hierarchy," Karl recited the old lesson, "except for the Jews who are the anti-race. Teutonic man has many enemies, including traitors in his own midst, but the Jew will always be the supreme enemy because he is anti-natural."

Alberg was nodding, partly in agreement and partly from irritation. All this was well and good, but the SS man was circling around the main point. "We all know that, Karl, but how does Atlantis help us?"

As far back as he could remember, Karl had been intimidated by the tyranny of ideas. Any ideas. His mother had wanted him brought up a good Lutheran but the father had wasted no time placing his son on the fast track to success with National Socialism; and Hitler's New Order was a jealous god. All the Nordic Christ meant to Karl was a way of giving people like his mother a way to go through the motions of their old faith without presenting any political problems. Atlantis was as far out of Karl's depth as Hoerbiger's cosmic ice theory or any of the other enthusiasms that engaged the SS elite when they held secret meetings in Burgundy.

Karl's discomfiture was like fresh blood to a tiger where Alberg was concerned; but a loud snicker from another SS soldier distracted the pedagogue's attention and got Karl off the hook. "You there," spat out the professor. "What's your name?"

"Uh, Ludwig," came the unhappy reply.

"Well, Ludwig, why don't you tell us why Atlantis is important to our mission?"

This one had more imagination than Karl. It didn't help him very much when he said, "Because of magic, Herr Doktor Professor. If we find the true Grail, it can only be touched by those with the blood of the Volk. Lesser races will become progressively sicker, and a Jew touching the Grail would rot away to nothing in an instant, his skin peeling, eyes falling out . . ." Ludwig's vivid description trailed off to nothing as he felt the attention of everyone in the cave settling on him in deadly silence. Then Alberg broke the spell by laughing.

"Only a juvenile mind would come up with something like that," the teacher's voice abjured the soldier. "Or a Jewish mind full of Talmudic nonsense." Sheer panic flashed over Ludwig's face but another hearty chuckle from Alberg put the younger man at ease. "Mind you," the professor continued, "your notion has a certain charm. It's a popular superstition born of the fact that every race has one soul, as Rosenberg has said. The Grail will communicate things to an Aryan that no one else could know. A careful reading of the Arthurian legend reveals our race-based truth."

Alberg began pacing back and forth in front of the symbol on the cave wall, making of it a blackboard and the vast cavern his classroom. Everyone slowly gathered around, except for the Tibetan guide who, even more slowly, was edging away from the company, back towards the tunnel entrance.

"There is no one truth for everyone," said Alberg, "but each race has a truth, far bigger than can be encompassed by any one individual. We believe that all civilizations worth the name began with an Aryan somewhere. Furthermore, I insist that no city of man was ever so old that it didn't look back to some earlier golden age. And yet there has to be a beginning. Or must there?"

He raised his eyebrows and assumed a mocking expression before continuing: "The Nordic Church soon to take its place on the world stage will deny the Old Testament idea of creation ex nihilo. We say the universe always existed; the eternal return is our truth, and nowhere is this more profoundly understood than among the great adepts of Tibet. Alfred Rosenberg first incurred the wrath of

Rome when he denied that God created man. The Nordic Church will teach that man and God have always existed, as equals. The Roman Church opposes the quest for the Grail because she fears all secret knowledge. And well she should, for Catholicism made the secrets herself by suppressing the Gnostic beliefs and branding them as heresies. In the end, Rosenberg won't care if Christ is proved to be all spirit, or completely physical so long as the physical side is Aryan!"

Alberg was getting red in the face. Excitement did that to him. The American Carter picked up the thread: "I get it! Atlantis was an Aryan civilization. The powers of mind come from her—extrasensory perception, telekinesis, and so forth."

"And healing powers," echoed Feuer.

"The power to make the lame to walk," came another voice.

"The blind to see," said another.

"To raise the dead," finished Alberg. "Yes, it is my belief that Christ was the last Atlantean; and in his body coursed the purest Aryan blood. The Jews conspired to have him killed. Then the Jewish Saul, later known as Paul, was sent to corrupt the pure racial message, and make Christianity dependent on Hebrew myths."

Alberg didn't have to drop the other shoe, or boot. They all knew that something would be found inside this mountain that would be dubbed the true Grail; and they would return to New Berlin as heroes of the Reich. Maybe a rock would do, after all. But given the size of the cavern, and the emblem carved in stone, they were sure to find something better than that.

The plan adopted was a simple naval search pattern. Baulmer had everyone gather in a tight circle at the center of the cavern, then move out in an unfolding spiral that would leave no inch of ground unexamined. The natural luminescence of the cave actually provided sufficient light for their purposes but Alberg had them using their electric torches as well. If anything were there, it would certainly show up.

Something did.

Carter found it. He started to laugh, but the sound choked his throat. "That can't be," he said. Karl was nearest to him and hurried over. What he saw, fossilized in the rock below, was a gigantic footprint, vaguely humanoid but subtly wrong in ways other than size.

"What's the matter?" asked Karl. Carter only shook his head.

"Over here," cried out one of the Swedish twins. The two men were near and hurried to her side. They found another footprint, only this one wasn't a fossil. This one was in a patch of brown dirt.

"I've always had a fear of words that begin with the letter Y," said Carter, suddenly. "I've just remembered the first story I ever heard about the Himalayas, when I was very young."

Meanwhile, Professor Alberg had found a giant footprint over by what appeared to be the crude altar but must surely be a natural shelf of rock. He was calling everyone to come see when the Gruppenfuehrer wondered aloud what had happened to their guide. Alberg was too preoccupied with his find to worry about that. And nothing would have distracted him short of the loud crash that suddenly drew everyone's attention to the tunnel mouth.

"We're sealed in," said the Frenchman who was nearest and skilled at stating the obvious. He walked over to touch the unyielding stone surface of a boulder—or was it some kind of door?

Now Alberg became concerned about the absence of the Tibetan guide. After all, the man was his lodge brother in the Vril Society, a fellow believer in the Thule. They knew each other's secret names. (Aryan secrets were acceptable, of course.) The man had worked ever since the end of the war to introduce the Third Reich to the Grail. Why should he disappear at their moment of triumph?

The altar moved. With a terrible grating of stone on stone, it moved, and the sound exploded in the immensity of the cavern. The Alberg expedition stood rooted to the spot, all but Karl whose instinct for survival burned hot in his chest. He ran toward the opening, his usual method of facing the unknown. Up until now his courage had served him well. Unfortunately, taking the wild chance didn't pay off this time. Karl was lifted by a hand proportionate in size to the footprints. He stared into the most perfectly blue eyes he had ever seen in his life. Then the leviathan placed Karl gently on the ground and he had a clearer view of the giant.

First impressions can be misleading. Given a height between nine and ten feet, and a body almost completely covered in hair,

Karl and the others might well have expected an ape-like countenance. But there were no heavy brows, no flatness of face, no heavy jaw or sloping forehead or thick, brutish neck. The features of the face were one of the few parts of its anatomy not covered in hair, as were the hands. And it was the most beautiful face Karl had ever seen, a face to match the pure light that seemed to stream forth from the eyes.

As the giant came into full view of the Alberg expedition, it was joined by others of its kind, all of them huge, all of them possessing the same delicate features and long fingers on their well-formed hands. "Welcome home," said the first one in perfect German. "Welcome," said the others in English and French and other languages. As everyone spoke German in the expedition, the first of the giants continued to address the party in the language of the Reich.

"I don't understand," said Alberg, displeased with the sound of his own lame words.

"You were brought here by a mutual friend," continued the mellifluous voice. "We have something for you."

One of them came up from the rear, carrying a golden goblet covered in runic symbols. The drinking vessel was of a size suitable to the great hands holding it. There was something red in the cup that almost spilled out.

"If you are of the true blood," said the voice, "your spirit eye will be awakened. If not, then your flesh will serve others who are awakened. Even the remains of the body will live, transformed into the humble creatures you have already seen in this, our home."

Ludwig, who had an imagination, was the first to panic. He screamed. He ran. He got absolutely nowhere fast. The giants didn't even try to stop him as he hammered his hands bloody against the boulder blocking the tunnel.

Alberg opened his mouth and tried to speak, but nothing would come out. The giant helpfully answered the unspoken questions: "He lives. He is still among us. He was always one of us."

Carter managed to say, "The cross must have been much larger than we ever expected." His words sounded like a moan.

"Now gather around, you men and women. This is His blood." The giant hand held up the cup. "You must drink."

Another voice spoke. Karl's voice. He was surprised to hear himself expressing the worry that must be on the minds of all his comrades. "How many of us will . . . survive?"

The beautiful face formed a beautiful smile. "There is no death here. But there is transformation, as I said. If you mean how many are of the true blood, and will become like us . . ." The startling blue eyes seemed to grow in Karl's sight until they became his whole world. "Only one in ten thousand awaken."

"The rest serve, and serve well," said the others in chorus, then continued: "Their flesh is our flesh; and their flesh dwells among us." Dark things moved on the cave floor around everyone's feet, but nobody looked this time.

"This is His blood," the first one repeated.

Professor Alberg fainted but they woke him up. His turn came as did everyone's. The people lined up and they took communion. It was abominable.

The Steel American

———— ✠ ————

S. P. Somtow

The steel American was different from all the others. Not that there was any real doubt that he was an American. He spoke English, after all, not Russian; besides, the Russians had just come through the village the week before with their annual promises of tractors and medicine.

He was different because he came alone. Because he was completely encased in platelets of jointed steel, like a television robot. And because he came to *me*. He was *my* American.

At the crest of the hill, past the old stone temple where the man who used to be my husband had meditated, hardly moving, for the last ten years, there was a waterfall where the women used to bathe, mornings, coyly draped in their sarongs. Behind the waterfall was a cave most people were afraid to enter, for it was inhabited by a malevolent spirit, but I've always been good with spirits. The back of the cave opens into a deep, still pool at the bottom of a well of rock. Nobody knew about this pool except me. My mother showed it to me the day after I had my first period, and she told me that its waters contained the secret of our family's youthful appearance. Indeed, until the day she died, my mother had an inexplicably smooth complexion, and it seemed that she aged all at once, within minutes, just before she passed away. It could have been the water, but then again my mother was a shaman; it could have been some other magic.

I too was beautiful. No need for false modesty in a story like this. Yet, in his fortieth year, my husband had turned from me, left

107

me sleeping, crawled out of the mosquito net, climbed the hill, entered the sacred brotherhood of *sangkha*. I was a widow and not a widow.

And every morning at sunrise I bathed in the secret pool, waiting, perhaps, though I did not know for whom I waited. Until I met the steel American.

It was the morning after the last Russian left. I had left my *panung* in the cave. That was one of the reasons I kept the pool so secret; although I was a married woman, I loved to bathe naked, like a child. In this private place, I could let the cool water invade every cranny of my body. As I stood embracing myself, it seemed sometimes that the water itself loved me. It was alive and it made me come alive. It touched places my husband had never learned to touch. It made me forget the shame of having been forsaken.

But not for long. I climbed back up into the cave. Sunrise was pouring down the limestone well. I sat in a shaft of light, drying my hair with my husband's old *phakhomah*. The void inside me ached. I wanted to pray to the guardian *vinyaan* of the hill, but I did not know what to wish for.

At that moment, I heard a crash—iron on rock—like a kettle clattering on the stove. I turned and saw the steel American. At first I didn't think he was human at all; the metal he wore glowed pink and orange in the circle of morning light. The television in the village had not worked in over a year, but I remembered the movie with the robot. No doubt robots were commonplace in America. At first I assumed he was no longer working; perhaps, like transistor radios, he ran on batteries. I did not cover myself, since he did not seem to me to be sentient, but merely a simulacrum of a man.

The metal visor slipped and I found myself staring into his eyes. It was too late for modesty, so I just stood there and gaped. The eyes were the color of the secret pool itself: sometimes brown, sometimes blue, depending on the light; a wisp of golden hair straggled from the helmet. His cheeks were lined and hollow; he seemed to have endured many lifetimes' suffering; but his eyes were the eyes of a boy. I thought he was beautiful, and I was ashamed that I thought him beautiful, and it brought back the memory of my husband, sitting in the lotus position in a pavilion at the monastery and gazing for hours at some inner beauty I could never impersonate. And I began to weep.

"Demons," said the steel American, "when you are tired of cajoling, you try tears. But I won't be moved."

I could understand him after a fashion because I had been learning to read the Bible with Father O'Malley.

"What are you doing here?" I said. "You're exhausted . . . wounded too. You're not a deserter, are you?"

"Of course not," he said. "Get thee behind me."

"I can't . . . you're leaning against the wall."

"Temptress! Whore of Babylon!" he gasped, and then he slumped back again. Father O'Malley used those words sometimes; it was hard to tell whether they were meant for insult or for lovemaking. Why would a wounded American call me names? I recovered enough of my sense of proprieties to slip my *panung* back on and tuck the fabric around my silver belt, and to throw on my blouse; then I took my plastic *khan* and filled it from the secret pool. I then knelt over him—he was stretched on the cavern floor, his hands clasped together like a corpse prepared for cremation—whispered an ancient formula for making lustral water, threw in a few petals from some wildflower that bloomed from a crack in the rock—I sprinkled the magic liquid over him and waited for him to awaken.

This time, he was a lot more civil.

"Are you an angel?" he said.

"Good," I said. "The last time I was a demoness." I went on sprinkling the water and whispering the meaningless syllables that came unbidden to my lips.

"What country is this?"

"That's a good question," I said. "The Russians have told us we're in a liberated zone; you people have told us we're part of a great free nation; all I know is that this mountain is called Doi Xang, that we're a village of Thai speakers, that below us there's a village where they speak Hmong. We're not actually *in* a country, though everyone around us thinks we're in *his*. We grow opium and raise pigs and ducks. I know that there's a war going on a few kilometers down the mountain, to the northeast of us. Sometimes, at night, we can look down on the flaming jungle and smell the smoke; it's a choking chemical smell mixed with the odor of burning flesh. When the television worked, we sometimes used to see news about the war. But we could never figure out what it was about, so we would switch over to *Lost in Space* or *Leave it to Beaver.* But then, you see, the war doesn't touch us. Nothing does, not even the monsoon. It's because our temple is built over one of the sources of the river."

The steel American looked at me, wide-eyed and only half-comprehending. I eased his helmet off and his hair, matted and unkempt, fell on to his shoulders. A rancid odor came from inside his iron casing. I wondered how long it had been since he'd removed his armor. I tried to tug off one of his gauntlets. He pushed me away. "No!" he said. "I've sworn to live inside this metal shell until the day my quest is fulfilled."

"I see. It's a bargain you've made with your god." That was easy to understand; I had tried to deal with the Four-faced Brahma for winning lottery numbers, but I never seemed to come up with the right offering. Or perhaps it was his way of telling me that my special powers were not meant to benefit myself, but the whole village.

"But it's not good for you," I said. "What you're wearing wasn't designed for the tropics. Your god would surely understand."

"I'm afraid not," said the steel American. "He's a hard god. Harder than the steel I gird myself with."

"I know," I said, thinking of Father O'Malley, tormenting himself whenever a woman crossed his mind.

"They said I would travel far and wide. And it's true. I've traversed the burning desert of time itself, and I'm still no closer to my goal. They said there'd be a castle of temptation atop a mountain, and a sorceress."

"Well, this is a castle of sorts, and I did tempt you. Though I didn't mean to. And I *am* a sorceress. I know how to curse, and how to heal. Though for healing I usually prefer penicillin."

"Your words are dark," he said. "Tell me your name, mysterious lady."

"My name is Mali," I said. *"Jasmine."* He looked at me with the kind of longing a pubescent boy has; he did not even know the nature of his longing.

"I am Sir Perceval."

"Should I call you Sir, or Mr. Perceval?"

"Tempt me no more," he said. I clutched his metal hands in mine. "I hurt so much I think I'm dying."

"We can heal you," I said. "It's the least we can do."

"But I have to find the grail!"

"You want the grail?" I said. Foreboding gnawed at me. Of all the things demanded of us through the years, by the CIA and the Russians and the Vietnamese and the missionaries and the land stealers, this was the first time someone had asked for something we actually possessed. And it was the one thing we could not give, because it would mean the death of our way of life.

"There's nothing for you here," I said. "When your wounds have healed, you can go on your way. Though you've wandered so far astray in space and time that I don't see how you can find your way back."

"You're lying," said the steel American. His jointed fingers dug into my hands and stained them with blood and rust. "You're the sorceress they told me of. This is the castle atop the hill, and this is the stream that heals all wounds."

I gazed into his eyes and knew that in his purity he saw past my dissembling. What could I tell him? "Yes," I said, staring past him at the sweating limestone, "yes, I was lying. I am that sorceress."

I had to move him out of the cave myself; I didn't want anyone to find out about the secret pool. He was delirious by then; our conversation had taken place in a moment of relative lucidity. After I had dragged him out to the other side of the waterfall, I saw my daughter Pailin pounding the washing by the side of the stream while her half-brother, Smaan, sat watching from the back of a water buffalo. I called out to them.

"We've got a new visitor," I said.

My daughter gathered her washing; Smaan went running back

to get help; they managed to heft him onto the village chief's Land Rover, and we drove him down to the temple hospice.

I left him lying on a straw mat, between a pregnant woman and a man with a gangrenous leg, who had crawled all the way to our village from a prison camp in the hope of being healed.

I didn't want him up and about and frightening the villagers, so I placed a sleeping spell over his eyes, and I told Smaan and his friends that if they said anything to anyone I would make sure they were reincarnated as cockroaches; they nodded and ran off to play among the ruined pagodas that jutted from the wild grass like the mountain's teeth. He would sleep at least until evening; by then, perhaps I would have a plan.

My daughter sat cross-legged, mixing a love potion on the veranda of our house, her baby slung across her back. Smaan was still trying to fix the television; he had been trying for years.

The baby squalled. "Oh, Mother, hold her for me," Pailin said.

I took the child in my arms. "You're using my mortar and pestle," I said. "I wish you'd use your own things when you do experiments."

She was pounding furiously: locusts, hemp, toadstools, a little horse fat. "Your things have more magic than mine do," she said, "and I need the strongest I can get."

She seemed barely older than my grandchild. I wondered whether she, too, would age all at once, in the minutes before her death. Although the baby was half-Russian—we hadn't been able to save the father—no one dared ridicule my daughter, because they were afraid I would send a spirit in the night.

"You don't need to attract a husband yet; you're only thirteen."

She smiled and looked away. There was no need to remind me that she had been offered five thousand baht for a two-year contract at a brothel in Chiang Rai.

"The new American," she said, "is the most beautiful man I have ever seen." Suddenly I noticed a strand of blond hair in the mixture and I realized that my daughter was in love. With a man who was forbidden to make love! I knew what it was like to love such a man, and my heart ached for her.

"Don't think about him. He's made a bargain with Phra Yesu, the Christian god; he is not allowed to remove his iron skin."

"That's ridiculous, Younger Mother," said Smaan. "How can he shit?"

"Who knows?" I said. "A sliding panel, perhaps."

"Well," said my daughter, "if he can have a sliding panel for that, he might just as easily have a sliding panel for the other."

"That's absurd," I said, but then I thought, why not? The Americans are not entirely human. The Vietnamese, the *montagnards,* even the Russians are easier to fathom.

I went to see Father O'Malley first, because of all our visitors he was the craziest. Madmen are best at penetrating to the core of things.

The father's church, like all the other buildings in the village, was on stilts, and thatched. It was the time of the year that we hang phallic fetishes from the eaves of our houses to make sure that the earth renews itself. The sandalwood phallus brushed my face as I walked onto the veranda. I knew Father O'Malley would remove it as soon as he found it, but someone would soon sneak another one back up; there are some things that you just don't trifle with.

I washed my feet from the rainwater jar and left my sandals in front of the threshold; then I took some holy water, crossed myself, and genuflected as I went inside. O'Malley sat on the altar, scratching his head: a fat, balding, sweaty man. An electric fan, powered by the battery of a van that idled outside, blew right in his face; the rest of the church was stifling hot. The air was thick with opium smoke.

"Oh, Mali," he said. "Come for your reading lessons? Or perhaps you're in need of religious succor? It's Sunday, isn't it? So hard to keep track."

"You haven't kept track for five years, Father." It had been that long since O'Malley staggered into our village, gibbering about women being raped to death and babies sliced in two. There were no wounds in his flesh, but his soul seemed ravaged beyond repair; even now he had barely begun to heal. We couldn't in all compassion send him back out, so he was allowed to build his church, though of course no one worshiped there.

"We were studying the apocalypse, weren't we?" he said, reaching behind the altar for a weatherbeaten Bible.

"Yes. But I don't want to read about religion today. Can we go back to what we were looking at last week . . . the Arthurian romances?"

He laughed. There was a whole pile of books—mostly reclaimed from corpses found rotting in the jungle—and among them was *A Child's Treasury of Arthurian Tales*. That was where I'd first read about the grail, and that was how I had been certain that it was in our village.

He opened that book and I got into position, that is to say I lay, face up, on the altar and unclasped my silver belt, and undid the buttons on my blouse. Father O'Malley discreetly turned his back and faced the bamboo crucifix. One hand held the book open; the other reached behind, grasped at the air for a few moments before landing, by accident it seemed, on my exposed breast. Lightly the fingers drummed as Father O'Malley read to me and I listened, filling in the words I couldn't understand with my own vision of how things must have been in the olden times . . .

> *Phra Yesu, the Christian god, who was an incarnation of the god Vishnu, made his disciples drink his blood from a silver cup called the Holy Grail. It was a magic blood which could heal the universe. But Phra Yesu was attached to material things and could not free himself from the sexual desire for Mary Magdalene, who was an incarnation of Maya, the deceiving one, who tempted Buddha under the Bo tree. So Phra Yesu was made to suffer crucifixion instead of being granted enlightenment. And the silver cup was lost.*

This was the gist of what I gleaned from the priest's discourse. I could not make out all the words, but oh, the severe beauty of their sounds! I loved the clash and grinding of those English consonants, the elusive imprecision of those vowels. Father O'Malley's left hand had worked its way to my pubes now, and his index finger was warily circling my clitoris. I tried to concentrate on puzzling out the story, but his touch had already begun to tease the waters within me.

The Fisher King lay wounded in his castle . . .

"Yes, yes," I said, "but who is Sir Perceval?"

"Let me find where it talks about him."

Softly his left hand skimmed the hair of my pubis. I trembled. I was thinking of the first time my husband touched me. He'd started to waken my body and then without warning he shuddered and fell still . . . the mosquito netting hung heavy, drenched with the moisture of night. Lizards barked as they darted from cupboard to cupboard. I lay awake while my new husband slept; sometimes, through the wire-mesh window, the sky lit up with the soundless fire of the distant war; I was sixteen; my husband was thirty-five; I cried as I fingered the amulet I wore to ward off the spirits that cluster around at night, when we are most vulnerable. In those days, the war was still far away. These days we could hear it as well as see the flashes in the jungle.

The pure fool came to Klingsor's stronghold . . . the maidens danced around him, displaying their wanton charms and daring him to fall into temptation . . .

Father O'Malley dropped his book. He sighed. Perhaps he had ejaculated beneath that sweat-soaked cassock of his. Abruptly he knelt at the altar, retrieved a bundle of *mayom* branches that he kept tied up next to his bag of frankincense; he unbuttoned his cassock, stripped down to his waist, and, gazing intently at the face of Phra Yesu on the cross, began whipping himself furiously. He showed more passion than when he had furtively caressed me. I lay on the altar, unfulfilled, just as I had with my husband. This was how our reading lessons generally ended.

When Father O'Malley finished flagellating himself, he eased his cassock back over his bruised flesh, went to the back, and got a bottle of Coke and two glasses. I buttoned myself up quickly and joined him in one of the pews, sipping my soda and watching him try to ignore his pain.

"I don't know why you beat yourself afterwards," I said. "Surely you know that the sex drive can't simply be flogged away."

"Then how does your husband manage?"

"He's a holy man," I said, and looked at the floor.

"So am I," said Father O'Malley. He too looked at the floor. A gecko ran past with a struggling dragonfly in its mouth.

"Perhaps you were a holy man once," I said, "but you have fallen from grace. Or so you claim."

"We are all fallen," he said.

"Don't you want to make love to me just once? Don't you feel hypocritical, clutching the book of learning with your right hand and groping me with your left, and feeling so filthy afterwards that you have to flagellate yourself?"

"Of course I want to make love to you," he said, his voice trembling, "but that is between you and your husband. It's what God has ordained."

"I'm afraid my husband is journeying toward the extinguishment of desire. And I'm left out."

To distract him, and to prevent him from falling prey to his temptation and having to hurt himself again, I told him about the steel American and his quest for the grail. I told him that the man lay up at the hospice in an enchanted sleep.

"He was wearing armor?" Father O'Malley paged through the King Arthur book until he found what purported to be a picture of Sir Perceval.

"That's him!" I said. "But more emaciated. And then, the artist doesn't do justice to his eyes. His eyes stare right past things as though they're not there. I wasn't even sure he felt anything when he saw me naked." A thought occurred to me. "He hasn't come to take you back, has he? I mean, you *are* a deserter after all. Or a spy."

"It's nothing like that. It's just that . . . well, he's not real, any-way. He's like everything else in this damned village . . . an illusion. You know as well as I do that I can't go back . . . that you're all part of some *Twilight Zone*-like hallucination that I'm having . . . that I'm really out in that jungle with my left arm shattered, drowning in a swamp of leeches . . . my death is still going on, a split second stretched out to forever."

"There, there," I said, stroking his hand. "Of course we're an illusion. Life itself is an illusion, according to the Lord Buddha. My husband could tell you more." A feature of Father O'Malley's madness was that he believed he was dead, and that this place was some kind of psychedelic purgatory. "But you'll want to be on hand when he wakes up. He might need another American to talk to."

"He'd be English, not American."

"Makes no difference . . . American, Russian, Martian, suit yourself."

"Maybe he'll need spiritual counseling," Father O'Malley said.

"You really miss being a priest, don't you? I mean, you haven't made any converts here . . . except for Nit, the village idiot, and she thinks that drinking the sacramental wine is just another word for giving you a blowjob."

"I've failed her. But I can't go back. I don't have the guts to face . . . what's out there. Beyond the—"

A sacred *saisin* ran the perimeter of the village. Every evening I would walk all the way around, making sure the cord was taut, looping it through banana trees and bamboo thickets, whispering the words that keep away evil. O'Malley was convinced that beyond the *saisin* was another universe, a world more real than ours.

Leaving the church, I saw that Smaan and his friends were kicking something around. It was a human head. Russian from the headgear. I yelled at them to stop.

"The head is the seat of the soul," I said. "Show some respect. The pigs will eat it if you don't give it a decent cremation."

"But we found it outside the *saisin*," said Smaan. "And it's only a *farang's* head anyways."

I glared at him, and at length he lifted the head up high, like a flag, and the boys marched off toward the jungle, whistling *She's got a ticket to ride*.

I had an exorcism and a childbirth that afternoon, so it was almost evening by the time I went in to look at the Holy Grail.

I don't know how long the Holy Grail had been in our village. Before the grail, there had been other relics. There used to be an herb called *moly* that could cure even death; a bearded adventurer named Gilgamesh had come for it. That was in my mother's time. Or maybe my grandmother's. We had a golden fleece once, but all that remained of it was a shiny hank of wool.

The Holy Grail took many forms. It was never that shimmering golden chalice hovering in the air, haloed with rainbow light, like in Father O'Malley's book. There were times when its power had resided in a broken Coke bottle. But for a few years now it had been that lowliest of household objects, the *khan* we use for drawing from the stoneware jars, tall as a ten-year-old boy, that we set out for catching the waters of the monsoon. Sir Perceval had already seen the grail; he had come within a finger's breadth of touching it.

There was a locked room in the temple that held these treasures. The women of my family had held the key to the room since the beginning, before there was even a temple, before the Indians came to our country and converted the people to the teachings of Buddha: in the days when everyone listened to the spirits of tree and rock. In those days they didn't need people like me to interpret the language of spirits. Then we learned from the Buddhist missionaries that the spirits were illusions; that we ourselves are but shadows.

Nothing exists.

In the main hall of the temple I knelt with three joss sticks before the ten-meter-long reclining image of Lord Buddha. I said my *namo dasa* three times, stuck the joss sticks in the burner, drank in the sweet smell of incense. Then, making sure no one could see me, I crawled on my hands and knees under the tiers of altars stacked high with fruit and flowers and fresh eggs, and I crept underneath the statue, past the stucco hem of Lord Buddha's robe, until I faced the wall with the faded fresco of a gateway guarded by angels.

The key was a mantra that I repeated three times; then I was inside the room.

The room that was also the well of rock above the pool of still cool water.

The plastic *khan* I had bought at the Sunday market in the next village for twenty-five satang ... which I'd filled with healing water and sprinkled over the steel American ... it lay on a slab of rock beside the pool, where I'd last left it. I felt an overwhelming relief. The relic had a mind of its own; there were times when it refused to be found.

I held the *khan* in my cupped hands. The room spun around me. I muttered the mantra three times in reverse and presently I found myself outside, treading across the stepping stones to the pavilion beside the stream.

My husband sat there in his saffron robes, in the lotus position, on a reed mat; my stepson, his *phakhomah* hitched up, stood thigh-deep in the water casting a fishing net.

I prostrated myself before him, keeping my distance so that he would not be polluted by the touch of a woman.

"Holiness," I said, "there's a new American. He's asking for the grail."

"Then you must give it to him," he said.

There were those in the village who believed that my husband neither ate nor slept, and that he had sustained the lotus position for over ten years. I knew better, but you can't argue with superstition.

"How can I?" I said. "We gave away the golden fleece. We gave away the golden apples of the sun. The magical herb. The mistletoe. The urn of the demon's heart."

"We are a very giving people."

My stepson held a wriggling fish in both hands. He held it up, laughing. "Breakfast, honored father!" he said.

"Don't wave it at me now," said my husband. "Temptation, you know." For monks may not eat after midday.

"But," I said, "everyone for miles around knows that this is the village that heals. The war rages around us and we're untouched. Wounded men come crawling past the *saisin* and we cure them. Without the grail—"

"Oh, nonsense. It's just an old plastic bowl that you bought for twenty-five satang."

My husband placed his prayer fan in front of his face and chanted for about half an hour. The words of the mantra spoke of transience and the insubstantiality of fleshly desires. Smaan gutted fish and tossed them into a bucket. The pavilion smelled of sandalwood and night-blooming jasmine; moisture was condensing out of the evening air.

At length my husband stopped his chanting. He continued the conversation as though no time had elapsed at all. "You see," he said, "we are in the business of fulfilling secret desires . . . that's why the travelers come here . . . and that's why they often find it so hard to leave. That is how the ones who come here are healed. That is why some cannot be healed . . . they just don't have the yearning to be healed."

"I can't believe that Father O'Malley's secret desire is to fumble around inside a woman's *panung* . . . and to whip himself afterwards."

"Yet he won't get up and walk away."

"If that *is* what he really wants, though, doesn't it mean his mind is sick and that we haven't succeeded in healing him at all?"

"It's not our place to say who is sick and who is whole."

As always, my husband spoke in riddles; as always, I knew that the answer to my dilemma lay somewhere in his words. He launched into another bout of chanting. I wanted to fling myself at him and shout, "What about *my* secret desire, what about my need for you to come back down from the mountain and put your arms around me and make me fully a woman?" But I knew he would only answer with an enigmatic smile.

"I'm taking the fish home for Pailin to cook," Smaan said, and he started to lope downhill, swinging the bucket and whistling.

"The boys were kicking around a human head this afternoon," I said. "Any moment, the barrier's going to break and the horrors beyond the *saisin* are going to leak into our world . . . don't you care about that?"

A bomber passed overhead. Behind the next ridge of mountains, the evening sky was bright with the aurora of warfare.

My husband said, "Remember the story of King Vessandar, who gave away his very children—those most precious to him—to a beggar, because he had managed to free himself even from love itself, that most persistent of desires. It was only when he had relinquished even love that he was free to be reborn as the Lord Buddha."

I went down to the hospice. I cured a lame child, and I let a man die in peace who had been consumed by tuberculosis, whose every breath was agony. Then I went to the room where Sir Perceval lay. Father O'Malley was already there; he sat beside the knight with open Bible, peering at the words in the light of a kerosene lamp.

On the walls, the frescoes of heaven and hell seemed to dance.

"Back off," I said. "I'm going to wake him now."

I waved my hands over the steel American's eyes.

"Don't listen to the woman," Father O'Malley said to him as he stirred. "She is a seductress; she'll lead you away from your quest." Always woman the evil one, woman the temptress, sex as the ultimate darkness; I marveled at the alienness of Christian thinking.

The eyes opened. They fixed on me. I knew that I was beautiful, like my mother, and that no man save my husband could resist me. I wondered whether he could still be moved by carnal passion or whether, inside that cage of steel, he had succumbed to atrophy. I had to know, because it was the only way to keep my village safe from him.

"You're the angel who tempted me by the pool," he said.

"Is the grail the thing that you truly desire?"

"Yes." But the eyes told me a different story, and I dared hope that I could win my people a reprieve from the entropy that afflicts all transient things.

"Then I'll have to give it to you," I said. "This village is the place that rewards all seekers with the object of their quest. If the grail is what you truly desire, meet me at midnight at the secret pool, the one only you and I know about."

I left so Father O'Malley could hear the knight's confession.

* * *

I found my daughter still concocting her potion, and I told her I was going to have to borrow it.

"Oh, Mother," she said. "At your age." I was twenty-nine years old. "You know it will only work if there's something there to work with."

"I believe there is."

"Oh, Mother! *I* wanted that man to make love to me! All day I've been dreaming about the milk-white skin beneath the steel, unburned by the sun and moon. It's cruel of you to take him from me."

"Trust me, Pailin." I embraced her. I was glad now that she had used my implements to make the potion. "There will be others. Your time will come."

I sat in meditation until I felt the spirit of my mother, and her mother before her, and so on, back to the beginning of time, take possession of me, one at a time. At midnight I walked back uphill to the temple, crawled behind the giant statue of Lord Buddha, and murmured the mantra that opened the wall to the secret pool beyond the cave.

The steel American was already there, kneeling by the side of the water, his hands clasping his sword. He had doffed his helmet as was proper in the presence of the divine. When I appeared, on the rock in the center of the pool, with my *panung* bound tightly about my breasts, he looked up.

"I have brought you your heart's desire," I said. The same words that my ancestresses spoke to the world's great wanderers. I held out to him the plastic *khan* filled with my daughter's potion.

"I knew you were an angel," said Sir Perceval. "I've kept myself pure. I've done everything I knew how to try to be worthy of this moment. *Deo gracias.*" Humbly he stretched his hands out to receive the relic.

I held the plastic bowl in my hand and I knew what he saw: a jeweled chalice, cunningly wrought, floating on a cloud of light. I stood above him as he knelt.

"Look into my eyes," I said, and as he gazed up at me and the moon behind me I poured the sacred water and the love potion over him so that the liquid grazed his lips and scalded the scales of reality from his eyes . . . and I said, "Perceval, Perceval, I am here to give you the thing you most desire. You have fulfilled your vow and you no longer need that armor. Free yourself, Sir Perceval." I did not add, *Free me,* but I felt myself strain against the cage of my ensorcellment, the cage I had crafted around myself, the cage of my self-inflicted shame . . . and the pure fool, whose eyes betrayed his true desires because he did not have the art of dissembling, he cried out, "Yes, I have fulfilled my vow!" and all at once the armor seemed to melt from him and scatter across the cool still water like a million beads of quicksilver.

Oh, he was beautiful. His skin was so pale it seemed to be wrought from the very moonlight. . . . His penis was like a fetish carved from teakwood. His hair streamed up toward the stars as though drawing upon their brilliance. And his eyes—in the moments before they lost their innocence—were the eyes of a child. I knew then that I loved him, had always loved him even before I knew he existed for me to love.

I unloosed the knot that held my *panung* over my breasts and it too swirled away; and he seized the bowl and drained the potion and then he kissed me; and I was awakened; and we made love, in the circle of moonlight, in the water that churned and lashed and trickled in time to our passion as though it were one with the waters inside us, our blood, our sweat, our sexual fluids. I was beautiful and I knew that he found me beautiful; I knew that my breasts were ripe and fragrant as young mangoes, and my breath as intoxicating as the jasmine of the evening. I gave him all I had withheld from other men. The void that no one had filled, I let him fill; took him into myself, like a mother receiving her child back into the womb and saying to it, *Do not be born, for the world is full of suffering.* It was my last and finest magicking.

And afterwards, when I held him in my arms, feeling the water's turbulence die down, I watched the steel American grow old and withered, and disintegrate into the pool . . . his eyes last of all, still fixed on mine even as his flesh lost all its substance . . . I watched him fade into the past whence he had come . . . and I still held the plastic *khan* in my hand, and knew that the village would endure.

Our television sputtered to life soon after that. But my eyes became too dim to watch it, and now I sit on the steps where visitors leave their shoes, chewing betelnut and letting my grandchildren describe the images they see. On this television, they tell me, brutal images of war alternate with reruns of *I Love Lucy*.

Today Father O'Malley came to visit me. He walks with a cane now. We read together from the book of the apocalypse, and for old times' sake he touched me; we made love as old people do, getting more comfort from our closeness than excitement.

"Will the steel American ever be back?" I mused, as we lay together beneath the mosquito netting.

"How should I know? I'm only a deserting army chaplain, not a shamaness."

The *saisin* had been brought in closer to the village, and now, when we walked over to the stream, it was rare to find that it was not red with human blood, or there were no bloated corpses floating slowly toward the main river. "Do you still believe that our village isn't real?"

"Yes," he said. "If I leave, I will find that a thousand years have passed, or that I am dead and buried."

Afterwards, he did not whip himself. He is coming to terms with his secret nature.

Tomorrow is my husband's funeral. Everybody is happy, as he led an exemplary life and we are glad to hasten him toward nirvana.

I no longer bathe in the sacred pool. For me there is no cave behind the waterfall. The mantra in the temple no longer works; it ceased to work shortly after I told my daughter the secret.

But I still try to go back. For, though I loved him and killed him, though I fulfilled his desire by relinquishing my own, though I lied to him by telling him the truth, and betrayed all that he believed in . . . I cannot exorcise him from my mind. All my life I waited for the void to be filled, only to find that no void can be filled, no hunger satiated, until the day the soul steps away from the ceaseless cycle of *sansara* and dissolves in the cool still pool at the heart of the world.

Sometimes I toy with the idea of leaving the village. Beyond the *saisin* there are many roads. Perhaps, circling back on myself, I will find the steel American again, and my own young self, unchanged, still charged with magic.

Looking for Pablo

✠

Wil McCarthy

Some nights are magical, even now. You know the ones I mean, when you come home smelling of kerosene and adrenaline and car-chase burnt rubber? When neon and starlight are so familiar that the light of dawn seems strange and new? When you know that en-chantment has not altogether passed away?

I will tell you of such a night. It was 1985, that wonderful pre-postmodern age, on that warm summer night when we went looking for Pablo.

There were three of us in the Bug. There was me, riding shot-gun with my arm hanging out the window. Bruce was driving, and his younger sister Megan rode in back, leaning forward with el-bows propped up on both seat backs.

The windows were all open and the air roared through at eighty degrees and forty miles an hour as we sailed through the thinning traffic of Academy Boulevard. The Beach Boys were wailing out "Wouldn't It Be Nice" for about the fifth time since we'd set out. I never liked those guys much, I guess, and they were starting to wear a little thin.

I switched off the stereo, popped the tape, and threw it out the window.

"Hey," Bruce observed.

"Hey yourself," I said. "Go buy some real music."

"That was Megan's tape."

"Oh." I turned around. "Sorry about that, hon. Bruce'll buy you another one."

126

"Don't worry about it," Megan muttered, staring past me into the night. "I'm just sitting here being bummed out. Even the best things in life are shitty, you know?"

She was on her fourth beer and waxing philosophical. Megan was fourteen, still girlishly cute but on the threshold of a womanhood so intense it seemed the world must shake.

"What's the matter?" I said. "You get dumped again?"

"Yes, I got dumped again," she mimicked sourly. "I don't understand. Like, oh right, there's something wrong with me?"

I patted her on the hand and smiled. I didn't understand it either.

"Good grief," Bruce called out beside me.

The wind howled through the Bug for a while.

"Good grief," Bruce said again, as if afraid we hadn't heard.

"What?" I asked.

He turned and flashed a grumpy look back at his sister. "I haven't even had a *date* this year."

I nodded, and raised my hand in a way that said, "This is true for me as well."

And that about summed it up.

I chugged the last of my beer and handed the bottle back to Megan. She took it and replaced it carefully in the cardboard six-pack holder, then polished off her own brew and completed the set.

"Make a wish," she suggested, and heaved the whole thing out onto the pavement, where it popped and exploded and became a field of glittery fragments skidding in our wake.

A traffic light swam into view, glaring malevolent red. Bruce shifted down and hit the brakes, bringing the Bug to an abrupt halt. The air seemed unnaturally still and quiet in the sudden absence of road-wind. The streets were empty. The night was ours alone.

"You know," Megan said, shattering the silence. "Love is just like anything else. It's like lightning, it's like a force of nature. People sometimes get in the way."

My lonely heart began a slow, sad violin concerto inside my chest. I sighed. "Some people do, Megan. Some people never even see it."

Seconds passed. The light remained red.

"That's true though," I said after a while. "Things just happen for no reason. It seems like love, at least, should be looking out for you, but it isn't. It strikes and goes away. Like lightning."

"People build lightning rods, though," Bruce chipped in. "And their houses don't burn down."

We all nodded somberly, aware that we had cracked a great truth. Aware, also, that like most truths it would bring us no joy.

The air was split with the wailing of a car horn behind us. There was a screeching of tires, and suddenly a white Continental materialized beside us in the right-turn-only lane. It materialized with a hearty initial velocity, however, and whipped around us like a rocket, returning to our lane barely three feet ahead of our front bumper, screaming off into the night.

Bruce looked up and cursed. The light had turned green! He shoved the Bug into gear and floored the accelerator, frantically trying to regain lost time. It was a comical game we played, one that involved going as far and as fast as possible. To fail to *go* the instant a light turned green was nearly unthinkable.

It was a comical game we played *all the time,* just like looking-for-women or trying-to-have-fun. The rules were nebulous but utterly inviolate, as important as the real traffic laws. *More* important, I guess.

Sometimes I think life is just a comical game we all play.

Anyway, Bruce took the Bug all the way up to sixty-five, as high as it would go on level ground, and howled like a madman. Ahead, the white Continental seemed to slow, then to back up as we started gaining on it.

I stuck my head out the window (where it was assaulted by a sixty-five-mile-an-hour gale) and imitated Bruce's yell. This was nighttime, this was fun in its elemental form. Streetlights and shopping centers flashed by, barely noticed as the white car came closer and closer.

"Pablo!" Bruce called out delightedly, pointing a finger at the Continental's license plate. Sure enough, against the green and white mountain background of Colorado were the letters P-A-B-L-O, barely legible but growing more so now by the second.

"Heey!" I agreed. "It's Pablo! Hey Megan, look, it's Pablo!"

Megan hooted.

The world lurched as Bruce made a sudden lane change, found a little more speed somewhere in the Bug, and pulled up alongside the Continental, braking to match velocities with it as the windows drew parallel.

"Pablooo!" I cried, sticking my head further out the window. "Hey Pablooo!"

The driver turned and looked at me through the glass of his own window, his face not four feet from mine. He was a dark-skinned man with a pencil moustache and a hairnet. His eyebrows were heavy, nearly joining in the center, and his eyes . . .

I yelped and pulled my head back inside. "Stop the car!" I shouted at Bruce in a frightened voice.

Bruce gave a puzzled grunt, but tapped the brakes and fell in behind the white car. "What's the matter?" he demanded.

I collected my thoughts. What *was* the matter? The man had given me a creepy look, but it was more than that. I felt like a deer that had sniffed the air and caught the smell of lions. No, that's not quite right. It was more like that dim, nightmare terror you feel when you're standing at the foot of the basement stairs and you flip off the light, and suddenly you're *sure* that Bela Lugosi is reaching out for you from the darkness . . .

I'd seen a ghost. An entity. The physical embodiment of all things Pablo, if you know what I mean. I like to think the Kiowa and the Arapaho had names for that kind of thing, names they uttered only in a kind of dread whisper as they huddled around their fires on haunting, haunted nights when the stars glared down coldly like the eyes of a million gods, and far away the coyotes cried out like tormented souls.

"What's the matter?" Bruce asked again, sounding impatient.

I turned and looked at him as the hairs prickled on my scalp and neck. Words bubbled up through my mouth. "It's Pablo," I heard my voice say. "Right through to its black and stinking core."

He nodded, misunderstanding. "Yeah, it's Pablo all right. Hey Pablo, can you sell me some drugs?" The question was rhetorical, posed in a phony Hispanic voice loud enough only for Megan and myself to hear.

"I think it could if you wanted it to," I admitted, shuddering. "It could put a knife in your stomach, too, and when you woke up in Hell it'd be right there waiting for you with a big old smile on its face."

"You betcha!" Bruce agreed merrily. Megan chittered something good-natured behind me.

Pablo's car put on a sudden burst of speed, gained fifty yards on us and turned off on a side street before we could so much as draw a breath.

"He's getting away!" Bruce shrieked, flooring the accelerator again, whipping through the ninety-degree right turn at a speed that lifted two of the Bug's wheels off the pavement.

I didn't think following Pablo was such a good idea, but this, too, was the game. It *had* looked like Pablo was trying to get away. Like our scrutiny had bothered him enough to alter his course. And if he was trying to escape us, the game required that we pursue.

The side street was residential, which in Colorado Springs meant convoluted and badly lit. It would be both difficult and dangerous to chase Pablo down here, which of course obligated us all the more.

At first there was no sign of him, but we glimpsed his taillights vanishing around a tight curve as we rounded the first bend. We saw him at the next bend, too, and the one after that. And we were gaining on him! Bruce pushed in the headlight knob and killed the Bug's eyes, giggling maniacally.

Even one such as Pablo, with a goddamn Lincoln Continental, was no match for Bruce and his little yellow Bug. Bruce always drove when we went out at night, and years of the game had made him a master of the chase. He knew which turns to make, knew just when to hit the brakes and when to shift the gears.

I felt my worries melting away. The game was not to catch, but merely to pursue, and Pablo was a fine quarry. He was clever, making sudden turns (even flashing his blinkers the opposite direction) and he was sure a good driver. But he'd never get away, not from the likes of us.

But suddenly, the white car was in view again, and showing us headlights instead of taillights! Pablo had somehow turned around!

The Bug pulled into a driveway. That is to say, Bruce worked the controls like a pianist at the keys, applying just enough brake that the tires didn't squeal, downshifting to first gear even while wrenching the wheel around two full turns. He killed the engine, and we lurched to a halt. In less time than it takes most people to pull up a zipper, he had turned the Bug into an inert, parked vehicle. All of us ducked our heads instinctively as Pablo's lights flashed by.

Had he seen us? Were we just another car in just another driveway, or had he noticed one final instant of movement, or caught sight of Megan's blond hair flashing in the glare of a streetlight?

"Damn," Bruce muttered, wiggling the gearshift knob. "Damn! Oh fuck, man, I can't get it back into neutral!" His voice rang with the frantic, mock-seriousness he reserved for the game.

"He's getting away!" I said. Incredible!

"Hurry up," Megan added wisely.

"Piece of shit!" Bruce yelped. His hand now pushed back and forth on the gearshift with quick movements, as though it were the handle of a pump. He gave it a hard jerk to one side, then slammed it the other way. It was moving, maybe, an inch to either side, clearly not shifting gears as it should do.

He tugged upward on the knob, and then tried wiggling it some more. No help. He sighed.

"What's wrong?" Megan asked. She sounded concerned, which was understandable since this was her car too, or would be once she got her license.

Bruce pursed his lips, and faced upward at an angle, looking at nothing. A theatrical gesture. He raised his right hand, placed it on his heart. "It's fucked, Megan. What's wrong is, it's fucked."

"Um." I cleared my throat. "The Pablo is getting away."

"Thank you," Bruce replied with evident irritation.

We were all silent for a moment.

"He *did* something."

It was Megan who spoke.

"He knew we were chasing him, and he did something to the Bug. He's trying to stop us from catching up to him!"

Megan's voice was light, the words more a make-believe sug-gestion than an accusation. And yet, there was an edge to it.

A certainty hit me like a wave slamming into a rocky shore. "A quest," I said, almost whispering, fearing the words even as I said them. "We have to go on a quest to find it."

I looked at Bruce, and over my shoulder at Megan, and saw their puzzlement, their skepticism.

"We have to go looking for Pablo," I persisted. The words were tumbling out of my mouth now, in a low tone like a chant. "The encounter with it was not an accident. The forces of darkness have played their Pablo card, they have unleashed the Pablo on the un-suspecting night! It prowls the city, purchasing cigarettes and lot-tery tickets, biding its time. And when the time comes, it will lash out with cobra-swiftness at the hearts of the young and the hopeful, and there it shall dwell. My friends, we must seek it out at all costs, and destroy it if we can!"

The look that Bruce gave me was the sort of cheerful amaze-ment people use when somebody says something totally, hopelessly asinine. Megan looked quizzical, as though she hadn't quite heard and wanted me to repeat it.

"What the *fuck* are you talking about?" Bruce inquired.

Something caught my eye outside.

A flicker of orange lit the sky, like the end of a lit cigarette. The orange became a line, a row of sparks headed by a single, bright coal burning its way across the starry sky. A meteor!

"There!" I cried. "There, the heavens have sent us a sign."

The meteor burned its way to the ground somewhere south of us. It had landed inside the city of Colorado Springs!

"Follow the shooting star!" I instructed Bruce, easily popping the gear shift into neutral with my left hand. "There lies the object of our quest!"

My voice echoed and died inside the Bug while the two of them stared at me. "Good grief," Bruce said.

"Hi!" Megan told the night clerk at the 7-Eleven as we strode in. A sour-faced woman of about forty, she glared back at us, mem-orizing our faces, measuring us against the tape marks on the door frame. And yet, there was a tentative friendliness about her as well. It was an aura of dull/frantic graveyard shift boredom, one that hinted she would strike up a long conversation if given the chance.

"Good evening," the clerk said. She stood there motionless as we shuffled past her, then, looking a bit uncomfortable, took a half-step sideways and started straightening the Twinkie packages in their racks.

Bruce stopped right in front of her and smiled. "Hello. How are you tonight?" He was always careful to be nice to the clerks, you see, and he typically started right up with a kind word.

"Oh, zombied out of my skull," she replied, her voice sliding out in long, weary breaths. "I've got five hours on already and I don't get to leave until 7:45."

She continued on that way for a while, with occasional comments from Bruce encouraging her along. I wandered off, uninterested. Some of the night clerks were neat folks, with real day jobs and all kinds of stories to tell. The majority, though, were dull, almost bovine creatures who (as we had proven on numerous occasions) were hard pressed to identify the guy on the five-dollar bill.

The air inside the 7-Eleven was cool and dry but had a still, indoor quality to it. The air of a hospital, maybe. Or a mortuary. Stark fluorescent lights, far too bright if you really noticed, lit up the shelves of brightly colored food packages, the Slurpee and Nacho-Cheez machines, the refrigerators full of pop and Perrier and 3.2 beer, and cast deep shadows in the spaces behind the video games. My sneakers squeaked and squealed unpleasantly on the freshly waxed tiles of the floor. Somewhere a coffeepot bubbled once and fell silent.

The unearthly convenience-store atmosphere, normally a comfort to me, seemed more sinister tonight, crackling with subtle energies capable of destroying human souls, or corrupting them irretrievably.

I plucked a long, cylindrical package of Spree candies from one of the shelves. A little farther on, I picked up a box of Vivarin and a stick of spiced jerky. Sugar, caffeine, and salt. Like the ingredients for a magic spell, one which could provide strength and wisdom to see us through the storm that was swirling in around us.

Megan was over by the rental video rack, happily scanning the covers of the movie boxes. She glanced at me briefly as I walked up, then turned back to the shelves. "I've seen that one," she informed me, pointing to a box which depicted a green, slimy hand reaching out from under a manhole cover. "And that one," she added, pointing out another movie. "And that one and that one. This one was really good. Have you seen it? Oh, and I saw this one, and that one . . ."

She turned and looked at me to see why I wasn't responding. I smiled a thin smile at her. "I've seen them all," I stated flatly, maybe a little bit nastily.

"Well!" she responded, pretending to be impressed. "I guess you're just too cool for me!"

My smile widened, and I felt some warmth flow back into it, felt some of my unease retreat. Ah, the power of friendship. The power of beauty, of youth. "Don't worry about it, Megan, I'll still let you hang around with me."

We grinned at each other, and made our way back to the counter, strutting together like Dorothy and the Scarecrow.

Up front, Bruce was still chatting with the clerk, and I saw her features had gained a certain animation they had previously lacked. Her cheeks had taken on a slight flush, her eyes a faint sparkle. The corners of her mouth turned up slightly, the beginnings of a smile, and I realized with some surprise that she was pretty. Sometimes all it takes is a little humanity to bring people out, you know?

But the image of the Pablo flashed out in my mind like a grease-spattered neon sign. The antithesis of human kindness, the very seed of corruption.

Striding forward, I placed my items on the counter and pulled out my wallet. "Did you see a meteor about twenty minutes ago?" I asked her, rudely breaking through whatever Bruce was saying. I tossed a five-dollar bill on the counter with my purchases.

The sour look snapped back onto her face like the visor of a helmet, and she gave a good glare at me. Bruce poked me in the arm and made an irritated noise. When the clerk (her name tag read "Sandy") picked up my candy and started punching cash-register keys with her left hand, I feared she wouldn't answer me at all. But she relented as she rung up the beef jerky, and muttered at me (looking at the jerky, though), "Yeah, I saw one. Do you want a sack for that?" She indicated my merchandise with one hand while snatching up my money with the other.

"Yes, please," I said quickly. "About that meteor. Did you see where it landed?"

Sandy, the clerk, turned and looked at me again. Her expression expressed a very tiny glimmer of interest. "Yeah, I did, actually. It looked like it was right in the middle of downtown. I say that because it definitely passed in front of the Holly Sugar Building, but it was definitely *behind* the hospital. I never saw anything like it."

I nodded thoughtfully.

"Actually," she added, "I'm glad you asked me that. I'd almost forgotten about it. That's strange, isn't it?"

There was some ruckus behind me as Bruce and Megan pushed each other or something, but I didn't turn my head; I was not to be distracted just then. I nodded instead. "Yeah, that is strange, Sandy. Would you say there was anything, well, supernatural about the experience?"

Sandy blinked, looking puzzled. She blinked again. The sour look snapped back down over her face. "Supernatural! Whadya go and ask me something like that for, huh? You want to know if I've seen any UFOs, too? Huh?"

I could hear Bruce and Megan suppressing giggles. I did not turn around. "I'm not making fun of you, Sandy," I insisted as reasonably as I could. "This is important. The three of us are looking for Pablo."

The clerk looked at me blankly while Bruce burst out in genuine laughter. After a moment Megan cut in, too.

I turned around and glowered at them. Bruce was guffawing shrilly, his face red, and Megan, while more sedate, had a great big turd-chomping grin stretched across her face.

"Very funny," Sandy humphed, slapping some change into my hand and stuffing a white plastic bag under my arm. "Ain't you kids got any better way to spend your time?"

I shot her a helpless look, then glared back at my friends again. "Nice going, guys. Really good work."

Still unable to speak, Bruce thumped me good-naturedly on the back and headed for the door. Frowning, I followed him, and Megan trailed after me chuckling faintly. Bruce pushed the glass door open and stepped out, then stopped short, causing me to slam into his back at full walking speed. (If this doesn't sound painful, then try it sometime.)

I yelped and grabbed my tingling nose, taking a step backward only to hit my back on the door frame, off which I bounced sideways into one of those big upright trash cans that sit outside the entrances of 7-Elevens. Two of the can's four feet lifted up slightly off the cement, but only a millimeter or so. My momentary fear that it would tip over proved groundless, and I managed to regain my balance without falling into anything else.

There was a big Hispanic person standing in front of Bruce like a wall.

I steadied myself against the trash can, got my bearings, and looked again.

Sure enough, a three-hundred-pound Mexican-American fellow stood there, hands on hips (Superman style), glaring down at us. No, at me. In fact, he was taking a step *toward* me, and the expression on his face was not a friendly one. He took another step. I was frozen, badly frightened by this apparition. It was not the Pablo, of course, but in some sense it was something worse, certainly something more *immediate*. It was a physical, flesh-and-blood human being towering over me with murder in his eyes.

I thought briefly of the butterfly knife in my left front pocket. I didn't know how to use it, not really, but I'd been carrying it around for a few years now, with some vague idea that if the chips were down it was better to have it than not to. It didn't occur to me until several years later that a good pair of sneakers and a willingness to run are a lot more useful. Anyway, at that particular moment the idea of drawing the knife occurred to me and was quickly discarded. Might as well pull a knife on an onrushing freight train, I mused with the quick, dreamy quality of panic.

"I want to talk to you," this large person stated. His breath smelled of onions and chili sauce, his body of sweat and motor oil. I stood motionless, looking up at him with large eyes. I should interject at this point, that I was by no means a short young man. This guy was seven feet tall if he was an inch.

In my peripheral vision I could see Megan standing in the doorway, her frame rigid. My view of Bruce was now blocked by the massive form of the man in front of me. The night air was cool and dry, and had a stillness to it like the air inside the convenience store. Somewhere, faintly, muffled by double-paned glass, a coffee-pot bubbled once and was silent.

"I heard you in there, talking to that lady," the human wall informed me. "And I'm gonna warn you *once*. Don't go looking for Pablo. You won't like what you find, or where you'll find it."

I was a hedge, a mailbox, a piece of sculpture. I had stopped thinking, was simply standing there with an expression of horror on my face.

The man's features softened a little, becoming concrete instead of granite. "Just . . . forget about it, okay? Go home, man, get some sleep. There's your warning."

He turned, slowly, the way an aircraft carrier might, and strode away. His footsteps didn't make any noise, and he wasn't twenty feet away before the darkness swallowed him up.

The night was still.

A cricket, as if sensing the passage of danger, began to chirp.

"Holy fuck," Bruce said.

I started to reply, but found myself shaking too badly to speak.

"Well," Megan suggested in a quiet voice that was almost a whisper. "Let's go downtown."

Bruce nudged me uneasily as we sat together on the hood of the Bug. Megan was still in the back seat fumbling with her shoelaces, humming some vaguely familiar tune. (Sitting here now, typing this, I realize it was probably "Wouldn't It Be Nice" by the Beach Boys, but maybe I'm letting my imagination interfere with my memory.)

"I don't know, Wilby." (That was what Bruce used to like to call me.) "I get a bad feeling about this. There's more going on than we're directly aware of, and I get the feeling, somehow, that things are not going to turn out okay."

I let out a breath, and shivered a little, even though it wasn't cold. "Maybe we should do like that Mexican said, and just go home."

Bruce nodded. "Yeah, that might not be too bad, except that I think we'd regret it for the rest of our lives. If we follow through, at least we'll have that much."

The strength of those words! An inspiration, to be sure, but not really a surprise. Bruce was the one who'd stood impassively before the tower window of Mairmont castle, while the ghostly nun turned the void of her face upon us and whispered like the night wind through the treetops. Megan and I, and Megan's friend Jannell, and Jannell's current would-be boyfriend, had all run gibbering in terror.

"Yeah," I agreed reluctantly, clapping him on the leg.

"Let's climb up on the roof of that parking garage!"

I nearly fell off the hood. Megan's voice had come without warning, from directly beside me.

"Jesus Christ!" I shrieked. "Don't do that, you stupid . . ."

I stopped myself.

"So-*ree,*" Megan said in a hurt tone. Her face wore a frown that was just visible in the glow of distant streetlights.

"Calm down, Wilby," Bruce said. He hopped off the Bug and, with an overhand "follow me" gesture, started walking across the street toward the five-story garage Megan had indicated. We were on the fringes of downtown, between the hospital and the Holly Sugar Building. Trees hung down over both sides of the street, nearly blotting out the stars from this angle. Dark shops were visible down past the parking structure, most of them vacant storefronts that had once displayed books and cameras and bright ski jackets. Nowadays the action was all in the shopping malls.

The thought galled me as I stood there, feeling the light evening breeze play coolly over my skin. Most of the kids Megan's age were wild about the malls, particularly the big ones. They hung around there after school, spent their evenings and weekends there browsing and shoplifting and buying french fries and Coke. They were, it seemed, a lost generation, an entire population ignorant of anything but the plastic world that was smothering them all.

Grim thoughts. I shook them off, slid off the car, and trotted after Bruce and his sister.

They were waiting for me inside, hiding behind the dim hulking forms of parked automobiles, and they leaped out at me with gleeful shrieks as I ducked under the black and yellow striped traffic gate. I yelled back in pretend startlement, then laughed to show I wasn't mad. The prank was so utterly typical, so much to be expected of the two of them, that I probably would have been more surprised if they'd skipped it.

Together we raced up the stairs, pushing each other merrily, giggling despite the seriousness of the occasion.

When we got to the roof, the sky seemed to blossom above us. The city lights were not bright enough to wash out the gleam of a billion stars, to hide the murky, roiling nimbus of the Milky Way. To the west, halfway down the sky, rested the dime-sized disk of a crescent moon, black on black, visible only as an absence of stars highlighted by that faint, faint blue glow known as Earthshine.

We stopped short, exchanged awed gasps.

"Look!" Megan whispered. "Look at the moon!"

But Bruce and I were already looking. How could we not?

"It's all worthwhile, you guys." The words spilled out of me quietly, like a mountain cascade on a bright spring morning. "Whatever happens tonight, whether we find Pablo or not. Whatever happens. It's worth it just to see this view. Everybody else in this town is sleeping, or else rolling around in bed wishing they could sleep. But we're right here!"

"Oh, man," was Bruce's only comment.

After a long while, he looked away, and ambled over to the edge of the garage's roof. He climbed up on the ledge, a dim figure in the night, and the zipper on his jeans came down with that distinctive noise that zippers on jeans have. He urinated out into empty space.

Actually, that seemed like a good idea to me, too, so I went over and joined him. Far below, I saw, was a small bridge made of metal and concrete, which connected the second floor of the garage to the second floor of the building behind it. The purpose of such a thing eluded me (as, indeed, it still does), but it sure made a handy target, and it reverberated like a kettle drum as our pee slammed onto it from above.

When we were finished, Megan came over and joined us.

"I looked out over the other side," she said, "but I can't see that 7-Eleven. If ol' Sandy was telling the truth, the meteor landed somewhere in a straight line between there and Holly Sugar."

I thought for a second, and shook my head. "It only takes two points to make a straight line; we have the hospital over there, and Holly Sugar over there." I swept my arm in a broad arc. "It must have come down somewhere along that line."

We stared out into the night, but could see nothing more helpful than leafy treetops and the roofs of houses.

"Wait a minute," Bruce began, snapping his fingers. "That looked like a big meteor. If it landed on a building or in the middle of a street, people would get all excited about it. There'd be police and fire trucks all around it. I don't see any fire trucks out there, do you?"

I protested. "Hey, it looked to *me* like it went downtown, too. It must be around here somewhere."

"I didn't say it wasn't here," Bruce corrected, shaking his finger at me in the dimness. "I said it didn't land on anybody's house. Look, there's your line, trace it out. Right *there.*" His finger moved across the town and came to rest. I looked where he was pointing, but there didn't seem to be anything there. I got my head next to his arm and sighted down along it. Still nothing, just a small blank area, dark with trees.

"Oh," I said, getting it. "Acacia Park?"

"Right," Bruce agreed.

After a pause, Megan stepped in between us, putting one arm around me and another around her brother. "Well, let's go, guys. Pablo is there waiting for us!"

Her carefree tone indicated that this was, in fact, the last thing she really expected. In spite of everything, Megan still didn't believe. She was unable, somehow, to perceive the *charge* that permeated the air, the ground, our bodies like some huge electric field.

I gave my head a mournful shake and laid it on her shoulder. "Honey," I told her gravely, "I think he is."

"Ow goddammit watch where you're going!!"

The hoarse cry pierced the night like a knife through soft flesh, and was accompanied by rustling and thumping ahead of me as Bruce stumbled and fell.

A stab of terror ran through me. It was too dark to see in this alley, but the voice had not been familiar, and now something had happened to Bruce!

But presently, my friend's voice rang out: "Sorry! I'm sorry about that. Are you okay?"

The hoarse voice called out again. "Y . . . Shi . . . You just knocked the wind outta me for a sec. You oughtta watch where you're steppin'."

"What's going on?" Megan demanded from behind me, her tone conveying more annoyance than fright.

I looked ahead, desperately trying to penetrate the gloom. There! I could just barely make out the figure of Bruce as he picked himself up off the ground, and beneath and in front of him, another sprawled form that looked like it might be trying to sit up.

"It's okay," Bruce assured us as his dim silhouette pulled itself upright. "I just tripped over somebody. We should have brought a flashlight. Are you sure you're okay, sir?"

Sir. Sir, he said! Well, that was Bruce for you.

The night was split by the sound of a huge glob of phlegm being hawked up. The sound of spitting, of something impacting wetly on the brick wall of the alley.

"Sir?" Bruce persisted.

I crowded forward, my hand reaching down for the butterfly knife. If only I could *see!*

"Aw, I'm awright," the hoarse voice croaked from below and in front of me. "I knew I shoulda curled up behin' yon Dumpster. I *knew* I shoulda gone over there by the Dumpster. What you all doing banging aroun' here late at night, huh?"

Suddenly, bony fingers wrapped themselves around my shin, a hand containing all the warmth of a dead tree branch. I shrieked, and pulled away. I hadn't known he was so close! The darkness was like a smothering blanket around me.

The voice hissed, like a wind blowing over an empty plain in the middle of a lifeless desert. "I tell your fortune, man. You marry this girl who doesn't love yeh, right? But your dreams, your hopes, they're like smoke. She leaves you, an' it cracks your heart like an egg. Like an egg! You recover, most ways, but you never the same bright boy again. You live a long life, but you fall off a cliff an' die all alone. It's three weeks before they fin' the body, an' the coyotes 'ave got to it by then. Nobody comes to your funeral. Nobody comes! How do you like that, huh?"

I took a step backward and hauled out the knife. "You! Don't touch me again or I'll cut you *bad!*" My right pinkie fumbled at the knife's catch, and with some awkwardness I flipped the handles open and exposed the blade. It caught a bit of orange light from somewhere and glittered coldly in the night. The way a knife is supposed to, you know?

"Wil!" Bruce called out, consternation evident in his tone. He couldn't see what was happening, he wasn't sure what he ought to be doing.

"Be careful," Megan warned behind me.

"Thank you!" I shot back. "Thank you very much! This guy is *crazy,* Bruce. He tried to grab ahold of my leg."

Below, the alley man made a rhythmic hissing noise that might have been a laugh, or an asthma attack.

Bruce held up his hands, a dim figure in the shadows. "Hold it," he said. "Everybody relax. Sir, why don't you stand up so nobody steps on you or anything. And Wil, if that's your knife I think you better put it away. Nothing's going on here, we're just walking through."

There was a pause. Then, the rumpling, rustling sound of the alley man struggling to his feet.

I lowered the knife, but kept the blade locked.

"You don't need to get so excited," the alley man declared with a wheeze. "I'm not a cannibal or nothin'. I'm sorry, though. I know better than to touch somebody who don't wanna be touched, an' tellin' fortunes is just plain mean."

I shuffled uncomfortably. "Yeah, well, you just scared me is all. I'm not here to hurt anybody." Reluctantly, I reopened the butterfly knife's catch and flipped the handles closed over the blade. Actually, it took me two tries.

"Guys," Megan called out worried and annoyed, "what's going on?" Should she scream, she wanted to know? Should she run and call a cop?

"Just relax," Bruce repeated. "Nothing is going on. We just accidentally disturbed somebody, and now we'll let him get back to sleep. Is that okay with you, sir?"

The alley man made a hacking noise, spat at the wall again. What microbes was he filling the air with? I wondered. What horrible diseases was he going to give us?

"I feel bad," the alley man said after a moment. He was facing me, looking as sincere as a dark silhouette possibly can. "Like, tellin' somebody's fortune. 'At's a cruel thing to do, an' I done it. Maybe you don't know it, but there's still a few hobos aroun' that know how to do magic. Not jus' bad stuff, but some good, too."

I squared my shoulders. "Is that right?"

I saw him nodding through the gloom. "Yeah, that's right. I bless ya right arm, fellow. Swiftness of motion, sureness of strength. Until the sunrise, one night only."

He made a motion I couldn't quite see, produced a puff of rancid breath. Tiny crystals, like grains of sand or salt, peppered my arm.

"Hey!" I protested.

"Sawright, fellow. You got a blessin' now."

I rubbed my arm. Nothing wrong with it, and none of the crystals had stuck. Humph. I stuffed the butterfly knife back in my pocket and squeezed past the alley man, pulling Megan after me like the caboose of a train. I heard the man as he fell behind us, settling back down to the pavement with a wheeze and a groan.

"Have a good night," Bruce offered back. The alley man made no reply, and so became a part of the past.

When we stepped out onto Tejon Avenue, God spoke and there was light.

* * *

The orange glow of the sodium vapor streetlamps blotted out the stars, made black velvet of the sky we had admired. The street and sidewalks were almost daylight-bright, but down the side streets it seemed darker than ever. We were strolling down a tube of brightness, a tunnel through the black mountain of the night.

We were walking down the middle of Tejon Avenue like we owned it, but there was tenseness in our steps. We had seen too much to kid ourselves anymore.

The park drew closer, its lush summertime greens turned dark olive by the orange-and-black of downtown. Deep shadows hid its interior, the spaces between the trees. It was a pleasant, almost garden-like site by day, but right now it looked like a hunk of Brazilian jungle that somebody had dropped in the middle of the city. And, as with a jungle, unknown and unseen dangers lurked within.

"We're off to see the wizard . . ." Bruce sang, but his heart wasn't in it. His voice trailed away, and the night swallowed its echoes.

"I *do* believe in spooks!" Megan tried, and we all chuckled, if a little uneasily.

Our feet seemed to make almost no sound on the pavement. The air was still, the trees of Acacia Park motionless and silent. The interstate was barely half a mile away, and usually pretty busy even at this time of night. But we heard nothing.

Finally, our course angled off to the side of the road, and we crossed a sidewalk and stepped out onto grass. We were in the park.

A darkness fell about us right away, as overhanging tree limbs blocked the streetlights of Tejon. Bruce drew forward slightly, and Megan and I fell back a pace. Like a platoon on jungle patrol, with Bruce on point. But then, platoons on jungle patrol are usually packing enough firepower to level a small town, and that has to boost your confidence a bit.

There was a rustling up ahead of us.

As one body, we stopped. My hand dipped into my pocket, seeking the faint comfort of the butterfly knife. "Pablo?" I whispered.

Bruce glanced back at me, then turned his eyes forward again.

"Fuck it," he muttered, and then, cupping his hands to his mouth megaphone-style, "Hey Pablo! If you're here we want to talk to you!"

A moment of silence came and (eventually) went, and then there was a commotion ahead of us, deeper in the park. A figure burst into view maybe twenty feet away. He was wearing blue jeans without a shirt (which even this warm night didn't quite warrant), and his skin was a chalky, unhealthy white even in the gloom of the acacia trees. His hair was a bright copper red, his nose prominent on his narrow face. I can picture him clearly in my mind, even now.

Something clicked when I saw what he was doing, and the chemicals of bright animal fear jumped out into my bloodstream. The guy, this white, flame-haired apparition, had spread his legs and brought his arms together. He had dropped into a shooter's stance, and in his hands there was, in fact, a shooter.

In a motion that shocked me with its suddenness, Bruce ducked and spun, dove toward Megan and tumbled her to the ground. Just in time, I think.

The muzzle flash was the same color as that meteor had been earlier. Around it puffed white smoke. The guy's face was just wild, the expression that of somebody who has found a nine-inch spider crawling out of his mouth.

A piece of copper-jacketed lead traveled through the spot Bruce had just been standing in, and then through the spot Megan had occupied. I saw it as a white streak, not really a motion but a whole thing, a line of death like a laser beam. But I *felt* the motion. The gunshot was not a sound, it was an *event,* and I was a part of it as the bullet ripped past my shoulder at supersonic velocity, and its shock wave hit me like a slap in the face.

My mouth fell open and I just stood there in dull amazement. I had just been shot at. Well, actually I guess it was Bruce he'd been aiming for, but he'd only missed me by about a foot and a half.

The gunman shuffled a little, adjusted his stance. The gun smoked in his hands. "No Pablo!" he shrieked, and fired again.

This time, the bullet passed through the narrow space between my left arm and my chest. A tube of expanding air followed behind it like a heavy pillow.

"No Pablo!" The guy shouted again, though my stunned eardrums could barely make it out.

Who the hell was this guy, and why was he trying to kill us? Suddenly, I was furious. I straightened up to my full height, filled my lungs, and *screamed*. The sound of primal rage.

"WHAT ARE YOU FUCKING DOING!" I demanded in a voice that shook the stars. "JUST WHAT THE FUCK ARE YOU TRYING TO PULL!"

My right hand was still gripping the knife in my pocket, and I pulled it out and flipped off the knife's catch.

The blade was a cold arc in the night. It didn't stand still, it danced through the air in a deadly, glittering ballet. My hand jumped left, jumped right, moved forward and back. The butterfly handles flapped like wings, they spun like the arms of a figure skater. The sound of it was frightening, the clicking and clacking of cool steel formed into an instrument of death.

The thought occurred to me, briefly, that I was not capable of this. You saw people wield a butterfly knife this way in the movies sometimes, turning it from a simple object into a *zone* of air and metal and I-mean-business motion.

Red Hair dropped his gun and ran.

I mean, this guy was twenty feet away and pointing a gun right at me. Even if I *threw* the knife, he'd have plenty of time to duck before he blew my head off. But he ran nonetheless.

And God help me, I ran after him. With a blood-boiling yell I charged his retreating form. There was murder in me, never doubt it. If I had caught him . . .

But I didn't catch him. I didn't pursue him for more than a second. You see, that big Hispanic guy from the 7-Eleven was in front of me all at once, like he'd materialized out of the very stuff of night. I pinwheeled my arms, and stopped running so abruptly that I fell straight forward, landing on my elbows and chest and very narrowly avoiding slitting my own throat with the butterfly knife.

I gasped in a breath, rolled over on my side. I would have popped up onto my feet, but in an instant the big Hispanic was standing over me. Not that he'd moved quickly or anything. He was just *there*.

"I warned you," he uttered softly, and his voice was like moonlight reflecting off a pool of oil. "You lookers for Pablo, you take no warnings. You blunder around, packing weapons, doing damage. For what purpose?"

In lieu of an answer, I stuck the butterfly knife in his leg.

He pulled back, and my fingers slipped off the twin handles suddenly slick with blood.

"For what purpose?" The man repeated, his tone utterly unchanged. I watched in numb horror as he reached down, lazily, and plucked the blade from his thigh.

"Did you hope to achieve some kind of enlightenment?" He glared down at me, not angry but reproachful, in the terrifying way that a father is toward a two-year-old. "No, it was an ego thing, wasn't it? You had a point to prove. 'At any cost,' you said. You've endangered not only yourself, but your friends as well. Perhaps you don't realize how close you cut it, just now.

"And speaking of cutting, it seems you've stuck a knife into a total stranger. Look at me!"

I looked. The man's jeans fit him tightly, and my knife had punched a triangular hole through which I could see wounded flesh. Blood flowed from the puncture in regular glurps, like milk pouring out of a carton.

The man shook his head sadly. "Femoral artery, man. Very bad news. You went looking for Pablo, and you found him inside your own heart. That's how it goes down, every fucking time. Don't say I didn't warn you."

I gaped for a while, as blood splashed the ground in front of me, as the man's right pant leg turned a crimson that was almost black in the gloom of the park. He just stood there, looking down at me, shaking his head.

"Who the fuck are you?" I yelped at him, pawing at the ground, seemingly unable to get a grip.

The man smiled. "I thought you knew me. My name is Jesus."

Hey-Zeus was how he pronounced it. The Hispanic name, you know?

I looked over at Bruce and Megan, and saw them sprawled on the ground, looking back at me with wide eyes. I turned my head back toward Hey-Zeus again.

There was nobody there.

Is there a moral to this story? Something simple and to-the-point, like "Don't go looking for Pablo" or "Don't mess with people named Hey-Zeus"? Well, I doubt it. Life rarely boils down to single sentences.

I learned many things that night, most of which I could never hope to articulate. Live well, my friends. Hold your joys out before you like lanterns, and keep your sorrows in your pocket where the butterfly knife used to sleep. Keep yourself pointed away from gravity, and remember to look up at the stars every now and again. You get it?

Perpetual Light

———— ✠ ————

Michael Cassutt

Four times each day the bell tolled at the Chapel of Perpetual Light, calling the brethren to atone. With the constant wail of sirens, the daily gunshots, and the eternal roar of the nearby freeway, Brother Stephen rarely heard the ancient bell. Fortunately the brethren of the Light lived in the graffiti-spattered chapel building itself, where they could be summoned in person, if necessary.

Brother Stephen was about to close the chapel door, but realized he would have to dislodge a sleeping vagrant who heard no bells and felt no pain. He decided to let him rest. It wasn't as though the chapel had so many visitors that services were often interrupted.

Brother Stephen turned and went inside, walking toward the altar, passing the gathering group of eight bare-headed men in brown robes. Not one of them was younger than fifty, a fact which occasionally disturbed Brother Stephen, who was far beyond fifty himself. He reminded himself that the Light would provide.

He made the sign of the cross and genuflected before the tabernacle. The prayers began automatically in all the wildly differing accents of the brethren. (Brother Stephen's own way with English had once encouraged a visiting Serbian priest to believe they were landsmen.)

"In the name of the Father and the Son and the Holy Spirit . . ."

"For those who make the children weep," Brother Stephen recited.

"We atone."

Brother Stephen found his concentration broken by the sound of a helicopter flying low over the neighborhood. There seemed to be more sirens than usual, too. He put it out of his mind as he opened the tabernacle.

"For those who bring the darkness."

"We atone."

Light shone from the tabernacle, a Light so bright it cast shadows. Brother Stephen knew, of course, that it was a trick, of sorts—engineering of a century past that allowed a candle, a chalice and a piece of glass to somehow represent the Face of Heaven. Still, it soothed and at the same time terrified Brother Stephen. It was the honor of being the keeper of the Light that had kept him content for so many years.

He bowed his head, prepared to let the power of the Light wash over him, when he realized something was wrong. The familiar chant of the brethren in prayer had changed—as if someone were singing out of key. Brother Stephen turned away from the tabernacle.

In the doorway was a young man, no more than twenty-one, expensively dressed in a white shirt and leather jacket, and holding a gun.

Brother Stephen quickly closed the tabernacle, genuflected, and went toward the young man. "Good evening. I'm Brother Stephen." For the first time he realized the young man was bleeding. "You're hurt."

Brother Stephen reached out, but the young man brandished the gun. "Don't."

"That's not necessary. Whatever we have, we share." The helicopter and sirens were suddenly louder. "Nor do we turn pilgrims out into the night." He nodded to Brother Andrew, who closed the chapel door.

The young man stared at Brother Stephen. His eyelids fluttered and the gun dropped. Brother Stephen caught him before he hit the floor. "Take him to the applicant's cell. Quickly!"

Two of the brethren took up the young man and carried him away. As if picking up a hot coal, Brother Andrew retrieved the gun and handed it to Brother Stephen. At that moment there was a knock on the door. "I'll handle this," Brother Stephen said.

As he reached for the handle, Brother Stephen noticed a spot of blood on the floor. He stood on it, concealing it, as the door opened. Outside was a Latino policeman, who crossed himself.

"Sorry to bother you, Brother, but we're checking all the buildings on this street."

"What is the problem?"

"Shootout at an AM-PM over on Twelfth. We think he's the same guy who's done a bunch of other jobs, and he was headed this way."

"Well, if we see anyone like that, we'll be sure to give you a call."

The policeman hesitated, looking past Brother Stephen to where four of the stouter brethren waited. "Well, ah, thanks, Father." He grinned. "You've got some linebackers here, anyway."

Brother Stephen closed the door and, for the first time in many years, bolted it. Then he crossed himself.

Brother Stephen realized it wasn't unusual for the wounded to find their way to the Chapel of Perpetual Light. Its location in a downtown area between Korea Town and the banking district was home to transients and those who preyed on them. At least once a month some poor soul, victim of a knifing or a beating or a shooting, would present himself at the door, or, more likely, be found there in the cold, pre-dawn hours by brothers rising for devotions.

So it was that Brother Andrew knew exactly what to do with the young man who, it turned out, had a bullet wound in his side. When Brother Stephen arrived to examine the young man, the wound had been cleaned and dressed. The young man had regained some of his color and was conscious.

"Let me take a look at that," Brother Stephen said, drawing back the blanket.

"Are you a doctor?" the young man said.

"We all have some medical training," Brother Stephen replied. "Brother Andrew will call for an ambulance."

"No!" The young man tried to rise. "No hospitals, no doctors. I'm feeling . . . better." He coughed.

"I see. Young man . . ."

"Call me Garrett."

"Mr. Garrett . . . you've been shot."

"Tell me something I don't know." He forced a smile. "He didn't hit anything vital. I'll be fine if I can just rest here . . . for a couple of days. I'll pay you."

"It isn't a question of money. No one will force you to see a doctor. You are welcome to stay until you are well."

The bells were sounding again. Brother Stephen realized Garrett had been in the chapel for hours. "What's that?" Garrett demanded.

"Midnight prayer," Brother Stephen said. "We pray four times a day, midnight, dawn, noon, and sunset."

"Sounds boring."

"It is anything but." He rose. "You're welcome to join us, you know. When you're feeling better." Brother Andrew headed for the door; Brother Stephen turned to follow, but hesitated. "Oh, Mr. Garrett. I believe this belongs to you."

He drew Garrett's pistol out of his robes and placed it on the desk.

Brother Stephen had just sealed the tabernacle following midnight prayers when there was another knock at the chapel door. "This is getting to be a habit," he said to Brother Andrew, who for all his many virtues, had yet to catch a joke.

Another man waited. "My name is Helprin," he told Brother Stephen. "I'm looking for someone." Helprin was short, olive-skinned, and balding. Brother Stephen could not accurately guess his age and placed him to be anywhere from thirty to forty-five.

"Do you have some identification?"

"As a matter of fact, I don't. I'm not a policeman."

"But you . . . want someone."

Helprin nodded across the street. "I've been out there for six hours. I saw you take him in. I saw you lie to the police. And I know he has not come out."

"You leave me speechless, Mr. Helprin."

"Whatever he told you, his name is Masum. Last week in Madrid he blew up a synagogue. Before that he put a bomb on an airliner. He has killed children, and I want him."

"What you say is horrifying, Mr. Helprin. But what goes on out there doesn't concern me. In this chapel we serve a different master. Even if he is a criminal, the young man is under the protection of the Perpetual Light."

"Don't pull the *sanctuary* crap on me. The man's a killer."

"Then we should call the police." Brother Stephen turned to Brother Andrew. "Will you call them?"

"Wait!" Helprin's eyes narrowed. For a moment Brother Stephen thought he would attack him. But Helprin merely jabbed a finger. "Have it your way," he said. "Masum will have to come out eventually. When he does, I'll be waiting." Then he turned and walked down the steps.

The movement of Helprin's arm had raised his jacket. Brother Stephen had seen that he, too, was armed.

It was after dawn prayers that Brother Stephen next saw Garrett. He and Brother Andrew, who had looked in on Garrett as he slept, found the young man in his bare feet staring out the second floor window, obviously contemplating an escape.

"You're up early," Brother Stephen said. "Just in time for breakfast."

Garrett stared at him. "I've got to get out of here."

"If that's what you want. But don't you think you'd be better off with some food in your belly and shoes on your feet?"

Brother Andrew set out a tray. Simple food: an apple, a bowl of cereal, a bottle of water. Garrett sat down and began to eat. With his mouth full, he said, "Who are you people?"

"We're members of the contemplative order of the Perpetual Light. The popular term is *monks,* though we call ourselves *brothers.*"

"Why aren't you afraid? I have a gun."

"As far as we're concerned, you're just a young man in trouble." Brother Stephen smiled. "The same could have been said for all of us—including me—at one time in our lives."

"I blew up a synagogue. I'm being hunted."

"I know. Mr. Helprin was here."

The news didn't seem to surprise Garrett. It did seem to annoy him, however. "His people murder mine daily. And he calls *me* a terrorist!"

"He mentioned something about the murder of children."

"Even if there were children involved, they were all Zionist pigs."

"Of course. One can never be too careful with Zionist pigs. Or any kind of pigs."

Garrett had finished. Brother Stephen took him by the arm. "Let me show you around."

He led Garrett downstairs to the chapel proper.

"I'm not going to debate these matters with you, Brother. You've locked yourself up behind these walls; you know nothing of the suffering my people have endured. We are fighting a war."

"A war you will eventually win."

"Yes."

"I know a little about war. I used to be a soldier, much like you, I suppose. Fighting for a cause I believed in. But ultimately I found it to be futile." Brother Stephen genuflected as they approached the tabernacle. "Is there such a thing as final victory?"

"Are you trying to tell me that violence never solves anything, Brother? History is full of examples that prove otherwise."

"Oh, yes. Wasn't there a war with Germany and Japan? Who won that? The British? Maybe it was the Spanish? Perhaps I have been shut away too long. I can't seem to remember just who was fighting, and who won."

"I don't think it would be easy to convince a Carthaginian that violence never solved anything—if you could find one."

"An interesting point. I'll keep it in mind when I ask the Romans who defeated Carthage." He smiled. "If I can find a Roman." He suddenly stopped. "How are you feeling?"

"Amazingly well, thank you. I'm not bleeding. I can walk without pain. In a few days, I will no longer be a burden to you."

Brother Stephen opened the tabernacle. "Oh, Mr. Garrett, I'm afraid we have a slight misunderstanding. You can't stay here past evening prayers."

He drew out the Light itself, stepping back and deftly dragging Garrett to his knees. Then he whispered: "You asked what it was we did here. I told you that we prayed. That we atoned for sins. But I didn't tell you everything."

"I was afraid of that," Garrett said, sarcastically.

"You see, what keeps us here—what has kept us here all these many years—is the Light itself. It is holy . . . purifying . . . miraculous."

Garrett couldn't help but look. For an instant he, too, wore the rapt expression of a brother of the Order. Then he shook his head and stood up. "This is stupid!"

He started to walk away. Brother Stephen quickly closed the tabernacle and caught up with him.

"You say you will give me shelter as long as I need it," Garrett said. "Then you order me out within a day! This isn't a monastery, it's an asylum!"

He kept walking away. Brother Stephen called after him. "There's no contradiction, Mr. Garrett! I said you would have shelter *until you were well!* And so you have. Ask yourself why you are no longer limping. Take off your bandage and try to find a wound!"

Garrett stopped. He pulled open his shirt and ripped away the bandage. There was nothing but new, pink skin where the wound had been.

"What the hell is going on?"

"It's the miracle of the Perpetual Light, Mr. Garrett," Brother Stephen said. "It has healed you." He took the stunned Garrett by the arm. "Now, let's get you some rest. You'll need your energy when you leave . . . tonight."

Garrett slept through midday prayers and into the afternoon. About five o'clock Brother Stephen went to see him. He found Brother Andrew there, holding Garrett's jacket. "There is a stain on it, I'm afraid. I was unable to get it out."

As Brother Andrew went out, Garrett wiggled a finger in the hole. Turning the jacket inside out, he showed Brother Stephen the stain. "Hard to believe I was ever shot at all."

"Thank the Light," Brother Stephen said. "Now it's time for you to—"

"What's the rush?" Garrett snapped. "Maybe I want to know something about this magic Light."

"Isn't it enough to know your wound was healed within a day? That you're free to go?"

"Tell me, Brother: is there a back way out of this place?" Brother Stephen shook his head. "So the moment I walk out the front door a Zionist assassin will have me in his sights. This is hardly what I call free. Suppose I want to stay." He brandished the gun. "Suppose I make you keep me."

"I hope you don't think I made these rules," Brother Stephen said. "The Light itself is very clear: if you remain in its presence for a day, you *belong* to it."

"Oh? And *it* would keep me here?"

"You wouldn't want to leave."

Garrett looked at the floor. Then he raised his head. "Amazing. This Light has all these powers. It should be famous. Yet where are lines of worshippers?"

"I don't know how famous it is. All I know is that before I joined the brethren, I knew about the Light . . ."

"How did I manage to miss it?"

"This was probably before you were born . . ."

"It didn't manage to make the history books, either."

Brother Stephen shrugged. "This was in another part of the world. Many real events have never been written in history books."

"What kind of an idiot do you think I am? Who would be stupid enough to believe that this magic Light could be so famous that everyone would know about it, but so obscure that it could be brought here and stashed in this rathole? It doesn't make sense."

"The customs rules were rather lax at the time. In fact, it was Brother Andrew who brought it here himself."

"The old man?"

"He was a soldier in the service of King Louis. He killed Saracens to free the Holy Land."

"The Saracens occupied Palestine a thousand years ago."

"The Light was quite famous even then."

"Which means that if Brother Andrew fought them, he must be a thousand years old."

"Yes."

"He's remarkably well-preserved."

"Thanks to the power of the Light. All of us live by its grace. Brother Cleon was a French agent in Algeria. Brother Harald tortured Moors in Spain. I myself was a legionnaire in the service of Octavian."

"That makes you twice as old as Brother Andrew. Yet you're clearly younger. Your story doesn't hold up."

"We stay the age we are when we enter the service of the Light. It gives us sufficient time to . . . atone." Brother Stephen glanced at the window. Shadows from the bank tower to the west had reached the chapel. "It's getting late. You have to go."

Brother Stephen turned toward the door. Behind him Garrett said, "You're right. And your Light is going with me."

Something hit Brother Stephen behind the ear. He fell forward against the wall.

He never lost consciousness. For moments, how many he didn't know, he was too dazed to move. He was aware of a commotion in the chapel. Shouts came to him. A gunshot.

Dizzily, he pulled himself to his feet and went carefully down the stairs.

Garrett had all of the brethren gathered in the chapel. He stood now by the open tabernacle . . . wearing a robe of the Order. Brother Stephen saw that Brother Andrew was waiting by the door wearing Garrett's ill-fitting shirt, pants and jacket.

"Just in time, Brother Stephen," Garrett said. "Pick up your magic Light and come with me."

"What are you doing?"

"As you said: I'm leaving. Unfortunately, the Perpetual Light is leaving, too."

"It won't work."

"I thought you were immortal, Brother: not a prophet." He grabbed the Light from the tabernacle and walked to the chapel door.

One of the heavier brothers—Harald—made a sudden move toward Garrett, but the gunman saw him and jammed the gun right in his face. "I'll kill all of you if I have to," Garrett said.

"Leave him be!" Brother Stephen shouted. "If we've learned nothing else, it's that lives are too important to throw away!" To Garrett he said, "Take the Light, but let Brother Andrew stay."

"Sorry. He's my decoy."

At that moment the bells began to toll the evening prayer. One, two, three. . . . Brother Stephen turned toward Brother Andrew, who smiled and spread his hands. "It's my time at last. Goodbye, my brothers."

Garrett opened the door and Brother Andrew walked out.

Brother Stephen saw a flash across the street, the door of a van opening. Helprin appeared holding a rifle. He aimed it at Brother Andrew as Garrett lowered his cowl and edged to one side, prepared to run. "Masum!"

The last bell tolled. Brother Stephen realized he and the other brethren were praying aloud. "And let Perpetual Light shine upon him . . ."

Suddenly Brother Andrew began to glow. Face, arms, body . . . in moments he was alight. Not on fire, but illuminated from within, like the Light itself.

Helprin dropped his rifle and covered his face. As did the brethren.

When they opened their eyes, all that remained of Brother Andrew was a dusty heap of clothing. As if blinded, Helprin fell to his knees, fumbling in the street for his rifle and finding Garrett's empty jacket.

And now Garrett screamed. Brother Stephen turned and saw him clawing at his robe. "I'm burning up!" He had dropped the Light. Brother Stephen gently picked it up as the other brethren guided an unresisting Garrett back into the chapel.

They closed the heavy door and took the gun.

* * *

"What happened?" Garrett demanded.

"Brother Andrew is gone. He couldn't live outside these walls," Brother Stephen said.

"But he just . . . disappeared!"

"The same thing would happen to me if I went outside. And to you."

Garrett pulled away. "What do you mean? I'm leaving!"

Brother Stephen opened the door. "Try it."

Garrett hesitated. Brother Stephen reached for his hand and pulled him toward the door. "I said, *try it!*" He thrust Garrett's hand outside.

"Stop!"

He jerked back his hand. "I was on fire . . ."

"Flesh is weak. Weaker than the Light. And now you belong to it. You stayed here for more than a day."

Garrett shook his head. "No! No, I can't stay . . ."

"You can't leave." Brother Stephen put his arm around the shaken man and led him toward the altar, where the brethren had restored the Light to its tabernacle.

"What good would it do you to leave? You're a fugitive. Out there you will be a dead man, if not today, then tomorrow, if not by Helprin than by someone else. Here, at least, you might do some good."

"Locked away forever with a bunch of crazy old men?"

"Not forever. The Light extends our lives, of course, so that we may fully atone. But one day we will be freed . . . as Brother Andrew was." Garrett couldn't take his eyes off the tabernacle. "Once upon a time, my friend, we were all like you. Killers. Fanatics. Assassins. Men who would commit any atrocity in the pursuit of some holy cause. Here is where, in a tiny way, we make up for the pain we've caused. It's a noble task. It's a necessary one. You'll find a place here."

Garrett rubbed his temples. "I have no choice."

"You made your choice," Brother Stephen told him.

When the bells next tolled, it was for the midnight atonement. Brother Stephen led the newest novice toward the altar. Garrett received solemn handshakes from the others. Brother Harald, noting Garrett's resigned look, teased him: "Don't worry, Brother. It only hurts for a while." A couple of the others laughed.

Garrett turned to Brother Stephen. "It hurts?"

Brother Stephen was already opening the tabernacle, intoning, "We are those who killed the children. . . . We are those who made mothers weep."

The Light bathed Garrett. "It's wonderful . . . so warm." He forced a smile. "Four times a day for what? A thousand years?"

"Who knows? Maybe longer."

Then Garrett frowned. His eyes widened. "Make it stop!" He fell to the floor and began to writhe. "It's hurting me!"

He screamed again. "Of course it's hurting you!" Brother Stephen told him. He had the strength to suffer on his feet.

"If you don't suffer, you can't atone."

The Power in Penance

—————————— ✠ ——————————

Edward E. Kramer

Halford swiveled his chair in short swift strokes, but could not find a position to sit at ease. His right hand gently trembled as he poured another shot of Jack Daniels; he emptied it in a single, fluid motion. The bourbon raced through his arteries and into his brain—he would be pacified for another hour or so. Resting his elbows on the edge of the desk, he surveyed his reflection in the shiny mahogany surface. *James Vincent Halford, you look like shit,* he thought to himself. And in comparison to his appearance just forty-eight hours earlier, he honestly did.

He nervously straightened the burnished bronze desk plaque that bore his name, centering it between an antique brass teller's lamp and an oversized leather-bound Bible. "Father Vincent Halford" read the plaque in Old English script, but to Bishop Mahoney it had always been simply "Halford." Surveying the new desk arrangement, he felt that something was still out of place— something was missing. He wasn't sure what it was, only that he'd never find it.

"Jesus, Mahoney," he thought aloud, "without you I feel so alone. . . ."

. . . so alone. A farm-raised boy of ten ripped from everything he knew, deposited with a single duffel bag full of clothes in front of the great wrought-iron fence surrounding St. Martin's massive cathedral. He'd read *Oliver Twist* almost two years earlier; Dickens's darkest imagery held nothing to the vast gothic structures stretched out before him.

"Dear God in Heaven, you can't be dead," Halford mused again aloud, shaking his head in disbelief.

AND YOU'RE DAMN GLAD HE IS, a voice piped in. IT'S BEEN LESS THAN TWO DAYS SINCE YOU FOUND WHAT YOU THINK WAS HIS BODY AND ALREADY YOU'VE TAKEN OVER MOST OF HIS DUTIES, MOVED INTO HIS OFFICE, AND DISPOSED OF HIS CAT.

Halford defended himself. *Until another Bishop can be assigned, I've only tried to make the transition smooth. How do you explain to your parish that their Bishop melted to death? Spontaneous combustion, maybe, but even the supermarket tabloid headlines haven't read "Bishop Melts: Details on Page 3."*

TOO BAD YOU DIDN'T TAKE PICTURES; THE STORY WOULD'VE SOLD. TO TOP IT OFF, YOU COULD EVEN MENTION THAT THE GRAIL DID HIM IN—MAYBE GET YOU A FEW HUNDRED BUCKS MORE AND A SPOT ON GERALDO.

Stop it, damn you! I did what I had to do, and that's it. Case closed. End of discussion. You're killing me slowly, you know that?

I AM YOU. AND YOU'RE KILLING YOURSELF. . . .

. . . killing yourself. The two closed caskets were laid out before him. Mr. Burton, the mortician, had recommended they be seen that way. "Jamie," Mr. Burton had apologized, "burn victims are the most difficult to prepare." He had imagined what the caskets would look like open; the thought sickened him.

Halford rested his head on the desk and wept silently. He'd been engaged in futile colloquy with himself ever since he broke into Bishop Mahoney's library two days earlier. A twenty-by-twenty-foot chamber built off the side of his office, it was protected by a huge oaken door that was generally shut and bolted. When he retreated inside, Mahoney would always lock the door from within.

Throughout St. Martin's, those who knew of the library's existence referred to it as "the vault." Copies of arcane volumes, not permitted in the Vatican by order of the Pope himself, were rumored to line its shelves. After thirty years, Halford's first view of the vault's interior came when Mahoney revealed to him, alone, that St. Martin's now possessed the Cup of Christ—the Holy Grail.

He allowed Halford to view the magnificent silver chalice, but warned him not to touch. The sterling vessel was surely fit for the King of the Jews—Halford could easily picture it in Christ's hand blessing the Passover meal at the last supper. When Mahoney failed to show up for Mass a second day, Halford forced open the vault with a crowbar to reveal the Bishop's fate.

Halford pondered. Maybe Mahoney knew it would eventually destroy him, that he had to tell someone should the inevitable occur. Perhaps it was a test by God—and Mahoney had failed. If a man as pious as Mahoney was stricken by the hand of Christ for maintaining such an artifact, Halford knew he too would face no less of a consequence. Yet, from the moment he first saw the chalice, Halford had known it was to play a role in his destiny.

A sudden blur of white and black arced toward him from the corner of the room. Halford jolted back in his chair, lost his balance, and landed squarely on the hardwood floor. Percy slid across the mahogany desk, crashed into the near-empty fifth of whiskey, and propelled it onto the floor a foot from Halford's face. Halford reeled back, prepared for anything else to come his way. He glared at the shattered bottle, then up at Mahoney's cat—staring innocently at him from its perch atop the Bible at the corner of the desk.

"What the hell are you still doing here?" Halford yelled, as if the cat could understand his query. Percy cocked her head ever so slightly, then looked toward the wall next to the vault where her food and water dish once sat.

Imagine, Halford thought, *I'm plagued by the thought of death at the hand of Christ Himself, and it's a fucking cat that nearly kills me!*

THEN KILL IT. NOW'S YOUR CHANCE—NO ONE IS WATCHING.

I can't kill his cat. You know that. Even though I hate that furball!

DON'T THINK OF IT AS A CAT THEN; THINK OF IT AS BISHOP MAHONEY. YOU GOT YOUR WISH—HE'S DEAD; THE STUPID CUP IS YOURS. YOU WANTED IT THE MOMENT YOU LAID EYES ON IT. NOW TAKE CARE OF HIS ONLY LIVING LEGACY.

I did not wish him dead, damn it! I loved him. He was like a father to me!

A FATHER TO YOU? SHIT! WE BOTH KNOW WHERE YOUR FATHER IS—AND YOUR MOTHER, TOO. AND WE BOTH KNOW WHO PUT THEM IN THEIR GRAVES.

"Go away!" Halford shouted at himself, the echo of his voice mocking him. Halford jolted to his feet, stepped around the smashed bottle on the floor, and reached for the telephone to call the Mother Superior's office.

"Hello? This is Father Halford," he said tersely. "Can I speak to Sister Mary Ellen?" He noticed the fingernails of his right hand unconsciously scraping into the desk's wooden surface—and stopped. "It's back. Please come get the cat and teach it that its food is downstairs," Halford snapped with increasing anger. "Yes, I know the poem 'The Cat Came Back,' " Halford mimicked in response. "Just get the fucking thing out of here before I kill it!" His voice rose to a scream as he slammed the phone's handset back into its cradle.

GOOD JOB. THAT MIGHT EVEN GET YOU DEFROCKED.

I can't believe I just said that. I've never cursed like that before to anyone.

YOU HAVE TO ME. AND I'LL TELL EVERYONE.

You don't count. You're not real. And you don't control me—and never will.

OH, NO? THEN WHO GOT ANGRY AT SWEET SISTER MARY? YOU OR ME? HELL, IF IT WERE ENTIRELY UP TO ME, I WOULD HAVE GOTTEN INTO HER PANTS A LONG TIME AGO.

What the hell are you talking about?

SEE, THERE YOU GO AGAIN!

A warped and rather sickly ring of the phone broke Halford's train of thought. "Sister Mary Ellen?" he asked almost apologetically as he brought the cracked handset to his face. "Excuse me, Your Excellency." Halford cleared his throat and sat up straight in his chair. "The remains of Bishop Mahoney's body have been properly disposed of. No one here knows about his death, but me. Everyone at St. Martin's has been told that Bishop Mahoney was called to your assistance at the Vatican, and that on your word, I was to be left in charge until his return." Halford had only spoken directly to the Vatican once—to tell of Mahoney's fate. He may never have spoken directly to the Church of Rome, had the Cardinal not phoned just as Halford made his ghastly discovery. "You'd like it when . . . ? Yes, Your Excellency, I will have the chalice prepared for transportation to the Vatican at four this morning. Thank you, Your Excellency."

I can't just let it go like that. They gave Mahoney the Grail because they knew he had the knowledge to uncover its mysteries. I must *continue where he left off.*

Now you're talking, Jamie! Let's plot together on this. We make one hell of a team.

You stay out of this. This is my problem, not yours.

So, are you going to take a sip from the cup next and become the savior of all mankind—or perish like Mahoney, and have some unworthy bastard, like yourself, find your blood and guts spilt out all over the floor?

It's none of your business. Please—just go away . . .

. . . go away. The cremation of his pet parakeet, Pete, took place in the cellar of the farmhouse, on a makeshift altar of bricks and cardboard. He had gently rubbed a small amount of kerosene into the parakeet's feathers. Softly crying as he lit a small fire under the creature's wings, Jamie hoped his rite would quicken its return to God. The bird had been a Christmas present when he was six; at times, it was his only friend.

Halford considered his alternatives, again scraping his fingernails into the surface of the desk. He stared for a moment at the vault, at Percy asleep at its base, then out the far window at St. Martin's Square below. Standing up with a newfound burst of energy, Halford rapped both hands on the desk. He had made his decision. He would succeed—or he would die in the process.

Nudging the cat out of the way, Halford smiled to himself as Percy sneered, and scurried to the far corner of the room. He fantasized kicking the cat across the room and out the window—he could even hear a dull "splat" echo in the back of his mind.

Opening the vault's broken deadbolt, he drew the door ajar and slowly entered. One couldn't help but immediately be drawn to-ward the silver chalice in the center. The dusky sun shone through the stained glass window of *The Last Supper* and reflected bril-liantly off the cup, resting on its black marble pedestal. Tracing a rainbow of colors mapped on the vault's interior, Halford studied the shelves upon shelves of ancient tomes surrounding him. To gain even a fraction of the knowledge Bishop Mahoney knew about the artifact would take Halford weeks, even months of research—if the information even existed.

With evening approaching, he glanced about the room for a lamp. There was no electricity in the vault. He walked over to a small desk in the corner, far less elegant than that in the outer of-fice, struck a match and lit an antique oil lamp. Opening each of the desk drawers for the first time, Halford found a small cistern of holy water, a sealed decanter of wine, a jar of olive oil used as chrism, a box containing the small wafers of unleavened bread used for the Holy Eucharist, and Bishop Mahoney's diary. It wasn't exactly a diary, as it only chronicled the Bishop's time spent with the Grail. His final passage revealed his fate:

> *I will now consecrate the Holy Eucharist, giving sacra-ment to Our Lord. Please, dear God, have mercy on me, your loving servant. Forgive me for any thoughts, words, or deeds I may have committed against you, your Church, or your chil-dren. If you wish to call upon me to return home, I am not afraid. I understand that one must be true in heart, mind, and spirit to drink from your Holy vessel. I only pray that you find me worthy. . . .*

YOU'RE GOING TO DIE, YOU KNOW.

If it is by the hand of Christ, then I'm willing to accept my fate.

YOU'RE FUCKING STUPID, YOU KNOW THAT? IF MAHONEY DIED JUST BY HOLDING THE DAMN THING, WHAT CHANCE IN HELL DO YOU THINK YOU HAVE TO DRINK FROM IT?

My God, you're right! The carafe of wine was still sealed. He never drank from the cup; he probably never even began the con-secration.

HE WAS PROBABLY TOO BUSY PLAYING WITH HIMSELF.

Halford shifted his attention to a series of short, brisk raps on the outer door. "One moment," he called out, replacing the book and gently closing each drawer. He hurried from the vault and quickly shut the door. Collecting the largest pieces of broken glass, Halford placed the remains of the bottle in the trash. He took a few seconds to catch his breath, and reclaimed his seat behind the desk while straightening his name plaque.

"Please come in."

A young boy of about twelve, dressed neatly in St. Martin's dark blue uniform, opened the door. Delicate in appearance, the child's deep blue eyes demanded attention. "Father Halford?" he asked, then without waiting for an answer, "Sister Mary Ellen sent me to retrieve Bishop Mahoney's cat."

"Step forward son," Halford replied. "Tell me your name."

"My name is Joshua, Father. Joshua Christian Tabor. But my friends call me Josh." He glanced toward the window and caught sight of the cat curled up beneath.

Ideas began shooting rapidly through Halford's mind. "Bishop Mahoney has told me quite a bit about you, Josh. I'm glad you came up here this evening; I was going to call for you tomorrow to chat." Halford wished he didn't have to stretch the truth.

"Did I do something wrong, Father?" Josh's gaze left Percy and focused on the priest. Halford suspected he'd never been in Bishop Mahoney's study; the boy was obviously uncomfortable with the setting. Halford knew the luxury about him, which far surpassed any he would have witnessed at St. Martin's, must surely add to his unease.

"No, not at all," Halford said reassuringly. "He asked me to talk to you about your confirmation. Bishop Mahoney personally requested that I be your sponsor."

"My confirmation? Really?" Josh beamed. "I never even thought Bishop Mahoney knew me."

Halford rose and walked over to Josh. "He knows each and every child at St. Martin's like they were his own," he said, resting his hand on Josh's shoulder.

YEAH, MAHONEY WAS A REGULAR SANTA CLAUS.

Not now. Go away!

WHAT'CHA GONNA DO—KILL THE KID? MAKE HIM YOUR SACRIFICIAL LAMB?

"Father Halford?" Josh asked. "Are you okay?"

The boy's voice did not break through his subconscious struggle. Sweat collected on Halford's brow.

You're trying to stop me, aren't you? Well, you can't. I won't let you.

WHAT IF I KILL THE KID FIRST?

Why are you doing this to me?

"Father Halford? Please let go. You're hurting me!" Josh pleaded.

Halford noticed his fingers pressing into Josh's shoulder, and immediately withdrew his hand. "Oh, excuse me," Halford stuttered, "I'm awfully sorry. I've been a bit ill lately."

"Can I take Percy and go now, Father?" Josh asked with the slightest edge in his voice.

Halford knelt before Josh. He reached to put both hands on Josh's shoulders, then changed his mind and cupped his hands over the boy's. "Please don't leave now. Not yet. I need your help."

The priest reeked of alcohol. He knew it scared the boy, but the influence he had over the youth would overcome this obstacle.

"I'll help you, Father," Josh responded without hesitation. Halford knew it was what Sister Mary Ellen would have instructed him to do.

"I need your help," Halford repeated, "but you must not tell anyone—*ever*—what I am going to ask you to do. Do you understand?" He could feel the boy's pulse begin to race.

"I understand, Father," Josh replied, bowing his head.

"Come with me," Halford said, standing. "I will show you something more glorious than you have ever witnessed in your life." He walked over to the vault and opened it wide. The light from within flickered an amber and crimson dance over the silver chalice, the only element of the interior that could be clearly seen. He imagined the scene might be quite frightening for the boy. Looking back, Josh had not moved at all.

Halford knew he must immediately change his tactics before he lost all cooperation. "We must go practice your confirmation now," Halford said, forcing a smile as he spoke. "I want to make sure you are ready when Bishop Mahoney returns."

"But my confirmation isn't scheduled for another—"

"It doesn't matter," said Halford, interrupting the boy. "Practice is important."

Josh peered over to the entry door, then back to the priest. Halford knew the boy could beat him there if he had the guts to betray his word and run. Halford wagered he didn't. Besides, he knew that if Sister Mary Ellen ever found out that Josh left Father Halford's presence before being properly dismissed, the boy wouldn't be able to sit for weeks.

Halford rifled through a small closet by the entrance to the vault. Searching for a white confirmation gown, he spotted one a bit too large for the boy. It would suffice. "Here," he said, tossing the gown at the boy, "put this on." Josh caught the garment and began to change.

With a renewed sense of urgency, Halford returned to the vault to prepare for the ceremony. Opening the carafe of wine, he carefully poured half into the chalice, without making any contact with the holy artifact. He feared a call or, worse yet, a visit by Sister Mary Ellen asking for the boy's return; after all, Josh was missing the children's evening Mass.

Halford had performed confirmation so many times that he knew the ceremony by heart; he would condense this one to its essentials. *Reader's Digest* would be proud. Peering through the crack in the doorjamb, Halford glimpsed the boy slipping into the gown. *If ever there was a soul pure enough to vessel the blood and body of Christ,* he thought to himself, *it would be within a child such as this.*

YOU'RE MAKING ME SICK, YOU KNOW THAT?

I will no longer allow you to distract me.

WHAT IF YOU FAIL AND THE WRATH IS TAKEN OUT ON ALL OF ST. MARTIN'S? CAN THAT PIECE OF SHIT YOU CALL A SOUL BEAR THE WEIGHT OF THAT? LEST WE FORGET SODOM AND GOMORRAH. . . .

"Father Halford," said Josh, peeking into the vault. "I'm

ready." Gently biting his lower lip, he slowly entered and approached the Grail.

"Then we'll begin," responded Halford, noticing a slight quiver in the boy. "Please, son, don't be frightened; there is nothing to fear."

LIAR.

Halford pulled a small leather Bible from his coat pocket. Standing beside the boy, he recited: "You have already been baptized into Christ and now you will receive the power of his Spirit. You must bear witness before all the world to his suffering, death, and resurrection. I ask you now to renew the profession of faith you made in baptism."

WHY DON'T YOU TELL THE LITTLE SNOT WHAT YOU'RE REALLY DOING?

"I do," Josh solemnly responded.

HE DOES NOT.

Halford placed his right index finger into the chrism and traced the olive oil onto the boy's forehead. "I sign you with the sign of the cross and confirm you with the chrism of salvation. In the name of the Father and of the Son and of the Holy Spirit."

DO YOU REALLY THINK YOU CAN TAKE SOME STINKING KID'S LIFE TO ATONE FOR THE SLAUGHTER OF YOUR PARENTS?

My parents weren't slaughtered, *damn you! They died in the fire. . . .*

. . . the fire. The cat grabbed Pete and raced for the stairs, seemingly oblivious to the fact the parakeet was on fire. Jamie lunged forward at the animal, knocking over the small blazing shrine. Smoke filled the cellar, as dried pine straw lit the cat's trail in flames. Coughing as he ran, Jamie cleared the stairs and raced through the front door. He collapsed outside, watching his home burn as he cried.

With both hands trembling, Halford quickly blessed the boy, repeating the actions he had done countless times before. "Be sealed with the Gift of the Holy Spirit."

ONLY BECAUSE YOU WANTED THEM DEAD.

The chrism on the boy's forehead began to glisten with a ruby glow. In holy reverence, Halford's voice rose up to a scream. *Accipe Signaculum Doni Spiritus Sancti."* The gleam increased with each syllable he pronounced.

Oh, God. Oh, Christ. Oh, no—!

Halford saw the radiance that reflected from the cup, shimmering in the oil on the boy's forehead. As Halford began his Latin proclamation, Josh's body trembled. With his final syllable, the chrism seared through the boy's skin, his forehead evolving into a burning ember; his body contorted in wild spasms.

This can't be happening!

Halford shut hit eyes tightly while screaming the Lord's Prayer, but his concentration shifted focus to the vision that haunted him for years—his parents aflame, leaping from the window of their burning loft.

I didn't mean for this to happen!

Halford's eyes opened. The boy's charred and burning torso was slumped onto the pedestal, the Grail resting beside the mulch that formed his head.

NOW WHAT'CHA GONNA DO—KILL SISTER MARY WHEN SHE COMES FOR THE KID?

"No, what I should have done much earlier," Halford yelled aloud.

AND WHAT'S THAT?

"I'm going to kill *you!"*

Without a pause, he clenched the Grail with both hands and lifted it to his mouth. Before the cup reached his lips, Halford felt a brittle crack above his eyes. His world went abruptly blank.

Alone in the study, Percy paced the room looking for her food and water dish. Discovering a newly opened passage, she entered the vault. Lapping the wine first off the floor, then from within the silver goblet lying nearby, Mahoney's cat was finally content.

Leaving the vault with a pristine sense of grandeur far beyond that of ordinary felines, Perceval strode down the halls of St. Martin's with the spiritual strength and wisdom of all mankind.

The Longest Single Note

───────────── ✛ ─────────────

Peter Crowther

"All music is life and all life is music," Uncle Nigel said to me almost matter-of-factly as the train chuckitty-chunked its way through the late-morning countryside.

I suppose I should have been surprised. Not at what he said but at the fact that he was even there at all. After all, the whole purpose of my journey was to attend his funeral . . . or, at least, that's how it had started out. But, somehow, I wasn't surprised. England seems to lend itself to strangeness.

I hadn't been back since my father's funeral, two years earlier, which was also the last time I'd seen Nigel, his grief sitting uncomfortably—even incongruously—on his round and usually jocular frame. Dad's death had hit him hard, though he had tried to cover up his grief for my sake. He needn't have bothered. Dad and I hadn't been much of an item since my university days, and my leaving for the States had been the last straw.

That was seven years ago.

In the intervening time, we had become estranged . . . like lovers who tire of each other's company. I knew something about that, too.

Nigel and I had maintained an infrequent contact, exchanging occasional letters filled with pleasantries and politeness but which were as devoid of breath and life as my father had been, lying still and silent in the lounge of his old house.

The final letter didn't even come from Nigel but, instead, appeared one day, in the box outside our house in Wells, covered in the faint, birdy scrawl of Aunt Dorothy. Just looking at it, you could tell it was bad news.

Nigel was ill, the letter said. Very ill. Cancer. My uncle had lost a lot of weight and they were simply waiting for the end. It couldn't be long. By the time Susan telephoned Dorothy, the letter and its contents were five days old. Nigel had gone.

Long before the arrival of that letter, my house had become a pioneers' trail and, Susan and me, we had become two ragged, road-weary wagons passing each other on a long, tiresome search for something we'd misplaced. We didn't know what it was, nor did we even understand it: we just knew it was missing. Ringing Aunt Dorothy was one of the few things Susan had done for me in more months than I cared to think about. I didn't even want to think of what *I* had done for *her*. I knew it didn't amount to very much.

It was Susan's idea that I come over and attend the funeral. At first, I hadn't wanted to but then I got to see the trip as some sort of pilgrimage. Back to the old country, travel the old roads, see my past again . . . neatly folded and stacked away like old clothes in a hidden drawer. Maybe the thing I'd lost was in that drawer, tucked between a pair of threadbare denims and a shirt I could no longer get into, smelling as fragrant and as natural as a lavender potpourri. Everybody needs a touchstone, something on which you can rest a hand and say . . . *yes, that's it . . . that's all that matters.*

I decided I had to find that touchstone . . . find myself.

With a minimum of preparation—and even less communication between Susan and me—I drove to Boston, caught the flight to Heathrow and arrived in England on the kind of summery mid-morning that I'd forgotten could even exist.

The journey from Heathrow to the King's Cross train station was filled with hustle and bustle, the tube train a kind of mobile Tower of Babel, packed with seemingly endless dialects and accents and languages. I felt immediately at ease—what are tourists except people searching for answers?

Me, I was also looking for the question.

The chaos of King's Cross gave way to the sober calmness of

a train bound for Leeds. There, I had to change for a local connection to get to Harrogate. My old hometown.

It was while we were passing through Peterborough that Uncle Nigel appeared, looking as large as ever I remembered him being when he was alive.

I turned away from the window, with its endlessly spinning stream of captured fields and trees, to look at him. He smiled and gave a small nod and then looked back out of the window. "It's all about us," he said with a soft satisfied sigh. "From the simplest birdsong to the most complex orchestral composition. It breathes. It lives." I closed my eyes tightly and then opened them again. Uncle Nigel closed and opened his own eyes a couple of times in an affected squint. "Yep, you're still there, too," he said with a chuckle.

"But *I'm* alive," I whispered, though there was nobody within earshot. By virtue of the fact that I was in a smoking compartment, the rest of the carriage was almost empty. Only one other passenger—an elderly man chain-smoking B & H and reading *The Times*—accompanied me through the countryside and he was down near the split into nonsmoking. The sunshine streamed through the windows, dappling the seat backs and bare tabletops, and shining off his bald head. All around him, swirling slate-blue smoke drifted lazily to the sound of the train's momentum.

"And I'm dead but I won't lie down."

"What's it like? Death, I mean."

The smile fell from Uncle Nigel's face and he seemed to stare at me more intently. "It's quiet," he said. "What is it that they say? 'Quiet as the grave.' Well, that's what it's like. No sounds. No music."

I shook my head and started to get up. "I'm imagining this," I muttered to myself. "Jet-lag . . . something I ate maybe."

"You're not imagining it, John. They're all gathering down at the house now. They're rehearsing their platitudes, their eulogies, straightening out their crumpled black ties, pressing dark trousers and somber dresses, practicing their expressions of grief and sympathy. None of it actually means anything." He made a facial expression as though he had just eaten something unpleasant and then, setting his jaw firmly, gave the merest hint of a smile. "More to the point, I'm not going."

"Not going?" I said, sitting down again. "Not going where?"

"I'm not going in the ground."

I remembered when he and my father would sit for hours listening to music. They would put one record after another onto the turntable and then sit silently, reverently, almost living a particular song and then discussing it while one or the other of them ferreted out another record. Music had been their passion, their raison d'être . . . a mythical chalice they would turn over and over in their hands, admiring it anew each time. Without it, they were nothing.

Sitting there in the train carriage on my way to my uncle's funeral, talking to his ghost—I presumed that was what he now was—I remembered a conversation with my father—back when we were still speaking—when I had asked him which of his senses he would be prepared to give up if he had to. It was one of those silly hypothetical questions concerning a situation that simply would not happen. But rather than dismiss it as so many would, my father had thought long and hard, stroking the memory of his beard as he decided upon the appropriate answer. The loss of his hearing—and, as a result, an inability to appreciate his beloved music—was what he had finally told me would cause him the most anguish. And then he had added, "But my memory comes a close second."

We sat for a while, my dead uncle and I, watching out of the carriage window until I resolved to find out what really troubled him. "Is it so difficult to cope with," I said at last, "being dead?"

My uncle stretched his legs under the table and shuffled himself back into his seat. "As I said, it's quiet and it's dark." He shrugged his shoulders and straightened his jacket lapels. "We come from darkness, you know."

He closed his eyes and, in a lilting voice, sang the opening lines of Simon and Garfunkel's "Sounds of Silence." When he opened his eyes again they seemed to focus from far away, as though they were returning to him—to the train carriage—from a long way away. And they were glassy and moist.

"Darkness is an old friend for us all," he said softly.

I nodded. It had been a perfect rendition of the song, even

down to the fact that I had imagined the rhythmic picking of a solitary acoustic guitar.

"And how about this one." He cleared his throat and opened his mouth slowly. Suddenly there was a waft of music, of distant instruments—a guitar, two guitars maybe—playing what sounded almost like a Scottish refrain—and then Uncle Nigel started singing in a gentle, warbling falsetto.

It was another song that seemed to concentrate on darkness but it was one I did not recognize.

"A band called The Youngbloods," he said, recognizing my blank stare. "From an album called *Elephant Mountain,* 1969. And what about this one . . ."

The carriage turned suddenly cold and alien, and there was the strongest sensation of something awakening, turning over in the seats around us. My uncle closed his eyes and seemed to drift into a trancelike state. His expression was one of pain, but bearable almost beautiful pain. The sweet pain of loss, of grief. And the sounds that issued from his mouth reverberated inside my head. For just a few magical seconds, it was as though Uncle Nigel's bridgework had scooped up a radio transmission from the ether and sent the sounds floating from his open mouth. It was all there, voices and instruments. Jim Morrison couldn't have performed it better himself.

As though coming around from a seance, Uncle Nigel opened his eyes and gave me a half smile. It seemed almost like an apology. "Morrison had it right, you know?"

I frowned.

Uncle Nigel waved a hand languidly. "Paul Simon talked about darkness being an old friend—which is true—but Morrison had it bang on the button about music being our *only* friend. He meant it's our *truest* friend."

I shook my head. I still wasn't following.

"Because it's music that gives light to the darkness."

I looked nervously at the surrounding seats. Whatever it was had ceased now that he had stopped singing, and the carriage seemed to have regained much of its earlier warmth.

"They were one of Dad's favorites, The Doors," I said in an attempt to fill the sudden void of silence.

He nodded, half closing his eyes.

I looked out as we sped past a small station lying weed-festooned and overgrown, forgotten from the great clampdown of the 1950s. "Have you seen him? Since you . . . went over? My dad, I mean."

"I know where he is," he said.

"Is he all right?"

"As far as he can be, yes."

"What does that mean? Either he's all right or he's not."

"He's all right."

I cleared my throat. "Does he ever . . . does he ever mention me?"

Nigel smiled. "Now and again."

Neither of us spoke again for a few minutes. Then my uncle said, "Know why we fear the dark? Because"—he went on without waiting for me to respond—"with the darkness comes the silence. It's why we're scared of death.

"We come from darkness, and it's to the darkness we return. But in between we have discovered the music. And it's the loss of the music that scares us the most."

Uncle Nigel brushed at a tiny piece of lint on the front of his jacket and then folded his arms. "Darkness is nothing. It is the none-ness of being." He paused and then continued. "Light, on the other hand, is energy. In turn, energy is life. Life is movement, no matter how small. Movement is sound, no matter how faint or distant. And sound, dear John, is music, no matter how free-form or avant-garde it might be.

"It is the thing we search for all of our lives . . . search for it as though it were a mystic talisman, a keepsake." He looked out of the carriage window and threw his smile beyond the glass and his half-seen reflection . . . threw it to the countryside that lay humming in the sunshine. "It may be the rubbing of two twigs or the leaves in the trees on a windy day," he said. "It could be the noise of that wind through the feathers of a mountain bird; a rockslide or a rainstorm; waves breaking on the shore; a car engine, a baby's cry, the sound of footsteps on the pavement . . . the sound of this train." He turned back to face me. "Do you hear the music of the train, John?"

I did. It went *chuckitty-chunk, chuckitty-chunk.* "Yes," I said, "I hear it. But what has all this to do with you not wanting to be buried?" Just saying it made me feel incredibly stupid. The man at the end of the smoking compartment suddenly stood up and walked away, presumably toward the buffet car. It was as though he was leaving a theater in protest at the banality of the performance he had paid good money to watch.

Nigel waved the question away with his hand. "Whenever I walk along—sorry, *walked* along—Shaftesbury Avenue I always used to think of a piece by Les Dudek called 'Central Park.' It seemed to epitomize the throngs of people, the hustle and the bustle. And when the evening gloom came to the house I would often walk out into the garden and think of The Moody Blues' 'Twilight Times.' It was like all things in my life had musical references." He laughed and threw back his head. "Hell, my life itself was one long musical reference. I loved life, John. Loved it. I didn't *want* to die."

"Nobody want—"

"Yes, I know, nobody wants to die. But with me it was something more. Who else do you know that placed such store in music?"

"Well, my—"

"Apart from your father, I mean."

I shrugged and shook my head.

"You see, it's lost on most people. They don't grasp the significance. Life is the single longest note of all, John. We are a musical species. We come from darkness and silence into a world of noise and light. We translate all of our existence into musical as well as visual images. Soundtracks for films, music in church and at funerals—I wonder what they'll be playing at mine. It certainly won't be Jimi Hendrix, and more's the pity. It'll be something . . . something funereal. You see! We even have a word for *that* kind of music. Lost and cold music specially produced to reflect off the alabaster strangeness of someone we once knew but no longer even recognize." He stopped for a few seconds and looked back at the fields and hedgerows speeding by. "You wouldn't have recognized me at the end."

"I'm sure I would have," I said. It seemed that he needed the reassurance of his own identity.

"I was thin, God was I thin. Like a skeleton."

"What is it that you want of me?" I asked.

He seemed not to hear the question or, if he did, he chose to ignore it. "Have you noticed how, in a western movie, when somebody walks into a saloon, the fellow playing the piano stops? It's the threat, the imminence of death. That's why he stops playing the piano. He stops the music."

"Yes," I said. God help me, it was beginning to make a kind of sense suddenly, a fractured logic.

"And how *all* movies always have to have a music soundtrack. Even in the days of silent films, we had to have somebody sitting playing the piano to emphasize what was happening on the screen."

Chuckitty-chunk, chuckitty-chunk, went the train.

"What do I want of you?" he said after a while. "I want you to dig me up."

The man down the carriage returned with a lidded plastic cup and a shrink-wrapped sandwich. He sat down and I watched him remove the lid from the cup and then start to eat his sandwich. I turned to look at my uncle and shook my head. "Why?"

"Why? Because the ground is dark and silent, that's why."

"But you won't be in the ground. Well, your body will be but you—" I waved a hand in his general direction. "Whatever you are, you're here now, and your body is . . . I don't know, lying in state I suppose. So why should you be affected?"

"John," he said, "I came to you because of your father. Because, of everyone I know—even Dorothy—you might understand what I've tried to tell you. It's quiet over there, deathly quiet. And the reason is that you carry with you the sounds of where you rest. Why do you think they stole Gram Parsons' body? Why do you think they did it?"

"Who's Graham Parsons?"

"Not Graham, *Gram.* He was a singer . . . a musician."

"They stole his body after he was dead?"

Uncle Nigel nodded. "And he wasn't the only one. There've been others, but Gram is the only one that's actually documented."

"Who? Who's stealing all these bodies?"

He laughed. " 'Who' isn't important, it's 'why' that matters."

I was entranced. "Okay, why?"

"To leave them where it's light, where there's some sound." He said it like he was explaining one-plus-one to a five-year-old. "And that's what they take with them."

"To Heaven?"

"Heaven is just a state of mind, John. Like 'Great,' or 'Marvelous.' 'The flip side' is how *we* think of it . . . we whose lives have revolved around music."

"Okay . . . who's 'we'?"

He looked at me, kind of frowning and mashing his lips together. I was immediately aware of the train slowing down—not slowing as if it were coming to a station but rather just becoming less frenetic, less agitated. Everything suddenly became very calm. "This is 'we,' " he said and then he pointed out of the window.

I had heard about Woodstock and the other huge music festivals held in the 1960s and 1970s from my father. And I had seen the film. Well, looking out of the train window that day was like looking out on the audience at Woodstock. Only, the people standing out in the fields were not merely watchers, they were listeners, innovators of sound. People to whom music had been everything.

There was the Big 'O', the Big Bopper, Benny Goodman, Elvis, Janis, Mario Lanza, Morrison, Jimi, Buddy Holly, Dennis Wilson— Uncle Nigel was pointing them all out because, don't ask me how, the train had slowed right down and we must have been doing only about five miles an hour. I looked around at the man down the carriage and he was sitting holding a cigarette half in, half out of his mouth, with his lips curled in a seemingly endless snarl, a thin freeze-framed trail of smoke curled around his face.

"There's Nat King Cole," my uncle said, "and Liberace, John Lennon"—I recognized him straightaway—"Karen Carpenter, who's no longer thin at all, Keith Moon, Glenn Miller, Rick Nelson, Bing Crosby . . ." The list was endless, names I knew and names I had never heard of before.

Suddenly I felt my uncle's hand on my arm. I turned around and looked at him, wearing a kind of dumb smile and suddenly fighting an overwhelming urge to cry. "Go out to the door and open the window," he said.

"Huh?"

"Go on, go out to the door and open the window."

I did as he said. The noise washed into the train like a scent of night-stocks, far-off and fragrant, impossibly beautiful and warm. Like a billion bees humming, or a zillion tree branches waving, or a thousand trillion waves strumming a distant beach.

And, as we passed the thousands of people, black people, white people, people all colors, I saw my father.

I went to Uncle Nigel's funeral that afternoon.

It was like he said it would be, somber, affected and depressing. For me, though, it was difficult to be sad. Even when Aunt Dorothy came up to me and wept against my shoulder.

They played a couple of hymns which I recognized but didn't know the names of. It was all I could do to stop myself from standing up and shouting "Hey, he doesn't want this. Put on some Hendrix!" But I managed it.

I didn't go back to the house. Instead I rented a car and bought a large spade, some sacking and a cassette of *Electric Ladyland*. Then I rang Susan and told her that I loved her. She was shocked, asked me if I was okay. I said I was. We spoke for a while, nothing important in itself but, somehow, just speaking was the real important thing. "I think I've found it," I told her.

"Found what?" she said.

"Me . . . us . . . I don't know. Whatever it was that we'd lost."

Before I hung up she said, "John?"

"Yes?" I said.

"I . . . I love you, too."

That night I went down to the grave again.

It didn't take me too long. The earth was still soft and I managed to get it all put back the way I had found it. Uncle Nigel was right: he *had* lost a lot of weight at the end. His body couldn't have been more than about ninety pounds.

We drove until we hit open countryside, playing "Crosstown Traffic" and "Voodoo Chile" at full volume. Then I parked the car and hiked for another forty minutes or so into some real wild woodland. There were no paths, so no evidence that people ever came here. Just as he had said. I took him deep into a dense wood, getting ripped and lacerated by the clinging branches while, all the time, I was protecting his body slumped over my shoulder. When we got to where he'd described, I propped him against a huge birch tree.

I heard a voice say "Thanks, John," but he never showed himself. Maybe it was just in my head.

On the way back, still playing Hendrix, I thought back to the train journey and our conversation. And I thought of what Uncle Nigel had done with my father's body.

There's a small gully out among the rocks near Pateley Bridge with a special little collection of bones resting in the bottom where nobody can reach them. Being daily windblown, rain-washed and sun-dried. Listening to the sounds of existence.

And as the trees drifted by outside my window I thought of what Uncle Nigel had said about life being one long note. I thought of Susan, waiting for me, and I wondered what my own note sounded like.

I think it sounds like this.

For Percival Crowther 1913–1972

Jesus Used a Paper Cup

— ✝ —

Adam-Troy Castro

At least this Jesus did.

He lived in a crass alternate universe where the events of the Bible took place sometime after the invention of the suburban shopping mall. On his world, the Last Supper was held in the International Food Court of the Galleria Atrium. He and the Apostles shoved three tables together, in open defiance of mall policy, left Judas to hold their seats, then separated to collect their calorie-rich burritos and pizza slices and gyros and french fries and overstuffed monster big-mouth hoagies, and returned bearing their trays to discuss their plans for the upcoming resurrection amid the shrieks of mall security who kept pointing to the prominently placed signs that decreed NO BARE FEET. And when they left—to meet this world's version of the crucifixion, a Volvo which ran Him down in the parking lot as He and His followers searched for the level where Simon had parked his rilly bitchin van—the paper cup He used was already being collected into a plastic garbage bag and brought out back for the regular mid-afternoon drive to the dump.

Admittedly, this did not make for a very dignified New Testament.

But the Quest for the Grail was immeasurably worse.

Long before the sun reached its zenith high above the reeking hills of the great Jersey landfill, the two knights sifting through the greasy newspapers and blackened banana peels were already easily as fragrant as the towering mounds of trash that surrounded them.

That was the worst of it: the plate mail chafed their thighs, and eliminated their peripheral vision, and was easily as heavy as a sack of bowling balls, but the worst of it was the way it retained heat and sealed in the body odor. On really hot days, it was like being locked inside a phone booth with the concentrated essence of everybody who'd ever run the Boston marathon.

"I do *not* pick my feet!" Galahad said, as he tried to peel a stack of half-melted roofing shingles from his gauntlets.

"You always say that," Percival said. "And then we go back to camp and you pull off those boots and you set to work spending the whole damn night spooning all the yellow cheese out from between your toes. It's really disgusting, I'm here to tell you."

Galahad muttered a disgusted curse, gave up trying to remove the shingles now thoroughly glued to his gauntlets, and tried to walk away so he could find some more private place to dig. He got all of two feet before he sank up to his knees in a soft melange of apple cores and moldy bread.

"Hey, look," Percival said. "Lancelot's coming."

Galahad moaned. Lancelot irritated him even more than Percival did. Giving credit where credit was due, the fellow had been a brave and noble knight, once. And he was probably still brave, even though the fifteen years they'd spent poring through potato chip bags and frozen dinner cartons hadn't provided any challenges more fearsome than the occasional stray cat. But noble he wasn't: not anymore. He'd discarded most of his knightly bearing years earlier, and these days eschewed the boiling hot armor in favor of Bermuda shorts, a T-shirt reading I'M WITH STUPID →, and a baseball cap bearing an impressive mound of fake doodie on the visor. He'd even all but abandoned the quest, preferring to spend only an hour or so each morning pretending to poke the accumulated garbage with a stick before spending the bulk of his day in a deck chair, guzzling six-packs, shooting rats, and telling highly exaggerated stories of his sexual prowess to the panting junkyard dog, Cujo.

The once-impressive, now potbellied, knight waddled over the rise on the discarded tennis rackets he used as snowshoes.

"What do you want?" Galahad asked.

Out of shape as he was, Lancelot needed several seconds to catch his breath from the long climb up the hill. "I . . . met this old bearded guy . . ."

"Well, if it's nothing, go back to camp. Tidy up. Make yourself useful instead of getting drunk with strangers."

"He showed me where the Paper Cup is."

Galahad paused. "Yeah, right."

"But he did. He walked up and he saw I had some beer and asked if he could have some and I said sure, and he popped open a can and said, Jeez, what a hot day, and I said, You're not foolin, and he said, A cold can of beer really goes down smooth on a day like this, and I said, Yeah, you sure said a mouthful there, and he said . . ."

Galahad's blood pressure was rising fast. "Can we press the fast-forward button, please?"

"Hey," Percival protested. "I was enjoying the story."

Galahad fixed him with the kind of glare capable of reducing a midsized city to a glowing crater. Then he turned his attention back to Lancelot and seethed. "The Paper Cup. He showed you where to find the Paper Cup."

"Well, that didn't happen until we'd been talking for a couple of hours. Basically what happened is that as he got up to go, I said, As long as you're here, would you happen to know where I could find the Holy Paper Cup? And he said, Sure, I just saw it. Turns out it wasn't of much use to him, because he happens to be looking for a Ring of Power, which is another epic quest entirely. But because I was such a nice guy he showed me the entrance to the Holy Place where it's kept. Turns out it's about a hundred feet from our base camp, which I guess is a big joke on us, considering all the years we've been looking for it. So, you wanna check it out?"

Galahad contemplated the alternative: spending the rest of the day here, wrestling with both the refuse of the modern world and the somehow even less appetizing Percival. He decided that he didn't much like being a knight. If this lead didn't pan out he'd peel off his armor, hitch a ride on the interstate, and find work in a nice roadside diner where the jukebox was always playing "Tammy" and the waitresses were always cracking gum. It would be nice, to spend the rest of his life in such a place. If this lead didn't work out. If. Then King Arthur could go climb a rock. But first he might as well check it out.

"Yeah," Galahad said. "Let's go."

It took the three knights half an hour to climb down the mountain of refuse, and return to the narrow little path that separated it from the mountains comprising the rest of the dump. The multicolored slopes rose almost straight up, held in place by steel netting that bulged dangerously from the sheer weight of the plastic and cardboard and rotted fruit pressing down upon it. Lancelot stopped before the place where a closed refrigerator door stood imbedded in the wall of refuse. "There," he said.

Galahad looked at the refrigerator door, and then at Lancelot, and at the refrigerator door, and at Percival, and then at the refrigerator door, and then at Lancelot. "THERE? That's the big secret hiding place?"

"I know," Lancelot commiserated. "Dumb, isn't it? We pass the thing every single day of our lives, and we never once think about opening it."

"I always think about opening it," said Galahad.

"Me too," said Percival. "I just never actually do. I'm too afraid of looking stupid."

"Actually," Lancelot admitted sheepishly, "I've always wanted to open it, too, but I'm glad you guys admitted it first."

The three of them stood there, as paralyzed as characters in a Beckett play, staring at the little footballs and puppy dogs and Fred Flintstone heads magnetically affixed to the door. Crows made jeering noises. And at long last, Galahad let out a sigh and pulled the handle. The door swung open, releasing a wave of unearthly cold that never should have existed inside a refrigerator that hadn't seen Freon since before the creation of network television. And when the mist dispersed, there stood revealed—

—the one thing they never would have suspected—

—a smaller refrigerator.

This one marked with words of screaming purple lipstick: THE

HOLY PAPER CUP. WARNING: PURE AND CHASTE ONLY BEYOND THIS
POINT.

"Well, that lets me out," said Lancelot.

Galahad whirled. "I never thought you'd be a . . . coward."

"Coward nothing. I never told you this before, because I didn't
want to get you mad, but the King didn't seriously think we'd find
the Paper Cup. He created this whole quest thing just to get rid of
us—you two because you're annoying, and me because I was
shtupping his wife."

The revelation left Galahad speechless. "Guinevere? MI-
LADY?"

"Yup. A lonely lady, too. Seems Arthur spends too many eve-
nings off by himself polishing Excalibur . . . if, uh, you know what
I mean. Anyway, looks like I'm exempt. What about you guys?
You're both in your forties. You still pure and chaste?"

Both Galahad and Percival turned red, looked at their mail
boots, and said nothing. Lancelot turned away and coughed into his
fist, then faced his friends once again, a peculiar strangulated expression on his once-noble visage. Finally, just as the two virgin
knights were about to turn purple, Galahad stepped forward,
opened the smaller refrigerator door, and the still smaller refrigerator door beyond that, and crawled helmet-first into the microwave
beyond that, through the narrow crawl space that lay beyond, and
into the vast cavern on the other side. The cavern was so large it
was clear that this particular mountain of garbage was mostly hollow; indeed, bits of daylight could be seen through the tires and
cabbage balls and old newspapers that made up the cave walls. The
Paper Cup stood on a pedestal at the base of the cavern, bathed in
a heavenly radiance that, in Galahad's humble opinion, suited this
reeking place about as much as silverplate would suit a dog turd.

Emerging from the tunnel behind him, Percival said, "Huh!
That it? Seems too easy, I would say."

"I would say, too," said Galahad.

The two knights began making their way to the base of the cavern, the soft splooshes of their steps echoing hollowly against the
distant rubbishy walls. The altar of the Holy Paper Cup grew
nearer. Nearer. The closer they approached, the more Galahad grew

certain there had to be another surprise awaiting them. The Paper Cup wouldn't have been left somewhere where it could be found by anybody willing to open a refrigerator door; if it had been, there were any number of overweight housewives who would have completed this quest years ago. There had to be something else. A ring of fire. An army of animated skeletons. A demon from hell. A carnivorous rabbit. A gigantic rolling rock. A steel-jaw trap. Something. Anything. Dammit, he needed it to be something. If it was just sitting there out in the open for him to take, no fuss no muss, he'd have spent the past decade broiling in plate armor for no good reason. He *wanted* something to fight. Something other than Percival, or for that matter Lancelot, who if this was some kind of joke was going to be one sorry sucker indeed.

And yet here he and Percival stood, at the base of the altar, within reach of the unearthly glowing radiance that obscured the Paper Cup from view. It was unnerving as hell. There had to be another shoe, but nobody was dropping it.

"Go ahead," Percival said. "Take it."

"I don't want to take it," Galahad said. "You take it."

"No," Percival said magnanimously, "you're the leader. You take it."

"I'm the leader, and I'm ordering you to take it."

"All right. I mutiny and tell you to take it."

"I mutiny back, times infinity, and I tell you to take it."

"You can mutiny infinity times infinity," Percival said with utter finality, "plus one, and I'm still not going to take it."

Galahad muttered under his breath, bowing to Percival's superior logic. He commended his soul to God, vowed eternal fealty to the Throne, dreamed one last time of that roadside diner with the gum-cracking waitress . . . and reached into the unearthly radiance to take the Holy Paper Cup.

The other shoe dropped.

There was a tremendous rumbling, as loud as two continents colliding head-on. And a vast section of cavern wall just slid away, revealing the single largest dragon Galahad had ever seen.

It had been a long time since dragons had roamed free in the wild; these days, they were only in zoos and TV commercials for brokerage houses. Even those were tiny specimens, scarcely taller than the average man. This was a dragon as dragons were meant to be: eyes black as pitch, scales that gleamed like polished gold, a body so massive that it must have been bigger than the cavern surrounding it, which was actually within the realm of possibility since, as everybody knows, normal geometry doesn't restrain dragons. Clearly the guardian of the Holy Paper Cup, clearly the beast Galahad and Percival would have to slay to complete their epic quest, it was clearly much more than they would be able to handle, even with a dedicated army of thousands behind them. Fortunately, it was also dead of starvation, having waited several years too long to be found by the knights that would have been its only form of sustenance.

This was a little bit of a letdown, to tell the truth.

After a moment of respectful silence, Galahad just grunted and took the Paper Cup from the altar. The sphere of radiance stayed where it was, revealing the Paper Cup to be nothing more than an ordinary-looking Paper Cup, covered with daisies, worn through with grease and other unidentifiable stains, and filled with a substance only somebody extremely charitable would have agreed to consider water. An old cigarette butt floated in that liquid, bobbing gently, reminding Galahad of nothing so much as a poisonous eel lying in wait for the first unwary traveler to place his bare feet within snapping range.

"There's only one way to know it's the true Paper Cup," Percival said. "We must drink from it."

Galahad's stomach lurched. "I don't want to drink from it."

"If it's the true Paper Cup it will bestow eternal life."

"If it's just a plain everyday piece of garbage it will bestow typhoid. Let Arthur drink from it."

Percival tsked. "If Arthur gains immortality, he'll be sending us on stupid quests like this one for the rest of eternity. The nail clipper of Moses, that sort of thing. No, thanks. I just want to know it's genuine so we can use it to make a bundle on the talk-show circuit."

"So why don't *you* drink from it?"

"Because I'm not crazy," Percival said. Again winning the argument.

Wondering for one final time whether the jukebox at that fabled roadside diner would take dimes or quarters, Galahad lifted the Paper Cup to his lips. Wrinkled his nose with disgust. Commended his honor and his blade to the eternal glory of all Camelot. Wondered whether the waitress would have been named Carmela or Trixie. Tried to come up with one good reason why he should do this, failed, and naturally went ahead and did it anyway.

He drank.

And, of course, it was indeed the Holy Paper Cup, the relic of Christ, the table setting discarded and left to molder beneath tons of refuse just because some other shoppers had once wanted to sit down; and though the water tasted a lot like an ashtray after a roomful of Republicans have been stubbing cigars into it, it was definitely filled with magic, and it definitely worked its miracle for King Arthur's faithful servant. Almost as soon as the first fetid mouthful went down, Galahad felt the magic surge through his limbs, felt his body chemistry change, felt himself change from a temporary thing of mortal flesh and bone to something indestructible, that would never age, never suffer injury, never weaken or decay or become less than what it had been. He became something that embodied the shape of the future, something that would endure forever, as long as the sun shone and the rivers flowed and the stars twinkled in the sky.

Percival, watching all this, merely blinked several times.

And then went out into the harsh light of the great Jersey landfill to inform Lancelot that the glory of God had just transformed their comrade-in-arms into a soiled disposable diaper.

Siege Perilous

---------- ✠ ----------

Jerry Ahern and Sharon Ahern

Myriad disadvantages existed to running a mission up river along the Amazon, but at least Damascus Santini hadn't had to wear the clerical collar. The mission of Saint Barbara was only a temporary assignment back in 1984, spiritual refuge for a priest and his doubts. Six years later, Santini was long overdue for leaving the jungle and the priesthood. His Indian congregation was both strong in their faith and self-reliant, ready to stand up for God or themselves as needed.

Requesting transfer for more than eighteen months, and hearing nothing, he was suddenly and mysteriously ordered to meet with a Papal Emissary in Rio. Their rendezvous was at a church, in one of the poorer parts of the city. The structure had been burned half to the ground and never rebuilt. This was not a cash-paying parish. Someday, because of the poverty, Brazil itself would go up, hot, fast and violent.

Bishop Reginald Matumbe, the Papal Emissary, didn't wear black, and when Santini began to genuflect and kiss his ring, Matumbe merely said, "Please, not now."

They picked their way along the rubble, sunlight filtering down on them through holes in the roof. The masonry dust, stirred by their feet, threw debris into the humid air, making ghostly columns in the light. Matumbe looked like someone whom Santini could have grown up with on Chicago's South Side or fought beside in Viet Nam. Curiously, he sounded more like David Niven. "Do you believe in the Cup of Christ, my son?"

"I've got problems with my priesthood, but I'm still Catholic."

"I know about your problems, Father Santini. May I call you Damascus?"

"Sure."

"What I mean, Damascus, was do you believe in the Holy Grail, the cup Christ drank from at His Last Supper, into which the Blood He shed for all our sins was gathered by Joseph of Arimathaea?"

"Sure, I mean—"

"What do you think happened to that cup, Damascus?" Sweat glistening hotly on Matumbe's shiny black skin.

"No disrespect intended, but beats me. I read all the Holy Grail stuff in the books about knights and everything, but they didn't hit on it much in seminary."

Matumbe smiled briefly. "Well, Damascus, ecclesiastical scholarship has always been divided on the subject. Some, for example, contend that the cup was not a cup at all, but a plate. Others defend the notion that the cup was, in reality, only a bowl made of wood. That was common at the time, of course, and the intervening years would almost certainly have destroyed it. There are those who believe that the cup's significance did not originate with its use by Our Lord, that its origins were far older, that it was given to humankind by whatever means suits the philosophy of such persons, theology notwithstanding. Many among this latter group suggest that the cup was the Golden Fleece of mythology, and was the Philosopher's Stone. Are you acquainted with any of the legends and myths surrounding that?"

"The Philosopher's Stone? Like alchemy and stuff? I've read about it, but years ago. Why?"

Matumbe pulled out a cigarette, Santini taking one of his own, lighting both with the Zippo he'd carried ever since his first day in Special Forces. "Tell me about the so-called Philosopher's Stone," Matumbe asked.

Santini scratched his head as he exhaled. "Well, Paracelsus and a lot of guys like him, alchemists, they wanted the Philosopher's Stone because they figured it was the key to turning lead or some other base metal into gold. Make themselves rich."

The Bishop started walking again, stepping over a toppled railing and approaching the altar. The center of the altar was removed, where the Eucharist would normally be kept. The altar looked oddly empty, cold. Despite the dusty heat, Santini shivered.

"As Catholics, we believe that we are inheritors of the Kingdom of Heaven because of Christ's suffering and death on the Cross and His Resurrection. There are various persons and groups who consider themselves inheritors of traditions even more ancient, like the initiates of the mystery schools."

"The Egyptians," Santini said, exhaling smoke.

"Indeed. Those who claim they are initiates have been known by various names throughout history, held various affiliations—Templars, Illuminati, the Intellecti, the Cathars, who were part of the Albigensian Heresy. Some say that the Prophet Moses may have learned these secrets as a young man in Pharaoh's court. Today, unfortunately, these men, regardless of how they are called, labor to bring about an age in which they will seize world leadership. They consider themselves the only ones fit. As we can see from standing here in what was once the House of God, wealth is the key to temporal power, my son. Its absence is helplessness. These men believe that the Holy Grail, rather than a sacred symbol of Christ's Divine Love for mankind, is the Philosopher's Stone, the vessel by which untold wealth and even world domination can be achieved."

"I don't think I follow you."

Matumbe smiled. "A group of such men—call them what you will—are about to gain control of what may well be the cup from which Our Lord drank at His Last Supper, into which He bled from the Cross. Rather than bringing the cup into the light as a possible source of inspiration for mankind, they will defile it, perhaps destroying it for their own evil ends. You and I cannot let that happen, Damascus."

"You and I?"

"In Germany, in the immediate wake of Adolf Hitler's ascendancy and prior to his invasion of Poland, there arose a group calling itself The Vril Society, sometimes better known as The Luminous Lodge, by some accounts a public manifestation of a much older secretive German-originated group, the Illuminati. They were spiritual descendants of the Knights Templar, some say. Two years prior to their actual formation, a young scholar, initially as devout in his allegiance to Hitler as he was in his study of history and language, traveled extensively in the south of France, ending up at Montsegur. The man became an SS officer, and his quest was sponsored officially by the Nazi hierarchy. Some say when he realized the true nature of that cause which he served, he became embittered and took his own life. According to his interpretations of Arthurian Legend and the Cathar Phenomenon, however, Montsegur was the real Montsalvat, or Mount of Salvation. The Grail was taken there, he believed, then spirited away to some hidden cave nearby when the two hundred Cathar defenders of Montsegur surrendered to Hugues de Arcis. The Cathars were burned at le Champs des Cremats and the Grail was lost. By all published accounts, the young man's initial and subsequent attempts to capture the Grail failed. But in light of information received by the Vatican almost two years ago, the truth of which has been acid tested by the finest scholars available, the Nazis may indeed have recovered the Grail in the early part of 1944, bringing it to Berlin. The Grail was subsequently spirited out of the country shortly before Hitler's death in the Fuhrer Bunker in 1945."

Perspiration, beading on the Bishop's temples, ran in rivulets along the sides of his face, almost like tears.

"Eventually, what we assume may be the Holy Grail found its way to New York City."

"The Holy Grail in the Big Apple. Wow," Santini said, amazed.

"Father Warren Hastings, a Jesuit, and himself for many years devoted to the quest for the Grail, was dispatched from Rome. There were unsuspected complications. He located the Grail, but he was not the only one seeking it. Father Hastings was injured, escaped and made contact with the Vatican. He needs help."

"So I've been volunteered, then," Santini said.

"Yes. Fortunately, Father Hastings' injuries were minor. He is in hiding, awaiting that assistance even as we speak. That is all you need to know, Father."

Santini nodded.

"Like yourself, Damascus, a surprisingly large number of men have come to reject the violence of the world and join the priesthood, but few with the equal of your skills. If the task at hand required a scholar, and I mean no offense, then we'd get one. The Church requires a soldier. You've asked for release from your vows. It is yours. The Church will accept your return, should you wish. That will be up to you." The Bishop turned his back, staring at the altar. "I consider myself somewhat of an intellectual, my son, and faith comes just as hard to the intellectual as to the man of action. Faith teaches that we believe that our Heavenly Father's Will is manifested in many ways. Perhaps it is His Will that your priesthood be given one more challenge, Damascus, to save it or to show you that your life path lies elsewhere."

"I'll go," Santini said, accepting the *Siege Perilous*.

When Father Hastings opened the door of the sparse Commerce, Georgia, motel room, the second thing Santini noticed was an open Bible on the unmade bed. The first thing Santini noticed was that Hastings was trembling. Santini flashed a Vatican passport.

"So, you're the one they talked into this. I suppose you're some trouble-shooter for the Vatican."

"No, just a priest like you, Father." Santini extended his hand, giving his name as he stepped inside. The room smelled stale, as if the door were infrequently opened. Hastings took Santini's hand in his own. The handshake was odd, at once firm yet weak. "Got you holed up here, huh? Where I grew up, we called it going to the mattresses."

"I'm sorry, Father, but I don't have anything to offer you except water. I only get out for one meal a day. That's all I can risk. And as you can see," Hastings gestured around the room, "there isn't any refrigerator."

"You feel these persons who are after—after what you have. That they're nearby, Father Hastings?"

"I don't know." The priest sat on the edge of the bed, putting his face into his hands. "I just don't know." Then, very suddenly,

Hastings looked up. "Are you sure that you weren't followed? And, how do I know you are who you say?"

"I wasn't followed. And I thought you were going to ask me for some kind of proof of who I was, Father. Bishop Matumbe figured you might, too. I mean, I was told that you took your vows in January of 1962, that your middle name is Cornelius, your mother's name was Theresa, that you graduated from Notre Dame in . . ."

"Anybody could know any of that. They do, I'm certain."

Santini smiled. Warren Cornelius Hastings, Society of Jesus. Not the layman's classic impression of Jesuit. That was some burly, curly-haired guy who used to play football and pumped iron when he wasn't praying. Father Hastings's hair wasn't just non-curly, it was almost not there, and the fringe around the edges was grey and straight. When his shoulders weren't slumped, Hastings stood close to six feet. Thin as a reed, the hollows of his cheeks were deep and dark. Santini took a lighter from his pocket, flipping it to Hastings. "Name's on there. I've got a driver's license with my picture on it. I knew there was a reason I kept getting the thing renewed. You've seen my passport. Enough? Good. So, who are these guys that are after you?"

"You know, I believe you, that you are who you say you are." Never moving from the edge of the bed, Father Hastings looked down at his shoes "Our foes? You should know."

"Neo-Nazis, or like that," Santini told him.

"Like that, yes, only older." Father Hastings leaned down further. His hands disappeared beneath the edge of the bedspread. They reappeared holding a leather briefcase, the old kind which opened at the top. The leather was black, cracked and weathered. Hastings brought the case up into his lap, both hands clenched over it. "I went in search of faith. Instead, I found its antithesis."

"I don't . . ."

Hastings smiled wanly. "No, but you will, Father."

Santini took a step closer to the bed as Hastings moved his hands over the surface of the briefcase. "If you had searched your entire life for something which, intellectually, you doubted ever existed—or perhaps existed, but was an entirely ordinary object. If you were given to believe that this thing did in fact exist, even was in your grasp. If you searched like that, and found that the object of your desire was a mockery. How would you feel?"

"All my life I wanted to be a soldier, I guess. And I was one. It wasn't what I wanted."

"As a very young man," Father Hastings said, a smile just fleetingly crossing his lips, "I often thought that if priests were allowed to be married it would be sacrilege. By the time I was well along into my thirties, however, I missed the comforts of a woman, a home and children. I longed for it, Father Santini. But, by the time I turned fifty, I stopped wishing that things were different, because I realized that while I could dream of the ideal in the perfect state of bliss, its reality might be something altogether different." Hastings' voice was almost a whisper.

Father Hastings opened the briefcase, and reached inside. He raised a chalice of dully gleaming metal, holding it before him, like a shield. Santini fell to his knees. Father Hastings stood, raising the cup above his head. As Santini made the sign of the cross, Hastings whispered, "Now I know I can trust you, my brother in Christ, because you kneel in homage to the vessel which by all rights you think is that of Our Lord. But, it is not." Hastings' voice was low, detached, almost disembodied. "It is the cup of grief, not Salvation, Father, which I hold before you."

"The Bishop told me you'd gone after the Holy Grail . . ." Santini's voice stumbled.

"I searched for one Grail," Hastings said, "and found the key to another. Graven upon it is the key to deciphering certain runes, runes inscribed on tablets that have come to us through the mists of time. These tablets, Father, antedate the Sumerian kings at Ur. They were old when the Sphinx was new. And this very cup, the key to arcane knowledge, perhaps, belonged to Imhotep, the scientist and wizard, architect to the Pharaohs, a man some say came from Atlantis." Hastings moved the cup in his fingers, as if it were so familiar to his touch that its every arc and angle were committed to memory. "This is the Rosetta Stone to the texts of the ancient mystery schools."

Santini rose from his knees and walked toward Father Hastings.

Slowly he took the cup from the older priest's hands. Santini's eyes followed the runic writings that ringed the cup at every level. Paralleling each line were minute symbols he could identify as the hieroglyphs of Egypt. They had obviously been more recently applied.

"Did Matumbe tell you, Father Santini, that the Nazis recovered a Grail in France during the spring of 1944, and, that this Grail was taken to Berlin, then spirited away?"

"Yes, Father."

"The Bishop was right, but the Grail of which he spoke, the one found by Hitler's SS in a cavern, was a set of tablets. Without this cup, not even the most sophisticated computer could translate the runes. By themselves, the tablets of the Aryan Grail are useless, merely a heathen object of veneration. With this cup, he who possesses the tablets can decipher the knowledge of the ancients, the transmutation of lead into gold least among them. He who has the cup and the tablets holds the key to molding all of nature to his will, the ultimate temporal power over mankind."

"Where did this . . ."

"Come from? I don't know, Father Santini. But it was discovered, shall we say, by an SS officer who was one of the commanders during the fight at the Warsaw ghetto. His name was Otto Rheimenschneider. He was a young man. He took the cup from the belongings of a man then as old as Rheimenschneider is now. The old Jew was a scholar, I learned, when I met with Rheimenschneider in New York. The Jew's garret was crammed with books, old scrolls and hand-illuminated manuscripts. Rheimenschneider only took the cup, never realizing what he had until his service in June of 1944 in Berlin. By then, however, he had become disgusted, disenchanted. Assuming the identity of a dead man, he fled Germany, the cup with him, the SS after him." Father Hastings took the cup from Santini and stared at it, moving his fingers over the symbols engraved upon it.

"Otto Rheimenschneider lost his faith, and so did I," Hastings said tossing the cup onto the bed. "Do you know what the existence of this cup signifies, my young friend? The passions of my life are gone. The true Grail, the cup from which Our Lord drank at the Last Supper and into which He bled from the Cross, may not exist. I spent my life pursuing a myth. And, if this cup is His cup, then why was it His? He was the Son of God. Why did He drink from the cup of arcane knowledge when He always was and always will be the Sum of All Time and Wisdom because He and the Father are One?"

The motel door crashed inward. Two men, long, bulky, efficient noise suppressors fitted to the muzzles of their machine pistols, filled the opening. Neither Santini nor Hastings moved. The men looked like actors out of a bad movie, in their black turtlenecks, matching slacks and soft-soled shoes. Their hands were gloved. They wore no masks, their stereotypically blonde, blue-eyed, well-scrubbed features something that would be dangerously easy to identify.

The door swung on a single creaking hinge. Through clenched teeth, Father Hastings said in a barely audible hiss, "You will not have this cup! Never!"

"Hand 'em the cup, Father Hastings," Santini urged.

Implicit in what Matumbe had told him about a temporary release from priestly vows was the unspoken dictum, "Do what needs to be done."

Father Hastings turned his face toward Santini, glaring at him. "How could you! How could you empower men like these?"

"Just give it to them, Father," Santini shouted. He moved toward the older priest, then turned to the armed men and spoke.

"Look, guys, we don't want any trouble. You want the cup? Hey, you got the cup. Just take it and let us alone," Santini told them, taking the cup from the bed.

"No. Not to them," shouted Hastings, grabbing for the cup as well. Father Hastings' fingers closed over the cup.

"Give it to me now, Father," Santini advised. He was positioned between Father Hastings and the two men, and he made a great show of tugging at the cup, trying to force it from the older priest's grasp. He jerked on the cup a second time, simultaneously but as gently as he could, straight-arming Father Hastings toward the bed and out of the field of fire. In the same motion, Santini whipped his right arm back, letting the cup fly toward the two armed men. He threw himself flat to the floor and rolled.

Santini slammed into the legs of the nearest man, bowling him back and down. Rising into a crouch, Santini hammered his clenched right fist into the second man's testicles. The machine pistol sprayed a burst across the room, but Santini was already to his feet, crossing the second man's jaw with a left hook.

The first man was standing, fumbling with his gun. Santini wheeled to the right, his foot impacting the gunman's head, forcing him down, hard.

Santini started to reach for the gun, but Father Hastings was racing through the open doorway, the cup in one hand, briefcase and suitcoat in the other. When Santini looked again for the gun, Father Hastings shouted, "Come on, Father! We'll use your car." A burst of gunfire tore into the doorframe, six inches from Santini's head.

No chance to grab the gun, Santini ran through the open doorway, almost crashing into Father Hastings. "Which is your car, Father Santini?" Santini grabbed the older priest by the shoulder and propelled him toward the rented canary yellow Geo Metro. Santini gunned the engine to life.

He had an advantage of several seconds, and reached the highway just as the gunmen reached their vehicle. "Oh shit," he muttered, more to himself than his passenger. "They're in a BMW."

Hastings laughed, bitterly. "At least we've got God and gas mileage on our side."

"Yeah, but no gun," Santini said. "The other G-word is theirs."

By all rights, odds against the two men finding Father Hastings in the middle of northeast Georgia were astronomical. Any amateur could have come up with the older priest's general destination by checking the outgoing flights from LaGuardia for someone matching his description. It was there that Father Hastings had his rendezvous with the one-time SS officer, there that he realized that the cup was the key to translating the Aryan Grail. It was there, as well, that Rheimenschneider, the SS officer, was stabbed to death and Father Hastings sustained a light, grazing cut.

Knowing that the killers of old Rheimenschneider would be after him, Father Hastings discarded his clerical collar and his tickets to Rome, instead paying in cash for a seat on the first available plane to anywhere. That took him to Atlanta's Hartsfield Airport. He telephoned the Vatican, informing Bishop Matumbe that he would be leaving the city to re-establish contact after he was safely in hiding.

The quickest untraceable way out of Atlanta was a cross-country bus routed toward Greenville, South Carolina. Without preconceived intention, he slipped off the bus at a truck stop in Commerce. He paid cash at a small, non-chain motel, registering under a name not his own. After more than a week, and certain that he had not been followed, he contacted the Vatican, this time reaching the Bishop's secretary, Father Ignatius Martin.

Father Hastings detailed all of this to Santini in a nonstop monologue. Santini did not have time to consider the importance. The full repertoire of counter-terrorist driving techniques flowed through his mind. None of them could help a Geo Metro outrun a BMW. At least he was in front, and had the choice of battleground.

Santini piloted the canary yellow car southward onto Interstate 85. The BMW could catch them more easily, but the quantity of potential witnesses might preclude anything overtly aggressive.

As Santini called up and dismissed items from an ever-dwindling catalogue of possibilities, inspiration struck. Though not quite the experience of St. Paul on the road to Damascus, it would have to do. A road sign proclaimed the exit for Gainesville, Georgia. Very near there, on a lake named after the poet Sidney Lanier, was a house shared by a woman who was the author of books on the unexplained, and an adventure writer who lived out the exploits of his characters. That man was the brother of Santini's old Commanding Officer, a friend many years deceased.

Santini took the road to Gainesville. As if God Himself were watching over their yellow Geo, when Santini turned off I-85 and the BMW began to close, a State Patrol car pulled between them. Santini smiled, and handed his wallet to Hastings. "There's a card in there for M. F. Mulrooney. Hope I haven't lost it."

"Who is this Mulrooney fellow?" said Hastings, seeming more relaxed by the sight of the police car.

"M. F. stands for Mary Frances. She lives with a man named Josh Culhane. They're good people, and they have weapons, if . . ."

"Just contemplating killing is a mortal sin!" Hastings declared.

"Look, Father, if you and Bishop Matumbe are right, letting the bad guys have the cup is a mortal sin. It's like saying it's gonna be okay if a year or two or ten years from now everybody wakes up and there's a new Hitler. Those two guys chasing us have Nazi written all over them. Not the wannabe clowns who apply for parade permits in Jewish neighborhoods, but the real ones."

Hastings shuddered.

"Ever hear the theory that Hitler might have been the anti-Christ?" Santini continued. "You wanna risk a mortal sin or give the cup to Satan and just roll over and die? I can stop the car now."

Father Hastings said nothing for a moment, then spoke. "Here's the woman's card, but the ink is so faded."

"I fell out of a canoe with it once."

"It's only a Post Office box and a telephone number."

"Start looking for some change. We're close to the city."

Santini did not spot a shopping mall until they were well past the downtown. The police car, lights flashing, turned and headed back in the direction from which it came, in ardent pursuit of a speeder.

"Looks like we lost our guardian angel," said Hastings.

"Yeah, but there are two more nearby if we can reach them," Santini replied. "Get ready."

Santini swung a sharp left turn into the shopping center, heading for an empty curbside fire lane. The Geo parked, he grabbed his soft-sided suitcase with one hand and Father Hastings with the other. Santini entered the largest store he saw, Hastings in tow.

The telephone was in the customer service area. Santini dialed the number on the card. There was a ring, then another.

"Are your friends answering?" Hastings was impatient.

"Not yet. Wait."

Josh Culhane's voice came onto the line. Santini started to speak, but realized the voice was only a message on an answering machine. Santini almost swore. While still debating whether to leave word or hang up, a woman's voice cut in, telling him to wait until the tape played out.

"Fanny!" Santini shouted.

The beep sounded. "Who is this?"

"Fanny, it's Damascus Santini!"

"Damascus?" she cut him off. "You still in Brazil?"

"That's a long story. Josh there?"

"No, but he'll be back in about a half hour."

"I need a place to hide out," he began.

"Damascus. Of course. Always." Her voice was firm, reassuring. "Where are you?"

"Think about it first. We've got some heavy duty bad guys around the corner."

"Got something to write with, Damascus? Where are you?"

"The sign said Lakeshore Mall. Is it close?"

"Yes. You gotta car?" she asked.

"No problem."

"Write this down, Damascus. You're on your way."

Santini fished out his airline ticket envelope and a felt tip pen. After reading back her directions, Santini hung up. Hustling Father Hastings to a sporting goods store, Santini purchased an eighteen-ounce Louisville Slugger. They returned to the parking lot, all the while watching for the two men who had pursued them.

"Father Santini, why did you leave the car where you did? It might be towed away," Hastings asked.

"Doesn't matter, Father. Our Holy Mother the Church can grease the rent-a-car company and the transportation we'll need is all around us anyway."

"What do you mean, Father?"

"We're stealing a car," Santini said flatly, his eyes scanning the parking lot.

So far, so good. Santini posted the older priest as a lookout. He found a likely vehicle, a car old enough not to have an alarm system. With the bat, Santini smashed open the driver's side window, then disabled, the steering column lock. Within another sixty seconds, and only because he was rusty at it, Santini had the engine cranked. As soon as Father Hastings slipped in beside him, Santini had the car moving.

Temporarily ignoring the directions given him, Santini drove crosstown, turning down residential streets, cutting through gas stations, checking and double checking that the BMW was nowhere in evidence. At last convinced, Santini took the ticket envelope from his pocket. "You're navigator, Father."

Twenty-five minutes later, he was pulling up beside Fanny Mulrooney's yellow Mustang in front of a lakeside cedar and stone A-frame. He gave Father Hastings his suitcase and told him, "Go knock on the door and tell Fanny I'll be back in twenty minutes."

"I don't understand, Father Santini."

"This is a stolen car, Father. I'm gonna ditch it, wipe it down for fingerprints, leave some expense money behind to cover the damage and hike it back. Go on, hurry!" Father Hastings got out, stepping back as Santini threw the transmission into reverse, Hastings still hugging his black briefcase to his chest.

A boat ramp by the water's edge was the perfect place to leave the vehicle, off the road but clearly in sight. It took only a moment to smudge away prints and stash two hundred dollars in the glove compartment. Santini had been aware of gathering clouds for almost fifteen minutes. As he jogged back along the road, raindrops touched softly against his skin.

Someone was standing in the A-frame's driveway by the time Santini returned, and he slowed his pace. It was unsettling seeing Josh Culhane again, the mirror image of his twin brother, Jack.

Santini approached the house. There was a steady, light drizzle now. Culhane's hair and eyes were dark brown, his facial structure, like his overall frame, lean but not bony. He stood about six feet, taller looking still because of black cowboy boots. He wore a grey shirt, its sleeves rolled up to the elbows, and black jeans with a wide belt. Protruding above his waistband was the butt of a pistol.

"Damascus, how you doing?"

"Ohh, great, Josh."

"I take it this is appropriate attire for the occasion?" Culhane touched at the gun.

"Well, I don't know, Josh." Santini lit a cigarette, Culhane doing the same. "That looks like one of those sissy 9mms. I thought you were a real man and carried a .45."

"Technology catches up with all of us. Come on in."

Santini mounted the three steps, shook Culhane's offered hand and followed him through the doorway. Beyond lay a vaulted ceilinged great room, a bearskin rug, a couch, coffee table and some assorted chairs positioned for conversation and convenient viewing of a flagstone hearth set into the far wall. A fresh-smelling fire crackled and hissed there. Father Hastings sat in a chair and Fanny Mulrooney—Santini was the only one besides Culhane that she let call her that—was just serving him a drink. She turned around and said, "Hi, Damascus." Her voice was a warm alto. A lock of her auburn hair, longer than Santini had remembered it, fell over her cheek. Mulrooney brushed it away with the back of her hand. She wore an off-white cotton sweater that seemed miles too big for her, and a chocolate brown skirt, very full and so long that it reached her ankles. Below its hem, bare toes peeked out from brown leather flat-soled sandals. "Father Hastings just told me the wildest story, and I loved it!"

"I told them everything, Father Santini, but you said that I should trust them."

Culhane crossed the great room, stopping near sliding glass doors overlooking a frame porch, beyond that the lake. The rain, its drumming on the windows something Santini was suddenly keenly aware of, came down in wind-driven sheets. "I would assume we'll have these people calling on us sooner or later. If they were somehow able to tap into that telephone line or have an agent inside the Vatican itself—and those are the only plausible ways for them to have intercepted the two of you in Commerce at the motel—then they'll have access to your personnel file, Damascus. It won't take them long to make the connection, maybe a couple of hours at most." Culhane turned around to face Santini. "Want a gun, Damascus?"

"Not yet, okay?"

"Okay." Culhane nodded.

Fanny cleared her throat over-loudly. "How's about some sandwiches, huh?"

Culhane paced back across the room, locking the front door.

The sandwiches were good. Late afternoon wore on into black and blue twilight, and then night, inky and all but impenetrable. The rain was unrelenting, the winds heightening, thunder rumbling over the lake. Culhane brought out several guns, stashing them strategically about the first floor of the house.

One of the few magazine subscriptions Santini had kept up these past years was to *Guns & Ammo.* Culhane's catalog of weapons readied against an attack they all considered inevitable was state-of-the-art. "Dangerous times call for extraordinary countermeasures, Damascus." The pistol thrust into Culhane's waistband was a SIG 228 9mm with Aimpoint Laserdot Sight.

Father Hastings, apparently adjusted to his status as wayfarer in an armed camp, sipped from a tumbler of Scotch and recounted the history of the cup, which was now between them on the coffee table. Culhane, Mulrooney and Santini lit cigarettes, the smoke drawn up through the fireplace chimney. From where Culhane sat, left arm around Fanny, the lakeside approach could be watched. Santini, opposite them, could observe the road leading up to the house and the woods on both sides. Heavy curtains were drawn over the rest of the windows in order to frustrate snipers.

"Secrets known only to the elect are as old as man himself. There are spirit paths among all ancient peoples which must be taken in order to achieve manhood or other elite status. As tribal culture disappeared, the growth of secret societies flourished. Many historians dismiss these organizations."

"Fools if they do, Father Hastings," Mulrooney interjected, leaning forward to throw her cigarette into the fire. As she did, Santini noticed a bulge in the right side pocket of her skirt. "Out of Catharism grew the Rosicrucian movement. Then there are the Templars. Their initiation into the teachings of the mystery schools, at least among the higher ranking personnel, is indisputable. That's the Middle Eastern link. When the Church declared war on the Templars, certain knights escaped and founded Freemasonry. And some branches, heavily influenced by Rosicrucian thought and the Templar tradition, used the Masonic societies as a cover. It's a very small leap from these men into the Illuminati movement in Germany. And, of course, the link between the Vril, the Luminous Lodge."

"Exactly, Miss Mulrooney!" Father Hastings enthused.

Josh Culhane picked up the cup. "There's a reason for the fire," he said, gesturing toward it. "This cup seems to be made of some silver alloy." Culhane stood up and walked to the hearth, picking up a chunk of something, then casting it into the fire. Immediately, there was a loud crackle and white hot flame licked upward, consuming the object. "The melting point of silver is 960.8 degrees Celsius, while the tinder point of average wood is about 400 degrees. Something that's quite common knowledge in these parts is that solidified pine resin—it's called fat lighter sometimes—can be used as a fire starter even with wet wood, because of the tremendous heat it generates. If we have to, the cup gets thrown into the fire along with all the blocks of pine resin in this scuttle. And the cup will cease to exist."

Father Hastings sprang to his feet. "The cup, Mr. Culhane, is an artifact of great historical significance!"

"What's the greater peril, Father?" Culhane asked, lighting a cigarette. "That we destroy the cup forever or let it fall into the hands of the Nazis, or whoever they are, and that they use the cup to translate the Aryan Grail?" He looked at Mary Frances Mulrooney. "You're into this occult stuff, Fanny. What's the lesser of two evils here?"

Mulrooney stood up, hands thrusting into her pockets. "I'd love to get hold of the Aryan Grail tablets, get you to translate the runes, Josh. They might be the writings of an extra-terrestrial race which came to Earth and interacted with early man. Or even the last remnants of a culture which pre-dated man on Earth. But, we'll never know unless we can translate them."

"And?" Santini asked.

She looked at him, then at Father Hastings, then at Culhane. "If the Nazis or Illuminati or whoever these jerks are get their hands on power like that, maybe God knows what would happen, but I wouldn't want to ask. Josh is right. If we must, we destroy the cup forever."

Father Hastings turned in his chair. "I can't allow this. There must be another way."

Santini started to say there wasn't any alternative, but a knock at the door made further debate suddenly senseless. Culhane turned toward the sound, right hand covering the pistol at his abdomen. The bulge in Mulrooney's skirt pocket took on the definite shape of a short-barreled revolver.

"Who is it?" Culhane called out. As he spoke, he inverted a small brass bucket from beside the hearth, then set the scuttle containing the pine resin chunks on top of that.

A voice called back from beyond the door. "I have come to provide a rational alternative to your deaths."

Mulrooney laughed softly. "Gee, what a nice guy!"

Father Hastings half-collapsed into his chair.

"Damascus? Want a gun?" Culhane asked in a whisper.

"Not yet."

Culhane walked over to the couch, reaching down along the floor beside it. What he retrieved was an SP-89. It looked like a submachine gun, but fired semi-automatic only. He set it on the couch, beside the armrest. "Locked and loaded, just in case."

"Just in case," Santini echoed.

"Fanny. You're in charge of the cup. And keep an eye on the lake side," Culhane ordered.

Mulrooney took the cup in her left hand, her right hand still around the gun in her pocket. She stood directly beside the scuttle full of pine resin.

Culhane took the gun from his waistband and approached the door, but obliquely lest someone should open fire from the other side. Santini's eyes spied the red dot from Culhane's laser. Under conditions such as these, its tactical advantage would be minimal at best, but the psychology behind its use was clear. If zeroed properly, a bullet would impact only millimeters away from wherever the point of light came to rest.

After a quick glance through the peephole, Culhane opened the door. Rain lashed across the porch, and framed in the doorway stood a man dressed in black. As if on cue, lightning flashed.

Father Hastings gasped. "Father Martin!"

Damascus Santini laughed at himself. The last time Father Hastings had used that name, they were escaping the motel in Commerce. Santini hadn't made the connection. Father Martin was the Bishop's secretary at the Vatican. Father Hastings had spoken with him instead of Matumbe when placing the second call to Rome, telling Father Martin exactly where he was so that the Bishop could send help.

Santini called out toward the open doorway, "Yo! Father Martin, trade in the old clerical collar for a Nazi armband, the Cross of Christ for the Swastika?"

"May I come in?" Father Martin asked. Culhane merely nodded, stepping aside, keeping the laser's dot on Martin's chest. "I hardly think that will be necessary, Mr. Culhane." Martin walked into the house, palms open outward. Culhane slammed and locked the door. "And this must be the famous M. F. Mulrooney, holding the cup! Two such well-known authors, and here I am without anything to have autographed."

"Josh keeps a few books on hand for moments like this," Fanny said, smiling. "And he doesn't even charge sales tax."

"Well, I'm afraid I came for a different sort of reading material, as it were," Martin responded, stopping only a few feet back from the couch. "If I am given the cup without further incident, you have my word—"

"As a Nazi officer, or as a priest?" Santini interrupted.

Undaunted, Martin said, "None of you will be harmed. The cup is important. You are not."

Culhane stood midway between Martin and the front door, eyes and red dot on him. "And if we don't give you the cup?"

"I have men surrounding the house."

"I heard Don Adams say the same thing just the other night on *Get Smart*," Mulrooney said with a giggle.

"I would rather reason than resort to violence. What is it to be?" Martin asked. "The cup or death?"

"There's a third alternative," Culhane suggested. "That scuttle beside the fireplace is filled with blocks of pine resin. All Fanny needs to do is drop the cup into the flames and, you'll pardon the expression, kick the bucket. Then it's no more cup."

Martin shouted, "Attack the house! Attack!"

Santini snarled, "He's wired with a radio!"

Culhane wheeled, the laser-sighted pistol covering the doorway. Too late, Santini reached for Martin, Martin hurling himself toward Fanny Mulrooney. She started to throw the cup into the hearth as she kicked over the bucket of pine resin. Flames leaped instantly from the fireplace, licking outward, catching at the hem of her skirt. Martin had her left hand in his right hand, bending it back, his other hand prying the cup from her fingers.

From Santini's left, there was the sound of glass shattering, a burst of gunfire. A bullet tore at Santini's left thigh and he stumbled. One of the two men from the motel was already through the shattered glass doors, swinging the muzzle of his machine pistol on line with Fanny Mulrooney. Shots cracked as Culhane's laser settled. The man fell, dead.

Flames consumed Mulrooney's skirt and in another instant would envelope her legs. Santini got to his knees, lurched forward. Throwing his body weight against Martin, Santini caught hold of Mulrooney, jerking her to the floor. Santini's other hand caught hold of the bearskin rug, hauled it up and flung it down over the lower half of her body, smothering the flames.

More gunfire.

Mulrooney panted, "I'm all right, Damascus—"

Flames licked and hissed from the hearth. Fighting there, the cup between them, were Father Hastings and the traitorous priest. Santini started to his feet. The second man from the motel was on the floor, already dead.

The front door swung violently inward, nearly ripped from its hinges. Culhane spun toward it, no time to shoot, two men swarming over him, bringing him down. Culhane's pistol skittered across the floor. Santini, despite the wound to his thigh, clambered over the couch. Another gunman was in the doorway, raising his weapon. Santini dodged left, then forward, throwing his body weight against the door, smashing it against the shotgun's muzzle. The weapon discharged.

Santini battered the door against the man, again and again, then grabbed for his gun. Twisting the shotgun free, Santini buttstroked it across the right side of the man's head. Santini slumped into the doorjamb, his wounded leg starting to buckle. No more of the enemy were in evidence outside the house. Just inside the doorway, Culhane decked one of his attackers. As Culhane grappled with the second man, Fanny Mulrooney shouted, "Nobody move!" Her little revolver was held tight in both fists. Culhane's right hand flashed from his trouser pocket, clasping a small, semi-automatic pistol.

There was a single shot from the far end of the great room.

Father Hastings and Father Martin stood beside the fireplace, frozen in combat, neither moving for what seemed an eternity. Santini blinked. Father Hastings collapsed to his knees. Santini raised the captured shotgun to his shoulder. Even as he took aim on Father Martin, Santini wasn't certain that he could take human life again.

But Father Martin's body began to sway, the fingers of his right hand opening, the cup tumbling from his grasp as a scream issued from deep within his chest. His pistol discharged a single bullet into the flames, the cup already vanished there. His body went limp, collapsing into itself, crumpling to the floor.

Culhane raced to kneel beside Father Hastings, bending over him, then looking up. He shook his head once, then went to check the others.

Santini knelt beside the old Jesuit. Blood drooled from his mouth, soaked his clothes from the abdomen downward. It was arterial bleeding and nothing they could do would keep death from making its claim. "I'm damned," Father Hastings rasped, the blood flowing more rapidly now. "I believed in a symbol, not Our Lord."

Santini leaned closer to the dying priest. "You said that you lost your faith, Father. That the passion of your life was gone. But you had passion, and faith when you fought with Father Martin. You weren't trying to save the cup. You wanted to destroy it, for the good of mankind. You said that if Christ drank from this cup, then why, who was He? Was He really the Son of God? I think you searched for the Holy Grail as a way of justifying your faith, to find rational proof of God. So, maybe that's why you never found His cup, but God led you to this cup, instead.

"You can't ask God to explain Himself just to satisfy your intellect. You've got to accept God for what He is, a mystery. If every morning when the sun came out you heard somebody who sounded like Charlton Heston say, 'Wake up, guys,' it'd be easy to believe in Him, there wouldn't be any challenge to it, and faith wouldn't matter. But He doesn't do that. So, maybe all He wants is that you trust Him. Do you have that trust, Father Hastings?"

Father Hastings tried to answer. He was gagging on his blood.

"Fanny. There's a Bible by the suitcase. Bring it." Santini spoke quickly.

Seconds that seemed like an eternity later, Fanny Mulrooney handed the Bible to the dying priest. Father Hastings closed his hands around it and smiled. He looked up at Santini, and then closed his eyes forever.

Culhane broke the silence. "Father Martin's dead. Not a gunshot. Heart attack or stroke, and he looks too young for either. His hands were burned pretty badly, too. He was reaching into the fire as he died."

Santini grimaced. "One priest saved, one priest lost. Assorted others living and dead. All fates debatable, ourselves included."

Culhane began tending to Fanny Mulrooney's leg, the burns not looking at all severe. Santini leaned back and lit a cigarette. There would be time enough to look at his leg wound. It wasn't hurting too badly, anyway. Time enough for a call to Matumbe at the Vatican to put in a fix with the law, too. Santini watched his cigarette smoke for a moment, then closed his eyes. The cup was gone, forever. Under his breath he murmured, "Amen."

The Sinner King

✠

Richard T. Chizmar

"But then the times
Grew to such evil that the Holy cup
Was caught away to heaven and disappear'd."
                                    —*The Holy Grail*

1

I stopped for a drink of water at the bottom of a grassy knoll and, when I finally caught my breath, I heard the dogs. Muffled barking off in the distance. A mile or so away. The frenzied, hungry sound of the hunt.

I returned the canteen to my knapsack, swung the bag over my shoulder, and started up the hill, picking up my pace. No need to panic, I told myself. I'd known from the start that my absence would not pass undetected, but I *had* hoped they wouldn't pick up the trail so quickly. The odometer on the Jeep had recorded sixty miles of progress before the terrain had forced me to abandon it, so I thought I'd had a decent jump on them. I'd even hidden the bright red vehicle under a copse of trees, in case they searched from the air. Now, I was certain they'd found the Jeep and were close behind.

I moved carefully down the opposite side of the hill, a half-jog, scanning the ground. If I lost my footing and turned an ankle or a knee, it would all be over in hours. I reached the bottom of the hill and ran for the treeline. The Canadian wilderness was beautiful in early autumn, and it served as both a curse and a gift for my cause. Unfortunately, it was one of the last remaining true wildlands on the continent and if I had been anywhere else at the moment I could have reached civilization—and help—by now. On the other

213

hand, considering the motives of the tracking party behind me, there were no better surroundings to hide in if forced to do so.

I moved deeper into the wilderness. Forty minutes later, chest heaving, legs feeling like rubber, I reached the summit of a rocky ridge. I resisted the urge to take another drink, and instead, leaned against a boulder the size of a mini-van. The rock felt cool and smooth against my shoulder and I rested my cheek against it, closing my eyes, savoring its touch. Within seconds, a vision of snarling dogs snapped me back, and I quickly unshouldered the pack and eased around to the backside of the ridge, which was lined with a cluster of smaller but no less impressive boulders.

The view was truly awe-inspiring. Miles of bright, sun-speckled autumn forest stretched before me like a quilt sewn with the richest cloth from every color of a rainbow. I could see acres of healthy woodland, peaks and valleys, streams and rivers snaking across the land like the pulsing veins of a giant, scattered lighter-toned green patches of rolling meadow, the occasional dark blemish of rocky bluffs similar to the one I was standing on. Not a single sign of civilization as we know it.

God's country, indeed, I thought, remembering one of Lucas Ransom's favorite expressions. He was such a dramatic bastard.

Somewhere in the distance, I heard the dogs. Impossible to tell if they were drawing closer, or if I was making some ground on them. I searched the landscape but could see no movement. Suddenly, I thought of the camp—the evil place I was fleeing—and what they'd done to pitiful Francis. A shiver tickled my spine. No way they were going to take me. No way. I reached down and touched the heavy cloth of the backpack, feeling the rough edges of the Grail. And as my fingers caressed the material, a dark realization came to me: taking the Grail had been a mistake. If I had just snuck out of the camp, they might not have followed me, thinking a city man could never cross hundreds of miles of wilderness. But they would never give up now. They would never stop searching until they'd found their Holy Grail.

I slung the knapsack over my back and jumped to my feet, inspired, actually energized, by the horrible thought. Drawing a deep breath, I ran—a bit too fast for the rocky terrain—up the slope of the ridge, pushing blindly through the heavy foliage ahead, out into—

nothing.

The ground beneath me suddenly disappeared.

Replaced by clear, blue sky.

A sheer cliff laughed at me as I fell—

—deeper into the hungry ravine—

—toward the rushing white water below—

Slow motion, spinning, arms flailing, knapsack feeling impossibly heavy, the sky so brilliantly blue it hurt my eyes—

—and then there was only darkness.

2

Darkness ... flames dancing dangerously close burning my face my body with their heat a screaming man inside the flames his face and mouth bubbling melting into a mask of blood his arms dripping black and yellow and red as he reaches for me he wants to take me with him into the fire a flame touches my hair my lips and i beat it out before it can taste me then the sound of singing a sickening evil sound then a gigantic cross jutting up into the air a white sword cutting the pure sky hundreds of kneeling men and women below the cross in flowing white robes singing singing ...

Slowly the darkness fades, is replaced by a dimly-lit room with a single small window, a sweet-smelling breeze kissing the air around me. I think I am safe until I try to move and cannot, my arms and legs restrained, until I hear soft music on the air, until I see a golden crucifix hanging on the wall, and then I know I am not safe. I must be back at the camp. They found me. I try to scream but the pain is too much ... and then there is only the darkness again.

3

I came to some time later to the sound of chirping birds and wood being chopped. Early morning sunlight streamed into the room through an open window. I stared at the empty walls, re-calling the crucifix from my nightmare, the music, the flames. All horrible memories I'd taken with me from the encampment.

I moved my head and a wave of pain and nausea washed over me. Bits and pieces slowly floated back to me. The dogs . . . the cliff . . . the river . . . falling! I was afraid to look down at my body. A dark vision flashed in my mind. That of a sideshow freak with no limbs. My arms and legs were not restrained at all; they just weren't there anymore. I lifted my head slowly, moaning, and caught a glimpse of two feet under a white blanket.

The bad news was it felt like I had a broken bag of bones for a body and was strapped to a bed in the middle of nowhere. The good news was I didn't think I was back at the camp.

From what I could see, head perfectly still, eyes still blurry, the room looked like it was part of a larger log cabin. The walls were un-decorated, a single naked light bulb dangling from the ceiling. I could just see the top half of a fireplace against the far wall, and I couldn't help but think of the flames. Real flames—like the ones back at the camp—not the kind that frightened me from my dreams.

"Hello," I croaked, mouth impossibly dry, not recognizing the sound of my voice.

The chopping noises stopped outside the window.

Footsteps.

A door opening and closing.

A long, breathless moment.

"Well, I'll be," a man's voice came from somewhere beyond my vision. "My good friend has awakened."

I didn't know the voice, so I kept quiet.

"Don't be afraid, partner. I imagine you're wondering where you are and how you got here." Movement in the room. "Let me pull this chair up and get you a sip of water."

A man's grinning face appeared directly above me and, for just a moment, I thought I was staring at the face of my long-dead fa-ther. The man had to be damn near seventy—the same age my fa-ther would have been—his face a friendly ball of wrinkles, a balding brow, deep tan, eyes the color of clay, a smile enough for two men.

"You just relax yourself and take this water down real slow like." He lifted a paper cup to my lips and I tasted the nectar of the gods. "Whoa, partner. That's enough for now. Too much will do you more bad than good. Trust me."

"Where am I?" I managed, water running down my chin. I wanted so much to lick my lips, but my tongue wouldn't cooperate.

"You're in the home of the honorable Lewis Perkins, that's me, halfway down the south side of the Levathian Valley. Where should you be?"

"How . . . where did you find—"

"I didn't exactly find you, partner. The river brought you to me. I was heading upstream, and instead of fish, I found you. Thought you was dead at first."

I swallowed and said, "I *feel* like a corpse."

The old man chuckled and whistled loud enough so that it hurt my ears. "Partner, you are one beat-up individual. Near as I can see, you got a broken leg, broken wrist, bruised ribs—don't think you broke any of them though cause you ain't been spitting no blood—and probably one whopper of a concussion."

I groaned.

He shook his head and real concern crept onto his face. "I fixed you up best I could. Cleaned the cuts. Set the breaks. But you were out cold for more than two days, partner. And when you finally started coming to last night, I had to tie you down to keep you from hurting yourself worse. You kept hollering about flames and crosses and other crazy stuff, sounded something like singing. Heck, I had to turn my music off, and yank that there crucifix off the wall just to keep you calmed down. Weirdest thing, it was."

"My God," I said, a tear slipping down my cheek. "You saved my—"

"No reason to thank me yet, partner," he said, loosening the ropes from my legs and arms. "You could die on me next hour for all I know."

I tried to smile. "Well, in that case, I'll hold off on the gratitude." He smiled back and gently patted my arm. He had rough, weathered hands, the hands of a good man. I decided right there that I would have liked this man even if he hadn't saved my life.

"Listen," I said, "this is very important. Could I use your phone?"

"Sorry, no phone this far out. Lines don't run anywhere near here. Closest place would be, umm, over near Rockton or in Riverdale. It's a tossup as to which is closer."

Riverdale . . . the camp was just north of Riverdale.

"Has anyone . . . anyone come around here looking for me?"

Another look of concern, mixed with suspicion this time. I didn't blame him. "No, no one comes around this side of the valley except for hunters from time to time. But my land's posted so they don't come in this far if they know what's good for them."

He paused, as if considering his next words carefully. "I found a knapsack that belongs to you."

My heart skipped; I'd forgotten about the backpack.

"And judging from what's in that there sack, I think you've got some kind of story to tell. And, if I'm gonna be caring for you, I reckon I've got a right to hear it."

I opened my mouth, but he "ssshed" me quiet.

"Not today, partner. You're a sight. You get some rest right now and we'll get some food in you soon."

"Thank you," I said, feeling helpless and foolish. A strong man like myself transformed into a child.

He patted my arm again, turned and left. A moment later, he returned. "You don't worry, partner. If anyone does comes here looking for you, as long as it ain't the law, I'll tell them I ain't seen a sign of you. I'll get rid of them real quick like. You don't go worrying about that, hear?"

I nodded and whispered a hoarse "thank you," suddenly exhausted from the conversation.

The old man winked at me and closed the door.

4

A full day passed before the old man mentioned the backpack again.

He'd spent the past twenty-four hours pumping food and drink into me and tending to my injuries best he could. The pain in my

leg and arm was just bearable, but I counted myself lucky that neither injury had broken the skin and neither limb appeared terribly
deformed. The old man sure wasn't a doctor and he wasn't the best
cook in the world either, but his genuine concern and gentle manner of care were more than good enough.

There was *one* thing the old guy—Lew, he asked me to call
him—was good at though, and that was talking. I was his first
company in years, he told me, and he was making up for lost conversation. By that first day's end, I'd learned everything I needed
to know about him, even though he still knew nothing about me.

Lewis Perkins. Sixty-two-year-old retired Air Force man. Aircraft mechanic. Living on just under 600 acres of his father's land.
Wife, Carmella, deceased. Cancer. Buried in a meadow a few hundred yards behind the cabin. No phone. No communication with
the outside world. Had supplies flown in four times a year to a lake
a mile-and-a-half north of the cabin. If the weather was bad, and
the flight had to be aborted, they flew in exactly a week later. Last
shipment came in less than a month ago. Spent his days hiking the
countryside. Fishing. Hunting. Some watercolor painting from time
to time. Most nights spent reading. Smoking his pipe.

It was during dinner on that second night—deer meat, green
vegetables, and hot bun rolls—that Lew brought up the knapsack
again. He did so in a sly, roundabout fashion, and as usual, it was
some time before he stopped talking.

"You know, Bill," he said around a mouthful of deer meat,
"you're not the first fella that river brought to me."

I stopped pushing my fork across the plate and leaned my head
back on one of the pillows he'd propped under me on the bed. A
fire crackled in the corner of the room, its warmth mixing with the
cool night air coming through the window. The painkillers Lew
had given me before dinner (he told me that he used them a couple
times a winter for his arthritis) were taking the desired effect. My
stomach was full and I was ready for a good story.

"No, sir. 'Bout two years ago, I found a man about a mile from
where you washed up. But this fella was still in the river, hooked
on some fallen brush like a trapped beaver, and he was deader than
dead. Had been that way for a few days. But, you see, this guy had

a full pack with him. Looked like he belonged out here. I even found his camp some ways upstream. Probably slipped on the rocks or, heck, he could've had a heart attack for all I know."

He stopped, and looked away, plucking a strand of meat from his teeth with pinched fingers. He swallowed a drink of beer and looked back at me. It was obvious that he was waiting for me to talk, and when I didn't, he continued.

"What I'm getting at is this. After I found you, I didn't find no camp and, believe me, I looked. And the only thing you had on you was some old backpack, all tangled around your arm. Just a few pieces of food, a canteen, a little old .38, some waterlogged notebooks, and a fancy-looking gold cup all wrapped up in a flannel shirt. No supplies, no warm clothes for the night. It looked like you'd lit out from somewhere in a big hurry and—"

"I'm a journalist," I said, pushing the dinner plate further down on my lap. I knew it was time for *me* to do the talking now.

Lew shook his head. "A writer, huh? I knew you were something special. I sure did."

I couldn't help but smile. "I'm not from around here."

"Oh, no kidding," he said with a smirk. "I thought you were a mountain man or something. Maybe a fur trapper."

I rolled my eyes and continued. "I live in Philadelphia. Have all my life, all thirty-nine years. Write features for a few of the national magazines. Public interest stories. I spent the last three weeks on an undercover assignment over near Riverdale, at the New Order camp. You heard of it?"

"Those religious folks?"

"Yeah. Exactly."

Most people had heard of the New Order. Founded three decades ago by New York business tycoon Lucas Ransom, the highly publicized cult of religious fanatics had built their own village—their camp—in the Canadian wilderness, where they worshiped a Holy God Of Nature and lived almost completely off the land. Many of their methods and practices were controversial and the group itself was under investigation by several law enforcement agencies.

"What were you doing there?" Lew asked.

"Last month I got an assignment to go undercover and infiltrate the New Order. Pose as a new member, a convert. Take a good look around, take a few pictures, talk to some people, and then disappear. We'd checked the area out pretty good and there was a spot close to the camp where a helicopter could land. I was to stay in camp for five weeks, then sneak out in the night and rendezvous with the chopper pilot and escape with my material."

"Five weeks, huh? That's a long time," he said, looking up at the cabin ceiling, thinking. "Then that's who you were running from. Something went wrong, huh?"

"Oh, yeah. Something went wrong all right. Murder went wrong. I watched them kill a man in that holy camp of theirs." My breath hitched and I reached for my glass and took a drink.

"Take it easy, Bill. Take it slow and start over again."

I took a few even breaths and asked, "Lew, are you familiar with the myth of the Holy Grail? Have you ever heard of the Sinner King?"

He shook his head.

"Okay, bear with me here. This'll take a few minutes but, when I'm done, I think you'll understand everything."

"Take your time," he said. "Ain't got no place to go."

I nodded. "According to history, the Holy Grail is the cup from which our Saviour drank at His last supper. He was supposed to have given it to Joseph, who took it with him to Europe, along with the spear which the soldier had used to pierce our Savior's side. Well, the Grail and the spear were supposedly handed down from generation to generation and the men who watched over these treasures were supposed to be men of great purity. But one of these men failed and thus began a terrible myth, that of the Sinner King. This man was supposed to have looked at a partially disrobed female and, according to legend, the sacred spear then fell upon him, inflicting a fatal wound, thus, crowning this man as *Le Roi Pescheur* or The Sinner King. Do you follow me so far?"

The old man nodded, clearly entranced by my little history lesson. "Yes, yes. Go on."

"Well, soon after arriving in camp, I discovered that the members of the New Order have their own Holy Grail for worship. Certainly not the Grail of historic legend, but a fine substitute with an undeniable power over the congregation.

"Now here comes the ugly part. You know the saying: history often repeats itself. Well, it certainly did in this case. One of the four guardians of this Holy Grail—a fella named Francis—was discovered to be having an affair with a teenaged girl in the camp. This man was brought before the holy men of the New Order and sentenced to death. I . . . I watched helplessly as they burned him at the stake."

"My God."

"It was horrible. Barbaric. I've been a journalist for twenty years and I've never seen anything like it. They held a ceremony and every person in the camp was there. It was like a celebration, singing and dancing . . . it was incredible!"

"So you decided to run?"

"No, I wanted to wait the final two weeks for my pick-up. But a few days later, while cleaning inside the chapel, I overheard two of the high priests talking in the confession room next door. It seems that somehow, one of the congregation had discovered my true identity and the priests were going to, that very night, spring a little surprise on me. On impulse, I grabbed the Grail from the altar, and took it with me. I grabbed my backpack and notes for my story from my room, stole a truck and drove as far as the airfield road could take me."

"And they came after you? Is that why you fell?"

"No," I said, smiling despite the nature of the conversation. "I'm a klutz. Always have been. I just ran out of ground to walk on and fell into the river. Thank God, you found me."

"Yeah, no kidding." He let out a long whistle. "What an experience."

"Lew, I gotta tell you, you may be putting yourself in danger, by keeping me here. In case you haven't guessed by now, that thing in my backpack is their Holy Grail, their highest treasure, and they're not going to stop looking for it."

"You can stop worrying about that. This is my land and I'll defend it against anyone who crosses the wrong line." He scratched his head, thinking again. "You know, there's a hunting cabin on the western border of my land. It's empty most of the time, but hunting parties use it from time to time to rest, grab a quick meal, or sometimes stay the night in bad weather. I could get out there in a few weeks, when you're up and around a bit, and leave a note for someone to send a plane up to the lake, get you out of here."

"Jesus, a few weeks—"

"You won't be up and walking for at least another week, and that's gonna be with the help of a crutch. Someone's gotta be here to cook for you, take care of you."

Again, I felt as helpless as a child. "I know, I know. Just thinking that a few weeks is a long time."

"Yeah, but you're lucky. Death's even longer."

I shut up. He had a good point.

The next hour passed quickly, both of us running our mouths until our throats were sore. I told him more about my experiences at the camp, about my life in Philly. He told me about how he'd met his wife, the time spent overseas while in the military. At twenty minutes past ten o'clock, we said our goodnights, and soon after I was asleep.

5

Two weeks later . . .

"All right!" I yelled. "That's the biggest one of the day."

I watched Lew as he walked slowly to shore, the clear water moving swiftly around his rubber waders, and plopped the fat trout to the ground, where it flipped from side to side. In the weeks I'd been here, under Lew's care, a bond had formed between us. It was as if the dire circumstances had allowed us to forgo the usual stepping stones of friendship, and progress directly to the strongest of bonds.

"I think I'll nail three or four more keepers and we'll call it a day, okay?"

"Sounds good to me. I'm going back and grab us a couple more beers."

He looked at me, the worried expression that I had already learned to dread creasing his face. "Maybe I'd better—"

"Now, don't go looking at me like that, Lew. You know damn well I can walk just fine with the crutch you made." I picked up the heavy pole and waggled it in his direction. "It's a two-minute walk to the cabin."

"Well, you be careful," he said, dropping his trout into the cooler with the other fish. "Look out for holes and rocks. And watch out for all those tree roots. There's some monster roots around this river. I've tripped on them a few times myself."

"I'll be careful. I promise."

"And, hey, some of those roots are hard to see."

I could still hear the old guy chattering away with his warnings when I reached the cabin. I took two frosty bottles of beer from the kitchen cooler and a pack of Oreo cookies from the counter and limped into the den, looking for Lew's pipe. He allowed himself two smokes a day, and I thought he'd probably enjoy one after all his hard work. I spotted the old bulldog pipe on the bookshelf next to a stack of thick aircraft reference books and what looked like a photo album. I grabbed the pipe, and absently flipped open the album cover.

Four rows of small black-and-white photos covered the page. Each picture, faded and yellowed with age, was attached by tiny adhesives on the corners. The first three pages of the album held childhood memories—images of a young boy with a baseball cap on backwards, riding the shoulders of an older man. A child atop a painted horse on a merry-go-round. On a tire swing. In a cute little dark suit, holding hands with a smiling mother and father.

The middle pages held memories from older years. Bare-chested men crouched on the wing of a WWII bomber. A young Lew trying to look street-tough in full dress uniform. A smiling beauty who must have been Carmella. A simply wonderful shot of Lew and Carmella, arm in arm, on their wedding day . . .

I heard something behind me and whirled, almost losing my balance.

Nothing.

Suddenly, standing there looking at the pictures from years long past, I felt guilty for probing into my friend's life without being offered an invitation. Hurriedly, I snapped the photo album shut and as I turned to leave, a single picture fell from its pages and fluttered to my feet. I pushed the photo across the floor with my crutch until I had a better angle at which to retrieve it, bent slowly, and pinched the picture with two fingers. I wiped the dust from the print and almost put it back in the album without looking at it. I spun it very slowly in my fingers, like a playing card, brought it to my face, and almost fainted dead to the floor.

Oh . . .

my . . .

God!

My heart trip-hammered!

Had to be a mistake!

Had to be!

I stared at it for a breathless moment, then stuffed the photo back into the album and started for the river, barely using the crutch, grunting in pain. Act as if nothing has changed, I thought. It *could* be a mistake. It truly could. But if it's not, I need to buy some time to think this over. Act as natural as possible.

But I knew that was going to be damned near impossible because all my thoughts—sad and very frightened thoughts—were on that photo. The small black-and-white picture which had showed a horrifyingly clear image of a smiling, few years younger Lewis Perkins, standing next to New Order's founder, Lucas Ransom, in front of the congregation's holy temple.

6

Dinner that night was a pair of fat trout and baked potatoes out on the front porch. Autumn twilights this mild were rare for the valley, and Lew wanted to take advantage of the pleasant breeze.

After the meal, I sat back on the step with the night's last beer and stretched my leg. Lew rocked himself in his chair, smoking his second pipe. We sat mostly in silence, which was rare for us. Finally, Lew broke the quiet.

"You been thinking of home today?"

"Huh?"

"You been mighty quiet all evening. Thought you might have been thinking about being back home, missing your friends."

"Yeah, I guess I have been. Wondering how much longer it was going to be."

"Shouldn't be too long now. A hunting party's bound to see my note anytime now. Just keep hoping."

"It's all I can do."

"You know . . . I'm really gonna miss you like the dickens when you leave here. Hate to say it, but it's almost gonna feel like when Carmella passed on. Like I lost a part of me. Just all quiet and lonely."

I wanted to say many things, wanted to say that he was like the father I never knew, wanted to stand up and embrace the old man right there on his front porch in the middle of the dark wilderness, wanted to ask for a simple and clear explanation for what I'd seen. Instead, I just took another swig of my beer and watched the stars dance their lonely dance in the night sky.

7

I could tell by the sun that it was mid-afternoon when I finally regained consciousness. Bright sunlight usually streamed through the window until just after lunch, when, at that time, the trees blocked the rays. The room was in warm shadow now. I tried to blink the fog from my eyes, but it didn't help. My head pounded, no doubt from whatever had been in that final beer the night before.

It had been pretty easy to figure things out after I came to and found my legs and arms bound to the bed once again. He'd fooled me good, he sure had; I just hadn't figured the old guy was going to make a move so soon.

Footsteps.

"It's not what you think, Bill."

I laughed and it came out harsh and angry. "And just what the hell am I supposed to think, friend? You drug me, knock me cold, and strap me to my damn bed. What am I supposed to think, huh? I'm being punished for leaving the toilet seat up?"

"I know you saw the pictures."

"I saw one damn photo, you bastard."

"Please don't be angry with me." His voice was trembling now.

"If you're a part of their crazy clan, why didn't you turn me in? Get it over with. Why didn't you tell them I was here with you?"

"I'm not a member of the New Order . . . not anymore. Haven't been for years. I lied to you. I lied to you about a lot of things . . . I never left a note in the hunters' cabin. Never went there at all."

"Jesus," I whispered.

"And I *do* know the story of the Sinner King, the story you told me about the Holy Grail. I know it all too well. Ten years ago, Carmella and I lived at the camp. Worshiped there. We had been there for four years and both of us were held in high standing by the priests. Carmella was an educational leader, and I was one of the guardians of the Grail. But I made a terrible mistake, misunderstood the evil advances of a neighbor's wife. Accidentally encouraged these advances."

He stopped, loud sobs shaking his body. "I, too, am what you call a Sinner King. I, too, like the man you watched them burn at the stake, failed in my duty to the Lord. But that was ten long years ago. I have *never* heard of the sacrifice you described, thank God. They excommunicated us, forced us to leave the camp and abandon the practice of their faith. My dear Carmella died three years later, ashamed, tortured by grief."

My journalist's mind working full speed, I spotted a ray of hope. An opportunity. "That's okay, Lewis. It's all okay. Help me get back to Philadelphia. Help me find someone to fly me out of here. I can write a story that will change the New Order forever, a story that will avenge both of our losses—"

His eyes widened in surprise . . . in fear.

He shook his head rapidly, silencing me. "No, no, no. Don't you see what all this means? Can't you see? It became so clear to me last night. You. The Grail. Falling to me from the heavens. It is a second chance. A second chance to prove that I am worthy. That I am pure enough to protect and watch over the Holy Grail."

I saw the madness in his eyes then. Eyes no longer tired or sad. Eyes that danced with desperate insanity. He brushed a strand of hair from my face, gently, lovingly, stroking my brow, and I thought I might be sick.

"You must stay here with me, Bill. I'm old and will not live forever. Don't you see? You and the Grail—you were sent to me. The Grail will need a guardian when I pass away and you ..."

8

Six weeks later ...

The restraints are no longer necessary. Even if I still *wanted* to escape, it is not possible. I know that now ... after two earlier attempts. My leg still bothers me, and I don't know the land well enough to survive a single night, much less an entire journey. To leave now, in the midst of winter, would be suicide. The cabin is my home now.

It's all rather strange. We still talk into the long hours of twilight. Comfortable, easy conversation, spotted with much laughter. We are rarely apart. Eat our meals together. Fish and hunt together when the weather allows. Read or play cards by the fire.

Lew keeps the Holy Grail on the mantel, balanced on a fancy wooden stand we spent the better half of a week carving. He kneels and prays before it each morning, and then again in the evening. He keeps after me to join him, like a father badgering his son to go to mass each Sunday. He swears that the Grail speaks to him in the voice of God, comforts him. That if I join him, I too will hear.

What he doesn't know yet is that I *already* hear. As each day passes, the voice inside my head grows louder, clearer, stronger. Tomorrow morning, I will join him before the Grail, and I will listen.

It is night now, a beautiful winter sky blankets the valley, but I anxiously await daybreak. Lew will be so happy with my change of heart. He never lost his faith in me. He tells me each morning, without fail, arms outstretched, that this will all be mine one day soon: the cabin, the valley, the Holy Grail.

And I think he may be right.

Lucky Lyle's Big Surprise

✠

Terry Black

They say you can find anything at Bieberman's. What I found was the worst moment of my life.

We were going someplace else. I remember: Mom just wanted to stop in for some hair cream or eye blemish or whatever it is that women buy. I was five at the time, maybe six, old enough to be interested in army sets and rubber creatures and anything involving chocolate, but not much else.

Now, Bieberman's wasn't my favorite place, but it had one thing no other five-and-dime could boast of: a Lucky Lyle Vend-O-Matic machine. Great stuff—you put in a penny and shook Lyle's hand and out popped a piece of gum or a little candy or one of those horrible licorice things. I know, big Goddamn deal, but what made it great was this little spinwheel, deep in Lyle's spring-loaded bowels; if it stopped at just the right spot you'd hear a loud ka-CHUNKA! and Lyle's hand would pop open with a special prize.

It could be anything. My best friend Larry got a Ninja Master Hide-Away Knife; it couldn't really kill you 'cause it was only rubber, but it looked so real Miss Ackerman called the police and they almost came out to our school. Another time Fat Steve got a bottle of Gross-Out Brand Fake Phlegm, but it backfired when he tried to make it come out his nose and it got stuck up there.

The *real* prize, though, was the Double Whammy Special.

That's when Lyle's eyes would light up and his head would spin round and his chest would pop open to bestow a prize "worth more than FIVE DOLLARS!" according to the sign. Lyle's big

229

jackpot was a local legend, but I never saw the mechanical bastard come across.

Except that once.

We were racing across the store that day, desperately late. Mom had her nose paint or whatever it was in one hand, and me in the other, frog-trotting toward the checkstand without so much as a Hershey bar to make *my* trip worthwhile. What I really wanted was the new *Famous Monsters of Filmland*—I liked to sketch little Frankensteins and Godzillas on other people's homework—but I'd overspent my allowance already; all I had left was a couple of pennies for the Lucky Lyle machine.

I dug my heels in, trying to turn Mom aside long enough to pump some change into Lyle's coin slot. I groped in my pocket for those last few pennies, fighting the suction of Mom's come-hither grasp—when I saw something amazing.

Lyle's chest had *already* popped open.

And there in his belly was a white container, about the size of a Pop-Tarts box, just waiting to be snatched away. In one heart-stopping moment I knew what must have happened: some new kid, either dumb or from out of town, had stuck in his penny and taken the gum and just sauntered away, ignoring the flashing eyes and the spinning head and the loud ka-CHUNKA!, not even noticing the priceless treasure—

But I did. I grabbed for it, came *that* close, only Mom's grip tightened and I was pulled right off my feet, hauled out of snatching distance, receding toward the checkstand. I remember sharp words, a hasty purchase, a frantic sprint through the parking lot to the beat-up Chevy with the cracked windshield and the dashboard Jesus that wouldn't stay on—then nothing. I can't even remember where we went in such a hurry.

But the next time I saw Lyle he was back to normal, hat pulled low and hand outstretched, leering at the shoppers with his roving eyeballs and painted-on mustache. I put in a penny and got a piece of licorice.

Two years later they closed the store.

* * *

I tried not to hold a grudge; Mom couldn't fathom the importance of X-ray glasses or windup werewolves, any more than a five-year-old could balance the checkbook or gas up the Chevy. But I wished she could see things my way *now,* when at the age of seventeen I had to wrestle with the thorny question of Life After High School.

Dad, being a dentist, thought I should be a dentist. He had the school all picked out, this snooty campus in central Delaware where someone famous had once graduated. But I didn't want to fight tooth decay until retirement rolled around; to me it was like climbing an Everest of extracted teeth, old and blackening molars without even the grace to turn into skeletons when you threw them on the ground like in *Jason and the Argonauts.*

"You can't watch movies for a living," Dad pointed out, not unreasonably. "Sooner or later you have to pocket a paycheck. How are you going to make ends meet if your greatest talent is making people want to vomit?"

He was referring, I guess, to the artboard propped in my lap, where under the guise of sketching my little sister I'd drawn a slimy creature with brittle claws and bulbous, probing eyes. Artist's conception, I'd argue, but Dad wasn't in the mood.

"I hadn't thought about it," I muttered. Strictly speaking, that wasn't true—I *had* thought about it, quite a bit, but I had yet to reach any meaningful conclusions. "I figure something will come along when the time comes."

"Well, you're wrong," Dad said. "Life doesn't owe you a living. It doesn't owe you success. Hang around, goof off, and you'll wind up in a trailer park grubbing for food stamps."

Of course, I'd heard all this before; it was like a vaudeville routine, tired and well-rehearsed. At some point I'd make a snide remark about dentistry and Dad would stomp away, groping for those Marlboros he wasn't supposed to smoke anymore.

But not today. Instead he took my drawing and held it to the light, not distastefully, but with a critical eye. "Not bad," he said, startling me with the compliment. "I used to draw," he added, as if the hairpin-turn subject change was the most natural thing on earth. "I wanted to do it for a living. That was my big ambition, to draw cartoons—for newspapers, magazines, even the movies. It was all I cared about."

I'll bite, I thought, and asked the obvious question: "Why didn't you?"

"Long story," he sighed. "But I tried everything to break into the business. I even wrote to Walt Disney once, asking his advice—and he actually wrote back."

"Really? What did he say?"

"He said my work had promise—but there were so *many* cartoonists, so many would-be illustrators glutting the market that it was hopeless to compete. He said I shouldn't even *think* about it, unless I was so obsessed I could do nothing else." He laced his fingers; I could tell he wanted a Marlboro.

"I thought about it, hard. But your mother and I had been married six months—you were already on the way—and I just couldn't take the chance. So I forgot about drawing, went back to school, and earned myself a Doctor of Dentistry." He rubbed his nose; it was an Irish nose, brick-red and big as a golf ball. "As for the moral of this story—well, I guess it's whatever you want it to be."

Dad's words stuck with me as I headed for Cavalcade o' Comix, looking to blow my spare cash on back issues of *X-Men, The Incredible Hulk* and *Cerebus the Aardvark.* I tried to imagine getting a letter from Walt Disney, the past equivalent of Stan Lee or Steven Spielberg. It'd be like a scroll from Mount Olympus; you'd want to savor every syllable—

The notion was so absorbing I must have lost track of where I was. Because instead of the beige-on-beige of Coastside Mall I wound up on a darker, quieter street, nosing the Chevy past shutdown storefronts with broken windows and FOR LEASE notices, mom-and-pop businesses up for adoption. The only sign of life was a sludge-colored tabby trying to poke its way into a dirty old box that promised "oven-fresh pizza."

Behind it was Bieberman's Five-and-Dime.

Oddly enough, it looked fine. I don't know how the place kept its pristine facade when all its neighbors resembled the victims of atomic testing, but Bieberman's looked for all the world like you could still go in and buy something. There was even a banner reading UNDER NEW MANAGEMENT/OPEN FOR BUSINESS. Intrigued, I pulled to the curb.

I left the Chevy next to the stump of an old parking meter, cut off like a gangrenous limb, and approached the double doors. I jumped when they opened automatically. From deep inside came a fatherly voice, saying, "Welcome to Bieberman's—America's top choice for your home convenience and family needs."

The place was a graveyard. No clerks manned the registers; no shoppers thronged the aisles; no self-important floor managers bustled about, poking at displays. Even the complaint department was unpeopled, a first for Bieberman's.

Only one thing moved. I shouldn't have been surprised; it was the obvious choice, the motive force, perhaps, behind this bizarre and unnatural grand reopening: the man with the roving eyeballs and the painted-on mustache—

Lucky Lyle. His eyes followed you everywhere.

I put a penny in the slot and shook Lyle's hand. He gave me back a piece of that blue-flavored gum, with the strange taste that occurs nowhere in nature. I wondered if there wasn't some weird, secret fruit, harvested deep in some some Godforsaken jungle, used to make all that blue-flavored gum, soda, and Sno-Kone juice.

In my pocket were seven pennies. I fed them to Lyle. He gave me three gumballs, two butterscotch candies, a piece of licorice, and a tiny whistle that didn't work.

"Welcome to Bieberman's," said the voice again. *A shoplifter's paradise,* I thought, eyeing the rows on rows of trashy convenience items: ladies' patent leather shoes, keychains labeled ABIGAIL, ADAM, ADELAIDE ... men's hats (who wears men's hats?), ugly neckties wide as your head—

Nothing in the store was worth swiping. I sighed and headed for the door. It was closed, stuck shut, locked behind me.

Lucky Lyle started to laugh.

I'm not saying he was alive, or haunted, or anything. He was only a machine. But when Lyle tipped his head back and let loose that chalkboard cackle, I nearly dove through the plate glass.

"Shut up, Lyle," I said stupidly.

Not until that moment did I realize why I'd come here. But suddenly it was my goal, my Grail, the top priority of my teenaged life to make Lucky Lyle fork over his Double Whammy What's-Its-Name, if it took every cent I could scrape up.

I went to the nearest cash register, hit NO SALE, found the drawer stuffed with cash. I paid no attention to the nickels, dimes, quarters, dollars, fives, tens, and twenties. But I took every penny from the rightmost compartment and stuffed them all into Lyle's receptacle.

There was an avalanche of gum and candy. No prize. I headed for the next register, wondering belatedly what I'd tell Our City's Finest if they blundered in to find me stuffing my pockets with Bieberman's smallest change.

"Hell with 'em," I said aloud, feeding this new hoard into Lyle's coin slot. With each new penny he seemed more lifelike, his features better defined, his face taking on a ruddier cast. His lip seemed to curl into a ceramic sneer.

Once I thought he winked.

The floor became littered with licorice and small candies, M&M's, jacks, and Super Balls. Lick 'em tattoos you could stick on your forehead. Rubber ants, spiders, and centipedes. Vampire teeth. Fake eyeballs.

"Come on, you son of a bitch," I said.

Bieberman's had eight registers in all. I emptied them of all their pennies, wondering if I should bother to replace the money. Hell, let 'em have the candy, I thought, kicking aside a snowbank of sourballs to feed in the last thirty-seven cents.

On the fifth-to-last Lyle went ka-CHUNK! and presented me with a Chinese finger puzzle.

Fourth-to-last was a set of chattering false teeth.

Third-to-last was a vial of fake blood.

Next to last was a skull on a chain.

Last was a rubber headstone.

"Damn," I said. "I'm out of change—"

* * *

For a long time I sat looking into Lyle's roving eyes, seeming to lock on mine even as they wandered left-to-right, right-to-left, with the coy hypnosis of a snake-charmer. Did he want to trade places, perhaps, leaving me to sit here hawking prizes while Lyle turned flesh and blood and went off to dental school—a sort of novocaine-squirting Pinocchio?

One more penny would tip the scales, trip the wire, hit the button. One cent more and Lyle would betray whatever secret sat waiting in his ribcage. I knew it somehow, I *knew* it.

One cent more—

When it came to me, I laughed out loud. Ask a silly question, I thought, heading for the shoe department. It took twenty minutes and several dozen shoeboxes to find what I was looking for; finally I bent back the penny loafer, extracted the coin, and clutched it in my hand.

"Gotcha," I said.

I swear he looked pissed when I showed him the coin. Even more so, when I jammed it home.

His eyes turned the color of molten lava; his head did a 360, Linda Blair-style; his laughter rose to a typhoon screech, with a shower of sparks and the stench of ozone; the air seemed gravid with pent-up energy, humming and crackling like a stressed power line—

Lyle's chest went ka-CHUNKA! and snapped open. Inside was a white container, about the size of a Pop-Tarts box.

For a moment I couldn't open it. I had to savor that delicious instant, the glee of not knowing, the sweet suspense of unknown reward. It was almost a pity when I could bear it no longer, and tore the top off that white box like a kid on Christmas morning.

It was like nothing I'd imagined.

The *least* of it, the smallest part of the surprise, was that the box was bigger inside than out. You could fill a steamer truck with the contents of that box, though it was no bigger than a pint carton.

The stranger thing was not how big it was, but *what* it was: a playset. Full of action figures and windup cars and a sprawling, snap-together landscape, spring-loaded, battery-powered, ready to burst into motion when you hit the switch and wound the gears and put the figures in their little slots—

—but it wasn't army men, or firemen, or astronauts, or police. It was *my own life*. There was action-figure me, and a mom and a dad and a sister, and a beat-up Chevy they could drive, and a college the "me" could go to where battery-powered dental instructors sat waiting to give boring lectures on Magic Slate blackboards, while toothache-ridden patients-to-be made lifelike moaning sounds and lined up outside the door of my toy dentist's office. There were even old toy magazines for them to read.

Lyle's prize, it seemed, was a glimpse of tomorrow. And the future wasn't a bright one.

For this I'd waited a dozen years, and squandered a fool's ransom of loose change? For this I'd burglarized Bieberman's, and risked getting jailed for the pettiest of crimes?

No.

I wasn't a slave to some penny-dreadful prophecy; I wasn't like those neurotic buffoons who can't leave home without consulting their horoscope, can't get out of bed without dialing 976-PSYCHIC. If I didn't want to jerk and twitch on supernatural puppet-strings, then dammit, I didn't have to.

Lyle seemed to sigh. He froze in position, like the robot he was. But the rest of the store came alive:

Rubber insects swarmed the toy college, devouring the professors. The Dean was gobbled by huge, chattering teeth. Fake blood spilled across the snap-together floor, as slimy spiders with drooling mandibles rode webs of spun licorice into scale-model dorm rooms, chewing the limbs off a pliant gaggle of coed Barbies. Headstones sprouted on foam-rubber lawns, only to topple as H.O.-Scale zombies with bubble-gum intestines clawed free of their graves and started munching the townspeople, drooling butterscotch saliva.

A regiment of G.I. Joes tried to fend off the invasion, roaring in on camo Tonkas, hefting die-cast M-16's. But every critter they blasted split into a dozen more; they were suctioned by blobby leeches, poisoned with sour-grape venom, mired in Tootsie Roll quicksand. The fall of Toy Town was swift and inevitable.

It wasn't Lyle's doing, I realized; it was *me,* upending this joyless matchbox universe with the force of my imagination. I was unstoppable—I could fashion cartoon carnivores to overrun the staunchest defenders.

I was an artist. I could do nothing else.

But I hated to leave a mess. When the spiders and lizards and crawly vermin were all done feasting, I packed each and every one into the little white box and slipped it back into Lyle's chest, where the ribs were still hanging open. Maybe someday, somehow, another five-year-old would find it there.

Who knew?

The doors swung open as I turned to leave. It's true what they say: you *can* find anything at Bieberman's.

Ashes to Ashes

-+-

Jack C. Haldeman II

I can't sleep on airplanes.

The man next to me certainly could. His head was back and he was snoring loudly with his mouth open. He wore an old corduroy suit that had been rumpled even before we left New York. That had been hours ago, hours of having the kids behind me kick my seat, listening to babies cry and mothers complain in a dozen different languages. Hours of bad food and a movie I'd seen before. The man shifted in his sleep and his arm flopped over onto my leg. I pushed it back. He didn't wake up. The moon reflected off the water an impossible distance below. We were above the Atlantic, somewhere between Greenland and England, heading for Amsterdam.

His name was Johann Schrijuer. Or maybe it wasn't. I should never have listened to him, but I needed the work. And the pay? Considerable enough for me to pass the three cases I was working on over to Sam, who has an office across the hall. Considerable enough for me to agree to take on this crazy job and to get stuffed into this cattle-car of an airplane, something I regretted even before they finished the oxygen mask lecture. By the time they showed me how to inflate my life vest, I knew it was a big mistake.

My name's Dan Harris and I'm a private eye, duly licensed by the city and state of New York. I'm not that great to be honest, but I do have a reputation for finding things that disappeared under questionable circumstances.

Most of the time it's simple; a spouse in a divorce case, or an employee helping himself to more than his salary. Once in a while they're complicated, and those are the kind I really like. It took a lot of legwork to find who switched Mrs. Bowen's diamond brooch, as it went undetected for more than five years. Or the time I chased the shadow of a "lost" Picasso full circle to a hidden room in the basement of the owner's house. I like the hard ones, the harder the better. Once I get to nibbling on one, I don't let go.

And then there are the two strange ones I can't explain.

The Bradshaw case concerned the theft of a near priceless urn containing the ashes of Bradshaw's grandfather. I found it in a random locker in Grand Central Station. I have no idea how I did that.

Then there was the mummy that disappeared from an Egyptian exhibit. Turns out it had been stolen as a prank by a street gang. I walked right to the building where they had stashed it.

In both cases something strange happened, and I felt guided more by a feeling of intuition than any interpretation of physical clues. But it wasn't exactly intuition, more like there was someone walking beside me, pulling me to the bones and ashes. It was very strange. Or maybe it was luck. I've had my share of that, too.

Regardless, those two cases don't appear on my résumé. I don't talk about them. Never. It scares me to even think about them.

Anyway, my preference for difficult cases is why Johann, if that's his name, was referred to me, and showed up at my office with an offer I could not refuse.

My office is a joke. I've got one room and a desk in a part of the city where rents are low and it's not safe to walk at night without a big dog. I share a secretary with three other people. Ray runs an executive apartment-seeking firm, which is really only Ray and the classified section of the Sunday *Times*. Larry is in the import/export business, but I've never seen him export anything. His imports all arrive in small packages and envelopes from a post office box in Queens and his clients never hang around very long. Claire runs the phones for an escort service, and her employees are a lot more attractive than Larry's clients. Our secretary is Louise, a sharp woman who knows her business. Nothing much surprises her, though she did raise an eyebrow that morning when she first brought Johann Schrijuer into my ten-by-twelve cubbyhole office.

I think it was disapproval over his olive-green corduroy suit. It was an ugly color I hadn't seen in years.

After we were alone, he pulled up a chair. "I want to hire you," he said, "to find some artifacts that were stolen from a group I represent. They have no physical value whatsoever, but to us, they are priceless." He could have been around fifty, give or take ten years. Wire-rimmed glasses, dark hair a little on the long side, neatly trimmed goatee. His suit, besides being that hideous color, had an odd cut to it. He spoke English with an accent I couldn't place.

"Exactly what artifacts are we talking about?" I asked. "I need some idea if what I'm looking for is possible to find before I agree to take the case."

"I can't reveal that to you at this time," he said. "If you agree to help us, you will be given a full explanation."

"I don't like the sound of this," I said.

Johann took a small velvet bag from his pocket and passed it to me. "A retainer," he said.

I loosened the drawstring and shook the contents out on my desk blotter. Diamonds. A lot of diamonds. I picked one up and walked to the window. Even in the weak winter Manhattan sun, it sparkled. I didn't know much about diamonds, but if these babies were real, an early retirement loomed on the horizon. I leaned against the sill and looked at the man.

"Just who do you represent?" I asked. "Is your group legitimate?"

"I am negotiating for your services on behalf of potential clients," he said. "More than that I cannot say until you meet with them."

"Ridiculous," I said, walking back to the desk. "I can't possibly . . ."

"I believe you will find the advance quite satisfactory," he said, nodding toward the diamonds. "The stones are of the highest quality and carefully prepared. They are of modest, yet sufficient size." I sat on the edge of the desk and moved the diamonds around with my finger. They *were* beautiful.

"Their modest size eliminates the possibility that they could be traced by certificates," Johann said with a small smile. "I'm sure that will increase your options. Yet they are of sufficient size to be mounted in exquisite settings, and should bring a substantial return."

"I would need to have them appraised," I said.

"No problem." Johann shrugged. "You can do that this afternoon?"

I nodded.

"Good," he said, rising from his chair. "Our plane leaves for Amsterdam tomorrow pm from JFK."

"But . . ."

"I understand you have a valid passport, Mr. Harris," he said. "I also understand that you are not likely to have any problems accepting unconventional retainers. And remember, these are simply a retainer; should you retrieve our material, your reward will be quite substantial." He handed me an envelope and walked to the door. "I suggest you have them appraised immediately."

I did. Then I packed my bag. The envelope contained a KLM airplane ticket and a hotel reservation slip for the Hotel Schiller Karina in Amsterdam. I put the diamonds in my safe deposit box at the bank. They checked out at a conservative $80,000. The appraiser said they were very fine stones and he could find me a buyer for the lot within an hour anytime I wanted, but that I could get more if I waited and broke it down into smaller lots. I decided to wait. There might be more where those came from.

So that's how I found myself strapped in this silver bird, hoping we could fool the law of gravity long enough to touch down in Holland. I hate to travel, even as far as New Jersey. The only reason I had a passport at all was that three years ago I'd planned on a week of fun and sun in Barbados with a new friend. By the time the passport had arrived, she was an ex-friend and I had long since turned the tickets into several bottles of expensive scotch, most of which were ex themselves.

As I watched the maybe Mr. Johann Schrijuer snore in the seat beside me, I wondered just how much he *did* know about me.

I'd slipped a peek at the name on his passport when we had entered the international terminal at JFK. I'd only gotten a glance at it, and couldn't make it out. Whatever it was, though, it wasn't Johann Schrijuer. I wondered about that, too.

Whatever his name was, he slept while I tried to read a paperback I'd picked up at JFK. Eventually, they served us breakfast just before landing. He slept through that too. Or he seemed to.

"Have you seen that flight attendant before?" he asked, as I was struggling with the sealed cap on my orange juice. "The man who gave you your tray?"

I shrugged. "I didn't notice."

"Ah, well," he sighed. "This changes things. Here, you may need this." He passed me an envelope. It was stuffed with traveler's checks issued in Dutch guilders. They were all 500-guilder notes and my signature had been neatly forged on each. At about $250 U.S. per note, I was holding several thousand dollars, assuming the checks were a tad more on the real side than my signature.

"What?" I said.

"Before we land, would you like to tell me how you came to find that funeral urn?" he asked. "I'm curious how you picked one locker out of so many." I looked at him. He had the hint of a wry grin that I couldn't interpret.

"No," I said coldly. "I don't want to talk about it."

"Nor the mummy, I suppose," he said with a smile. "You *do* seem to have a knack with long-dead objects."

"Fasten your seat belt," I said. "We'll be landing in a few minutes."

He reached under his seat, got his briefcase, rose, and stood in the aisle. "Take care, Mr. Harris," he said, and headed toward the bathrooms at the end of the plane.

"Wait," I said, and followed him, catching up just as he slipped into one of the rooms. I waited for a couple of minutes and tried the door. It was unlocked.

He was gone.

I stepped in to make sure. The room was musty and damp, with a faint, acidic smell. In spite of having been used all through the trip, every surface was now covered with a fine, undisturbed layer of dust and mold. It reminded me of a long-deserted tomb. I shivered, and made my way back to my seat. What was happening?

"Mr. Harris." It was the flight attendant Johann had asked about.

"Can you tell me where Mr. Smith is?" he asked.

"Smith?" I said.

"Your traveling companion," he said, indicating the empty seat.

"I don't know him," I lied. "Never saw him before the flight. Maybe he changed seats."

"Perhaps," said the man, waving to another flight attendant. He wasn't buying it, but there wasn't much he could do, not here. "Enjoy your stay in Holland," he said in clipped tones, without an ounce of sincerity.

It was another half-hour before we landed. I spent the time with an unread magazine in my lap. Now I had another disappeared item to deal with; a man who couldn't make up his mind in the name department. A man who knew a lot more about me than I liked.

When we landed at Schipol Airport it was in the middle of a cold rainy drizzle. I was alone, I didn't know a soul in Amsterdam, or in all of Europe for that matter. The rain somehow seemed appropriate.

On top of it all, they had lost my bag. I filled out numerous forms and was interviewed twice by suspicious officials. While I was doing this I cashed two of the traveler's checks without any problem. When I'd signed the last piece of paper, I walked easily through customs, and out into a foreign country for the first time in my life.

I just stood there for a minute, taking it all in as busy people hurried by. Airports have a sameness about them, which was about the only familiar thing around. The signs and billboards were all in a language I couldn't read. Conversations I couldn't understand floated around me. It had an alien feel to it, and New York seemed a universe away.

I thought about taking a cab into Amsterdam. I could certainly afford it. At the last minute I saw a pictogram pointing to trains, and headed up the escalator. A cab would only insulate me from the country, and if I was going to do this right, I needed a feel for the place. I might as well get started.

Luckily, the woman at the ticket booth spoke English, or I might have gotten stuck right there. She said most people in Holland spoke English, so I shouldn't worry. I worried. It's in my nature to worry. It has saved my ass more than once.

The train was crowded, but I got a seat by a window. Flat countryside, green even in winter, rolled by under the gray sky. The people around me all seemed to know one another but I couldn't understand a word they said, and soon their voices were just background noise to me as I stared out the window at endless fields filled with cows and sheep huddled together in the rain.

Small backyard gardens stretched from the houses to the tracks, even as we got close to town. Since my knowledge of vegetables starts and ends with the salad bar at Wendy's, I couldn't identify anything.

The train station was chaotic, and the instant I hopped off, I was hopelessly disoriented and confused. The place was packed with people, mostly young men and women with backpacks. On the street outside, a calliope was playing loudly. A group of dancers were performing enthusiastically to the raucous accompaniment of drums and battery-powered electric guitars. Long, segmented trams clanged importantly, missing the milling pedestrians by inches. Culture shock pounded in my ears and I caught the first cab I saw.

The Hotel Schiller Karina was an old building in the middle of a block facing a park. It may have been handsome or historic, but I was dead tired and jet-lagged to the bone. It was all I could do to check in and go up the winding, narrow staircase to my room.

The room was small, but tidy. Louvered windows looked out over the park. The room was too hot, so I turned the heat down and cracked the windows. For about three seconds I considered taking a shower, but ended up just kicking off my shoes and flopping on the bed. I slept like a dead man.

A knock on the door woke me up. The room was dark. I'd managed to sleep through my first day in a foreign country. Some traveler. I fumbled for a light switch, found one, stumbled over one of my shoes, and opened the door.

"Your suitcase has arrived, Mr. Harris," said the young woman, as she entered the room holding my bag in one hand and balancing a tray in the other.

"Thanks," I said, taking the bag. She set the tray on the desk. "I didn't order anything," I said.

She shrugged. "It came from the kitchen." I gave her a few large coins, hoping it was enough of a tip. The money was still a mystery to me. She smiled and left. The tray had a small carafe of coffee, three bottles of Dutch beer and a basket with hard rolls, cheese and cold cuts. A card was underneath the basket.

Escape Cafe, it read. *Midnight.*

The card was unsigned. I checked my watch. It was still on New York time, so I reset it. Almost nine.

I poured a cup of coffee and opened my suitcase. As I was digging out a shirt, my hand hit something hard. I knew immediately what it was, just as I knew I hadn't packed it.

My gun. Still in its shoulder holster.

I set it on the bed and stared at it. I've had it almost twenty years, and it's a hell of a lot more constant than most things in my life. But here in an Amsterdam hotel room it looked alien and sinister. There's no way I would have considered taking it on a plane. Who? How? Why?

Going through my suitcase, I found a box of ammunition. I opened it. Seven rounds gone, just like I left it after my last trip to the shooting range. Someone was playing with me.

The shower was nothing more than a corner of the bathroom with no tub, just a drain in the sloping floor. I figured that out a lot quicker than how to flush the toilet, which had some weird thing on top I pushed about ten times before I discovered you had to pull it. At least there was lots of hot water for the shower.

I was still angry about the gun when I got out of the shower, but at least I was cleaner. I made a sandwich and opened one of the beers, which I'd set out on the window ledge to stay cool.

I sat in a chair and looked out the window. The park was surrounded by shops, restaurants and bars. The buildings were narrow and jammed together. It reminded me a little of parts of Brooklyn. People were walking up and down the sidewalks, in the middle of the streets and through the park. I felt better after my nap and shower, and tried to think a couple of things through.

Someone was jacking me around, that much was clear. But they were paying a lot for the privilege. I wasn't sure how much leeway that bought them. I finished the beer and decided they'd bought at least enough leeway for me to see what they wanted. That, and figure out how they'd smuggled my gun into Amsterdam. I strapped it on before I went downstairs, loading it first. Like I say, I have a tendency to worry.

The desk was no help at all. My suitcase hadn't been delivered by the airline, but by a young man who simply dropped it off. The tray from the kitchen had been paid for by a stranger in their restaurant. No one had ever seen him before. They gave me directions to the Escape Cafe, and advised me that if I was foolish enough to go there, I should take a cab. It was in the middle of the red light district, and not safe at night.

I took them up on the cab, not because I was especially hesitant to walk around at night, but because the map they gave me was confusing. There didn't seem to be a straight street in all of Amsterdam; they all curved around the canals, which looped around the inner city in more or less concentric semicircles. A New York boy like me was guaranteed to get lost, being used to a city where streets are laid out in tidy grids like streets ought to be.

It was cold, but not too bad. The streets were slick with the afternoon rain, not quite turned to ice. We drove quickly through a dark residential area and then past a street full of closed shops. The central square, all wet cobblestone, was deserted, though scattered people sat on the steps of the buildings around it, huddled in doorways and under overhangs. We turned a corner and the city came to life. Here there was noise, lights, many people. I looked at my watch. I was early.

"How much further?" I asked the driver as he stopped to let some pedestrians cross in front of us.

"Three blocks to the canal," he said. "Then left for two blocks."

"I'll get out here," I said.

"If you like," he replied politely.

The area was crammed with shops and milling people. Most of

the people were young, and most of the shops featured, in one way or another, sex or drugs. A significant percentage of the people looked stoned.

The "soft" drugs—marijuana and hashish—though technically illegal, are tolerated in Holland. They are sold openly in dope bars; even licensed and taxed by the government.

Louise, my secretary, has been here a couple of times on vacations. She made a point of warning me about the space cakes, a kind of super-powerful hash brownie. She needn't have bothered. I'll take Heineken over hash any day.

On this street I could take my pick of almost anything. Every third building seemed to be a bar, and most were crowded. With a few exceptions, most of the beer bars were loud and packed. Dope bars came in all flavors, from filthy ratholes to elaborate, expensive places. Some had loud music, some soft. Pick and choose.

There were shop windows full of pipes and rolling papers; other stores displayed magazines and tapes of every sexual combination I could imagine, and a few that had never occurred to me. In between were all kinds of ethnic restaurants and assorted carryout shops. A good number of people were carrying paper cones filled with French fries, dripping—yuk—with mayonnaise. It was, for the most part, a good-natured crowd out for a fun night. I caught sight of a few characters with trouble written all over their faces, but they stayed in the doorways or off the main drag.

When I reached the canal, I knew I was in the right place. Red lights lined the narrow streets that ran along both sides of the water. Red lights hung from the bridges that crossed the canal. Red lights burned beside most of the windows and doorways. I turned left.

The road was very narrow, and people were elbow to elbow. Once in a while a car, usually a taxi, would try to get through, but it was clearly quicker and easier to walk. There were more sex shops here than on the cross street, and the owners were much more aggressive, standing at their doorways, calling out why their shop was better than any of the others. Even more aggressive were the doormen for the live sex shows, who grabbed at people walking by and tried to entice them to pull out their credit cards for a guaranteed good time.

Many of the large ground floor windows had women sitting carefully posed with their props, which ran from teddy bears to whips. I noticed that white lace lingerie under UV lights seemed to be very popular. Within a block, I'd figured out the routine: point to the side door and negotiate the arrangement. I saw a few ex-NFL linebacker types lurking in the shadows as the protection. None of the men I saw walking out of these places were smiling. Too bad.

It's a crazy world, but I didn't make it, and I'm slow to judge it. People need people, I guess, and if they have to pay or sell to do that, it's none of my business. It made me kind of sad, though.

By the time I reached the Escape Cafe, I'd been offered hard drugs three times, approached by free-lance hookers twice and had one dumb pickpocket try to get my wallet. He won't be using that hand for a couple of weeks. Times Square at this time of night is a lot rougher.

The Escape Cafe was a half-flight down from the street. It was dark, wood-paneled, and nearly deserted. I stood in the doorway a moment and looked around.

Two tables were occupied. One table seemed to be a Japanese tour group and the other held a couple of lovebirds exploring each other's fingertips over glasses of wine. No one looked up. All the seats at the bar were empty, so I walked in and sat at one.

The barmaid came over and smiled at me. She was maybe twenty-five, dark hair, and had a warm, friendly smile. "A beer, please," I said. She walked over to a large decorated porcelain jug that held the tap and pulled the beer, scraping the foam off the top with a plastic knife.

"Three guilders," she said pleasantly as she sat it in front of me.

I pulled some funny money out of my wallet and stared at it. I guess I stared too long because she pulled a bill out of my hand, held it in front of me and said "May I?" I nodded, and she made change.

"American?" she asked.

"Good guess," I said.

"Been here what? Two, three days?"

"Close enough."

She laughed. "I have a sister who lives in Chicago. She does modern dance. Do you live near Chicago?"

"New York," I said.

"Close enough." She made a pathetic attempt to mimic my voice.

We both laughed.

Her name was Anna and she was easy to talk with. For the first time in days I relaxed a little as we made light, casual conversation. She had been born in Germany, but was a Swiss citizen. For the past few years, she'd been living in Holland. She was curious about New York, having been all over Europe, but never to the U.S.

I didn't see him come in, but Anna's voice suddenly turned cold and distant. I looked in the mirror and saw Johann coming up to the bar. He was wearing the same dumb suit, but with a matching overcoat this time.

"Come with me," he said, standing behind me. "Now, Mr. Harris. Hurry."

I stood up. Anna had turned her back, and was busy polishing a counter that didn't need to be polished.

"Thanks," I said. She didn't reply.

I followed Johann out the door. We turned left into the crowd.

"You weren't followed," he said. It was a statement, not a question.

"Were you expecting someone to tail me?"

"One never knows," he said. "Turn here."

I had other questions, and asked them, but he clammed up, shoved his hands in his pockets and walked without answering.

We crossed over the canal and into a side street. It wasn't deserted, but there were considerably fewer people walking around. It seemed to be a mix of residences and businesses.

After a couple of blocks, Johann turned into a dope bar. Thankfully, it was a quiet one, with sitar music playing softly in the background. A few couples sat at small tables covered with burlap, smoking and talking.

Johann went straight to the back and through a door. I followed him up a very tight circular staircase. The steps were only about four inches deep, and I hoped that none of the customers downstairs would have to negotiate these to find the bathroom. We went up two flights and through several very sturdy doors, each guarded by a heavily armed bruiser.

I needn't have worried about dope-impaired customers. Upstairs was clearly off limits. The floor was one large room running the length of the building, with a bathroom and kitchen partitioned off. The furniture was, for the most part, old, bulky and very expensive. Three desks, which were probably older than I was, held modern computers. There were five people in the room when we arrived; four men with shotguns and a woman. Of the group, the woman—tall and gaunt—looked the most dangerous. I thought about pulling my gun, but the odds were awful.

And then I felt it. I didn't recognize it at first because it was weak. But it was the same odd feeling I had when I was trying to find the mummy. It felt like there was somebody half inside me and half outside, pulling me. Without thinking I took two steps toward the far end of the room, where an ornately decorated screen hid whatever was in the corner. I had to will myself to stop walking, and even so, I took another half-step in that direction. Four shotguns were aimed at my head. "Good," said Johann. "Very good."

I didn't see one damn good thing about it.

"You all may leave," he said. Three of the shotguns quit pointing at my brain and headed for the door.

"You sure?" asked the fourth.

"It's okay, David," he said. "Everything is under control."

That left three of us. The woman sat at the head of a glass-covered conference table and indicated that we join her.

"He doesn't look like much," she said as I sat down.

"Mr. Harris is exactly what we were seeking," Johann said.

"I sincerely hope so," she said, and turned to me. "You see, Mr. Harris, our group has lost some items that have considerable value to us. We have reason to believe that these items will not remain in this country very long, and it is imperative that we retrieve them before they are lost to us forever."

"And what am I supposed to be looking for?"

"Bones," she said. "Bones, ashes, and a small wooden bowl."

A chill sent shivers through me. The feeling was strong now. "Bones?" I stifled a nervous laugh. "You brought me halfway around the world for bones?"

"There is a lot at stake here, Mr. Harris," said Johann. "Several organizations would stop at nothing to get these artifacts. Do you realize how much influence it takes to replace the staff of a transatlantic flight with your own agents on such notice? Consider that, and understand that such action is minor compared to what they—and we—are capable of."

"Like disappearing?" I asked. "Where did you go?"

"A magician's trick," he said with a wave of his hand. "Nothing at all. It was a minor inconvenience, but necessary. I could not be detained."

"And my gun?" I asked. "Was that another magician's trick?"

"We could easily have provided you with one," said the woman. "But this is an important and delicate issue. A person such as you is likely to feel more comfortable with a familiar weapon. It may give you the slightest edge, and we need all the help we can get."

"It sounds like you need an army," I said.

"We can provide one if necessary," said Johann. "We are, as you are aware, not without resources. All we need from you is the location of the artifacts. We will handle it from there."

"But why me?" I asked. "I couldn't even find the library in this city, assuming there is one."

"You know very well why we picked you, Mr. Harris," said the woman.

I nodded. That was true.

"So what's so special about these bones?" I asked. "Whose are they?"

"Some say they are the bones of a saint," said the woman. "Others believe the person was quite the opposite of a saint. It doesn't matter. What is important is that they have immense power,

power that we have used over the years to amass a great fortune. We need them back."

"And the bowl?"

"Ah, yes," said the woman. "The bowl. Some have called it a chalice, a grail. To me, it is simply a bowl. It will be with the bones and ashes. It has power too, but only certain people can utilize that power. If you locate the bowl, do not attempt to physically touch it. It is said that only the pure can come in contact with it. Purity, in this day and age, is a rare commodity. I myself would not qualify, nor—I assume—would you."

I had to admit that was true.

"What's behind the screen?" I asked.

She looked sharply at me and then to Johann. He smiled.

"You *are* the man for this endeavor," she said, getting up and walking to the screen. "Come over here." She moved the screen aside, revealing a small table with a pad of green felt on top. I was drawn to the table, and could not have backed away if I wanted. On the pad was a very small sliver of bone, maybe a half an inch long.

"They missed this when they stole the rest," said the woman. "It has limited power by itself, and not much range. But this will give you an idea of what you are looking for."

She touched the bone and her face melted.

It was as if she was a wax dummy too near a flame. All her features blurred and slipped, moving constantly as if there were living creatures sliding around between her flesh and bone, twisting and turning. Slowly her face shifted and reformed.

It was my face. Exactly, except that my eyes glowed red and smoke drifted from my nostrils. Terror grabbed me and would not release me. It was like looking at my own death. I tried to move, and couldn't. Every muscle was frozen.

"I could kill you," she said with my voice. "I could simply stop your heart, or force you to do anything I want. And this, all from the small piece of bone they overlooked. When they are all together, there is no limit to our power. It has proved quite helpful in our business endeavors. You must understand how much we want them back, and how we will stop at nothing."

I gasped, unable to speak.

She grinned, and maggots spilled from my mouth. My eyes became hollow sockets swarming with insects. The flesh slid from my face like rotting tissue.

Mercifully she stepped away from the table. Her face slowly shifted back.

"We know the artifacts are still in the city," said Johann. "Find them."

Somehow I managed to get down the stairs and out into the street.

I was in a cold sweat, shaking with fear. There were too many things here I didn't want to know, but I could not ignore them. The same force that led me to the mummy was with me now, and would not leave, I realized, until I had seen this thing through.

I was walking aimlessly, sucking the cold night air with ragged breaths. I didn't want to be here. I didn't want to have to face whatever it was that was pulling me, but there was no choice. And then I saw her.

"Anna!" I shouted. "Wait up!" She turned away, walking quickly. I ran, and caught up with the closest thing to a friend I had on this side of the planet.

"Leave me alone," she said.

"But, I . . ."

"You work for him," she said. "I don't want to have anything to do with you."

"I don't understand," I said.

She stopped, turned and looked at me.

"He smuggles heroin, you know."

"I didn't know," I said.

"Maybe you didn't," she said, cocking her head. "I can usually read people fairly well and I had you pegged as a pretty straight guy. That loathsome man destroys people's lives."

"I thought he was a diamond merchant, something like that."

"You work for him, though. Right?"

"I'm not sure," I said truthfully.

"Which way are you headed?" she asked.

"Schiller Karina," I said. 'Do you want to share a cab?"

"I'm going that way, but I'd rather walk. Join me?"

"Sure," I said.

It was getting late and the back streets we walked were almost deserted. We talked in the cold night, mostly about nothing much. I'm afraid I did most of the talking, to keep from thinking about what I'd just seen. And through it all, the force within me was looking, looking; seeking out bones and ashes in the darkness.

We crossed a couple of canals, and came to the hotel. I rang the night bell and waited for someone to come to the door.

"What's the best way to see most of the city?" I asked Anna. "Should I take a tram?"

"A tour boat would be better," she said. "Trams mostly run in straight lines, the boats circle around. But you don't look like the tourist type to me."

"It's something I have to do."

She looked at me in that funny way of hers, and seemed to reach a decision. "If you want to take one," she said, "I'll go with you."

"That'd be great, thanks," I said. "Nothing like a native guide."

"Meet me after work, and we'll catch one."

"At the Escape Cafe?"

"No," she laughed, pulling out a piece of paper and scribbling on it. "That's what I do to make enough money to stay alive. My real job is here. Two o'clock this afternoon?"

She passed me the paper.

"Safe Place?" I read aloud.

"That's the address underneath it."

The night clerk opened the door.

"I'll see you tomorrow, Anna," I said.

"Good night." She turned and left.

The moment I walked into my room I knew someone had been there. It was a very professional job, and it took me a few minutes to find the small tell-tale signs. They had gone through everything and put it back very neatly, exactly as they found it. But nothing is ever exact. I have a bad habit of leaving the top of my aftershave unscrewed a little bit. It was tight. A book I was reading was open to the wrong page.

I was sure the desk would be no help, especially the night staff. There was nothing to do about it now, so I went to bed.

My sleep was an endless procession of nightmare images, each worse than the one before.

My cab driver found Safe Place without any trouble. It turned out to be a large old building a little outside the central city. There was a wrought iron gate out front and Anna was waiting there.

"Come on in," she said, opening the gate. "I just need to get my stuff."

Inside, there were kids everywhere. It was a madhouse, but a happy madhouse. Posters and crayon drawings lined the walls. It was mostly one large room, partitioned off into smaller areas by waist-high bookcases. There were different activities and different age groups in each area. Some were reading by themselves, some sitting around an adult. Over in the corner a group seemed to be putting on a play. Piano music drifted from upstairs.

"Dan, I'd like you to meet Sarah Burton, the founder of Safe Place." Sarah was a slight, elderly woman. She had a warm smile that put me instantly at ease.

"Pleased to meet you," I said. Her handshake was firm. "Interesting place you have here. Is it a school?"

"We do some teaching here," she said, "but mostly it's a haven."

"Pardon?"

"These are all children who have fallen through the cracks of society for one reason or another. Some live in abusive families, some have no real family at all. We provide a safe place for them, a place where they can feel secure and unthreatened."

"I'm impressed," I said. "It sounds great."

"We couldn't do it without people like Anna and the others," she said. "All our workers are volunteers. I wish we could pay them, but we exist entirely on donations and it is all we can do to keep the buildings open and buy supplies."

"Miss Burton has established three Safe Places," said Anna. "The others are in Germany and France. Plus, she's got two sites lined up in Africa."

"Those are dreams, Anna," she said. "The money just isn't there."

"We're nothing without dreams," said Anna, and then she looked at her watch. "Time to go."

"It was nice meeting you, Miss Burton," I said. "Good luck."

"And good luck to you, too," she said.

We took a tram back to the center of Amsterdam. Anna had a pass, but I had to buy a *strippen-kaart,* a long slip of paper with incomprehensible instructions written in tiny letters in a language I didn't understand. Anna folded it and slipped it in a box that stamped it. All the way into town that buried part of me kept looking for something it couldn't find.

The tour boats were docked right down from the train station. We got the last seats on one that was just leaving. I sat by the window and slid it open as the pilot backed the small, low boat into the canal.

The narration started. It was on tape in several languages. English was last, and by the time a point of interest was noted, we were usually past it. No problem; I wasn't looking for the narrowest house or where the Mayor lived. I was looking for bones. And a bowl.

They were still here, that much I was sure of. I felt a kind of trembling or resonance as the boat circled around. Sometimes it was stronger than others, but it was always there, pulling at me.

I scanned the houseboats and the narrow houses that lined the canals. Somehow I knew it would come. When I found the mummy back in New York, I'd had a cabby drive me around. He probably thought I was crazy, and I would have agreed with him right up until the moment I busted through the door and saw it propped up against a wall.

Something stirred when we passed the Anne Frank house. It grew stronger when the boat cut through a side canal and under a low bridge. Then it hit me.

There! That house in the middle of the block. The pull was so hard I had to hold the seat to keep from going out the window and swimming over to it.

"What's wrong, Dan?" asked Anna, an anxious look on her face. "Are you okay?"

"Address," I stammered. "Red door, cracked window. Right there. I need the address."

"It's fifty-two," she said. "See the number?"

"Fifty-two what?" I snapped.

She said the name of the canal. It went right past me; too many consonants and not enough vowels.

"Write it down for me," I said. "I *need* it!"

She fumbled in her purse for paper and pen as I shook and sweated, deep into the grip of something I didn't understand.

It lasted until the boat turned into another canal. I sat there white-knuckled and breathing hard, while Anna stared at me.

"Dan?" she said. "What's wrong?"

"Something frightened me," I said. It was the truth.

"That house?"

I nodded, and sat quietly until we got back to the dock. Amsterdam passed by me in a watery blur. I had other things on my mind.

Anna, of course, noticed, and when I tried to leave after the boat ride, she protested.

"I'll take the night off," she said. "You don't look well at all, Dan."

"I need to be alone for a while," I said.

She finally agreed, if I promised to call her at Safe House tomorrow. I did, and we separated.

I wandered for a while, and stopped at a cafe to wait for dark. I had a beer, and on a whim ordered a bowl of mushroom soup. It was rich and creamy. I followed that up with three leisurely cups of coffee. What I'd heard about European cafes was true, they didn't rush me. I could have stayed all night without anybody bothering me.

And so could the man at the table by the front door. He'd sat down just after I arrived and had been matching me coffee for coffee. When I asked for my bill, he did too. I didn't like that a whole lot.

I left the unpaid bill and my umbrella at the table and walked to the bar, as if to ask where the rest rooms were. Instead, I asked if they had a back door. They did. I gave the bartender ten times what my bill was and indicated I wouldn't mind if they ran interference for me with the guy by the front door. He agreed. I slipped out.

The back door opened onto a pedestrian walkway. I buried myself in the crowd and took the first turn, cutting through a clothing store. There didn't seem to be anyone behind me, but I kept twisting and turning. I'm used to the cat-and-mouse game, and I felt pretty sure no cats were following this particular mouse.

I didn't want to call the number Johann had given me. Sure, he'd hired me, but that display last night had been a little much. And I trusted Anna one hell of a lot more than I trusted him or that creepy woman. What I wanted to do was check the place out by myself and get a feel for what was happening.

Luckily, it got dark early this far north in winter. With the help of the hotel's map and the weird pull those bones and ashes had on me, I located it easily. It was much harder to stay outside, so strong was the wrenching force on me.

I hid behind a parked car and watched the house. Through the lace curtains I could see several men walking around on the first floor. The other floors were dark. The lights from the house and several houseboats danced on the canal. I was trying to make up my mind about what to do next when someone made my mind up for me.

"We've been expecting you, Mr. Harris," he said, making his point by shoving something hard in the small of my back. "Hands behind the head. Go to the front door."

I make it a point never to argue with superior firepower, so I did as instructed. The door opened and I went inside.

Maybe half a dozen men stood around the room. They were smiling, but there wasn't one friendly or funny thing in sight. One of them took my gun and set it on a table about five feet away. With a healthy lunge I could get it in a second. They didn't seem to care.

Me, I only had eyes for a wooden box on the table next to my gun. It pulled at me with incredible force.

"You're in way over your head, Mr. Harris," said a heavy-set man in jeans and a sweater as he leaned against the table, his hand on the box. Another man slammed me down into a chair.

"You want me to tie him up, Mark?"

"That won't be necessary," said the man leaning on the box. "Isn't that right, Mr. Harris?"

I nodded. I couldn't move my legs. It was the same effect as last night, but weaker. Sufficient to keep me in my chair, however.

"You see," said Mark, "I don't have to touch the bones to use them. Proximity is enough. And I . . ."

He was interrupted by a noise at the door. A man shoved Anna into the room. "She was outside," he said.

"Anna!" I cried.

"I'm sorry, Dan," she said. "I was worried about you. I thought you might come here."

"Shut up," said Mark. "Put her in the chair next to Mr. Stupid."

When Anna had come in, I felt the hold on my legs weaken. Either the power was limited or the thug didn't know how to use it effectively when he was distracted.

"Who are you with?" snapped Mark, glaring at Anna. "United States? The Frenchman? Who?"

"Dan!" cried Anna. "What's happening? I can't move."

"Leave her alone," I said. "She doesn't know anything."

"And you don't seem to know much more," he said.

"I know you searched my room," I said.

"Why would we do that?" he asked. "You are a minor player in this drama. Actually, it was a group from the United States that searched your room. They also staffed your plane with their people. The group represents a certain Texas millionaire with connections to the CIA. They have a lot of money, but they couldn't offer me what I want. What I want is power. And with my new friends, that is exactly what I will have."

"Friends?"

"If you know them at all, you know them as a terrorist group. They are, however, well-situated and have a great deal of oil money at their disposal. They intend to diversify, and the bones are the key."

"Bones?" gasped Anna.

"Ah yes, the bones," said Mark. "And the ashes. There are many stories about them, some of which may be true. I have heard it said that Hitler had the bones, as did the Kaiser before him, but that they were stolen by the Russians toward the end of the war. Others hold to different theories. History makes no difference to me. They are powerful, and I have them. That's all that matters. Your Dutch friends, Mr. Harris, sadly underestimated their potential. They used the bones for many trivial things, such as stock market manipulation and assuring their heroin shipments arrived undisturbed. A colossal waste for something with global power."

"And the bowl?" I asked. "The chalice?"

"Worthless," he snapped. "The power of the grail cannot be used for personal gain, nor can it be used for any evil purpose. It may only be used to better the fate of all mankind. Of course the bones can do that too, if the holder is stupid enough to have a weakness for benevolent actions. But the bones do not carry the same restrictions as the grail."

A series of gunshots echoed in from the street. I could feel Mark's attention waver, for my legs were free. Using everything I had, I lunged for my gun. I almost made it.

He was watching the door, but saw me out of the corner of his eye. I fell to the floor, gasping for breath, my chest burning. I was two ticks away from a heart attack. My gun levitated from the table and shattered as if it were made of glass.

Then all hell broke loose.

The door burst into flying splinters and a creature drawn from every bad nightmare I've ever had exploded into the room, spitting smoke and sparks while tossing fireballs at everything in sight.

Mark, distracted, released my tortured heart just this side of the grave. He flipped open the wooden box and pulled out what looked like a piece of a leg bone. A green shimmering light surrounded him and two fireballs bounced off it, ricocheting around the room, starting a number of small fires.

The creature roared, and I saw the small sliver of bone hanging on a silver chain around its neck. It was the woman, and behind her was a grotesque parody of Johann, all fangs and claws.

"Dan!" Anna screamed. "Dan!"

I got up, and threw my chair through the front window. "Out," I yelled. "Get out."

Anna dove through the window. The woman-creature and Mark, who had shape-shifted into a disgusting beast covered with slime and scales, were locked in a deadly embrace. Smoke and fire were all around and an Uzi splattered the wall above my head.

I grabbed the wooden box and followed Anna out the window. The beast roared. I landed in the small front yard and sprinted to the street that ran along the canal.

"Look out, Dan!" yelled Anna.

It happened quickly. I saw a subhuman creature at the window and a ball of lightning spun toward me. I could smell the ashes and the bones pulling at me. The bowl in the box glowed a faint orange. At the very last instant, that thing that lives inside me said *protect* and a weak green shield surrounded me. Anna was holding me as the lightning hit and we were both knocked backwards into the canal just as the house exploded.

It was spectacular. Everything seemed to be moving in slow motion. As I sailed to the canal I saw the brick house rise about five feet into the air and collapse, taking parts of the buildings on either side of it. Then I hit the water and the box flew out of my arms.

The bones and ashes scattered in the air. As they hit the water they burst into blue flame. For a brief moment, the canal seemed to be on fire, then all was quiet except for the distant sirens and the low sizzling as the bones burned themselves out.

I saw the wooden bowl, the chalice, floating on the water. It wasn't far away. I swam to it, but as I approached it, the bowl began to glow a cherry red and the water around it boiled and churned. Regardless, I reached for it and the skin on my hand blistered and burned before I touched it. I screamed in raw pain.

"Dan!" yelled Anna.

"Over here," I cried, treading water. She swam toward me. "That bowl," I said. "Can you reach it?"

She could, and she did. That's when I knew things would work out okay. And I guess they will. Safe places for a lot of people.

So the flight back to New York was not too bad. But I cheated a little bit. I had a lucky piece in my shoe. A tiny sliver of bone I managed to salvage.

A man can't be too careful, you know.

Here There Be Dragons

✜

P. D. Cacek

Dr. Leo Matthias studied a rat-gray pigeon waddling the ledge outside his office window, then returned his gaze to the dapper old
man sitting across from him.

"Would you mind repeating that, sir."

"No, of course not. I would like a Paranoid-Schizophrenic with
Delusions of Grandeur, please," he answered. "To go."

"Ah."

The handy professional "Space Saver" was promptly marred by
a quick note. In Leo's $125-an-hour opinion, the old man had un-
doubtedly described his own mental aberration.

Which was something, at least.

Leo had walked into his office that morning to find the old man
sitting behind his desk, calmly leafing through the latest issue of
Psychology Today. The receptionist swore she hadn't let him in and
his appointment book showed no one scheduled for another hour.
But the polished nails, neatly trimmed beard and $500 Brooks
Brothers suit—along with the unusual request—piqued Leo's financial if not professional curiosity.

"For any particular reason, Mr. ... ?" Leo put down the antique ebony fountain pen to make eye contact. Usually that was
enough to initiate dialogue. Today it wasn't.

The old man looked straight back. And winked.

"Well, of course there's a reason, Doctor. To make such a request without reason would be ... madness."

You can say that again, buster. "And what would that reason be?"

"To participate in a quest."

Leo picked up his pen. "For what?"

"The Holy Grail, sir."

"Ah-*hah.*" He wrote *Don Quixote* on the notepad and underlined it twice. "And may I ask why you've decided to look for a Paranoid-Schizophrenic with Delusions of Grandeur for so lofty a mission? It would seem to me that a Knight Errant would be the more appropriate choice."

Leo never tried to argue or bully a patient out of an illusion—it ended the sessions too quickly and cut into profits.

"Welllll . . ." The old man chuckled and tugged on one corner of his beard. "Actually, it was Gordon Bradshaw's idea."

"Gordon Brad—" Leo set the pen down carefully and leaned back in his chair, moving his foot toward the recessed alarm button under his desk. One never knew when even the most sedate patient would become violent. "You mean the mass murderer?"

The old man found a piece of lint on the sleeve of his jacket and just as carefully removed it.

"Yes," he said, without looking up. "Not that he was my first choice, mind you; but you would be surprised at the number of *good* men who refused me."

When he finally looked up, the old man's face was slack with sorrow.

"They lacked the courage, you see . . . so I finally decided to go against tradition and look for men with—well, with perhaps less than a heroic reputation, but who have demonstrated the courage to go against society's norm." Deep-set eyes, the color of Leo's pen, sparkled as he spoke. "Gordon Bradshaw seemed a likely candidate . . . given that criteria. He proved even less willing to cooperate than the others had. However, he did offer me an option I had previously overlooked."

"And that was?" Leo asked.

"Well, to paraphrase the man's colloquial terminology . . . he was of the opinion that a man would have to be crazy to accept my offer.

"He then went on to suggest I engage in an activity which was physically impossible—considering how the neck is attached to the body . . ."

"Ah." Leo moved his foot away from the alarm and picked up his pen. The old man was a loon—plain and simple and harmless. Gordon Bradshaw would no more be allowed visitors than he would be given a flaying knife and bag of candy and told to go back to collecting children.

"Oh, and by the way, I don't think myself to be Don Quixote. *He* was a literary character spawned from imagination and fancy. *I* am quiet real."

Leo chuckled and turned the pad over. *Well, the old boy's got excellent eyes. I'll give him that.*

"I have excellent eyes, Dr. Matthias. As befits my name."

Coincidence. "Ah . . . I mean, yes. Mr. . . ."

"Myrddin Merlinus Emrys—the Falcon." He paused for effect. "But you may call me Merlin."

Leo had to fight the urge to clap his hands together. *Yes!*

"The Merlin? Like in *Le Morte d'Arthur?"*

A cloud suddenly blocked the sun and Leo heard the distant rumble of thunder echo through the deep high-rise canyons of glass and steel. Out of the corner of his eye, he saw the fat ledge-walking pigeon take to the air. A single feather, lost in flight, swirled in the gusting air.

"Yes," the old man said softly, *"that* Merlin."

Leo swallowed carefully, as visions of T-bills and time shares danced in his head.

"But I thought you'd been trapped in the Crystal Cave by whatshername"—Leo snapped his fingers as if he'd just remembered—"Morganna LeFey."

A brilliant white light, followed by a sizzling crack and the smell of ozone, filled the room. When the after image faded, Leo watched five more feathers—scorched and smoldering—spiral downward past the window.

"The bitch."

Leo blinked as a charred lump followed the feather's descent. "What?"

The old man twisted a corner of his mustache while a small tic began mamboing under his left eye. Leo dutifully added the information to his notes.

"I gave her the gifts of enchantment out of love and she . . ." A weary smile eased the tension from his face. "You have a saying that fits the situation I believe—*There's no fool like an old fool.* Unflattering, but unfortunately so true. I believe she's now selling real estate."

Leo set the pad aside, after jotting down the time and adding an hour's "Inconvenience Time," and folded his hands.

"Well, we've made an *excellent* start, Mr. . . . Merlin. And one that I'm sure we can continue to work through in the sessions to come. But now . . . if you'll excuse me, I do have other patients to see."

The old man didn't move except to drape one leg over the other. Getting comfortable. *Goddammit.* Leo stood up to show him how it was done and took a step toward the door.

"Just make an appointment with my receptionist." He smiled. Took another step. Went so far as to nod.

The old man nodded back. And stayed seated.

"Sir . . ."

"No, I'm afraid I was never knighted. True I am Arthur's cousin and counsel, but I thought it best not to place myself beneath his will. He needed a strong hand and if I were knighted . . ."

"Enough." Leo was toying with the idea of breaking one of his own rules and toss the potential Swiss Bank Account out on his ear. "The session, *sir,* is over. If you'd like to come back and talk to me about these delusions of yours—"

"Delusions?"

"—then make an appointment. Or, if you prefer, my receptionist can give you the name of another doctor equally qualified to treat your—condition. Either way, I'm afraid I must ask you to leave. Sir."

Leo had his hand on the doorknob when he turned around. The old man was standing: Red-faced, closed fists, set jaw . . . but standing.

The old man drew himself up and squared his shoulders. Leo

had originally placed him at about five seven to five eight—now he seemed closer to six feet. And heavier. Much heavier. Flesh seemed to be filling the wrinkles from the inside out.

"I am not psychotic, good doctor, nor will I leave until I have obtained that for which I have come."

The man's voice was deeper than it had been a moment before, and carried a lilting British accent. Leo mentally applauded the transformation—it took a real sickie to produce details like that—and opened the door a crack. If there were any threats going to be made, he wanted his receptionist to be able to testify later on.

"That's right, you wanted a paranoid-schizophrenic with delusions of grandeur." He patted the breast and side pockets of his sports coat with his free hand. "Sorry, fresh out. But just for your edification, *sir,* I'm not in the habit of handing out my patients. Even to the Wizard of King Arthur's court.

"Now get the hell out of my office before I have you physically ejected!"

Leo threw open the door and came face to slavering jaws with a dragon. Or, at least it appeared to be a dragon for the few nanoseconds he stared up into its bile-green eyes.

All three of them.

The door felt less than adequate as he slammed it shut and leaned back against it . . . considering the amount of snarling and clawing coming from the other side.

"What the hell is that?"

"A pet."

As if encouraged by the sound of its master's voice, the "pet" tried to drive the doorknob through Leo's spine. He barely felt it. Something far more interesting was happening in front of him.

The dark blue business suit which had fit the old man so perfectly a moment before suddenly looked ten sizes too big. It hung from his body—bunching at his ankles and elbows like a poorly chosen Goodwill hand-me-down.

In the brief respite between snarls and guttural hisses from the reception area, Leo heard a gentle ripping sound and watched the seams simultaneously tear themselves apart. The strips of material fluttered against the old man as if buffeted by a gentle breeze, then slowly melted into one another.

A mewling sound curled through the door just behind Leo's right ear as the old man took a step forward.

The hem of the midnight-blue gown whispered against the nap of the carpet as he stopped. Crude symbols stitched across the bodice and shoulders glimmered beneath the high-intensity track lights. The old man cocked his head and let his hand caress the sheathed knife—grip bound in leather, a milky-white stone set in the pommel—hanging at his waist. The tip of the sleeve, wide and full and edged in crimson, brushed against the arm of a chair and left a charred, blackened swath in its wake.

A thin coil of silver, crafted to resemble a living snake, curled around the old man's forehead. Leo caught a flash of emerald green from the thing's eyes as the old man turned and slowly walked to the window. He shook his head as he looked out, arms crossed over his chest . . . wisps of smoke curling upward from the hems of his sleeves.

"There are no more heroes, Doctor," he said without turning around. "It is a sad fact but one I cannot allow myself to dwell upon. Come here."

Leo wasn't about to move away from the door but discovered he had little choice in the matter. He glided over the plush 100-percent virgin wool without moving a muscle.

"Look down there."

Leo's nose squashed into the double-pane glass.

"Seven point three million people . . . and not one of them with the balls God gave a gnat."

Leo gurgled.

"No. No, don't try to justify their poor showing to me." The old man flicked a finger and Leo slid off the glass like a slug. "You people have been industrialized, sanitized, civilized . . . lobotomized into accepting one and only one reality."

He uncrossed his arms with a flourish. Smoldering etches appeared in the glass where his sleeves brushed against it.

"I offered them another realm."

Leo worked his jaw with one hand until he was satisfied it wasn't broken.

"There's a name for that," he said, "it's called Fantasy. And we have special places for people who live there."

The old man turned his head and smiled. "And dost thou not believe what thy eyes tell thee?"

"What? That you really are Merlin? Give me a break, okay."

Standing, Leo brushed past the old man and seated himself behind his desk. While giving the outward appearance of a calm professional from the waist up, his left foot was tap-dancing with gusto on the concealed alarm. Ten minutes . . . fifteen on the outside, if the building security guard was in the john . . . and the old man would be history.

But, in the meantime . . .

"I'll admit the suit trick wasn't bad." Leo offered a half-dozen perfunctory claps. "Bra—vo. Although I have to admit I saw it done better at a local comedy club. Guy turned into a gorilla. Great effect . . . now *that* was magic!"

A fist-sized ball of lightning crashed into the window directly next to Leo's skull. Silver spiderwebs appeared in the glass.

"Dost thou think this *magic?*" The old man leaped onto the desk seemingly without effort and glared down at Leo. The headband's tiny green eyes flashed. "Magic is an illusion, Doctor, a parlor trick any dolt could perform. I am a Sorcerer."

"And one hell of an actor," he mumbled, double timing the alarm button. There'd be no question about the man's sanity when the guard rushed in—thank God. One look and the old coot would be hog-tied and headed for the nearest Mental Reclamation Center.

Clearing his throat, Leo removed his pen from under the old man's left foot and tapped it against his chin. "My apologies. I'm just not used to having Fifth Century Sorcerers popping in for a chat."

"Sixth Century, to be exact."

The old man jumped backward off the desk with the agile grace of a cat and sat down . . . hovered actually, in midair three feet off the ground. Leo smiled, having seen mimes pretend to sit on invisible chairs many times before.

The explanation faltered however when the old man raised his feet onto an invisible ottoman. Leo hadn't even seen David Copperfield try that one.

"Now, back to business," he said, getting comfortable, "simply give me what I have come for, Doctor, and I'll be on my way."

"Well, I . . . it—I mean . . ." Taking a deep breath, Leo picked up his pen again and slowly—thoughtfully—began tapping it against his chin as his feet went into overdrive under the desk. "I cannot simply *give* you one of my patients . . ."

Thunder deepened the cracks in the window. A crystal shard fell to the carpet.

". . . I mean without a good reason."

The old man—*Merlin*—considered it for a moment and nodded.

"All right, then I shall explain. Again. I require someone who will not become overly upset if . . . *reality* should suddenly change. Become fantastic. And what better choice then someone who doesn't have a clear grasp on either?"

Leo frowned. That kind of thinking could be bad for business. "But that's crazy."

Merlin smiled and a golden beam of sunlight poured into the room. The office door vibrated with a low throaty purr.

"Exactly, Doctor. I've tried this before with men renowned for their wisdom and knowledge . . . and look what it got me: Death, dismemberment, betrayal, royal bloodlines severed for all times . . . Myself set down for all history as a doddering old fool done in by a pair of shapely thighs—

"But not this time. This time *I* shall choose the Defenders of the Faith." He glanced toward the window as another splinter of glass fell. "Not leave it up to a still-green boy with more of his brains below his belt than under his crown."

Leo snuck a quick peek at his Rolex. *Anytime now . . . anytime . . .*

"Am I keeping you from another appointment, Doctor?" The old man asked courteously.

"NO . . . no, not at all." Leo swallowed and straightened his tie—almost poking out his eye with the pen in the process. "Now . . . about this quest—"

"For the Grail?"

"Yes. Isn't it . . . well, a bit ambitious?"

Merlin crossed his arms over his chest and huffed loudly. The purr behind the door instantly turned vicious. Leo glared. Whoever it was in the dragon costume was going to get theirs soon enough. He just wanted the privilege of signing the commitment papers.

"Now you sound just like Arthur."

Leo's gaze drifted back to the seemingly floating psychotic. "Arthur?"

"The King."

"Ah."

"No, Arthur didn't think too much of the quest first time around. He even had the nerve to try and convince me that the Grail was nothing more than a myth. Convince me . . . ME who taught him how to wipe his nose. HAH!"

Three more pieces of window tumbled to the floor as the old man's accomplice echoed the thunder from out in the reception area. *Where the hell WAS that guard?*

"But not this time," Merlin said slowly as if measuring his words. "This time we shall find the Holiest of Chalices and set history straight."

"Well, I wouldn't worry too much about that if I were you . . . Merlin." The name left a bad taste in his mouth. "Every kid knows the story about King Arthur and the Quest. Hell . . . there've been books written about it, movies made . . . even a really *great* musical—"

An entire panel of glass struck the floor and shattered. "Yes . . . and my character didn't even get one bloody song. No. The Grail is still missing and it was my sworn quest to retrieve it."

Levitating until the top of his head brushed the acoustic ceiling, Merlin uncurled one long-nailed finger and pointed it directly at Leo's still throbbing nose.

"Wilt thou give me that which I seek?"

Jaw unhinged, and sphincter threatening to follow suit, Leo

quickly went through his mental list of paranoid-schizophrenics with or without delusions of grandeur, and came up empty-handed.

Nothing.

Not one paranoid or schizophrenic or delusionist. The majority of his practice seemed to consist entirely of burned-out baby boomers who were troubled by the fact their fathers never cried.

Shit.

"Ummmm."

"Doctor"—the floating apparition growled—"bring forth that which I have asked or suffer the consequences."

"Ahhh . . ."

"Doc? Hey, Doc?" a powerfully masculine voice called. "Are you okaaaa————?"

The question lengthened into a bubbling scream which ended in a wet smack.

Leo shoved the chair backward and stood up. "What the hell was that?"

Black eyes focused on Leo's face. "My pet was getting peckish so I allowed you to order his lunch."

The guard. Purrs mixed with slurping crunches vibrated through the door.

"Well, Doctor?"

"Well *this,* asshole."

Leo made it to the small office bathroom just as the outer door exploded inward. Better to be found hiding like a naughty little boy than to face whatever had just burst into the room.

The rational portion of Leo's mind concluded it was probably Gordon Bradshaw inside the elaborate costume; the other 99 percent refused to comment.

Leo glanced back just as the thing regurgitated a ball of liquid fire. He could feel the heat liquefying his flesh as he fell backward . . .

. . . onto a clover-strewn knoll.

The sunlight overhead stung his eyes, making them water. Lifting one arm to shield his face, he scraped his cheek raw with the studded leather glove.

"Careful, boy, I've no use for a one-eyed knight."

Leo blinked around the glare and pain. Merlin was standing a few yards away, leaning on a gnarled staff. A small hawk . . . no, a *falcon* glared down at Leo from the old man's shoulder.

"What the fuck?"

"Very good, Doctor . . . speaking like a native Saxon already. Excellent. You'll make a fine Sixth Century Knight."

Leo stood up . . . tried to stand up. He was wearing a stiff leather tunic overlaid with sheets of hammered metal linked together with rings. Beneath it, next to his naked skin, was a coarsely spun jumper of raw wool. His legs were bare, his feet wrapped in shapeless leather boots.

"Knight?"

"Of course." A deep chuckle caused the little bird to ruffle its feathers. "Why, you really didn't believe in those 'knights in shining armor' fairy stories, did you?"

Merlin crossed the distance between them in three strides and squatted, using his staff as a balance.

"Sorry to disappoint you, Doctor. But *this* is reality: pair-of-plate armor, studded leather, hand-to-hand combat with short swords. Mud, blood and outdoor facilities . . ." The smile widened on his face. "And the quest for the Holy Grail."

Leo tried to scoot backward only to run into a half-buried rock. It hurt too bad to be an illusion. "What do you want with me?"

Merlin stood up and took a deep breath. "Again, not my first choice, but beggars cannot be choosers. Besides, my friend, you *do* have some of what I've been seeking. After building your own fantasy world of expensive cars, gold wristwatches and investment properties, assimilating mine will be relatively easy. You see, Doctor, you do qualify in a way. See your destiny, sir! These are not mere trappings and delusions, I'm offering you a chance at achieving *true* grandeur!"

Lifting the staff, he raised it over Leo's head. The sun seemed to surround him. "Thou hast been chosen, Sir Knight, for thy valor and courage to seek the Holiest of Grails. How speaks thee?"

"You're nuts." Leo pulled his legs in under him, tried to push himself and fell back under Merlin's staff. "Okay, so you're not nuts ... you're just a *real* good hypnotist or illusionist or you slipped something into my morning coffee when I wasn't looking or you planned this with my wife to get my insurance money or"— Leo licked his lips, tasted dirt and grimaced—"or *I'm* crazy."

Merlin shook his head and moved the staff away. "No, you're not crazy, Doctor, I assure you. I *am* Merlin, this *is* the sixth century, and you *will* seek the Holy Grail. And this time, with luck and by the grace of God, we shall succeed in our quest."

"And if *we* don't?" Leo asked.

The smile twitched again as the falcon took flight.

"Then I shall have to keep trying." Bending down, the old man offered Leo his hand and pulled him to his feet. "There now, shall we be away, Sir Lyonel? Methinks, I remember a banquet being planned in thy honor. Percival brought down a stag this morn for the sole purpose, and Arthur himself has ordered new mead served up."

Leo looked into the old man's eyes—deep hollows that led into the man's soul.

"But stay close, Sir Lyonel, and do not tarry in the deepening shadows." Merlin smiled and tossed an arm lightly over Leo's shoulders. "Here there be dragons."

Judas

—✠—

Connie Hirsch

If beginnings cast shadows, the day Maggie Katze moved in with me counts for a total eclipse. I thought knew what I was getting into: a roommate straight out of a women's shelter, who made a side trip under police escort to remove her belongings from her boyfriend's.

The police presence didn't bother me; I was an Army MP, and I'm now working for the Campus Police to finance my degree in Political Science. My friend Shanice had let me know that Maggie needed a place to stay, and since my extra room was vacant ... I've done this before, for women with potentially violent ex's. If a woman lets out that her roommate is a cop, it can go a long way to cool loverly ardor.

In my experience, some battered women have the aura of victims, no kidding. I mean, something in these women makes them go out and find partners who'll oblige. Others—most others—are fairly emotionally healthy until they become abused, and when they get out they're as much bewildered as betrayed—"How could I let that happen?" I heard one say once.

Maggie sounded like one of the betrayed.

I was waiting on the front porch of my apartment building, a grand old house converted to flats, feeling the spring breeze when the caravan drove up—the cruiser, Shanice's Yugo, and what must be Maggie's Toyota. I hopped out to the curb to help them unload. A peach crate of ferns emerged from Shanice's car, Shanice somewhere behind it. She's a frizzy-haired bottle blonde, thin to the point of gaunt, and given over to wearing crystals, but I like her anyway. "Paulita, this is Maggie," she said, tilting her head toward the brunette struggling to pick up a box marked "Books" from her hatchback.

"Can I give you a hand with that?" I said.

Maggie had dark eyes and an infectious smile. "I should have remembered how much books weigh!" she said. "Would you give me a hand—oh—nice to meet you, Paulita!"

I laughed. "Nice to meet you too," I said. "Stand aside and let me get at it." I hefted the carton easily and decided not to show off by asking for another. I lift weights five days a week; in my line of work you need the upper-body strength.

We got Maggie's stuff in the house in fifteen minutes, maybe less. I waved bye-bye to the escort—who'd stood on the curb looking bored—and went in to find Shanice and Maggie collapsed on my big plaid couch. "Can I get anyone anything?" I said. "Ice tea, lemonade, beer?"

"If you don't mind, I'll have the beer," said Maggie. "I want to make a toast."

"And lemonade for me," said Shanice.

"Wild and crazy girl," I said to her and she smirked.

Maggie hadn't even asked what kind, so I got out the Sam Adams, one for me as well.

Maggie held up her beer like a glass of champagne. "I'd like to toast 'Good Riddance' to Joe Bridgman, out of my life forever!"

"Amen," I said, and we all clinked together.

"And another toast," said Shanice, after we'd drunk. "To Maggie, who had the courage to get out, and to the future."

"Sounds good to me," said Maggie. "Believe me, all this fuss is worth it, even all the stuff I left behind."

"You should have taken more," said Shanice.

"We did buy stuff together," she said. "But I decided . . . calmly and rationally . . . that the hassle of fighting him in court over furniture and shit isn't worth it. Being shut of him is."

Later I volunteered to unpack the kitchen stuff. Maggie didn't have much there either: a box of battered pots and pans—"Joe is a cook and all the good stuff was his anyway," she said—a nice set of Corelle dishes, for which I planned to retire my stoneware; and a box marked "Mugs." I saved that one for last after shuffling the china cabinet around.

The last box was similar to the others—odd, worn or chipped cups, mugs, and glasses, wrapped in newspaper. It's a good thing I don't have many cups; there was lots of room to stow them away. I keep the number small or else the unwashed dishes tend to pile up when I'm on my own.

At the bottom of the box was a wrapped lump half again as large as anything else, like a stein or vase. Maggie'd packed it like something precious; there was enough wrapping to make an onion proud.

It was more like a ceramic cup or goblet, done in a white crackle glaze with an illegible design on the side. It had a wide base, good to hang onto, comfortable in the hand. I was reminded of the vessels for the Japanese Tea Ceremony, plain, yet highly sophisticated and balanced. This wasn't a factory-turned product, but the result of an effort by a master craftsman, or all those hours in Mr. Vincoure's ceramics class back in high school had taught me nothing. This was like finding a swan among ducks.

The cup seemed to invite me to hold it, to look into the bowl and think about what liquids it must have contained, what other people must have held it and thought. I had the feeling—call it an intuition—that this cup was way old, and special. Very special.

Running my finger over the base, I caught my finger on an irregularity on the rim, like a little thorn. It was a sharp stabbing pain and I put the cup down and looked at my finger, beading up a miniature drop of blood, like a ruby. I ran some water over it and pressed down on the pad with my thumb while I looked at the cup and tried to see where the projection had been, but it seemed the only way to find it again was to run another finger over the area. Stupid, I'm not.

Right then, Maggie called out for some help—she was up on a ladder trying to hang a picture. I stowed the cup away on the shelf for safety, and forgot entirely to ask her about it.

* * *

Our first week was trouble-free. Maggie turned out to be as nice as I'd hoped. I pulled some double shifts because of illness in the department, so I was out quite a bit. But Monday crawled around and my week from hell was over; I was relaxing in the living room, drinking coffee in my bathrobe and watching a Daffy Duck cartoon, when there was a hellacious banging at the front door, and the bell rang repeatedly.

There was something truly urgent in the rhythm, not like an overinsistent salesman or a prankster would produce. I jumped off the sofa and headed for the door by way of my bedroom, where I keep my gun on top of the armoire. I stuck it into my bathrobe pocket, making sure it was chambered on an empty cylinder.

I could see a slim figure through the hazy glass—Maggie?—and heard the scrabbling of a key in the lock. There are two locks; one has a tendency to relock if you don't keep pressure on the door. I'd had to show Maggie how; it took her a couple tries to get the trick.

I opened the locks from my side and jerked the door open. Maggie practically trampled me trying to get in. "He's here, he's following me," she said. She ducked down the hall, shaking, pale, in that shocky way people have when they're really scared, eyes wide and flashing back and forth.

I closed the door and turned the locks. "Joe?" I said, though it wasn't much of a question.

"He's in his car, he followed me from the market," she said. "He's right across the street."

"Let's see," I said, nodding my head toward the living room. I had to catch her arm before she walked right in front of the window. I could feel her tremble. "Don't make a target," I said, and led her around the room so we came up on the curtained side. "From here he can't see us," I said.

"That's him," she said. Across the street a red Jeep Cherokee was parked in front of the fire hydrant. I couldn't see the occupant except for an outline: he might very well be looking toward us.

"That's his car?" I said.

"I'd know it anywhere," Maggie whispered. "I was driving and I noticed him behind me. I drove all the way over to Memorial

Park and back, on Route 30, changing lanes, but I couldn't lose him."

"Damn," I said. "Next time, flag down a cop car or drive straight to the police station."

"I'm sorry, I did the best I could," she said. She sat down on the floor, small and huddled, and I realized she was crying silently.

I crouched next to her. I should have kept Joe under observation, but some things are more important. "You did do the best you could," I said. "It's not your fault that he's a jerk."

"I know," she said. "It just keeps going on and going on. . . ."

Outside, someone was yelling. Maggie looked up at me as I peeked over the sill. Joe had gotten out of his car and was walking across the lawn, carrying what looked like a tire iron. He was medium height, with dark brown curly hair, and a compact build; he looked like he could use that crowbar to good advantage. *"Maggie!"* he yelled.

"Maggie," I said, slow and forceful. "Go to the kitchen, and call 911 *now.*"

"What's happening?" she said.

"Just go now," I said. "I'll meet him at the door. I want the police here as soon as possible. Tell them it's Code 55."

It helps to keep an even tone of voice; she headed off for the kitchen phone, keeping low. I went to the front door, thinking about the thin glass that separated us.

I got there just as he started ringing the bell: long, angry buzzes. "Maggie, I know you're in there!" he yelled, a sinister outline behind the hazy glass. "I want to *talk* to you." Talk, my ass. I always have my best conversations with a crowbar in my hand, let me tell you.

I took the gun out of my pocket, advanced the cylinder and held it at my side. "This is Officer Paulita Cadiz of the University Campus Police," I said in a loud, flat voice. "Mr. Bridgman, you are in violation of a restraining order forbidding you to contact or come within a hundred yards of Maggie Katze, and I hereby direct you to leave these premises immediately."

I could see his outline sway back. I wondered how he must feel to hear that Maggie had a protector . . . would it make him turn away or get angrier? "Tell Maggie I want to speak with her!" Joe yelled. There was a loud bang that made me raise my gun: he must have hit the building for emphasis. "Tell her I know that she has it and I want it back, now." His voice was hoarse, and sure with the clarity of madness.

I repeated my warning about the restraining order. "Tell her I want *it,*" Joe said. "Tell her I'm not going away until I get *it.* MAGGIE DO YOU HEAR ME?" He screamed out what he'd said before, repeating crazy variations of it.

Maggie came up the hall corridor behind me. "They're on their way," she said. "The dispatcher says hold him off if you can."

I backed up a few steps, never taking my eye off Joe's dark figure waving shadowy arms. There was a tinkle of broken glass; he must have hit the porch light. "Maggie," I said just loud enough so she could hear me, "get your pocketbook and coat, and go wait by the back door. If he does break in, I want you to scoot—head for the variety store two blocks over and *don't* look back, okay?"

She nodded, pale in the half-light of the interior corridor. I could hear Joe crunching things with his crowbar. My landlady had set out potted plants on the porch to enjoy their first taste of spring, but not anymore. "I'm going to get it," he repeated for the umpteenth time, his obsession unblunted and endless.

Half a dozen times I thought "this is it" and got my gun up, expecting him to crash through the glass. Another time I was sure he was prying at the door, ready to pop it out of the locks. I didn't want to force a physical confrontation; I didn't want a judge to conclude I had somehow provoked an attack.

I've traveled to a number of violent confrontations in the course of my profession, but this was the first time I'd had to wait on the police. It seemed endless, but from beginning to arrival of the police it could have been no more than ten minutes.

The cavalry drove up with sirens blaring. I could hear the officers getting out of their car, telling Joe to put the crowbar down and come forward with his hands over his head. I started to relax but tensed up again when I realized Joe was not cooperating. I went down the long hallway that runs through my apartment, back to the kitchen where Maggie was clutching her pocketbook next to the back door.

"Are we leaving?" she wanted to know, ready to bolt. I couldn't blame her.

"Shhh," I said. I could hear the officers outside, trying to talk Joe down from the porch with no success. "Stay near the door," I whispered. "If he makes a move they may have to shoot, or if he busts in here trying to get away. . . ."

The standoff went on long enough that officers came to the back and led us away to safety, me still in my bathrobe and slippers and gun. Maggie and I ended up over at Shanice's as Joe held out on the porch for nearly three hours, refusing to give up his crowbar, attack the police, or tell anyone what "it" was that he wanted back.

There was never any question that Maggie was going to press charges, I'm happy to say. I might have been tempted to push if she'd been hesitant, but she was out of victim mode and ready to claim her rights. All I did was offer moral support and a friendly face at the hearing.

If anything, Joe looked worse in court, more wild-eyed and paranoid-acting. He kept having whispered arguments with his court-appointed attorney. When the time came the lawyer entered a plea of guilty, but asked if his client could make a statement. The judge frowned but said as he allowed it.

"Your Honor, a possession of some importance was taken by Miss Katze when she retrieved her stuff. All I wanted was to get my . . . stuff back," Joe said, nervously shuffling.

"Mr. Bridgman, you were expressly forbidden from directly contacting Miss Katze, were you not?" the judge said.

"Yeah, but I had to get my stuff back."

"You could have asked your attorney to contact her representative, and pursued your claim that way," said the judge, unperturbed. This must have made sense to everybody in the world except the defendant.

For a long moment Joe glared at the judge, who lowered his glasses and stared right back. He turned his gaze right to Maggie, who was sitting behind the prosecutor. "I want it back, *bitch,*" he said, with a stare that lifted the hairs on the back of my neck. I swear he didn't blink.

"You will address the court with your remarks, young man," said the judge, but it was as if Joe was in some different world.

"I said I want it back, and you'd better give it to me or I'm going to come and take it," Joe said. "You think you can get away with stealing it . . ." He started to climb over the stand, fell onto the floor, knocking over a bailiff who sprang to intercept him. I was on my own feet, the judge was banging his gavel, Joe had half-dragged the other bailiff and his attorney across the floor toward us before he was stopped. I was reaching for my gun, not sure if I was going to have to shoot in this crowded courtroom—a cop's nightmare, all these people around.

The judge called for a five-minute recess, but Joe kept screaming that he was going to get "it" back. "I'm going to hold you in contempt of court," I heard the judge say between outbursts. After ten minutes of this, the judge asked that Joe be removed, then told Joe's attorney that his client had a choice of six weeks of voluntary psychiatric admission or county jail for violating his restraining order. "And I would advise you, Mr. Wagner, to contact Miss Katze's representative and see if this possession thing can't be worked out."

"That's just it, Your Honor," said Joe's attorney. "I can't get him to tell *me* what it is." He looked over in Maggie's direction. "If you have any idea, miss . . . ?" he said.

Maggie was white and trembling from Joe's outburst, but she popped to her feet like she was being called upon in Sunday school. "I swear, Your Honor," she said. "I'd give him anything to be shut of this, but I haven't the faintest idea what it is that he wants."

Maggie was shaking in the car on the way home. Aside from a few soothing phrases, I left her alone. She was still pale when we got home, so I decided that medicinal drink was called for. I walked her straight into the kitchen and announced that we were going to have Irish coffee to celebrate.

While I started the coffee perking (there was no way I was going to use instant) Maggie went to the cupboard to get mugs.

"What the *hell* is this doing here?" she said with such distress that I nearly dropped the coffeepot turning to look. For a moment I had the wild idea that Joe had somehow broken in and left a severed head or something else nasty.

But Maggie plucked the strange white goblet off the shelf and put it down on the counter as if she was afraid it was going to bite. "How the hell did this get in *there?*" she said. "I hate that ... *thing.*"

I put the coffeepot on the burner. "It was packed in your box with the mugs," I said. "You didn't know it was there?"

Maggie stared at me. "No ... I loathe that thing ... I'd never have packed it."

She was upset, so I wasn't going to argue about how the goblet had gotten there. "What's not to like?" I said, picking it up. "It's pretty ... and pretty old, I'd bet."

"That's not the half of it," Maggie said. She sat at the kitchen table, hugging herself. "Joe stole it from some professor he hated. Around the time things first started going bad."

"Stolen?" I said. I turned the goblet over in my hands. "Is it valuable or something?"

"I don't know," she said. "Joe had this faculty adviser he really didn't like, said he'd been screwed out of credit, stuff like that. That's why he dropped out and went into cooking full time. Anyway, to get back to this professor ... Maurice? ... Joe stole some of his research materials and anonymously reported irregularities, to the department head. Evidently this professor had been concocting false research for years ... I forget the details, but he lost his job eventually."

"Okay," I said. "So Joe hung on to this goblet and some other stuff. You don't suppose," I said as an idea hit me, "that this is the 'possession' he wants back, do you?"

"I don't even know how it got here," Maggie said. "I packed most of the kitchen stuff and I certainly don't recall seeing it. I don't even like touching it."

"Shanice probably saw it and thought it was yours," I said.

"And Joe assumes you took it on purpose, therefore he harasses you but won't tell his attorney what it is he wants."

Maggie looked doubtful. "Well, not a lot that Joe does makes sense, but this fits," I said. "So all we have to do is turn it over to the police, so the court can prosecute him."

"Oh, no," Maggie said. She folded her hands together tightly, the knuckles showing white. "This is going to sound silly . . . but I don't want to get him into any more trouble."

"It not only sounds silly, it is silly!" I said.

"Just a minute!" she said. "I've been to enough courts and seen enough lawyers. I'll go after Joe for anything he does to me now . . . but I draw the line at stirring up trouble for stuff he did in the past. There's a difference between standing up for your rights and vindictiveness."

"It's *your* ex-boyfriend," I said reluctantly. I put the goblet on the shelf, well back where it wouldn't get hurt. "Y'know, if we were to return it anonymously, and let Joe know about it, he wouldn't have any reason to harass you anymore."

"You think so?" said Maggie.

"Well, if the cup is what he wants," I said. Privately, I was certain that the cup had to be "it."

Maggie put her head in her hands. "This just goes on forever . . . ," she said.

"I'll take care of it," I said. I wanted to take the offer back immediately. But, hell, Maggie looked so grateful. "I'll find out what department, what professor, and contact them anonymously."

"That would be wonderful," she said.

"It won't be any trouble at all," I said.

The next day I asked Shanice, who worked in University Records, to check Joe's enrollment records on the computer for me. Bridgman had a good academic record through the first two years of college, when he'd changed his major from biology to political science. Fall semester of senior year he'd pulled three Incompletes and a D; records didn't have him listed as matriculating now.

Maggie had said that Joe had stolen the goblet from his faculty adviser; that was easy enough to determine: he'd had three, a biology professor, and two history professors. The last one, Roland Murphy, was still teaching at the university, but the first, Sidney Sumner Maurice, wasn't.

On a hunch I went over to the police log and researched Maurice. Several incidents in the past two years had been recorded: a physical fight with one of his students; two arrests by campus police for public drunkenness; charges of sexual harassment that were dismissed before they came to court; escort off campus when his office was cleared out. I vaguely recalled hearing about one of the arrests for drunkenness. The rest had happened during the day shift, which I hadn't been assigned to in my first year on campus force.

I still had some time before my shift started, so I walked over to the Provost's. I'd befriended a secretary there, when I'd removed a crazed grad student who said he had a bomb. I didn't get into police work to curry favors, but I wasn't going to complain if they came my way.

Emilie was pleased to see me, not busy, and eager to help until she heard it was Maurice I was interested in. "Oh, my," she said. Emilie dressed like a refugee from a beatnik film, black turtleneck, stirrup pants and pointy glasses on a librarian's chain. "He's bad news, all right. What's up? Did they find out that he stole something else?"

I blinked and remembered I didn't want any suspicion to fall back on Joe . . . just yet. "Just some routine fact checking," I said and winked.

"What do you want to know?" she said.

"What was he dismissed for?" I said.

"Technically, he isn't dismissed, just on an unpaid and indefinite sabbatical," she said, waving a finger at me. "Tenure."

"Yeah," I said. "Go on, why was he 'dismissed'?"

"Just about *everything,*" she said. "Except for outright rape or murder, he missed those. Faking research, selling antiquities from the University museum, fencing rare books from the library."

"Last two sounds like he developed a drug habit," I said.

"I heard"—Emilie leaned forward, her glasses clinking on the desktop—"that he was placed into a drug program after he finished his sentence for embezzlement a few months ago."

"If, say, materials came to light that belonged to the University, who should they be given to?" I said.

"History Department," she said. "That is, assuming the police don't want to be involved."

"Well ... let's just say they aren't involved yet, and might never be," I said. And left it at that.

As I walked back to the station I debated the advisability of hanging onto the goblet. The more I thought about it, the more I could see that having the goblet as a bargaining chip made sense. We could hand it over if Joe continued to be a problem; he probably wanted to sell it to finance his drug habit.

I thought about it all through my patrol that night. When I got home, I hid the cup away in my dresser and neglected to tell Maggie what I'd done. Better she should think herself clear of any wrongdoing. Later I could mention it if it came to that, but perhaps Joe's imprisonment (he'd chosen jail) would have driven some sense into him. I could only hope.

Maggie and I settled down into a month of blissful normality. No maniac ex-boyfriends, just the regular end-of-semester craziness. Maggie managed to pass her courses with a heroic last-minute effort, while I finished my single afternoon course with little trouble.

The goblet stayed in my dresser drawer. It kept showing up in my dreams, a product of my guilty conscience I suppose. I took it out once or twice just to look at; it was such a nice piece of art that I didn't wonder that Joe wanted it back. Well, he couldn't have it, I had it now, and I was much more worthy.

Maggie decided to go visit her mother in New Jersey for three weeks before summer session began. Unspoken was the fact that Joe was scheduled to get out of jail a week before she came back. If he decided to come around and look her up for an odd bit of terrorizing, he'd find only me, and I was ready for him.

The day after Maggie left, I pulled a T-shirt out of the dresser drawer and nearly dropped the goblet. I'd like to had a heart attack! Drawers aren't the place to keep cups, so I moved it back to the kitchen cabinet. It seemed to be happier there, even if it did often slide around to the front the way some glasses do.

I took some comp time, and vegged. I still had graduation duty to look forward to, almost three solid days of telling students, parents, and alums where to park and which way was the stadium. So I hung around in my bathrobe, read a little bit, and watched a lot of TV.

I got behind on the dishes. If it's just me I keep three plates and three sets of utensils, and wash them when they're dirty. With Maggie's additions, I could spend two whole weeks before having to do the dishes . . . which I did.

The more I looked at it, the more gross the stack of dirty dishes became. I decided to have milk and cookies, and then I'd tackle the mountain of washing up. But when I went to the cabinet, the only two drinking vessels left were Joe's goblet and a Flintstones jelly glass, which would hold about three sips.

I decided to live dangerously and go with the goblet. It was kind of a fun idea, actually, drinking my milk out of a potentially valuable antique, like a maid lounging about in her mistress's mink. I rinsed the old cup as a precaution, wondering about lead in the glaze: white isn't so bad, I remembered hearing. And besides it would only be one drink.

I remember walking to the refrigerator to get the red and white milk carton, the waxed paper slick beneath my hands. This must be how a Japanese Tea Ceremony feels, the exact and neat motions, the elegance of the vessel, the anticipation of pleasure in the act of drinking. I carried the plate of cookies and the goblet, cool and pleasant, to the living room, each step like an intricate dance movement. It felt like a magical spell.

I took a bite of cookie and picked up the goblet with both hands. How long had it been since someone had held this cup and drank from it? Certainly not Joe nor Maurice, or even the man Maurice had gotten it from . . . further back than that, a black magician of the darkest stripe. And what substance had he drunk? I laughed a little nervously at the fantasies running around in my head. And then I drank.

I can't properly describe the taste; I don't think it was like anything you'd ever encounter in a normal life. But I can offer something by way of analogy: once, browsing in a used clothing store I chanced upon a white fur stole of amazing softness. I pulled it out of the rack and ran my hands over it, like a cloud, soft and silkier than silk. "Oh, you've found the seal fur!" said the proprietor. I remember looking at the lovely whiteness in my hands and thinking that I wouldn't really mind bashing in a few baby seal skulls for something this beautiful.

The taste from my cup was like that, only ten or a hundred times stronger.

I drank and I learned. The cup spoke to me without words: images and emotions. It had wanted me, it had chosen me, and it had influenced events to bring it to me.

And I? I had been waiting all my life for knowledge, for power like this. I was an eager bride, ready for my wedding night.

I couldn't let the cup out of my sight after that . . . well, not for a while, anyway. I took it into my room and buried it at the bottom of my trunk, but I had to go and check on it every once in a while, to make sure it was okay.

I called in sick for several shifts, knowing (because it told me) that I wouldn't get in trouble. During the next week I would lie awake in my bed, and hear it whispering, saying things I wanted to hear. I didn't dare ask it questions; it didn't seem to be that kind of relationship.

But I had to know the answers, just the same.

When Maggie came home I was waiting for her in the living room; the cup had told me when she would arrive. "Welcome back," I said, holding my cup of power, watching approvingly as the smile slid off Maggie's silly face and she fell to her knees, white and shaking. Before her I was the master of this power, but to the outside world, for a while longer, I was the same cop, same defender of the law that I had always been.

The next morning, I was up early, way before my shift. Maggie was wandering around in her slippers; I mostly ignored her, only making sure that my trunk was locked securely. She thought I was going out jogging, and I wanted it to look that way.

I knew where Joe lived, in an apartment complex on the West End, swinging singles and would-be yuppies; I used to date a guy who lived there It wasn't hard to find his door, and his car was right in the breezeway.

I knocked with my jacket loose and the safety strap off the holster, just in case. Joe was a wuss, I knew in my bones, but sometimes wusses can grow a little courage when it's something they want badly enough.

I had a good idea what Joe wanted, and how bad.

I knocked again, more loudly. I could hear a masculine grumble from inside, and the clink of a chain being pulled back. Fool, didn't he know that was the best security device he could have on his door?

Door opened, I stepped forward, my foot firmly planted so he couldn't close it.

"Hey!" he said, his hand reflexively pushing the door toward me.

"Hello, Mr. Bridgman," I said. I wondered what my expression looked like, because he recoiled when he met my gaze. "I've come to have an important talk."

He didn't look as though he'd groomed himself for a few days: scraggly beard, red-rimmed and puffy eyes, runny nose. Probably he'd been up since he'd gotten out of jail.

"Perhaps we should talk inside," I said, pushing my way in. Joe was waking up, trying to figure out how he'd come to be on the defensive. I shut the door and walked to the middle of his living room, casing the area for potential weapons. Unless he tried to brain me with a TV tray or an empty beer can, I wasn't in much trouble.

"Just what the fuck do you think you're doing here?" he said, a little of his favorite demeanor returning.

"I came to talk," I said, my hands on my hips. "You kept saying you wanted 'it' back. I thought we'd make a little . . . deal, y'know."

Joe's eyes widened. "I knew it, I *knew* it," he said. "Damn bitch, damn *lying* bitch. She had it all along, didn't she?"

"Maybe she did," I said.

He made the mistake of getting excited. "You're in it right with her, aren't you?" He tried to grab me, maybe just to shake me, but I wasn't going to have it. I don't think he'd ever fought outside of grammar school brawls and beating up on Maggie; he had no idea that a simple foot sweep combined with a push could bring him crashing to the floor with such violence.

I was right on top of him; one thing I learned in self-defense is that you don't wait to see if your opponent will recover. I had him on his stomach, his arm twisted just short of dislocation. "Care to repeat that, asshole?" I said in his ear.

He started to squirm, cried out in pain and thought better of moving. "What do you want?" he hissed.

"I want you to give up on any claim on . . . it," I said.

He was silent, breathing heavily. "*You*—you've got it. Fuck you, you crazy b—" I twisted his arm enough that he uttered a hoarse cry and a little moisture squeezed from his eyes. While he was distracted, I pulled my gun out one-handed and cocked it, loudly. It was on an empty cylinder, but he didn't have to know that. Shooting him now would be . . . inconvenient.

"Take a look, Joe," I said, holding it near his face, so he could have that very inspiring view down the barrel. I guarantee you it's a sight that concentrates the mind wonderfully. "I said, I want you to give up even thinking about it. You weren't worthy, and you lost all claim to it, never mind that you never had much of one." I didn't know what I was saying, it was all coming out in a rush. "Just leave me and mine alone, and everybody will be happy, right?"

"You're crazy," he said. I stuck the gun so the muzzle pushed against his right nostril. I almost laughed to see his expression, cross-eyed, nose all scrunched up.

"Doesn't matter if I am or not," I said softly. "Does it?"

I got up. "Stay down," I said. He didn't take his eyes off the gun and he didn't move except to breathe. "I wouldn't recommend going to the police on this," I said. "First of all, I *am* the police, and they'll believe me long before they'll believe you." I took a few steps back toward the door for effect. "Secondly, if you managed to kick up enough of a fuss, I might have to turn ... *it* over to them, having discovered stolen material in the house ... and who knows what they'd do with it."

He looked pained, worried. Damn, I wasn't going to be able to scare him off permanently; no way would he give it up. "And if you've got any thought of coming to get it ... remember, it'll warn me you're coming, and I'll be ready."

I stared at him another minute, letting him sweat, then I let myself out. I knew I wouldn't have to worry about my back for another couple of days. As for what I'd do then ... well, I could think of a few possibilities. In the meantime, I had to find Professor Maurice.

I didn't want anyone connecting me with the professor, so I discreetly made a side trip into the Bursar's office on my regular rounds and copied his employment records. Social Security and car license numbers in hand, I ran it through the state computer and got several matches. He'd been prosecuted for various offenses, beyond the charges the university had brought: drug possession, driving under the influence. He'd lost his license for the last, but the car registration was still in his ex-wife's name. No current address listed; the parole board probably had it but I wasn't going to ask them about it.

A personal visit to the wife was definitely in order.

Maggie didn't say anything when I got dressed in my uniform hours earlier than needed. She didn't say much of anything, not since I'd caught her snooping through my room. I hadn't really had to hit her, just shake her up a bit, and the tongue-lashing, of course. Joe's physical battering had been nothing compared to my power.

The address Mrs. Maurice kept these days was considerably less grand than in her husband's heyday: now she lived in a modest suburb of row houses on half-acre lots, their sameness disguised by trees grown tall and cheery paint jobs.

She was a small woman with a well-lined face, with that look of betrayal I'd come to recognize. I explained I was investigating several antiquities thefts and I'd like to talk to her husband.

She looked at me with hostility. "We're divorced," she said.

I waited. "He never discussed his work with me, and all of his possessions were cleared out when he moved," she added.

"Do you know where he is now?" I said patiently, the right note of boredom in my voice.

"I—no," she said. "I don't, I'm afraid."

Like hell. "Well, if I can't talk with him, the DA might have to go ahead with a search warrant for these premises. It would be very inconvenient for you."

I hardly needed the power of the cup to see her change her mind. "Would you wait a minute?" she said politely. "I believe I've thought of something."

She disappeared for the amount of time necessary to feign looking up an address she'd forgotten she had. I waited in the living room; I could recognize the furniture that had survived the divorce versus the cheap items she'd bought since.

Mrs. Maurice brought the address written on a small piece of notepaper, in her even, spidery handwriting. "Will that be all, Officer?" she said.

"Assuming he answers my questions, it will be. We'll be contacting him in a few weeks, routine questions, nothing to be worried about, if you speak to him," I said.

"I hardly ever talk to him anymore," she said.

My curiosity got the best of me. "What sort of man is he?"

"I used to think . . ." She looked sad. "Until near the end, he was the same sweet man I married. But he changed so, as though he'd become a stranger. I've heard he has changed again, but . . ."

I nodded. Nothing the cup hadn't told me already. "Thank you for your help," I said. I'd given her a fake name and number, of course.

That night I dreamed I drank urine from the cup. It tasted bitter, but it was the bitterness of strength. I woke and got the cup from the chest and slept with it next to me, hand curled around the neck.

* * *

But I didn't confront Maurice right off. There were certain preparations I had to make.

I got a picture of the professor from the student paper back issues. It showed a smiling, professional man, stocky and fit, sitting in a book-lined office holding a textbook he'd written on Catholic cults and heresies. The story was almost four years old, long before the cup had come into his life.

Even with his picture, I was unsure at first that I had found Sidney Maurice. I parked in front of his rooming house all day, watching the inhabitants come and go, matching names to faces and eliminating his neighbors one by one. The cup would whisper to me, almost audibly, and the whispering rose to a furious pitch when Maurice walked past my car unaware. He was a changed man, stooped and skinny, his skin loose where he'd lost weight, and lined with defeat.

Another day of watching and a discreet bit of tailing showed me where he spent his days, at a halfway house running self-help groups for drug addicts. He kept a regular schedule, excellent for my plans.

I made my preparations most discreetly; including a visit to the Evidence Room at the station. The cup whispered to me when the coast was clear so I could ascend via the fire stairs and break into Maurice's room using a skeleton key,

His rented room was barely lit by tiny windows at the far end, like a long dark boxcar on a train going nowhere. The furnishings were shabby and painfully neat; Maurice even turned back the covers of his bed before leaving. The bedside table had an arrangement of dried flowers; a desk/dining table had a flowered tablecloth that didn't show the burn spots too badly, one corner taken up by a huge typewriter and a manuscript box filled with written pages.

I read through them as I waited: a nonfiction book about artifacts used by Christian cults, and their curious history. Saint's relics, pieces of the True Cross, and the Holy Grail, too: the mummery of the cult of a dead God, the flotsam and jetsam of belief.

I was a bit nervous; I was depending on Maurice coming home

alone. Things might get complicated and ... messier than I intended, if he brought a guest. But the cup whispered soothingly, tucked safely in the bag beneath my shoulder, that Maurice was on his way home alone, and I had only to wait patiently.

I stood out of view as Maurice turned the key in the door, making sure he locked it, and moved away before I walked out of the shadows behind him. "Professor Maurice," I said quietly, and was gratified to see him spin and gasp.

"How did you get in here?" he said.

"Super let me in," I said. "I'm from the University Police, Mr. Maurice"—I flashed my badge, quick, so he wouldn't notice that I was only an officer, not a detective—"and I'm here to talk to you about the theft of an artifact from the University collection."

I held out a Polaroid I'd taken of my cup, photographed against a neutral background, showing its indistinct design. Maurice held it with a trembling hand. "Where did you get this?" he said, looking wildly at me.

I smiled smoothly, I'd anticipated the question. "I'm not at liberty to say."

"This is terrible," he said. "I knew I had left this undone, and here it's come back to haunt me." I shook my head slightly, to remind him I didn't know what he was talking about. "Miss—?" he said.

"Smith, Barbara Smith," I said promptly.

"Miss Smith, this cup ... this artifact, is very evil."

I gave him a look any normal detective would give a statement like that. "Who would be interested in stealing it?" I said.

"Oh, many people, I should imagine," Maurice said. "It has been the central relic of a number of cults over the centuries, for which it has considerable value to collectors, let alone those who would perpetuate such worship."

"And it's evil."

"Miss Smith, I do not use such a word in jest," he said primly. "Aside from my personal history with the cup, it is easy to trace the baleful course it has had on human affairs."

"Such as?" I said.

"I could give you a complete lecture, Miss Smith," he said. He gestured toward the dented filing cabinet. "I can cite history books, old diaries, alchemical grimoires. I have researched this cup as far back as Spain in the thirteenth century, where it was supposed to have traveled from Constantinople earlier. It was later believed to have been a possession of the Borgia popes, and to have traveled to France where it was the object of veneration of a heretical cult of monks. In 1614 it was captured and walled up in the Notre Dame de Paris."

He took a breath, ran a hand through his thinning hair. "That would have been the end, one would think. The men who walled it up were careful to conceal its location, lest it fall into evil hands again."

"Why didn't they destroy it then?" I said.

Maurice shook his head. "It is said . . . they tried. I never put the cup's indestructibility to the test, myself. Perhaps it would have been better if I had.

"I have been unable to trace the cup until it turned up in the hands of a Jacobin faction during the French Revolution. From there it was passed to a German Masonic order, and used in certain esoteric rites. The order collapsed in 1918, at the close of World War One and the cup became the property of the Strausse family."

He paused as if he expected me to react, but he wasn't ringing any of my bells. "Go on," I said.

"Ernst Strausse is notorious as the commandant of the Oberhausen concentration camp. When he was executed for war crimes his personal possessions were seized and put in storage while his heirs squabbled. It was only four years ago that one of the claimants died and the antiquities he collected were put on sale in lots; my collecting trip on behalf of the University happened to coincide, and I bought the cup, in a lot of worthless porcelain, without the seller ever being aware of what it was he possessed."

"That's very nice for you," I said. "But aside from the cup passing through a few questionable hands, I don't see how you can call it evil."

Maurice stared past me, at the bare wall with its slightly cracked plaster and faded paint. "More than once . . . many times in fact, the records show a striking personality change in the owner." He turned to look at me. "Young woman, I scoffed at such thoughts; I am a scientific researcher, not some popularizer for television."

"Why did you buy this cup, Mr. Maurice?" I said. "You say yourself you didn't believe the stories . . ."

"I didn't know half the stories at that time," he said sadly. "Not that it would have stopped me if I had. Sometimes, you must go with your gut feelings, on half-remembered reference, and the look and feel of the object. I couldn't believe the other browsers were not clustered around that cup, wishing to touch it, marveling at its perfection and mystery.

"Sometimes I wonder if it wanted to come to me." He picked up the photograph. "To look at this flat representation is to see a vessel of the early Christian Era, not a prime example by any measure, interesting for its historical value but certainly not the object that secret wars have been fought over. Yet, to look upon the cup itself . . ."

"Is it really that old?" I said. "I thought you said fourteenth century?"

"As was common of holy relics, it was believed to be far older. Most, of course, do not stand up to scientific dating methods, but this cup's glaze is consistent with such a date."

"Whoa," I said. "Wait a minute. 'Holy relic?' What are we talking here, the Holy Grail or something?"

"No, Miss Smith, not the Holy Grail. If such a vessel exists on Earth, it is in a very secure place, far from the knowledge of antiquarians such as myself. No, the apocryphal provenance associated with this cup is very persistent and quite precise: this is the very cup that Judas drank from at the Last Supper."

"So . . . ," I said, the breath hissing out of me.

"Some cults venerated it, some used it for power in magical ceremonies. Others collected the blood of sacrifice in it to woo the darker powers."

"Professor," I said, "you sound more like a believer all the time."

"I am a man of rationality," Maurice said. "But when it was in my hands . . . it was as though I were the one possessed. The doctors say I had a breakdown, that I imagined the voice that whispered, and allowed me to . . . Yet I remember what it was like, no hallucination could be so real."

"I see," I said. "Tell me, what would happen if someone were to drink from this cup?"

He looked up at me in horror. "You are not a detective, are you?" he said, blinking and wetting his lips. I said nothing, letting the power of Judas's cup flow through me and intimidate him. "Only the leaders of the dark cults dared to drink from the vessel; they and their followers, sealed unto death."

"And their victims," I said: fact, not question.

Maurice had a look in his eyes like a deer my father had wounded and tracked down for half a day on a hunt when I was twelve; lying there on the ground, too exhausted and injured to run, watching us come, breathing heavily, desperate for just one moment more. "And their victims," Professor Maurice said.

I pulled my evidence gloves out of my jacket pockets; they're what we wear on a crime scene so we don't leave fingerprints. My duffel contained the Judas cup and a bottle of carefully doctored wine.

I handed the bottle over to Maurice; it was a screwtop. "Go ahead, pour," I said, so his fingerprints would be where they had to appear. As under a spell, he performed, spilling a little but getting most of it into the cup. "Now, drink," I commanded.

His hands, both about the cup, trembled, as he fought the compulsion. "You—I could be most helpful, I know so much about the Judas cup . . ."

"Thank you, Professor," I said pleasantly. "But you've provided all the information I needed; I can figure out the rest. Now, drink."

Maurice drained the cup and put it down on the table, shuddering.

Strychnine is quite bitter, and so is cocaine, but I wonder how they must have mixed with the strong red wine, the taste of betrayal. It's unusual to take cocaine mixed with wine but not unheard of, and neither is it unheard of for cocaine to be cut with strychnine for a bigger kick; sometimes the proportion is wrong and the user dies. I'd dissolved enough cocaine and strychnine in the wine to kill with a single glass, though with the power in the cup itself I probably hadn't needed to.

Maurice slumped to the floor, jerking and quivering as the strychnine took effect, convulsing until his heart stopped. I watched, cradling the cup in my hands. I left half a Baggie of cocaine and a nearly empty bottle of strychnine on his table, and put a clean sheet of paper in the typewriter. I typed "I'M SORRY," a suicide note that would satisfy the coroner. No one saw me when I let myself out.

There would be no stopping me, ever.

I spent the next few days as if nothing had happened. I turned up regularly for work, wrote the required number of tickets and reports, even joked with my coworkers and volunteered to make brownies for the Memorial Day picnic. And watched the obituaries for any news of Maurice.

It took five days, but the landlord found him when somebody complained about the stench. It rated about two column inches in the *Globe;* the obituary got three inches two days later. "Died abruptly at home," it said, "survived by his ex-wife Marilyn Maurice and second cousin Adam." I liked that, neat, all ends tied up.

The days I spent like normal. The nights . . . the nights I came home; Maggie creeping around as if she might offend me. Well, she might, I kept her cowed for now. Going to my room and locking the door when I wanted to be alone.

I'd take out my grail, my Judas cup. The design was growing ever clearer; every time I'd take it out and lovingly nick my wrist and let the thick blood flow, it grew more distinct. It never seemed to hurt; it never seemed to weaken me, only to make me stronger, more a part of it and the great pattern. Lots of Hebrew letters, I thought, but I didn't need to know what they said.

A week later I noticed Joe skulking in the bushes outside my house. It was after midnight, when even the neighborhood dogs take a break from watching. The cup told me he was out there. I walked into the living room in the dark, holding the cup in both hands, to the big window, then I let the cup call him to step out so I could see him.

I don't blame him, really. He can't stop wanting the Judas cup the way a moth can't stop wanting the candle flame.

Through the cup, I told him to go away and not come back. I watched him walk away, reluctantly dragging each foot. It would only hold a few days at best; the call was too strong.

"Is—is something wrong?" Maggie said behind me. I turned and she edged back, as though I might hit her. "I heard you get up . . . I wondered," she added.

"Nothing, nothing that needs concern you," I said, planning how I was going to kill Joe. For a moment I considered setting up a murder-suicide, for after all, Maggie knew the cup had originally come from Maurice and was going to have to die, too. But efficiency isn't always wise; I wouldn't want that much scrutiny put on three deaths so close together. Better I should manipulate Joe into confronting me or the police so he could be shot down like a dog; Maggie's death could wait. Perhaps an overdose of sleeping pills . . .

"Go back to bed, Maggie," I said and she shuffled away, obedient. In the dark room, with the moonlight trailing wispy fingers through the window, I contemplated my future, my degree, law school, a career in politics. I thought of all the good I would do, with this power, making the world a better place for the strong and the brave.

Grail

— ✠ —

Richard Gilliam

The looseness of the chest straps surprised Buck Walters. Straining forward, he tested the limits of his confinement. The straps held. He could breathe easily, though he could move less than an inch.

Breathe easily, Buck thought. Of course. That's what they want me to do. I'm sitting in the death row gas chamber. They're going to make me suck the pipe.

Through the right window, Buck looked to the ceiling light. He didn't want to look at Warden Davis, or at any of those gathered, except for Maria. The light and Maria—all that was worth looking at now anyway.

The warden stood next to a table on which rested a silent red telephone. The phone would ring. Of this, Buck was certain. The ring wouldn't matter. Of this, Buck didn't care.

Through the left window peered a video camera. The court-appointed lawyer had asked Buck to die badly, for the benefit of the camera, and for those left behind on death row. Buck had asked if maybe the lawyer should die first, just to show him how. Next to the camera stood the lawyer, his sight not focused on the chamber or its contents.

Ten witnesses waited by their chairs, none seated. Seven of them Buck knew. Six were from families of his victims. Only Maria was his friend. The other three were "interested parties," or so he had been told.

The press section sat separately. Buck didn't care to look toward it. Thomas O'Conner, the state's attorney, stood with them.

Buck did not want his last earthly sight to be that of Thomas O'Conner, so he looked instead at Maria. Buck had asked Maria to stand as far away from O'Conner as possible.

Father Terrance wondered how Maria could believe she loved this killer. Or how an attractive thirty-year-old woman could remain faithful to a man who had been on death row for nine years. The priest walked toward Maria, placing his arms around her. He felt Maria feign thanks. That neither she nor this killer accepted the church, he was certain. He really couldn't work up a good forgiveness for either of them. That would be God's job, the motions of absolution notwithstanding.

Buck saw the doctor enter. He was a fat, stubby man whose suit never seemed to fit, and Buck often pitied him his job of keeping prisoners well enough to kill. Even a farm vet had the satisfaction of knowing that when his charges faced slaughter it was for the purpose of providing food. The doctor attached his stethoscope to the long tube which led into the chamber and to the harness around Buck's chest.

It's not like the electric chair where you usually die on the first try, Buck considered. When you suck the pipe they leave you locked up till they don't hear your heartbeat no more. Trouble is, it takes a long time to stop breathing. Twelve to seventeen minutes for most, and you're awake with your lungs wrenching until the end. Twelve to seventeen minutes of lung-puking agony. It's not even a pipe, anyway—that's just what everyone calls it. It's a bowl under your chair, where they got poison in a bag connected to a chain. And you got no choice. You gotta breathe it. Holding your breath delays it a little, but when your lungs burst finally and you suck in what you wish was gonna be air, it don't do no good. You got less than twenty minutes to live, cause you just filled your lungs with poison.

This is wrong, Buck thought, looking to Maria. Her soft, gentle smile reassured him. That's right. No need to get pissed. They're just doing to you what you did a bunch of times to yourself. They're killing because it makes them feel good. Dyin' pissed ain't

gonna help none. Gotta think about where you're going when this
is over. Getting thrown out of this place ain't nothing to be embar-
rassed about. It's finding enough forgiveness to get into the next
one that matters.

Thomas O'Conner walked toward Maria and the priest. Buck
smiled. Nothing he could do to save himself, but there was sure a
good chance O'Conner's day would be ruined. Maria pushed
O'Conner away as he began to embrace her. Buck smiled again. She
ain't the only one trying to get away from you today, O'Conner.
She ain't the only one.

"Lockdown is the best time to try to escape from maximum security," the old man had told young Willie during his first turn as
an adult. "Lockdown is when they feels real in control. You gotta
find some way out of a lockdown. Then you got it easy, 'cause
most of the guards are watching the general population."

Been real nice of the old geezer to show him some ropes. He'd
even cried when he'd heard the old man had passed—let's see, that
was the third turn, Willie figured. Wasn't rightly sure. That's what
counseling officers were for, to keep track of all your turns so you
didn't have to.

Only one turn left. It's get out real soon now or suck that same
pipe they're gonna shove down Buck.

Good thing Willie had gotten sick. He'd come to know the hospital pretty well. What a fucking pig that Doc Baker was. Addicted
to his own needle, to the point he stole morphine from the patient's
dosages. That fucking pig Baker. Good thing Willie knew about the
needle. Lot easier to get into the hospital when you got something
big to hold over the doctor.

Baker had even smuggled him a gun. A junkie is just a junkie
no matter inside or out or in-between.

Willie had always stayed clean, a reliable pro—the best contract killer around. Everybody said so, even Thomas O'Conner
when he asked the jury for the death penalty. O'Conner. Another
fucking jerk. He'd watched O'Conner's wife as she sat in the seats
behind the prosecution table. For the television cameras, of course.
O'Conner didn't miss a chance to make himself look good.

A major bimbo with nice tits, Willie thought. O'Conner wouldn't have married anything else. Sure like to get inside her as soon as I get out. Yeah, Willie thought. I'll make it a point to get inside her.

He looked at the clock on the stand by his bed. Ten minutes. Almost time.

Thomas O'Conner was careful not to grimace as he put his arms around the Mexican woman. A show of compassion always played well for the press. The little slut had shown him up, pushing his first attempt away, and he had heard the press snicker as she did so. Thomas O'Conner smiled, and leaned toward her to whisper in her ear. "Angelo, your brother. He has no green card, and we know where he is staying. Play it my way and we'll leave him alone."

Maria broke into tears, which is exactly what Thomas O'Conner had wanted her to do. Now he took her to him, pulling her taut bosom against him as she sobbed onto his shoulder. "That's good," he whispered, in a soothing tone that belied his cynicism. "Just keep on crying. The press likes it when the killer's whore suffers. Just keep on crying and we'll leave Angelo alone."

Thomas O'Conner felt Maria being pulled away from him. It was the priest. "I heard," Father Terrance said. "Leave her alone. Give her some dignity." Thomas O'Conner smiled again. He knew all about the priest and his gunsel. Priests shouldn't have a second apartment and a young boy kept there, and the ones that did should be very careful to retain the favor of those who knew.

Father Terrance studied the prosecutor. Detectives had interviewed his landlord last month, and had watched Ramon on his way to school. He had expected to be arrested any moment, but took no steps to hide the boy, so strongly did he believe their love to be just. Ramon had felt the same, saying over and over each time they lay together that he could never leave Father Teddy, no matter how much others disapproved.

Ramon's skin was even softer than Maria's, and his hair all the more fragrant. Ramon knew how much the priest enjoyed rubbing his face in Ramon's hair, and the boy took special pleasure in the scented shampoos that his lover brought him. Not so much difference in age, twenty-four versus fifteen, only nine years. It would make no matter once Ramon was grown, save that the Church should find out, Father Teddy thought. But that was what his inheritance had been for, to give him a second life hidden from the Church and its prying eyes, though now this ambitious prosecutor threatened all he had.

Thomas O'Conner looked deeply into the priest. No, not now. Not something this strong. The Church was a powerful tool, and wasting a major secret wouldn't be necessary. They were both perfect, the sobbing slut crying into the waiting arms of the faggot priest. O'Conner stood by and watched, his veneer of concern unshaken by the girl's rejection.

Maria felt the arms of the priest slip around her, their comforting warmth held close against her dress. How sad, she thought, that such a tender man would never know the pleasures of a woman. She had misjudged the priest, she decided. Here was someone who could love more than just the power of the Church, someone very unlike the many priests she had known so many times.

Buck was pleased when the priest took Maria from the prosecutor. He had continued to hate Thomas O'Conner for several years after the conviction that sent him to death row. Maria had told him not to hate, not to ruin the last years of his life in dreadful anger. Maria, who always listened, who always loved him. Maria, the one good thing in his life he hadn't killed. Maria, who had taught him to forgive himself, and enabled him to face his fate with dignity and confidence.

Willie smiled as the nurse unlocked the cuff that chained him to his bed. The ruse had worked. A normal loose bowel movement had been made to look like diarrhea, which meant both Willie and the bed had to be cleaned, and thus Willie would have his chance to beat the lockdown.

Though an attendant sponged his buttocks, Willie wiped him-self clean. He'd chance it just after he put his hospital gown back on, thought Willie. They'd cuff him again afterward. He'd have time to reach the gun under the table first.

As the attendant turned to take the soiled linen, Willie noticed the nurse gazing inattentively out the window. In a single motion, the gun was in his hand, and pointed at the nurse.

"Take off your clothes," Willie said calmly, but determinedly. "Start with the shoes. I want the shoes, too."

The nurse looked at the gun, started to raise his hands, then did as instructed. No one had noticed, thus far. Three minutes till the hour, Willie saw on the clock. The pellets would drop at one after. The timing was just as he wanted it.

The black and white security monitors weren't closely watched by the guards. He'd easily be passed through the exit door into the administrative area. The crowd of protestors outside the prison walls was his ace in the hole. If he could just get outside, outside a little bit, Willie thought, he could blend into the hundreds in the open field. Get to the reception area, thought Willie. Find a re-porter, take his clothes and credentials, and walk out the gate. One thing for sure about reporters, Willie knew. They were always pok-ing around where they shouldn't have been. Finding one alone shouldn't be hard.

Buck's thoughts drifted back to his father. He was ten, his mother two years dead, his father just out of prison. Fourteen months wasn't long for killing his mother, Buck thought. DUI manslaughter always carried less if the victim was a passenger in your car. That was before the DUI laws got tough anyway. Too tough, Buck thought. Ordinary people who did no one harm got tougher sentences than career criminals with long arrest records. Justice was a funny concept.

The trouble had started the first night his father was home. Come here boy, he had been commanded. Lie down with me. I want you to put it in your mouth. Buck had refused, or tried to at first, until his father grabbed Buck and stripped down his pants.

Two ways we can do this, his father said, and you should wanna do it the way that hurts less.

Buck's anus had bled for days, and never again did he refuse his father. It was an agreement between them. Only in your mouth, so long as you do what I want.

Maria had helped him stop hating his father. Hating the dead was worse than hating the living, she had said. It is too late when you hate the dead.

Sometimes Buck was sorry the old man had died so badly, lingering in a prison hospital while his liver rotted away. They'd given him serious time when the second crash had occurred. Serious time for causing the deaths of the family of three—all gone in an instant. The old man had cheated the law one more time, having served only eight months when he died.

No one came to the funeral. Just Buck, the priest, and the prison detail. Drake's Crossing wasn't going to miss Lenny Walters, and it sure didn't care about his fourteen-year-old son. Folks in the east Tennessee hills figured fourteen was plenty old to take care of yourself, anyhow.

Buck thought his funeral would look much the same. Just Maria, Father Terrance, and the burial detail. Certainly not Thomas O'Conner, who'd be too busy preening for the television cameras to worry with the disposal of his kill.

Willie looked through the window at the prison gate. So close. One last barrier. The alarms would go off soon, though the nurse and the attendant were locked in the supply room. Maybe enough time. Gotta find street clothes and press credentials. Either that or make something happen, fast.

There was a tall truck parked next to the perimeter wall, the yard overflowing with vehicles. Excellent cover, should he go for the wall, Willie thought. Yeah. Maybe the wall was a better option. Easy to climb the truck and then the wall. A few cuts from the razor wire, perhaps. On the other side of the wall was a woods. He'd find a stray protestor and get new clothes that way. Not have to risk fooling the gate. Sure. That's right. Don't risk the gate.

* * *

Thomas O'Conner addressed the reporters, standing to the side so as to face both the witness area and the sealed chamber. He cleared his throat to gain their attention, then began.

"The Governor has called and has ordered the execution to proceed. Let me remind you that even though Ernest Buchanan Walters stands convicted of only two murders, he has confessed to three more, plus numerous other violent crimes. The father of his first victim, Denise McIntyre, is here today. Miss McIntyre was kidnapped, tortured, and raped repeatedly over a three-day period before she died from loss of blood. The husband of Lucy Wollaston is not here. He took his own life in the year following his wife's death at the hand of the condemned. Their son is now twelve, and lives with his grandparents. You have the particulars of these crimes detailed in your press kits. Both I, and the people of this state, are pleased to see this killer now brought to account."

The speech was good, Thomas O'Conner thought. They'd remember it next week when he announced his plans to run for Governor. TOC IS TOUGH ON CRIME the bumper stickers would read. He'd have an easy time against this incumbent, who had almost been persuaded to commute the sentence of this "reformed" killer.

The girl was good, O'Conner thought. He'd have time for her soon. She'd support his candidacy, or see her brother sent back to Mexico. KILLER'S GIRLFRIEND ENDORSES O'CONNER the headline would say. She was even pretty. Maybe he'd see how far she would go.

Same for the priest. Father Teddy could keep his little pet, just so long as the Church got out the vote. The Cardinal was already in his pocket anyway, O'Conner mused. Smart move letting the Cardinal in on those apartment deals some years ago, just before his elevation.

Father Terrance let go of Maria and looked at the death chamber. The autopsy after the execution would take most of the morning. The burial was scheduled for 3:00 P.M. He'd be home to

Ramon by early evening. Thoughts of Ramon brought a smile to the face of the priest. Why was it so wrong for him to love Ramon, when he loved the Church as well? Was not love God's most precious gift? Did God need so much love there was none left for Ramon? And what of Ramon? Was it right for the Church to deny Ramon his needs? Would a just God create mankind in His own image and then damn to Hell the souls of those He created imperfectly?

Maria stood stoically. No more tears. Not in public. It was important to give no further satisfaction to evil ones who were doing this. There would be much time to cry when this thing was done. She knew she'd have to deal with the prosecutor and her brother later. Perhaps she'd seduce O'Conner, then let them be "found" together. That would stop this evil man, who was about to kill Buck for no reason other than his ambition for power. The power hungry were the most easy to seduce.

The warden raised his arm and signaled the pellets to drop. Buck looked toward the light and waited.

Willie knew he was spotted. Crossing the yard had taken too long, and he'd made too much noise as he'd climbed the truck. No warning, no siren wailed as the first bullet from the tower guard tore into his left arm. The top of the fence was within reach. His right hand grabbed onto the razor wire. No time left to be careful. No time left at all. The second bullet slammed into his right shoulder. A third missed.

Willie fell back onto the hood of the truck. Slowly, painfully, he tried to raise his injured arms in surrender. More bullets came at him, in the leg, in the chest, in the shoulder again, in the head, until it no longer mattered.

Damn that O'Conner, thought Willie, face upward and squinting at the sun. Damn that fucker! Damn that bimbo he sleeps with. Damn them all! Damn them all! Damn them . . .

The sun was no longer bright, Willie realized. Bullets no longer struck his flesh. He'd fool them. They only thought it was over.

* * *

Buck wanted to forgive his father, but there was nobody in the chamber to tell. The gas seared his lungs, and a giddy wave of nausea struck at him. I'm lightheaded, Buck strained to think. Lack of oxygen. Don't breathe too deep or too shallow. Let it happen naturally. Best to die in peace.

Buck drew his thoughts to Maria and their final night together. He recalled the contours of her body, and the love within her touch. Maria. Who had taught him to let go of the past. Who had taught him to accept her love, and then to give his. Maria. Forgiveness. Love . . .

The light in the chamber had become much brighter. The straps on the chair were loose.

What a disappointment, thought the lawyer. This tape was no good at all. He hadn't fought it. He'd just died. Seven minutes. The fastest on record. Just three minutes of consciousness and seven minutes until the fat little doctor said he was dead. The lawyer looked at O'Conner. You're the winner, he thought. You've taken this round cleanly.

O'Conner smiled, quite satisfied, and watched as the woman and the priest made a hasty exit. Others followed. The room was unpleasantly noisy as the fans roared, clearing the chamber of the poison gas. O'Conner followed the final reporter, vaguely aware that an alarm was ringing behind the din of the fans. He turned and looked at the room. Only the warden, the doctor, and the orderlies remained.

O'Conner felt a vigor, a strength in his loins. He'd hurry home. He wanted his wife. There was nothing, absolutely nothing as good as sex after an execution. To celebrate the kill by taking the body of a woman. Maybe she'd get pregnant this time. A baby would look good in the campaign pictures. Wow! What a day. It's hard sometimes to believe life can be this good.

Willie was surprised to see Buck. "Got me too, the fuckers," said Willie. "Got me about thirty seconds short of the other side of the wall."

"Sorry they got you, old friend. Didn't take so long as I thought it would for me. Kinda glad it came easy," said Buck.

"Easy? Shit! I'm gonna get those fuckers. I'm gonna go back tonight."

"Why hurry? Look at the light all around us. It's warm and soft, and peaceful. Why would you want to walk away from that to return to there?"

"Why? Revenge. Get even. Hurt the fuckers who hurt me. Got me something special in mind. Got me a special person I wanna visit. A real special surprise for a fellow we both know." Willie grinned.

"That's fine, if that's what you want," Buck said. "Wouldn't be right for you not to go back and learn a little more. There'll still be time for you up here yet. There's time for everyone to get here. Even killers like you and O'Conner."

Willie laughed. "Guess you know me pretty well, Buck."

"Yeah, Willie. I've had some time to study on it."

"Well, I got a ride to catch. Gonna pull an inside job tonight," said Willie.

"So long, old friend. Maybe next time we meet things will have been better for you," Buck replied, a smile gathering on his face.

The light seemed brighter, so bright Buck could no longer see Willie. There was a figure in the distance. He thought it looked like his father. A rush of emotion poured into him.

"Paw! Paw! It's me, Buck," he said, running forward.

"Son!" the man shouted, moving quickly toward Buck.

"It's okay now. It's all okay," sobbed Buck as he hugged his father.

And for once, for the one time it very truly mattered, Buck was right.

Lacey O'Conner shifted, trying to keep the fluid within her. Don't make a wet spot, or at least don't make it any worse. Besides, she held a very special gift within her. She knew it. The lovemaking had been strong, and she had felt her power meshing with that of her husband. This was the time, she was sure. The son Thomas wanted, and from the glow she felt inside her, one whose spirit was much in the image of her husband. They'd name him William, after Thomas's father. Yes. Just like Thomas and his father. So much to teach him. So much for him to learn. So much to be passed on from father to son. . . .

Lost and Found

————— ✠ —————

Lawrence Schimel

There is an instinctive recognition of one's own possessions; luggage is visible the moment it is placed on the conveyor belt; a mother peeking into a classroom immediately spots her son among the rows of backs of heads. Call it a woman's intuition, call it what you will, as I stepped down from the cable car I recognized the kiddush cup on the sidewalk.

It was not exactly mine, belonging in truth to my mother. But it had lived my life with me, sealing off each week of my childhood with its dark liquid, as if all the week's joys and traumas were locked into a Ziploc bag and placed in a freezer that was my life, to be taken out and defrosted at a later date, when I could digest the import of each item.

A week always ended on a Friday, and always in trauma. We would sit down for Shabbat, the cup so full I feared it would spill when Dad rested his elbows on the table after a long week at work, when my mother's chair bumped the table as she sat after lighting the candles. Once, when I was six or seven I had climbed onto the table to get the cup. I no longer remember why, just the wanting of it. It had knocked over, Manischevitz spilling across me dark as blood. The tiny wine handprints I had made on the tablecloth never came out no matter how many washings they went through. They stared at me each Friday, peeking out from under my plate in silent recrimination.

After the kiddush was said the cup would be passed from oldest to youngest, crossing over the table as it made its way toward

312

me, the final destination. And every week, just as it had almost reached its goal, Debbie, my older sister and the penultimate stop, would drain the cup completely.

"You're only supposed to wet your lips," she told me by way of an apology as she handed me the empty cup each week.

She knew she was guilty, but she said it as if she had only done what she was supposed to. I always wanted to scream back at her, "Then why did *you* drink it all?" But I never did. She would have calmly answered me with something like, "So you wouldn't drink too much," and sounding as if it were *for my own good* that she had made such a sacrifice. That's just the way Debbie was. She could get away with anything.

To console myself I was always thankful that she hadn't added, "Because you're too young." It didn't matter that I never really had these conversations with my sister; I lived in terror each Friday when it played itself out again that this week she would say those hated words.

"Spare some change, miss," the homeless man sitting behind the cup asked. I stared at him a moment, trying to bring his face into focus. He was old, and obviously a Jew, with the black skullcap and long, dangling *peyot* of the Hassidim. A tallis peeked from under a yellow and purple ski parka torn down the left side to reveal its synthetic innards.

You hardly ever saw a Jew like that begging. They're always too proud.

I hadn't even noticed him, lost in memories. I looked down at the cup. It was empty, dry as the days between Fridays when it sat atop the breakfront, between the candlesticks.

"It can't be the same cup," I whispered to myself as I continued up the street toward work. Sometimes you grab the wrong luggage off the rack; a mother confuses another child for her own.

Darlene didn't like us to make personal long-distance calls, but as soon as I was sure she had left (I didn't simply trust the ding of the elevator doors closing; she usually forgot something) I called my mother.

"Hi. Ma?"

"Esther! What a surprise. Is everything all right?"

"Fine, I just decided to call, that's all."

"That's sweet."

"How's Dad doing?"

"Oh, he's fine, fine."

"Good, and you?"

"The same. You know how it is. Things are always busy this time of year, parent-teacher conferences, that sort of thing. But I love working with the kids."

"That's great. Listen, I want to ask you something that may seem a little strange. Where's our kiddush cup right now? You know, the one we used to use every Friday."

"How did you know? It was stolen last week. We don't know by who, yet. Isn't it funny you sensed it?"

Last week and it had already made its way here. To my mother I said, "I found it today."

"What? Don't be ridiculous."

"I'm sure of it. That's why I called."

"Well, where was it, in a junk shop or something?"

"No, on the street."

"What?"

"A homeless man was using it for his change cup. It was on the sidewalk in front of him."

"In that case he needs it more than we do."

"But, Ma, it's been in the family forever."

"Then it's even more of a *mitzvah* to let him have it. How could it be the same one, anyway? You think some homeless man broke into our house in Baltimore and walked to San Francisco in a week? Ours was stolen, but this is a different one. Coincidence."

"I'm sure it's the same one."

"It can't be. You're just feeling the loss of it. Maybe you're sensing how distraught your father is over this."

"You said Dad was fine."

"Well, he *is* fine. Just he hasn't been feeling too well since it was stolen . . ."

"Why didn't you tell me? What is it?"

"It might not be anything. The cup's been in his family for so long; he feels responsible for having lost it. His mother brought it from Poland. Her father-in-law had given it to her when she married. That's probably why you felt it; he was going to give it to *you* when you got married. Debbie got the linen, you were supposed to get the cup."

The elevator dinged a warning. "Look, Ma, I gotta go. But it was good talking to you. Love to Dad, and let me know if anything happens, y'hear? Kiss, kiss."

Lunch is the working woman's great escape. I had fought with Darlene when she came back, or rather stood there while she yelled at me over things that were her own fault. If I had stayed in the office a moment longer, I would have gone insane. Or maybe punched her.

The homeless man was still in front of L'Uomo when I got downstairs. I took another deep breath to forget Darlene, then walked up to him. "That's a very nice cup you've got. How much would you like for it?" I said it fast, staring at the cup.

"I can't sell that. It's the Holy Grail. It's my salvation."

Great. A kook. Out loud I said, "It looks just like this cup my mother has. They could be a matching set. I'd love to buy it for her."

He looked up at me and I glanced away into the window behind him. His clothes looked worse because of the fancy suits. He probably chose this spot for that effect. "Weren't you listening, it's the Holy Grail. Not for sale."

He was very good at his act, sounding like he sincerely believed this nonsense he was spouting. But I could detect the cunning. After all, he was a Jew. "A hundred dollars?"

"Miss, do you know who I am? I'm who they call the Wandering Jew. Almost two thousand years ago I saw this cup used at a Passover seder which they now call the Last Supper. It's taken me that long to find it again. It's *not for sale!*"

Everyone had his price, even a lunatic. "Two hundred?"

"Spare some change, miss?"

"Excuse me?"

"Spare some change, miss?"

"Three fifty."

"Spare some change, miss?"

"Four—"

He cut me off. "Spare some change?"

Bastard.

I turned away from him, walking up the street toward Bush and Cafe Du Monde. I needed something to eat rather than to waste my lunch fighting with him. First Darlene, now this guy. I didn't need this.

Even though I don't like eggplant I ordered a sandwich of sautéed eggplant with roasted peppers because it was Sam's special for today and it was half price. I think I have a crush on Sam. Or maybe my stomach does. He studied cooking in Switzerland. Mom would kill me, though; he's from Palestine. She'd laugh at me anyway, *Thirty-two years old, and still getting crushes. How about finding someone you can marry?* Maybe she's right.

Thinking back on our conversation this morning I realized she hadn't asked me if I was seeing anyone. Things must be worse than I thought. Probably Dad. Damn it.

I didn't see the man with the cup again until lunch the next day. I was feeling calmer, my anger having dissipated while I slept. Sleep has always been my downfall in terms of grudges. Not knowing if he would be gone by the time I got back from lunch (at Du Monde again, of course) I decided to confront him.

"Yesterday you started telling me about this cup. I'm curious where you got it. Maybe they've got another one like it, y'know?" I almost glanced into the window again when he looked up at me, but I refused to be cowed by a mask he used for his begging and glared back.

"Baltimore."

"I knew it! You bastard! You stole that cup from my mother." I tried to grab the cup but he pulled it back from me, stuffing it into his parka.

"Don't you have anything better to do with yourself than pick on a poor old Jew?" he asked, whining nasally like a teakettle. Then he switched gears to, "Tell me, what do you do?"

"I'm a travel agent. What does it matter? Give me the cup back."

"A travel agent! That's nice, do you like it?"

"Stop changing the subject." I nodded. "Yeah, I like it."

"And do you get all sorts of perks? Like, free tickets to fly all over the world?"

"I don't have time for that. I work. I get two weeks vacation in August, and— Listen, you stole that cup from us." I held my hand out for it.

"You should try it some time. Travel all over the world, that is. You learn a lot."

I tried to work within his framework. "How can it be the Holy Grail if you stole it? Doesn't it need to be quested after? Battles fought, challenges overcome. Chivalry and all that."

He wasn't paying me any attention. His eyes were unfocused, staring toward the street but seeing someplace else. Softly, he said, "But there comes a point when you've seen it all. Really seen all there is."

"Doesn't it mean anything to you that it's not yours?"

He looked up at me again, suddenly here again. "Why do you bother me? Isn't it enough that Christ cursed me?"

"What does Christ matter to you? A Jew."

"I can't die. Not until he returns. That is my curse."

"Real tough life, immortality."

"Yes. It is. All there is is pain. Pain without release of death. Without any hope of surcease."

"That's a mighty big word for a man out on his luck. *Surcease*. Five hundred dollars would be a lot of surcease."

He smiled. "I've been a professor in my time. But I always leave before I get tenure. Imagine if they gave it to me? Tenured until Judgment Day. Wouldn't they be surprised?"

He had ignored my attempt to buy the cup.

"I see you don't believe I'm who I say. I really cannot die." He pulled a bottle from his parka and took a sip. "Want some?" When I shook my head, he poured the rest into the gutter and smashed the bottle against the sidewalk.

I took a few steps back. He was crazy, and drunk on top of it.

And now he was getting violent. I glanced around to see who could help in case he attacked. Could Darlene hear me on the seventh floor if I screamed? Would she even care? He picked up a large shard and sat again. My stomach tied itself in knots, and I had the absurd thought of my intestines as a macrame plant hanger. "What are you doing?" I asked. My voice quavered.

"It's just a little pain. In the grand scope of all these years it is nothing." He pushed the left sleeve of his parka back, exposing his arm. The tear in the yellow and purple fabric gaped like Christ's stigmata. "I tried many far more painful ways before I fully realized the futility of trying to kill myself."

"Don't!" I cried, but he brought the glass down, slicing into his wrist and cutting along the vein until he came to his elbow. For a moment I thought it looked like one of those flat hoses to water plants, with holes poked into its side and arcs of water falling in all directions, before bile rose into my throat and I ran from there.

"See? There is only pain," I heard, as I turned the corner. Ohmigod. What was I going to do? I just made a man kill himself. It was all my fault. If I hadn't pushed him to sell the cup he never would have done this.

Esther, stop it. You have a guilty conscience. He was only a street person. And he was crazy. And drunk. Maybe he would have done this anyway. Maybe he just needed an excuse, someone to blame.

I've got to call the police. An ambulance.

There was a phone on the corner. My legs felt like I was walking with cement shoes on; my arms refused to lift, dangling limply at my side. When I finally forced one to lift I saw why: a long gaping slit from wrist to elbow, the skin peeling away, bone showing through underneath.

No.

I closed my eyes and drew in a lungful of air, telling myself: *It was not me. I am okay. Now, call the police.*

I dialed without looking at my arm. Why was it taking so long? Maybe I had dialed wrong. What do they do about emergencies? This *is* an emergency.

Okay, Esther, when they pick up don't say: *I just killed a man.* Don't say: *I just killed a man.* Don't say—

"911."

"Yes, can you send an ambulance to the corner of Sutter and Powell. A man just slit his wrists."

"One moment, let me transfer you."

Let me transfer you? What is this, airline reservations? Someone's dying, fercrissake!

At least they didn't play Musak.

"Paramedics."

"Yes, I need an ambulance at the corner of Sutter and Powell. A man just slit his wrists."

I mumbled an answer to his questions and hung up. I had to go back and make sure the ambulance would get there in time. I didn't want to see him sprawled on the sidewalk in a puddle of blood, knowing it was all my fault.

And the cup. I had to get it before someone else did. Someone from the Tenderloin would think it was manna from heaven, a body ripe for the picking and no knifing to bother doing. My bile rose again at the thought of touching him. I'd never touched a dead person before. And what if he wasn't dead yet? I began to run toward Sutter, hoping I would get there in time to get the cup.

And what of the man? a tiny, nasal voice inside of me asked, whining like a teakettle.

What of the man: he was gone. There were drops of blood still slick on the sidewalk, the shattered glass and reek of whiskey in the gutter, the same mannequins and suits in the window—the only witnesses besides me—but no man. And no cup.

I left when I heard the sirens coming.

I needed to talk to my mother, to tell her everything: that it was my fault a man had killed himself, that I had lost our kiddush cup forever now, that I hated my job and still didn't know what I was doing with my life. But my parents weren't in when I called.

It was too late, but I felt a need to find out about the Wandering Jew, in memory of the man who stole our Kiddish cup. I had found myself on Post Street in front of the Mechanics Library and gotten books. It was always calming for me to go there after I had fought with Darlene, to watch the men playing chess on the second floor, or wander through the stacks of books.

Though I would always resent his haunting, I tried to forgive him. I lit a yahrzeit, hoping to burn my anger with its flame, purging myself, but the fire reminded me of the blaze in Oakland.

The Yahrzeit had burned nearly halfway when I looked up from Eugene Sue. It was too late to call home, now. Tomorrow, then.

I had to pass his spot on my way to work tomorrow I realized. Would the drops of blood still be there, brown paisleys against the sidewalk? The glass shards? The smell of whiskey? Fear and death hanging in the morning fog, a miasma obscuring the pale, bloodless mannequins in the window?

I marked my place with a napkin and placed both book and candle on the nightstand. I could not get comfortable when I faced away from the light, the darkness looming at the edges. I lay on my side, staring at the yahrzeit—too afraid to close my eyes, even— and watched the spots before my eyes until I fell asleep.

When I stepped down from the cable car I didn't even notice the cup. I stared at the man sitting behind it. Was I seeing a ghost? Did I simply remember him there out of guilt? "Hello," I asked, wondering if the people passing me would think I was crazy, talking to myself, or worse the mannequins.

"Morning. Spare some change?" was his answer.

Had it all been a part of his act? A ploy for sympathy, money? I wasn't sure. "What's your name?" I asked at last.

"I have a thousand."

He was still playing his story. All of yesterday had been a sham, a joke for his sick amusement. My innards tied themselves into a knot of hate. I remembered the yahrzeit I had lit for him, the struggles to forgive him, the books read out of guilt. My bitterness made me play along with his game, taunting, "Well, I don't like the sound of Ahasuerus so I'll call you John instead. For Johannes."

He smiled, thinking I was won over, perhaps. "You've been doing research." He rolled up the left sleeve of his parka, like a stage magician proving he had nothing up his sleeve. There wasn't even a scar.

"And what if I have?" I wanted to hurt him. Slap him, bash his face in with my attaché until the blood pooled on the sidewalk like I thought it had yesterday.

"I'm flattered."

"Screw you." I turned away, fearing I might actually lash out at him. "Screw you, *John.*"

"Thank you, Esther."

The knot in my stomach grew cold with uneasiness. How had he known? I'd never told him. What if he'd been following me home at nights? The Wandering Jew! Why have I been buying into his stories? He's a kook, a drunken kook. The Holy Grail, indeed. A Monty Python lunatic, maybe. What could I do to protect myself from him? What if he tried that stunt from yesterday on me, only the real thing this time?

I turned to confront him once more, but the street was empty. I went up to the office, wondering if he would be back on the corner at lunch, or when I got off work. Better than finding him in my apartment tonight. What was I going to do?

As I sat down at my desk I realized I hadn't even noticed if he had the cup.

He was sitting atop the blue mailbox on the corner when I came down from work. "Spare some change for the strange?" he cheerfully asked.

"How did you know my name?" I demanded.

"Divine inspiration?"

I waited.

"Lucky guess?"

I would get a straight answer from him.

"From following you around all day and night to find out where you live and reading it off your mailbox?"

I started to gasp, thinking he'd confirmed my worst suspicions, but caught myself before giving him that satisfaction. Was he for real? I didn't think so. Look at yesterday. I wasn't about to let him gloat again.

He pointed to the tag hanging from my attaché. "It's on your business card," he said with a laugh. My body betrayed myself, blushing, giving him the evidence to gloat after all.

"Why are you doing this? Do you expect me to believe it's a coincidence that you stole a cup from my mother, then came all the way across a continent to sit on the corner of the block I work on and torment me? You want me to believe that was all by chance?"

"Of course not. It must have been destiny."

Damn him and his games. "It's illegal to interfere with the U.S. Postal Service," I said.

He grabbed his feet and extended his legs, making a V. I was sure he was going to fall, slide off the curved top of the mailbox and splatter his head against the ground like an overripe melon. I could see it happening, the fall, the impact, the seeds scattering out from his head and the melon-flesh, orange like a Cranshaw, in pieces on the sidewalk.

"Go right ahead," he said, breaking the vision. Why was I listening to a talking melon head? I remembered the handful of letters to be mailed. Glaring at him, I reached for the mail slot, tempted to slam it after I had dropped them in. But he looked so precariously perched (legs up in the air) I was sure he *would* fall if I did. This time it would be real when his blood spilled onto the sidewalk, this time it *would* be my fault.

I turned away and muttered, "Asshole."

"You got a pretty view of it, just then, you did."

Despite myself, I giggled.

When I got home and found the yahrzeit still burning I remembered I hadn't noticed if he had the cup. Could he have sold it to someone else to spite me?

As I snuffed the flame I resolved to steal the cup back from him, if he still had it tomorrow.

"You're late," Darlene said, as I walked in.

"Sorry," I mumbled. "Trains."

"Your mother called."

"What?" Something happened to Dad. I rushed to the phone and dialed. Where could they be? The hospital? Was it that bad?

I called Debbie, hoping Mom had gotten through to her. Someone answered on the second ring, but it was only her answering machine.

"Did she say what it was about?" I asked Darlene.

"No. Have you done the Landis tickets yet? That itinerary needs to be faxed to him."

I jumped every time the phone rang, wondering if it would be my mother, calling from the hospital. I had to remind myself to answer, "Warner Travel, this is Esther," rather than "Mom? Is he okay?"

When I couldn't stand it any longer I told Darlene, "I'm taking my constitutional." Mom would call as soon as I left, but the waiting was driving me crazy. Now would be a good time to steal the cup back from John. At least I would have a small bit of good news to tell Mom.

Outside, I glanced down the sidewalk in each direction, then began running. I grabbed the cup with one hand and bolted for the end of the block. As I took the corner, the heel on my left shoe broke off. I limped to the next corner and turned left once more, constantly looking over my shoulder, expecting him to be chasing me. But it seemed as if I had gotten away with it.

I leaned against the wall to rest, cradling the cup with both hands. I felt as if, at last, Debbie had left me enough wine in the bottom to drink from it. Thirsty from my run I lifted the cup to my lips, to drink the cool liquid. I tilted my head all the way back, trying to find any drop of wine left in the cup, but it was empty.

He never had any change in it either. When I worked as a waitress the summer between high school and college the piano player would stuff a few bills in the tips jar every evening, to get the crowd started. He sat with his back to the patrons (though he could see them in the mirror hung above the piano) and read the *Wall Street Journal* as he played.

John didn't start the crowd off. I'd never seen anyone give him money either. I remembered Mom telling me: *In that case he needs it more than we do.* Was it really the same cup after all, despite all the coincidences, despite holding it in my hand and *knowing* it was?

Even if it were didn't make it right for me to steal it now. I didn't want to sink to his level just because he had stolen it from us first.

Rather than retrace my path—it felt too much like defeat—I limped down to Grant, then up toward Sutter again. He was sitting in the same spot. Hadn't even moved.

Angrily, I limped up the street and threw the cup at him. "Damn you."

"Thank you," he said, taking the cup back as if it were his due, "but I already am. I already am."

I was on the line with a client when Mom finally called. She came right out with, "Your father had a stroke, I'm in the hospital."

"Migod. How bad was it?"

"We're not sure yet. There's been some memory loss. Loss of use of the left side." I called up flight charts to Baltimore.

"I can fly out after work tonight. A red-eye, get in Friday morning, late. Which hospital is he at?"

"Sloane Memorial."

"I'll take a cab directly there. Yes, I love you. Take care of yourself too, y'hear? I'll be there soon."

"Sorry," I told the client on the other line, hurrying through his plans. When I hung up I called Continental and had the twenty-one-day advanced purchase waived. Finally, I told Darlene. As I sat at my desk again, wishing I could skip out on the last hour of work, I reflected that Darlene had accepted it better than I had feared. I tried not to think about my father. Finally, five-thirty and I dashed out. John was still on his corner. Out of spite I dug a quarter out of my pocket and went over to him.

"You can't realize how much pain you've caused by stealing this."

"You're going to lecture *me* on pain?"

"No. I don't think you'd understand." I dropped the coin into the cup, satisfied with the loud clink of metal on metal. I walked on toward the Muni. At the escalator into the station someone called my name. What was he up to now? I waited for him, hoping I wasn't wasting my time and missing my train.

"Here," John said, handing me the cup. "You forgot this."

I made some sort of sound, a mix of pleasure and surprise and speechlessness, all at once. "Ar—are you sure?" I was afraid he'd snatch it from my hands any moment, one last cruel joke.

"I'm sure," he said. I saw a flash of silver in his palm from the quarter. "You're going to miss your train."

"Thank you!" I cried, rushing down the escalator two steps at a time.

There is an air of melancholy and suffering which permeates a hospital, and leads one to fear the worst upon entering. Dad's room was small, seeming full of people when there were really only three: Mom, Debbie's husband, Peter, and Dad himself. And now me. Mom sat in the chair by his side, her head resting on the bed. I crossed to the other side of the room, clutching the cup like a security blanket. Dad looked frail, and so much older than I remembered him.

The cold metal brushed his arm and woke him. I couldn't tell if he recognized me or not. With his good hand he reached over to hold the cup. "What did you bring this for?"

"It's Shabbat."

"Did you bring wine?"

"I'll run out and get some," Peter said.

My mother had woken when he spoke. We waited in almost-silence, not knowing what to say to each other, afraid to say anything at all. Debbie came in and (surprise, surprise) noticed the subdued atmosphere in the room. Married life seemed to agree with her. At another time Mom would probably point this out to me as an opening into: was I seeing anyone, and why not?

Peter came back with the wine and opened the bottle. While Mom raised Dad's bed, Peter filled the cup. Dad said kiddush over it, and using both hands raised the cup to his lips. As he passed the cup to Mom, a feeling of warm happiness suffused my body. But when she passed it to Peter I suddenly found myself cold, worrying if this would be the time Debbie said: *Because you're too young.* This is ridiculous, I told myself, but still I stared at her as she lifted the cup to her lips. She took a sip, then walked around the side of the bed to hand me the cup.

"Here. You look like you could use this."

I stared at the cup, still full of wine and in my hands. I recalled all I had gone through to get it back: fighting for it, pleading for it, stealing it. And then him giving it to me, just before I came here. His words from atop the mailbox came back to me: *It must have been destiny.* How much of this had he known would happen? Was this his ultimate joke, what he had been working toward all along? If he really was the Wandering Jew, and immortal, what else was there for him to do while he waited?

Looking around I felt comfortable with my family for the first time. If I wouldn't have spilled wine everywhere, I would have given Debbie the biggest hug.

I *hope* so, I thought, bringing the cup to my lips.

"How's your father?" John asked on Monday morning.

I smiled. "Much better, thanks. It was good for him to have the whole family together again. We had a Shabbat ceremony, everything the way it used to be, even the same type of wine. It helped him to remember. It helped all of us."

"Good. You want a drink?" He offered me a cardboard container of eggnog, decorated with red and green tinsel letters.

"Isn't it a little early for eggnog?"

"Hoping for Gog and Magog."

"What?"

"Forget it. Anyway, 'tis the season to be goyim, fa-la-la-la-lah la-la-la-lah."

I laughed. "Darlene's going to kill me for being late. But I'm in such a good mood, I don't mind."

"Good, then look at this. I've got something to show you." He began unzipping his jacket.

"Really, that's all right." Was he planning on stripping for me? What was it, a pierced nipple? I hoped it was just a tattoo.

He unbuttoned his shirt and pulled out the tallis. "See this?" He held it up for me. "It's the Shroud of Turin."

"The Shroud of Turin," I repeated. What I had thought was a tallis was actually a tablecloth. I wondered if it had tiny wine handprints.

No, I didn't want to know.

A Deal with God

✠

Pat Cadigan

My new acquisition and I took the slow way home from Seattle. I think it was slow. It might as well have been home.

In fact, I had no idea how fast I could move with my new prize. Just because I had come by it carelessly was no reason to treat it carelessly, after all. It was breakable, as are most things you get from art galleries, the kind of things that don't always travel well.

But as soon as I'd rented the car, I knew I'd done right. It was large, similar to the sedans and town cars I'd driven back and forth to the airport in my old job. I set my prize next to me on the luxurious bench seat, pointed the nose of the car more or less toward the southeast and pressed the accelerator until I reached a comfortable cruising speed. After that, a car will practically drive itself, if it and the driver are any good.

My last job had been like any other time-filling bill-payer but I'd liked it better than most; while I was driving, I could think all I wanted. Now, with the miles rolling away under the wheels, I went through my mental trunks and cases and crates, reconsidering everything. Most people would have called it a mid-life crisis, but in terms of living actually accomplished, I was really much closer to the beginning than the middle, thirty or not.

I suppose I could have felt some kind of anger or bitterness toward my parents, but first I'd have had to figure out who to be madder at, my mother or my father. Then being mad itself would

328

have taken energy and attention that I could put to better use elsewhere, especially with this new acquisition to look after.

My acquisition, yes; I contemplated it with mixed feelings. Some things are beautiful because that's their nature and purpose—they're supposed to be beautiful and when you look at them you're meant to be glad that there are beautiful things in the world. Then there are other things that are beautiful because of what they mean—you look at them to remind yourself that there's still innocence or generosity or some other goodness in the world; it's a long list, take your pick. (*It might not be true, but that's something altogether different.*)

My new acquisition was, as I've said, strictly ornamental, art for art's sake, beauty for beauty's sake. Any deeper meanings were up to me. I could think them up, but on the whole, I tend to think it's generally best not to overburden anything breakable.

Sometimes I joked with myself that I'd have to be much more careful from now on about going into art galleries and similar places. Then I'd wonder if I were really done paying for this ornament to my own vanity, and if that was really all it could be: a trophy. And a voice in my mind that sounded not quite like my mother and not quite like me would say, *If you wanted medicine, you should have gone to a pharmacy.*

But was medicine what I was looking for? Sometimes things don't become apparent right away; it might even be years before you understand why you made some choice and why it was right, or wrong, or of no significance whatsoever. Most people find that last so horrible a prospect that they go around imbuing anything and everything with meaning. Even incorrect meaning is better than admitting your life makes no real difference. For some people, anyway.

Being mindful of that very human tendency makes me think twice about having any grand notions about my new ornament. In spite of all that I know and all I can do, I'm very human, no more and no less, and my mistakes would all come out of those very no-more-and-no-less human motivations.

Needing more time to think, I slowed the pace even more by taking a more circuitous route toward home ... "home" being defined as my most recent address. Might as well have been home, yes; a place that, unlike Seattle, could provide some past and a little context for my new acquisition, who seemed completely amenable. But of course, whatever I wanted to do was fine; all things considered, he could now live completely in the present and for the moment, not for what had happened six months ago or what might happen next year. The self-imposed vow of temporary silence didn't hurt his tractability.

I still marveled at how easily I had divined his Name in Seattle. At the same time, two things were going around and around in my mind like two animals chasing each other's tails: *Anything cheap is worth what you pay for it* and *Cheap is dear in the long run.*

At least he didn't look cheap—quite the opposite. But then, think of an art gallery and who you'd expect to find in charge: Michelangelo's *David* with a good haircut and designer clothes, perhaps. I wouldn't have gone that far in describing my prize, but he was pretty enough to be anybody's ornament. After all, that had been the role he'd chosen for himself long before I had come along to Name him and claim him. It occurred to me belatedly as we rolled down Route 84 with a fine grey mist blowing over everything like rags in a wind that the whole thrust of his life had been to await my moment of impulsiveness. From here on, it was my show and I'd learn much of what I needed to know by taking care of him.

You give a child a pet for a similar kind of learning on a smaller scale. I was smiling about that when everything went wrong.

There was a period of time I experienced as a series of jump-cut freeze-frames, except it wasn't just visual. I could hear strange, distorted voices calling to each other while cold mist drifted over my face and wet my lips, but I could see nothing. Then I *could* see: someone's feet running toward me while the moisture on the pavement splashed up and out, but I could feel nothing. And then there was something hanging above me that, after a long time or no time at all, resolved itself into my new acquisition's face, concerned and helpless: I could feel broken bones waiting for shock to wear off, and a hard pressure against the side of my head, but I could hear nothing.

Vision went away again; there was a sensation of rising up, or starting to, and then nothing at all.

When awareness came back, I was in the healing place. Apparently, I wasn't bad enough for departure, it was all fixable. I wondered if my mother and father would know, whether my damage could raise a blip within the stand-off that was their life together, or whether holding each other at bay kept them too engaged to know about anything else.

Not that it would have mattered. You go to the healing place the same way you come into the world or go out of it, and you stay as long as you have to and hope that the healing time doesn't get too out of joint with your outside living time. It seemed like a century before I could do even that—i.e., hope. There was so much wreckage.

Eventually, I began to feel more gathered, more focused. The light in the healing place became less scattered as I progressed toward a more coherent state of existence; random sensation resolved itself into sequences of real things. I became re-acquainted with the feelings that indicated the presence of my ornament, his physical proximity as well as his bewilderment and dependence.

I could perceive other presences as well, some of them standing out more sharply from the texture of the background than others. They exerted a subtle pull, as all living things will. Life calls to life, and power to power, as my mother had told me. Warned me.

At first, I thought it was just a particularly strong life calling to my own, and then I thought it might be my mother, suddenly made aware and coming to see if she could help. But as my senses recovered their sharpness, I realized that the power wasn't there with me in the healing place, or even in the immediate vicinity. It was somewhere back in the world that I had temporarily stepped out of.

Some impressive force, I thought, to have an effect on me in the healing place without actually being there with me. If it was that powerful it had to leave a trail.

I found it easily enough, but before I could pinpoint the source, I woke up in the hospital.

* * *

The ornament was asleep in one of those cheap frame-and-cushion chairs next to the bed, a well-worn flannel blanket over him. His head was resting on his left shoulder at an angle that was comfortable only when you were unconscious. He was going to wake up stiff, I thought; the least I could do was rouse him so he could shift position. I started to call out to him when the door to the room swung open.

At first, I thought it was a nurse's flashlight shining directly into my eyes, blinding me. But even as it moved from the doorway to the foot of my bed, it didn't get any less blinding. And then there was the silence—not just the quiet of late night in a hospital, but a complete absence of any sound, no rustle of clothing, no soft pad-and-squeak of rubber soles on antiseptic floors, not even the distant hum of fluorescents burning all night.

I got out of bed. My acquisition went on sleeping without so much as a twitch. I let him be; I was much more concerned with the light. This was not a flashlight's canned beam; it was more like something alive. Shielding my eyes as well as I could, I padded after it barefoot in one of those too-ventilated hospital gowns. Whoever was carrying it didn't have a steady hand—the light moved with a kind of bobbing motion, like something floating on a wave in a calm ocean.

Suddenly, I could see again; the light had moved behind the curtain drawn around the other bed in the room. Now there was something I hadn't thought of, that there would be someone else in the room, although it made sense. Strangers brought in off the highway didn't usually get private hospital rooms with round-the-clock nursing attention, especially if they weren't carrying anything to prove they were insured. I was probably fortunate not to find myself stacked with cordwood in some crowded basement charity ward.

In any case, my first impulse was not to violate my roommate's privacy, but the light was so strong that the translucent curtain became all but diaphanous. I had no trouble seeing the old woman sitting up in the bed or the dish she was reaching for. Maybe it was more of a platter, since it looked much larger than a dinner plate and the edge curved up a little more sharply. It was easy to see that, too, because there was nobody holding it—it was just floating there over the side of the woman's bed and she was reaching for it with the casualness of someone who did this every night.

I held my breath, hoping I could tiptoe back to bed without her hearing me. Talk about secret people and their secrets, I thought, feeling slightly giddy. When my mother had explained about secret people and strange worlds, had she been thinking about something like this? Or was this something else I was privy to as a knower?

The old woman removed something round and white, about the size of an old-fashioned silver dollar, and held it carefully between the thumbs and forefingers of both hands. The silence was still utterly complete, but I could see her lips moving. Ritual. Praying?

She put the thing in her mouth and it clicked for me then. The communion rite. I had never participated in any form of it, but I got the gist. Except this particular version was not really an act of faith; this woman *knew* what she was getting out of it. And what she wasn't getting.

I wanted to know, too, but apparently this wasn't one of those things I could just know, and I couldn't exactly barge in on her and ask her what she was up to.

They were around me and past me before I even knew they were in the room, two nurses and a doctor moving quickly but unhurriedly. Not that I could have hidden or anything, but to my surprise, they ignored me as if I weren't even there. One of the nurses pulled the curtain partially aside while the doctor stepped around the floating dish platter to carry something to the tray table. The other nurse went to the opposite side of the bed and unrolled thick strips of some kind of cloth, laying them out next to the woman on top of the covers.

The curtain in front of me had not been moved, so I was still watching everything through it and wondering how they could all see what they were doing. The way they moved had the feeling of routine; maybe they'd done this so often, they didn't actually need to see any more to do it? The nurse who had pulled the curtain moved to the foot of the bed, blocking my view; at the same time, the light began to damp down from blinding to merely bright.

What the hell, I thought; if I were going to be this nosy, I might as well take it the whole way. I stepped around the curtain just in time to see the doctor unroll the towel she had placed on the tray table and remove the lance.

Still, no one paid attention to me, not even the old woman who looked right through me with an expression of serenity as profound as the silence still in force. I was mildly shocked to see that she had a tracheotomy tube coming out of her neck, like someone in a coma, a detail that hadn't been visible through the curtain. The nurse on her left was turning back the sleeves of her hospital gown to expose her forearms. I figured I knew what was coming next, but what I really wanted to know was why. And why no one cared that I was standing there watching.

The doctor held up the lance. It was actually more like a broken-off spear and nothing at all like a surgical instrument. The doctor's elegant hands seemed to emphasize its brutal quality, even though she was treating it as if it were something fragile. Or sacred. The nurse on the other side of the bed bowed his head with unmistakable reverence, averting his eyes as he lifted the old woman's forearm for the doctor.

The tip of the lance or spear pressed against the flesh just under the wrist for a long moment before it finally plunged all the way through and out the other side.

I had expected the blood to spurt. Instead, it flowed out gently into the dish platter, which had obligingly come down into position to catch it. The doctor had averted her eyes now, too, along with the nurse at the foot of the bed, while the old woman stared into space, not watching but not deliberately looking away, either. Her expression suggested a state of transport or rapture. Only I was watching now, and if they weren't going to try to stop me or force me out of the room, I was going to continue.

The woman's blood kept flowing into the dish, enough that it should have spilled over onto the sheets, except that it didn't. An unmeasured time later, as if in response to some hidden cue, the doctor pulled the lance out. The blood stopped immediately.

The old woman seemed to rouse from a waking dream and offered the arm to the nurse, who wrapped a strip of cloth around it, in spite of the fact that there were no marks, no scars, not even a scratch to show where the lance had pierced her.

They went through the whole thing again with the old woman's other arm, lasting a little longer, I thought; or perhaps not. It was hard to tell. In that persistent silence, something funny seemed to have happened to time anyway.

Not to mention space, or at least the part defined by the dish. There was still no overflow, not so much as a drop spilling over the side, and yet I could see the surface of the blood collected in it, reflecting the old woman's face like a red mirror.

This time the doctor pulled the lance out and left it on the dish, which then floated upward as if to deliberately move itself out of the way. No one looked at it. The nurse on the woman's left removed the blood pressure cuff from the wall and wrapped it around her upper arm while the doctor started to examine her. Suddenly it was all very ordinary except for the dish hovering in mid-air with the lance lying in it.

And the silence, which was really beginning to bother me. Was this the only way I could witness this ritual, to see it but not hear anything? And what kind of ritual was it—a healing ritual, or a book offering to an especially obscure medical demigod, or something else I couldn't imagine at all?

The dish began to glow more brightly again; in a minute, the light would be blinding. The doctor lifted her hands to it and it floated down into them. She picked up the lance and held it close to her face. A bead of blood was shining on the point. The doctor touched her thumb to it and then used the same thumb to trace a triangle on the old woman's forehead. The woman closed her eyes and collapsed against the raised bed, unconscious, as the doctor turned away to wrap the lance in the towel on the tray table. On the other side of the bed, the nurse bent over to kiss the top of her head. Nice, I thought, taking a good look at him for the first time. This certainly gave a new dimension to personal care. Then I noticed the doctor was looking at him as well, in an expectant way. The nurse shrugged and turned to the nurse at the foot of the bed, who was making some notes on a patient chart. Not being able to hear them was frustrating, as was having them ignore me so thoroughly. I had to remember the ignoring trick, I thought; under the right circumstances, it could be quite effective. . . .

The dish began moving away from the bed, leaving the room exactly the same way it had come in. The light it gave off was blinding but I managed to see a little more this time. I tried to touch it as it passed but it eluded my fingers and sailed out into the hall. A moment later, as I tried to readjust my vision, I saw the back of the male nurse pulling the door shut behind him. His back was pretty nice, too.

My ornament shifted in his chair but didn't wake. *Little man, you've had a busy day?* And more than one of those, by the look of him. His sleeping face had no real repose in it, as if all his troubles had followed him into unconsciousness so he could wrestle with them in his dreams. Which was exactly how things were with him, no doubt. But what else could the poor boy do? Just wait and hope for the best, of course, but it couldn't be easy for him. I still owned him, even unconscious.

"It'll be okay now," I said to him. Or tried to. I sensed my voice, but I couldn't actually *hear* it. Oh, Christ, I thought, irritated; wouldn't you know that the accident would have deafened me. Well, it wasn't as if I couldn't reverse it, but it was annoying to have yet one more thing to do.

I started to get back into bed and then saw it was occupied.

There was a moment of confusion—wishful disorientation, I'd guess—in which I thought I'd gotten all turned around and I was back on the old woman's side of the room. But it wasn't the old woman in that bed. It was me.

Well, that explained the silence, I thought staring at myself.

I didn't look good. Of course, the tracheotomy tube didn't help appearances, even if it was letting me breathe more easily. My body tended to shudder and sigh on the exhalations, as if I were suffering for every breath. It wasn't peaceful, like the old woman. No wonder the ornament looked so upset, even in sleep. I wasn't able to tell him there was no suffering, no discomfort. Not even any sound, just nothing.

Nothing? Was that really true, I thought suddenly, or was there nothing only where I was . . . which was *not* where my body was.

And, come to that, why wasn't I? If I wasn't in the healing place anymore, I had no reason to be anywhere else but within the corporeal.

Maybe I'd slipped out inadvertently when that strange dish had floated in—power called to power, and all that. It made sense. So all I'd have to do would be to figure out how to slip back in again. Maybe retracing my steps would do it. I tried, moving as if I were still corporeal and it was all just a matter of getting back into bed again after all.

It didn't work. I could sense the body around me like a strong electrical or magnetic field, but I wasn't *in* it. A matter of concentration, I decided hopefully, and I was concentrating hard and heavy when the nurse came in and exposed the feeding tube in my stomach.

It was a different nurse, and she was just making sure I was clean, I guess; anyway, at the sight of the feeding tube, I went crazy. It wasn't any worse than seeing a tube coming out of my neck, though of course it wasn't any easier, either. I think it was just that the two of them together were too much. I ran back and forth screaming and yelling—or I would have been screaming and yelling if I could have made a sound—while the nurse bent over me and my ornament shifted again in the chair, still looking troubled.

After a bit—quite a bit, I think—I pulled myself together, ashamed at being so squeamish over my own body and found the ornament had woken up and was talking with the nurse. No—he was listening while the nurse talked to him.

The ornament did have a name: Gus, short for Augustus. Gus the ornament. Right. If I could remember, that had to mean I wasn't really *gone*. Naturally, I couldn't hear a thing the nurse was saying to him, and trying to read her lips in the semi-darkness was just an exercise in frustration. But at least I could see by her face that she was being kind, while Gus was being polite. Not yet the totally helpless lump he would become if I didn't find out how to slip back into my life soon.

She beckoned to him. He got up and leaned over me, taking my hand and stroking it. Trying to pull me back. I wanted to run up and down screaming and yelling again. *Power calls to power, Gus,* I thought sourly. *Power pulls power. Get me some of that stuff you slept through and* then *try me—*

And suddenly, I felt him touching me. Or *almost* felt him. It was like feeling the faint vibration of a radio running on the last drop of juice in a used-up battery, just before it dies altogether. I tried to seize the feel of him and hang onto it, build a bridge out of a thread, but there just wasn't enough.

Power calls to power.

I turned away from the sight of him bent over my inert form and found myself standing next to the old woman's bed. She was slumped against the raised portion of the mattress, eyes closed; her bandaged arms made her look like a failed suicide. There was no trace of the triangle the doctor had drawn on her forehead with her own blood. I began to wonder if I'd dreamed or hallucinated the whole thing as part of the situation I was in.

Then she opened her eyes and looked at me with that same expression of benign serenity.

Shocked, I waved both hands in front of her face to see if she was really looking at me. She didn't draw back but her expression faded slightly, as if my actions had unsettled her. She didn't *see* me, I realized, but she *sensed* me . . . sensed *something,* at least.

I tried touching her and that unsettled us both. It was as if I were oil and she were water, with a layer of plastic wrap between us just to make sure things stayed impossible. For a little while, I fumbled around while she sat looking bewildered. Then she reached for the drawer on the night stand. There was a pen, but the only paper was a box of tissues. The felt-tip pen wouldn't write on the box, and made big blotches on the tissues. She gave up and wrote on the sheet in big, unsteady letters:

DR. GOWAN
YOU

It was meant to help. I just wasn't sure how. I moved back to my own bed. Gus was still standing beside me, holding my hand and stroking it from the palm out to each finger. And I tried, very hard, but I couldn't feel a thing.

The pinpoint swelled gradually to a brilliant, deep red bead. For a moment, it hung distended from the point of the lance; then it fell heavily into the tube the doctor was holding. No one held the lance. It floated above the table in the lab, a sight that would have made me giddy if I'd had anything to be giddy with. Hell of a lot of floating equipment in this hospital, I thought, watching another drop of blood form on the tip of the lance. Well, all right, only two things, a dish and a lance, but that was probably two more than any other hospital in the country. The dish was nowhere to be seen, or sensed; the power was concentrated in the lance now.

Or rather, the power was concentrated in the blood that came drop by drop out of the point. Gowan and the two nurse-accomplices flanking her watched intently. The woman on her left had a rack of empty tubes they apparently hoped to fill; in front of the man was a rack empty except for one tube, capped, labeled, and half-full.

It was a slow process but nobody was in a hurry. The nurses had the look of people who were equally prepared to wait hours or days. Gowan's face showed the same feelings mixed with a kind of urging, as if it were her own concentration that produced the blood. It's the kind of expression you see on the faces of people who believe that their prayers can be answered if they say them right.

Except Gowan wasn't praying; like the old woman in my room, she *knew.* It wasn't faith, but hope—hope that the power, whatever it was, would choose to work for her.

As the lance continued to bleed, I could sense the slowness of the process extending outward; as long as the lance was active, time in the hospital passed more slowly, and not at the same rate in every location—it was slowest here and in the immediate vicinity, and dissipated farther away. Somehow it would all even out later, though probably no one would notice. Time always seemed warped in hospitals.

It slowed even more with each drop that welled up from that

point, I realized. As each drop fell, I could see it shake within itself the way things will do when seen in extreme slow motion. The movement of the nurses' chests as they breathed was all but imperceptible, their eyes like unseeing glass. I thought of my body lying in the room elsewhere in the hospital, Gus running his fingertips along my palm, the old woman sitting up in her bed, and outside in the hall, a different nurse plodding to the desk at the nurses' station, caught in a shift that seemed endless. Only I was outside the effect.

Correction: only I and Gowan.

Her eyes gave her away; she blinked slowly, but not slowly enough. It wasn't humanly possible to move that slowly, and when I realized, I wondered why she was bothering, what she hoped it would do. I moved in close to her, studying her nondescript, middle-aged face. She looked like anybody, everybody, somebody. Not a secret person, but someone who had become privy to a realm of secret people and had to deal with it, because there was no one else to do it.

Her Name should have become known to me then. I hadn't really been looking to divine it, and I certainly didn't want to say it, but the fact that it was obscured from me meant that quite a lot was out of kilter, at least where I was concerned, and it wouldn't be put right until I got back into my body and woke up.

For that to happen, I realized, I needed some of the blood.

And as soon as I realized that, I also realized Gowan could see me.

Not *see,* exactly, but *perceive,* I amended. Gowan could perceive that I was there. Only I wasn't supposed to know.

But why not? I wondered, as another drop of blood swelled so slowly that it was literally painful to watch, even with nothing that could feel any literal pain. The drop took hours to detach from the point, days to splash down in the tube in the doctor's hand.

Gowan didn't move and I knew it had ended. The lance had produced as much as it could for now: three tubes, counting the one she was still holding. Not a lot of return considering how much blood they'd taken from the old woman sharing my room, perhaps half a pint, total—but, I was sure, very potent.

And now, who would get it? Who would benefit? I could tell this was a familiar dilemma for Gowan as she finally capped the tube and put it in the mostly empty rack with the other two. She pulled a clean white towel out of a drawer under the table and raised it to the lance, cradling it for a few moments before wrapping it up. I felt the change in the power; suddenly it wasn't floating anymore, and she was carrying it to a cabinet across the room. I had a glimpse of the dish as she put the lance on the shelf next to it.

The two nurses hadn't moved; they were still caught in the slowdown. Gowan didn't pay any attention to them as she grabbed a handful of disposable syringes and then stuck the three tubes of blood in the breast pocket of her jacket. At least they didn't float too, I thought as I followed her out.

I'd known that she was going to visit the children's ward. Half the contents of one tube went into an IV connected to a too-skinny three-year-old, asleep or comatose. After a long period of pacing through the ward, the rest went to a husky ten-year-old with a head injury. Caught in the temporal slowdown, no one there noticed; from their perspective, Gowan probably hadn't been there long enough to register visually.

Time was moving a little faster in the intensive care unit, but then I imagined that was probably true normally. Time was something nobody had much of in intensive care. After considerable thought, Gowan passed up one cardiac case and dosed another in the next room. That took an entire tube, leaving one. My room was on the next floor up. I stepped in front of Gowan as she headed for the stairs.

I know you know I'm here, I thought at her as she pushed along, pretending she felt nothing. *I know what you can do; please help me.*

Pretending was a serious effort now. Her forehead wrinkled unhappily as her gaze came to rest on me, or whatever she perceived of me.

It'll work. Just help me get out of here and no one will ever know about any of this.

She stopped at the door leading to the stairs and leaned against the wall with a weariness I could practically feel as a tremor in the ether. The elegant hands covered her face for a moment and then smoothed back her greying brown hair as she looked up at the exit sign over the door.

"Nobody knows," she whispered to the sign. "*Nobody* knows. Even my nurses forget afterwards, until I need them again. It's a deal with God. Make your own deal. We all have to."

She shoved through the door and stumped down the stairs. I thought of going after her to work on her some more. It was the last thing I thought about for a while.

I came back to awareness in my hospital room. Not a bit like waking up; most like a switch flipped from off to on. I was looking up at Gus from a vantage point somewhere near the floor. He was asleep in that chair again, the blanket rumpled and probably smelly as well—he looked like he needed a bath. He also looked like he wasn't going to get one until I woke up.

And if I never woke up? How big a tragedy would that be, I wondered. Subtracting one secret person would leave a remainder of: one helpless possession who would probably spend the rest of his life sleeping on sidewalk grates. Anything else? Two parents, but they were so busy with each other I doubted they'd become aware of my absence for a long time. So, what else, then? Could I honestly say that the universe would be thrown out of balance if I weren't in it? This universe, at least?

The universe doesn't suffer from a lack of anyone; I didn't have to prove it needed me, I just had to want to be in it badly enough to stick. Which meant making sure someone else wanted that as much as I did. Or even, if possible, more.

Years from now, I'll tell someone the story of how Lassie saved me from drowning, I thought, concentrating.

Gus woke with a start and looked over at the bed where my body was still huffing and sighing.

I did call your name, but not from there.

The uneasy expression on his face deepened as he sat up straighter and looked around.

Wait, I thought at him, *it gets weirder.*

If I'd told him to wait for Armageddon, he would have started doing crossword puzzles. This wasn't supposed to take quite as long. After an hour of nothing but waiting, I was the impatient one; he was uneasy, knowing something else was wrong, but not knowing what.

Power calls to power: come in, power.

Nothing.

I thought of the old woman in the next bed and then, like before, found myself beside her. She was unconscious, lying back against the raised mattress as if she had been tossed there and forgotten. The covers were jumbled around her hands, but I thought I could see bruises on her wrists in the semi-dark. Perhaps they were just shadows.

Wait, I told Gus again—needlessly, but it made me feel better—and went in search of Dr. Gowan.

She was alone in her little laboratory domain, passed out on a roll-away cot. This was the goddamnedest hospital, I thought; what wasn't levitating was unconscious. Or comatose, like me. I knew what she was trying to do—apparently, she had much less understanding of the power than I'd realized.

Seriously disapprove, doctor. This won't damp the power, it doesn't depend on you. And what if somebody needed you, not in a way that called for a miracle but just some plain old medicine to practice, what then?

The sense of my thoughts reached her where she had taken herself. She couldn't bring herself back, of course, and that just about summed up humans for me: once they get anywhere, they're through.

Goes double for secret people, said a voice in my mind suddenly. *Test it out sometime.*

Not right now, thanks all the same. I hovered over the doctor on the narrow cot, concentrating until her trail became visible to me and I could follow.

* * *

I think it comes of the human condition—the modern human condition, anyway—that when humans are actually able to go elsewhere, they usually have to be incapacitated by some kind of drug so potent as to be toxic to them. And rather than finding their way to one of their superficial notions of paradise, they somehow instinctively head for exile in the dead ends of nowhere.

The doctor had put herself in solitary in what she thought of as nowhere. She hadn't bothered to visualize her idea; it reminded me of being under a restaurant-style covered dish. Or maybe hospital-style was more like it, considering the circumstances.

She knew me right away, but it took a little while to get past her pretending she was too poisoned/intoxicated to perceive or understand. That was embarrassing for her as I'd known it would be but I couldn't allow her to indulge in her feelings about being caught in a blatant lie.

Time to sober up, straighten out, and come home, Dr. Gowan. I can guarantee your miracle will work for me. I want to go home and live my life. I need to find home and figure out what my life is, I can't do that with a tube in my throat and another in my stomach.

Nowhere became Dr. Gowan as a good setting will show off a gem. Because it wasn't just nowhere, I realized, but Entropy itself, and Dr. Gowan saw herself as a one-person battalion dedicated to beating back Entropy in its most insidious forms: disease, injury, death. She was blessed with the perfect weapon, the ultimate magic bullet, and no shortage of people to use it on. But, like all good things, there just wasn't enough of it to go around.

So instead of being able to walk through her hospital as its resident savior-healer, she spent part of her time engaged in triage and the rest of it hoping she had chosen well. No human should have been forced to carry that kind of burden, I thought in a veritable seizure of self-righteousness; if I had been offered this thing, I was sure I would have refused it.

Because you're *not a doctor.* I'm *a doctor—a* real *doctor. No* real *doctor would refuse the chance to be a healer.* She turned restlessly in her realm of nothingness, resisting the urge to leave and not wanting to stay there all at once.

Better have a dose of your own medicine, doctor. Like the saying goes, Physician, heal—

Myself? Her laughter pelted me like small, hard stones. *Can't. That's part of the deal with God, you see . . . that I never, ever partake, that I never use it for my own benefit. If I get hit by a truck, if I have a heart attack, if I get cancer or AIDS, it's just too bad for me. Someone else will come along who'll make a deal with God and keep it.*

Not a healer but a custodian. A real doctor for a custodian. It wouldn't have been enough for certain secret people I could think of, who would never settle for being only a conduit. But then, that type didn't usually turn up as healers, either, and most likely for that very reason.

And while we're at it, whatever offer you did *accept seems like a good enough burden for anybody. Even you, whoever you are, and whatever. Secret people, what's that? What can you do besides have out-of-body experiences and make some young guy too handsome for his own good keep a vigil like a lapdog?*

In confronting me, she made the nothingness into a territory. The geographer's instincts I had inherited from my mother the traveler kicked in, and within moments I knew her territory better than she did. And being a knower, as soon as I knew that, I knew her Name.

If it had not been for my experience with Gus, I might have been foolish enough to Name her on the spot. Name 'em and claim 'em, as the saying goes—was there a saying like that?—except the claiming is the catch. I was still in the process of finding out what it meant for me to have claimed Gus back in Seattle; I didn't need to complicate things with another acquisition.

Especially not this one. I didn't know how I'd do having absolute control over her the way I did Gus. In its own way, it might have been as bad as my parents, irretrievably locked in their dance of death together, each watching for signs that the other might be weakening. No, this would be different, but just as bad, I could practically see it. Having had some power herself, she would understand far better than Gus what she had lost to me, and no opportunity to club me with it would ever, ever go unused. If she were to give up everything to me, she would make sure she leaned on me deliberately, without let-up, until I broke, or she ran out of demands, whichever would come first. I knew damned well what that would be.

However, she didn't know any of that *yet,* and that meant she could be bluffed. Instead of Naming her, I *almost* Named her; I took it to the brink, letting her see the process by which I could divine her Name and then stopping short—as far as she could tell, anyway. I let her know that I could go on to divine her Name, tell it to her, and take her; but if I chose, she could rush in and learn her own Name herself.

The implication was if she cooperated with me and gave me the book so I could wake up, I'd let her be privy to her own Name. For some reason, this made her unhappy. Instead of moving to shield her Name from me—actually possible, but only temporarily—she left it where it was and let go of the nowhere-turned-territory as she allowed consciousness and her world to come back.

"The blood," she said, opening the cabinet doors, "is payment from the ones who benefited in the past. The old woman in your room, she was helped. So she kept her part of the deal and allowed her forearms to be pierced and her blood taken. *This is my body; this is my blood.* Mean anything to you?"

A knower can know a lot of things, but that doesn't mean there aren't empty spaces as well. Religious ritual was one of those for me.

"It's all right. You'll be part of the communion too; you'll give back the blood. It takes a lot of blood, it takes ..." She paused with the rolled-up towel in her hands as the dish sailed slowly out of the cabinet and hovered almost a foot above her eye level. "It takes a *lot* of blood." The dish started moving through the room toward the door. Gowan turned to look in my general direction with a funny smile-frown on her face. A square-shaped face, very solid, very plain, and somehow looking much younger now. "You can't stop the process once it's begun, so you shouldn't even try. Remember that."

I remembered that every moment the lance was in a three-year-old forearm, impossibly big and crude. The child stayed quiet while she watched. Only later, as we were leaving did she start to cry, but it was someone else's job to console her.

She took everything up to my room and woke Gus to help her. He was cooperative enough, if suspicious. Gowan kept looking at him as if she couldn't believe he was for real, which was rather amusing in someone who took levitating objects and miracle cures for granted. Or possibly instructive—i.e., she probably wasn't going to be the last person I'd met who could believe in anything except the commitment of one person to another.

But then again, you couldn't call Gus's situation a commitment, exactly, could you? Commitment implied something entered into voluntarily, and with expectation of it being reciprocated. Gus, on the other hand, had lost his soul because he'd been careless with it and I had been just as careless in claiming it. But if that was the only way I could have gotten any help out of him to save my own life, then good for me and I could call what I'd done to him inadvertent foresight instead of carelessness or arrogance.

Gowan held a syringe under the lance and it seemed to me that the blood dripped a bit more quickly from the point this time, or maybe it was just that the time distortion wasn't as marked. Gus wasn't affected by it, something that she found unnerving but not worth commenting on.

The syringe was three-quarters full when the blood stopped. She capped it, set it aside, and took another empty one from her coat pocket. Before she could even get it open, the lance dropped down on the bed. For a long moment, she could only stare at it, startled. Then she picked it up and set it carefully in the dish, which was on the night stand.

"I guess that's everything and you get it all tonight." she said to my body, still shuddering and sighing. She didn't bother to swab the crook of my arm with alcohol, just uncapped the needle and slid it in. "Everything," she said over her shoulder to Gus.

I thought of the old woman then and went to have a look at her.

But the other bed in the room was stripped and empty; there had been no one there recently.

Something funny that had happened with time . . .

And then I understood—

The cool grey mist hit me in the face like a blow from a ghost as I got out of the car. There were flashing blue and red lights all around, disembodied voices calling to each other and a strange pain in my throat that was fading even as I became aware of it.

"I said, are you sure you're all right?" The police officer seemed to congeal out of the mist. I moved past him to the front of the car. The wheels on the right side had gone off the road onto the soft shoulder. Through the windshield, I could see Gus sitting motionless in the front seat with both hands on the dashboard as if he had to anchor it. His expression was beyond terror. Perhaps I should feed his denial, I thought, tell him he had a dream; I would have to decide that later. The police officer was saying something to me.

". . . only one in the line of cars that didn't plow into the jack-knifed truck. If you're sure you're okay, I don't mind telling you they could use some blood donors up at the hospital. The supply there is pretty depleted and this was a real bloody one—"

I had to ask him for directions, since I hadn't been awake for the first trip.

It was noisy, crowded, and chaotic at the hospital. They gave Gus a number and sent him to wait in a room with fifty other people. Me, they ushered directly to a laboratory—two nurses, that is, a man and a woman—where the doctor was waiting.

"It so happens we have a serious need for your type," she said, sitting me down at a table, "which is, as I guess you know, rather rare." She cleaned my arm herself. Nearby, I could see the usual equipment for drawing a pint of blood; no lance, no dish.

"What happened?" I said.

"Big accident on the highway," she said, "tractor-trailer jack-knifed and overturned. Your blood, however, we'll be giving to a little girl in the children's ward. We were completely out. You showed up at just the right moment."

I put my free hand on my neck. "Not quite what I meant."

"Oh?" She bent over my arm with her back to me. "What *did* you mean?"

"I think you know." Anyone who walked in would have seen a long plastic tube leading from my arm to a plastic bag. I couldn't see, but I could feel how the lance was stuck through my forearm just below the wrist. It didn't really hurt that much.

"Actually, it's a little late to ask," Gowan said in a low voice. "Certain questions you have to ask at the proper time. Like when there's something to ask about. Because sometimes, there can be as much power in the asking of a question as in the answer." She looked over her shoulder at me, her body still blocking the sight of my arm. "You didn't know *that,* did you? If you'd asked the right questions at the right time, something quite ... *unusual* would have happened. You might even have called it miraculous."

"What? I asked.

She shook her head. "It's hard to say. So many healings. So many lives saved. Perhaps ultimately, an end to suffering."

"That sounds a bit grandiose to me," I said.

"Does it?" She moved aside and I saw the lance piercing my arm. "I guess it does. I guess that's why it makes such a good bed-time story in the children's ward. Children love stories that have miraculous, happy endings." She pulled the lance out and plunged it through my other arm. I didn't feel at all weakened, but I could feel what she was actually trying to draw from me, and it wasn't blood.

"When it's distilled," I said, "you'll get a drop about the size of a fingernail. Give it to someone who believes in miracles."

Her face was cold. "I made a deal with God—"

"*I* didn't. But if God ever wants to make a deal, God knows where to find me." I pulled the lance out of my forearm and handed it to her. "*Without* a go-between."

"I wanted more," she said darkly.

"Even if I would give you more, this is all you'll be able to use. Even miracles have limits." I looked over at the nurses standing near the door. It was hard to tell if they were aware or not. "How many years ahead was I seeing in the room?"

"Many," she said. "So many lives saved, so many healings. And you didn't suffer. You were comatose most of the time and we took good care of you." She gave a short, hopeless laugh. "I remember a future that never was."

"You remember a dream you had," I corrected her. "Sorry, but I had to wake up. It wasn't my dream. Or my deal. Or my God."

I turned away from her and headed for the door.

"I just wanted to do some good," she called after me.

"Next time," I said, "ask for volunteers."

I collected Gus from the donor waiting room; they let him go without question. He didn't say anything of course, since his vow of silence was still in effect, but I could feel him looking at me for miles.

"It's okay," I said finally. "I paid it back. It wasn't my deal, but I didn't walk off with something for nothing anyway. Besides, what do you think would have happened to you if I'd let myself become that old woman in the bed?"

He just kept looking at me, and for a moment I saw what he'd been seeing during that time, the decades spent free and on his own, subject to no one. Another one who'd had a dream that didn't belong to him.

I sighed. "Not this life. Maybe next time you'll do it the right way."

His eyes seem to plead, but I knew he really didn't know what to ask for.

Maureen Birnbaum
and the Saint Graal

—————— ✠ ——————

by Elizabeth Spiegelman-Fein
(as told to George Alec Effinger)

What can I tell you? The last time Maureen Birnbaum zetzed into my life, I was five-ninths pregnant with our darling little Malachi Bret. My husband, Josh, never got along with Muffy, and so he wasn't like terribly brokenhearted when she said she was probably never going to bother us again.

Me, on the other hand, I was glad at first and then like I started to miss her. Not that I missed the gold brassiere and G-string she wore on her interplanetary jaunts, or the way huge broadsword named Old Betsy (no relation) she dragged with her into my nice clean Queens apartment. And not that I missed her endless braggy narrations of her really, really *hard-to-believe exploits. What I missed, I'm thinking, is our old Greenberg School friendship, which belongs in the dim, dark past. What I missed was my evaporating youth.*

See, Muffy still looks like a high school junior, and who wouldn't hate her on account of a thing like that? I, on the same other hand mentioned above, have become a little old housewife lady. I'll be thirty years old before I even get to the next paragraph. That was probably an exaggeration.

Okay. It was a rainy summer day and I'd dropped Malachi Bret off with Mums so I could like do some personal time gazing wistfully at crushin', killer leather shoes that'd probably fit, too, *but I couldn't buy them because now I'm a militant vegetarian after reading Sidney Sheldon's remake of Sinclair Lewis's immortal novel* The Jungle.

I was driving into the city in the maroon Renault Alliance Josh bought me (used, although he's a doctor with a healthy practice and like he could certainly have gotten me a better car and I don't see why not a new one) after the little Mazda died. I was halfway across the bridge when I heard this sort of fwumping sound and felt a gust of wind inside my car. Like I'm sure if the windows hadn't been rolled down, they'd've blown right out. I almost lost control of the steering wheel, and then I heard her.

"Whoa Nelly, sister! Get a grip!"

It was guess what Muffy.

Oh, and by the way, I didn't mean Sinclair Lewis before, I'm so sure (now, I mean). It was Upton Sinclair! Is my face red! I always get them mixed up.

Like anyway, I shoot Muffy a quick glance and I was shocked. I mean I was almost never shocked by the weirdo outfits she showed up in, but this one was a weensy bit over the top. She was wearing a tight white dress hiked halfway up her chubby thighs, and it was made out of—I knew it right off—honest to God samite. I don't even know how I knew, but I did. I mean, I'd never seen samite before, like it's not something they sell by the yard at Korvettes' or anything.

So she goes, "Miss me, Bits?" Now it was "Bits." It made me long for the good old Bitsy days.

I turned back to her and stared for a couple of seconds to establish the mood. Then I go, "Can I drop you somewhere, Muffs?"

Now like I really wish I had.

Look, I'm tell you, Bitsy, Fate can be cruel. Cruel to a heart that's true. How I've yearned—and like it's no big secret, right? because I keep telling you and I'm not even sure you believe me anymore—O, how I've yearned to whoosh back to Mars! Mars the red! Mars the terrible! Mars the bloody! Mars the home of the totally awright Prince Van, the buffest, tuffest babe in all of dudedom! Yet what does the universe do to me? It schlepps me to

Sherwood Forest—and a Sherwood Forest* like spotlessly *sans* Kevin Costner, no less—and then schlepps me to your house, then schlepps me to God—and I do mean *God*—knows where, then schlepps me like *I don't believe this* not to your house, but to your terminally skanky *car*. Forgive me, Bits, but like it's skanky and I'm so sure you know it.

Where was I? Like don't ask me. I aimed like I always do for Mars, and like I always do I missed. Not my fault, I was carrying a lot of weight what with Old Betsy and the rest of the accoutrements I've gathered in my world-saving travels. Maybe like I forgot to allow for windage or something. Whatever. I opened my eyes and saw that I was definitely not on Mars. It's getting to be easier for me to identify *not on Mars*. It's a gravity and blue sky thing. Yeah, huh.

There was a road. There's always a goddamn road, even in the center of the Earth or wherever. So I stood in the road and nothing was happening and nothing was happening, so finally it dawns on me that this time I had to like walk.

So I hefted Old Betsy across my shoulder and marched onward into adventure like any sun-bronzed warrior woman would do. I was like unafraid and ready to turn the tables on the evildoers. Just like roads, there's always evildoers, know what I mean?

So I'm bookin' it along this dirt lane, and I'm watching the sun. It's going up. Then it's like noon, you know? and then it's going down. I'm still walking. I haven't seen anybody or anything, not a cow, not a field, not a castle on a hill, not anything. Of course, being a fierce fighting woman, I'm not like dismayed or nothing about having to spend the night in the sheltering roots of a primeval oak tree, because although some male-dominated mythologies have this cockamamy idea that oaks are dudelike in their treeness, oaks have historically been shown to be the temples-houses of druidesses, from which we get the word, what is it? druades or something. And if the tree nymphets could live in an

*Like how could you have forgotten? This triumphant feat was spellbindingly recounted in "Maureen Birnbaum Goes Shopynge," in *The Fantastic Adventures of Robin Hood,* edited by that sweetie, Martin H. Greenberg, and published by Signet Books in 1991. We'll wait here if you want to go read it first.

oak, I didn't mind sleeping with one. Sisterhood is, you know, like powerful and all.

I was just about to wrap myself in my combat cloak, if I'd had a combat cloak (and while I'm wishing, I could have used a down-filled vest from L.L. Bean, too) when what should happen but a gnarly old man (and I *do not* mean that in any good surfer-dudelike way) hobbles into view along the dusty road. Figures, huh?

Oh, my *gawd,* I go, it's like the first person I see and already I have a moral dilemma. See, that's how the Goddess tests you, like she keeps scattering moral dilemmas around like carpet tacks. It's much more obvious to a heroine like myself, but I'll bet even you, Bits, has to make R & I decisions now and then, for sure, huh? That's "radical and intense," honey, don't give me that look.

Here were my choices: I could curl up prettily and hit the rack, or I could like introduce myself politely to the raggedy dude and find out where the hell I was *this* time. No, you don't have to worry, Bits, like they always speak English. Another function of the universe, I guess, and I see no need to overtax my splendid brain worrying about it.

It was a real poser, let me tell you. I held a secret ballot, and interviewing the venerable old gentleman dude won over flaking out by a tally of six to four. So I put on my medium-power smile, the one that goes "I bear you no ill will but I'll slice you like a radish if I catch so much as an evil flicker in your eyes."

"My good man," I go, stepping into the road and gazing levelly at him. Gazing levelly is like a vital fighting person kind of trait. Some of us are born with it, huh.

"Good my lady," he goes. "What would you of me?"

And I'm like, whoa, funny English again. I just knew I was in some grody prehistoric time before people discovered the truth and traded in their Louis Vuitton handbags for Fendi.

"I would of you like your name, for openers," I go.

"Hight I merely Joe," he goes.

"Joe." A guy named Joe, and he's going around woulding and highting. "And je suis Maureen Birnbaum, bravery like personified, and don't you ever, *ever* call me Muffy. I left that part of me long ago and, you know, far away."

Joe nodded thoughtfully, then gave me one of those shrewd, calculating looks, you know, where you feel like your thoughts are, oh, laid bare and lying there etherized upon the table like when old Miss Grau tried to make us understand "Prufrock," remember? Talk about a pair of scuttling claws. Jeez.

Well, now that you ask, Bits, I truly don't know *what* that has to do with my awesome adventure. It was an image, that's all. No biggie. Like forget it if it's too deep for you.

So he's like, "Wittest thou what I wot?"

Just the latest in un-key, dear. And they don't sell like Cliff Notes for real life, huh. I go, "No, I wit not."

"Wot I that thou art in the way of the Saint Graal."

I looked around quick, but nothing was coming. The wrinkly grandpop was operating on E.C.T. Estimated Cloud Time. I wasn't in anybody's way, for sure. "Well," I go, "in that case I'll just be moseying."

"None but the gentlest and most parfait knight may hope to achieve that goal."

Gentle, I'm thinking, hey, I could be gentle if I had a reason. Parfait, though, would take some thought. Hot fudge, definitely. Whipped cream, definitely. Six or seven maraschino cherries, most definitely. Ice cream? A tough choice, but I leaned toward mint chocolate chip and a scoop of bubble gum. "I think I can hack it," I go.

Joe give me this little smile like "Yeah, we'll see." I wot like instantly that I might have to watch myself around this guy. "Wouldst thou then accompany me?"

"I dunno," I go. "Maybe *you* could accompany *me.*" I was like there first, you know? It probably doesn't seem important to you, Bits, but billing is heavy stuff to a brawny warrior. Image is like everything, and you got to let people know from the getgo that they can't dis you without immediate and terrible retribution.

"As thou wishest," he goes.

So we walk maybe a half mile, neither of us saying much of anything. It's getting dusky and dark and stars are coming out and I look for Mars in the sky but the strife-torn God of War was like totally absent. When I look down again, what to my wondering eyes should appear but *another* shabby dude in a filthy robe and hood. He looked like the Hermit in the Tarot deck if the Hermit had gone residentially challenged—that's, come on you know, like homeless—for a year or so. Definitely not Block Island Race Week, Bits.

"Hola!" I go, but like soft.

"Behold, it is my brother Bohort."

Honest to goodness, honey, I could've sworn he said the most insulting thing. He didn't, though, I found out. "Your brother," I go warily. "What a whatchacall, a coincidence."

Gives me him that same dumb smile, all sort of bemused and condescending. "Not that we are twins of the womb, but yet are we brothers in Christ."

"Christ," I go. "Well, yeah, huh."

"Bohort!" he goes. "Well met!"

"God's grace to you, brother Joseph!" goes Bohort.

"And to you, good man. Behold Maureen, a lady knight errant who seeketh that which we wot of."

"Ah," goes his friend, "then gladly will we share our company."

"Fine," I go sternly, "but you can drop the 'lady knight' business. I'm a knight, period. None of this setting me off in a special category just on account of my gender."

Joe looked at Bohort, and Bohort looked at Joe. "Shall we continue on toward the Castle of Seemly Joy, or take our rest?" goes Joe. I'll like stop reporting their weird antique English if you don't mind, Bits.

Well, again the vote went for moving on, and so like we did. Okay. Now it's nighttime and we're still marching along. For once I didn't have to worry about where I was going, although like I didn't know what to expect from the Castle of Seemly Joy when I got there. The name of the place sounded like, you know, a massage parlor or something.

So I was lost in thought, something I try to do every few days—a healthy mind in a tuff body, n'est-ce pas? I wasn't paying much attention to the scenery until I noticed that we'd come to a fork in the road. "Aiee," I go, "a fork in the road."

"Even so," goes Joe. "A leftward turning and in likewise a rightward turning. Whichever shall we choose?"

"Don't look at *me*," I go. "I mean, I'm following you guys, like for sure."

"Then we ask you to choose," goes Bohort.

"I know," I go. "I'll choose the fork that takes us to . . . the Castle of Seemly Joy."

"Excellent brave choice!" goes Joe in an exclamatory kind of way.

"Uh-huh. Now which road is it?"

"Alas, we cannot tell you," goes Bohort. "The way differs for every pilgrim."

"Pilgrim?" I go. "Do I *look* like a pilgrim? What is this, a Thanksgiving pageant or something? Last time I looked, it wasn't even the Fourth of July."

"Choose," goes Joe.

And I'm like, "What the hell? This castle moves around over the countryside or something?"

Joe and Bohort looked at each other. They didn't say a word.

"We'll go to the right," I tell them.

"How now," goes Bohort. Don't ask *me*, Bitsy.

So we hike it off to the right, and lo and behold not a quarter of a mile farther on we come to a knight in full armor on horseback with a couched lance, just sort of idly sitting in the road waiting hour after hour after hour for us to come by. Like some people don't have anything better to do with their lives.

"What ho, varlets," goes the knight. He had a big shield with black stripes that divided the shield into three parts, like a peace symbol without the middle leg thingy. In the upper left section was sort of a pig with tusks all rampanty. In the upper left section were three red shapes like Lego blocks. In the bottom section was a gold-colored crown with bright enameled jewels. And like not a ding on that shield, like he just bought it that morning and nobody had bonked it yet.

"Who you calling varlets?" I go, stepping to the fore, see, 'cause I was like the only one in our group with courageous battle-hardened nerves.

"Y'all I'm calling varlets," goes Sir Froot Loop.

"Why don't you get off that horse and try it?" I go.

"Try what?" he goes.

"Try this." I waved Old Betsy around a couple of times. I had a feeling that inside his tin helmet, this guy was no rocket scientist.

He didn't say anything. He set his lance upright in some kind of socket thing, swung his legs heavily over the saddle, and landed with a noisy clanging on the ground beside his horse. Then he drew his own broadsword and came at me slowly. He moved sort of like Robbie the Robot, you know, huh? Clanking and shuffling. I figured he had one good swing with that sword of his, and if I kept out of its way, I had maybe fifteen minutes to dice him up while he recovered for the next swipe.

" 'Ware the knight," goes Joe. "He is the first Guardian of the Pearly Path, and your first Test."

I glanced over my shoulder. "You didn't say anything about tests. I would've taken this adventure pass/fail if I'd had a choice."

"Good my lady," goes Bohort, "you made that choice when you took the rightwise turning."

"Uh-huh," I go, watching my opponent awkwardly hoisting his sword for the first strike. "And like what would we have met on the leftwise way?"

"Alackaday, the selfsame Guardian."

I would've put down money that he was going to say that.

Like I'm turning my attention back to the lethal threat in front of me. "Who are you!" I go.

"I am Sir Sanspeur," he goes.

"And you've got a brother named Sansreproche or something a little farther on, don't you?" I am like so clever sometimes, Bits, I amaze myself.

By way of reply, this Sanspeur dude tried to whang me a good one on top of my head. If that blow had landed, I'd be sitting here dead, split from my skull straight down to my highly prized groinal area.

But you'll be happy to learn the blow didn't land. I neatly sidestepped—I mean, I had all the time in the world, like you know?—and while he was trying to unstick his blade from the ground, I just gave him a little sideways whack with Old Betsy, not hurting him much but sending his own sword flying away.

"Oh, I am undone," Sanspeur goes in a quavery voice. "You have bested me, and you are therefore a most terrible strong Maid."

"I'm nobody's maid, buster," I go fiercely. "Now, do we get to pass by you without any of your nonsense?"

For answer, Sir Sanspeur merely hung his ironclad head. I didn't even look behind me to catch Joe and Bohort's reactions. I kind of relished the moment of victory, which I knew wasn't going to last very long, because whenever there's a first Test, you can bet your Bernardo sandals there'll be another.

So I'm like, "What is this Saint Graal when it's at home?"

And Joe goes, "Saint Graal is Frankish for Holy Grail."

"Ah," I go, "the Holy Grail. You mean the Sacred Cauldron."

Joe looked at Bohort, and Bohort looked at Joe. "I don't believe I've ever heard the Grail called that," goes Bohort.

"Not surprising," I go, stifling an imaginary yawn. "Holy Grail is a male-supremacist, sexist, revisionist term using religion to hide the devious conspiracy to rob women of their innate power and authority granted to them by the Goddess."

"Goddess?" goes Joe. I thought he was going to strangle on the word.

"Don't pretend you don't know what I'm talking about," I go.

Well, they did so pretend. Bohort goes, "Of course, the Saint Graal or Sangreal, the Holy Grail as you would have it, is the chalice used by Jesus at the Last Supper. Its history is long and magical. It was fashioned from a gigantic jewel, a gem that had once been part of a magnificent crown given by sixty thousand angels to Lucifer, when that archangel still dwelt in Heaven. During his fall into Hell, the jewel fell from his crown to Earth, where it was fashioned into a cup. The cup came at last into the possession of a certain good man, who gave it to Jesus."

"Nuh-uh, that's not the way the secret traditions of women have it," I go.

"What secret traditions?" goes Joe. I thought I saw a flicker of fear in his eyes.

"The chalice is actually the Sacred Cauldron, the symbol of

women triumphant, the symbol of female power, as the cross is the symbol of male power."

Bohort looked horrified. "How can you claim the Holy Grail is a feminine symbol?"

And I'm like, "Isn't it a treasure that all men seek?"

Joe goes, "Wellll, yes."

"There's more," I go. I was getting into this. I don't know if I got all my facts straight, though, 'cause like I was trying to remember what I learned from Miss Stickney in sophomore Women's Studies. "The Three Sisters are the counterparts of your divine Trinity. They show up everywhere: The Triple Goddess, the Norns, the three Graces, the three witches in *Macbeth,* the three cauldrons of Wise Blood that Odin stole, there's no end to it."

There was silence for a while. Finally Bohort spoke up. "It doesn't make any difference, anyway," he said. "Sir Galahad achieved the Saint Graal because he was the only knight of the Round Table who was still a maiden."

"Galahad?" I go. "Like a virgin?"

"Certes," goes Joe. "Only a person untainted by profane love may long to see such a holy relic."

"Well," I go, drawing myself up to my full height, which is impressive to these short little ancestors of ours. "I myself am a maiden and about as taintless as you can get. But if you tell anybody—*anybody*—I'll damn well tear your lips off." I had been meaning to lose my virginity, Bits, but I'd been busy, first with you know school and all, then with hacking apart green Martians and God knows what. Now it looked like hooray being a virgin was going to get me somewhere.

"As my brother said," goes Joe, "Sir Galahad achieved the Saint Graal, following which it was removed unto Heaven forever. Now and then someone like Lancelot will have a vision of it, but not physical contact."

"And who knows from visions?" I go. "Jeez, I've had some visions—"

"So in these latter days the Queste has another goal," goes Bohort.

I felt my eyes narrowing like suspiciously. "And what may that be?"

"The Saint Nappie," goes Bohort. "The berry bowl used by Jesus at the Last Supper."

"Berry bowl?" I go. See, I was like fabulously dubious. "I don't remember berries at the Last Supper. I mean, if they'd had berries, they'd be part of the Catholic mass now, wouldn't they? Between the bread and wine?"

"I suppose," goes Bohort. "But I didn't say they had berries. I said they had a six-inch bowl. It is part of the Mystery what the bowl contained."

"Could've been rose water," goes Joe.

"Could've been Judas's petty cash bowl," I go.

Silence again.

"And the Saint Nappie?" I go.

"It is lodged on Earth, man wot not where. Perhaps it rests within the Castle of Seemly Joy, awaiting those who may find that holy shrine," goes Bohort.

I glanced from one to the other, a determined look on my face and the light of true conviction in my eyes. "Follow me, men!" I cried. I felt kind of like Gregory Peck in *Pork Chop Hill*. Ever since I first whooshed my way to Mars, I've known that I was born to command—and like not only command, but I was born to rule. I saw myself as a female Odysseus, wandering hither and yon in search of my own true love, fighting the worst battles against overwhelming odds and emerging all, you know, triumphant and stuff. Then someday I'd go found my own city and rule it benevolently until it was time for me to disappear magically and then there'd be all these like too strenuous to believe myths about where I was buried and how I was just waiting to return whenever my realm needed me no matter how many centuries had passed. See, I did too read that Joseph Campbell stuff. And I thought it was pretty dumb. I mean, don't you wonder what his wife thought about it all, huh?

Anyway. I had the feeling that there was something ho daddy weird happening around me because we'd been like making tracks for hours and I'd already been involved in one deadly combat, and I was still wide awake, I wasn't tired or hungry or thirsty, I didn't even have to pee. And jeez, Bits, you know my bladder's about the size of a walnut. So I had the feeling that I was caught up in some eldritch mystical Queste, on account of you never hear of like Sir Perceval having to stop and pee.

The trees—heavy oak action all around—arched over us like a green tunnel. It was shadowy and quiet—*too* quiet, like just before one of the camp counselors gets his head cut off by a chainsaw in a *Friday the 13th* movie. There was, as Mr. Stumpf would say, Gloomigkeit all over the place. Of course, I was concerned only for my fellow travelers, who did not have my strict and noble warrior woman code of behavior to fall back on. Yeah, huh.

Okay, like the road turned sharply to the right, and when we rounded the bend, there was this like rock right in the middle of our path. "Gladsome tidings!" goes Bohort. Like he was *such* an enthusiastic dude I wanted to slap him silly sometimes.

"Pardonnez moi," I go, "but what is so gladsome about a boulder in the road?"

"Why, good my lady," goes Joe, "mark you not it is a magic boulder?"

"I mark nothing, pal," I go. "All I see is something that would rip the bottom out of any wagon wants to come by this place. And if that rock has been sitting here all this time without somebody digging it up and heaving it off to the side, I think probably no wagon ever did come by here. That leaves me with like one question: Then what is this road for, if nobody ever comes by here?"

"It is a magic stone, forsooth, and a magic road," Bohort took pleasure in assuring me.

"A magic stone. I spieth nothing in the way of an enchanted sword sticking out of it. Or am I too late for that."

Bohort and Joe thought that was somewhat amusing and uttered like several ha ha's each. Then Joe goes, "Look thou not upon the stone, yet verily beneath it."

"Under the stone," I go. "Lemme see if I got this straight. There's something really neat under this stone. Like worms, maybe. Or Japanese beetles. Or a trapdoor into a vast and eerie subterranean wonderland of fabulous riches and you know nightmarish Lovecraftian gel-creatures."

Bohort looked at Joe, and Joe looked at Bohort. They were smiling, but answer came there none.

I grumbled a little and hoofed it over to the boulder. I did my rally best, putting my mighty thews to work rocking the stone. I prayed to the Goddess, or any one-third of her that might be listening, for sufficient strength, but it was like N. G. No go, Bits, at least. I can think of two or three other things N. G. could stand for, how come you can't? You should watch *Wheel of Fortune* every once in a while, that's what you should do, huh.

Well, it was like plenty clear that I wasn't going to roll that rock out of the road. I thought about the problem for a while. Then—in the famous words of my role model, Wonder Woman, "Praise Hera!"—I had a sudden insight, you know? Ever happen to you, Bitsy? A sudden insight? No, I thought not. So what I did was, I used my multitalented sword as a simple machine—no, not a pendulum. A lever. Wasn't it Einstein who said, "Give me a lever and a house in the country and I can move the world?" Or something like that. What do you mean, "fulcrum"? I'll use your head for a fulcrum, you don't let me finish my saga.

Well, to make a long story come to an end, I clean and jerked that boulder out of the dirt. Then I bent way down to see what Bohort and Joe had been talking about. It was a dirty number-ten envelope with a sheet of paper inside. I took the paper out and read it. It said:

"Hello, pilgrim!

Welcome to Clue #1! You've evidently surmounted the great difficulties put in your way, and you are to be congratulated! Now, if you keep up your courage (and stay pure! Pure is the way to go, whatever your disgusting fleshly senses may counsel you) you will soon acquire that which you heartily desire! So here it is, the first important clue!

The Saint Nappie rests on a deep blue satin pillow in the Great Hall of the Castle of Seemly Joy.

All best, and may God bless!

* * *

I crumpled the sheet of paper and the envelope into a ball and tucked them away in my utility pouch. A true barbarian swordsperson may revel in slaughter and all that kind of thing, but one does not litter the forest-ho.

"Now what?" I go.

"Onward!" cried Bohort. "Onward to the Castle of Seemly Joy!"

"What about the boulder?" I go.

"Oh," Joe goes in what you call your offhand manner, "someone will be by to reset it."

"With a new clue underneath?"

Joe looked at Bohort. "If that is the Lord's will," goes Bohort.

"Uh-huh, you bet," I go. "The Goddess wouldn't have any part of this nonsense."

Before we'd traveled much farther, Joe put his hand on my arm. "Forgive me, good my lady. I have a garment which will profit you much to don. It will mark you well as a holy pilgrim, and you will receive therefore the aid and succor of our allies."

He held out to me the very white schmatte in which I am even now encladded. I didn't think much of it at the time. I mean, *no designer label at all,* even on the *inside!* These two guys had never heard of the Talbots catalog. They probably never even heard of *Lane Bryant,* for God's sake!

So I took the raiment and garbed myself behind a set of bushes. I just like threw it on over my primitive but serviceable Ruler of the Everywhere gold bra and G-string. The white dress fit okay except it was snug across the you know *ass,* if we can speak freely. I would've liked to dab on a little Chanel #22—did I tell you I've moved up to Chanel now? Seems like I've never run into a single other warrior who wore *Je Reviens,* Not that I just follow the crowd or anything, Bits, but like who wants to be T.B.A. just because you smell wrong.

To Be Avoided, dear. Are you putting on fat between your ears, Bitsy? We used that one at Greenberg.

I'll be goddamned if I can remember what I was about to tell you. Maybe we can stop along here somewhere and have just the smallest little Bloody Mary? They're like just so *good* for you, too, you know, with all the vegetables and stuff. No? Too early? Ha, Bits, I think you'd positively freak if you saw how we savage fighters consume food and liquor shamelessly, in a free-flowing celebration of life and victory and not being pinned to the ground by a very sharp pointed thing.

Lemme see. Oh, yeah, like in another fifteen minutes or so we came to a falling down stone building. It looked like someplace the Vandals had lunch on their way to sack Rome, and they enjoyed the hospitality so much they made a point of trashing the place again on the way home. I looked at Joe and Bohort, and put forth the postulate that this, then, was the Castle of Seemly Joy, famed in song and legend.

They really shot me down, huh. "No, fair maiden," goes Bohort, "not so easily wilt thou arrive at that precious goal. This that thou beholdest is the Gladsome Abbey."

"Yeah, duh," I go. "It doesn't look so gladsome to me."

Joe shrugged. "There were more wonderful days, all long since," he goes. And like even if he didn't wink, he was implying it for all he was worth. I had to tread carefully here, Bits, 'cause I could sense Metaphorical Significance all over the place.

We went into the abbey, and boy howdy was I surprised that there wasn't any knightly dude in full battle array trying to stop us. There wasn't much of anybody, really. It looked worse on the in-side: crumbling stone and fallen blocks, caved-in ceilings and shredded tapestries, scuffed and warped planking on the floor, rats scurrying around, and best of all nothing but moonlight to keep the orcs away.

We poked into one chamber after another and didn't see hide nor hair of any human residents. After we'd gone through ten or twelve rooms, I found a suspicious pool of light in one corner. I turned around and saw that a silver beam of moonlight glimmered through a chink high up on the wall. I could hardly believe our luck, that the moon just happened to be in position to illuminate the very corner that like just happened to also be indicated by a big, wide, bright red arrow painted about knee-high on an adjacent wall.

"How fortunate," goes Joe.

"Really," I go. "How about that."

"What do you think it means?" Bohort goes.

I just squinched my eyes shut in like, you know, mock pain. I didn't bother to answer him. Instead, I got fully into hacking away at the dry-rotted floorboards with Old Betsy. In like a few minutes, I'd biffed open a hole big enough to put my hand into, so I put my hand into it. What should I find but a small leather pouch with a drawstring cord! How thrilling, huh?

Joe goes, "I wot not what mayest in the bag be." Joe wot not a lot of things.

"Perhaps we'll find out," I go, giving them like this little up-on-Mount-Olympus sneer. I pulled the bag open, and inside was a golden key, wrapped in a piece of paper. The problem was that mice or whatnot had gotten to the bag and the paper long before I had. Now the paper said:

—key.

—may use it—

Good—   —bless.

"What is it?" goes Joe.

I looked fully at him and did not blink. "It's a key, Joe," I go. "It's probably clue number two. Maybe it unlocks something here in the abbey."

"Well, no," goes Bohort.

"How do you know that?" I go.

Bohort looked like a guy who had sent in his subscription money to *Penthouse* and started getting *Architectural Digest* by mistake. "It just doesn't look like it would, that's all," he goes. Pretty lame, huh?

So we bailed out of the abbey on account of I figured Bohort probably knew what he was talking about, even though he was just ever so grieved that he'd let it slip. We hit the Pearly Path again until we smacked up against the second Test.

It was a big hairy serpent. Oh my *gawd,* Bitsy, no, the snake didn't have like *fur* or anything. It was hairy. *Hairy.* It's slang, Bits. Oh, just figure it out. So anyway I go to work on the serpent, all the time fully realizing that this was a thinly disguised phallic threat to my maidenhoodedness. Like the serpent in the Garden of Eden, huh? No big surprise that Eve was tempted by a big old charming male member, and like the mother of us all *just couldn't resist.* Of course, Bitsy, men wrote that book.

So I like lop the head of the snake and *by golly* two more grew back. I wasn't fighting a monster, I was fighting a literary allusion. I didn't have to lop any more heads to test my working hypothesis, so I went after the other end. I biffed off the snake's scaly tail, maybe eleven inches, enough for a whole 'nother meal if you'd wrap it in tinfoil and put it in the freezer. Well, the snake didn't grow his tail back, so I whanged another chunk of tail, and then another and another. I kept slicing that two-headed son of a bitch until I had left tail and was clearing into neck. The heads turned to watch what I was doing, and they were most evidently worried.

Finally, all I had left was this little V-shaped bit of monster, the two heads joined to maybe three inches of body. The heads just lay on the ground panting and looking pitiful. I left them like that, and we continued on our way.

"Excellent slicemanship!" Bohort goes. "You know that in my youth I myself carried a sword in the service of my king—"

"Arthur, would that be by any chance?" I go.

"—yes, King Arthur," goes Bohort. "And I was a stalwart of his Table. But never in all my days have I seen a soul so skillful with a blade. Except Lancelot, of course. And Perceval and Galahad, too. And Gawain and—"

"Yeah, huh," I go. "That was the second Test. How many are there altogether?"

"Now, that too differs with every pilgrim," goes Joe. "Most usually there are three, however."

"One more test and one more clue, right?" I go. "Things in threes?"

"Things in threes," goes Bohort. "Mirroring the holy and glorious Trinity."

"The Triple Goddess," I go. I watched them shiver. It was like good for them now and then.

Jeez-o-man, Bitsy, I could tell that I was getting close to the end of this exploit. I've got a sixth sense for knowing that by now. No, it's *not* women's intuition. Women's intuition is a male sexist demeaning fraudulent counterrevolutionary concept invented to put a name on something men can't ever understand because of their stunted and wholly unromantic natures. If you buy into the intuition thing, you might as well climb back on that pedestal they set up to trap your ass.

What do you *mean,* Bitsy, you *like* being on a pedestal? Hell, next time I come back from some mind-shattering adventure, I'll bring some of my pamphlets with me. God, honey, you need a little consciousness-raising. And a fanny tuck wouldn't hurt you, either, if I may make a personal observation just between close friends.

Just never mind, okay? Just drop it, Bitsy, I'm coming to the gut-wrenching finale here. See, even though I guessed not more than two or three hours had passed, I noticed the sun trying to peep over the horizon. "What time is it?" I go.

"Dawn," goes Bohort. He was like ever so helpful.

I shrugged. If I could accept two-headed dreadful serpents, I could accept three-hour nights. Maybe I was in some warm polar region or something. It didn't make any difference. I didn't have much time to like ponder, on account of there was a giant blocking our way on the Pearly Path. A *big* giant, Bitsy, resting his elbow on the crown of a mighty oak tree.

"The third Test?" I go.

"The third Test," goes Joe.

I chewed my lip for a few seconds. It looked like the giant was ready to give me all the time in the world. "Say," I go finally, "where are all those allies you mentioned? I mean, that's why I'm dragging around in this white outfit, huh?" A magical white outfit, too, Bits, 'cause it never got dirty and serpent blood came clean with just a damp cloth.

"Why, we are those selfsame allies!" goes Bohort.

"Yeah, duh," I go. They still looked like two fully rasped-out fugitives from the Dumpster behind Ernest and Julio Gallo's place.

"Behold!" goes Joe. And right there he whipped off his hooded robe, and doggone if underneath it he was wearing a tunic and like pants made out of the same white threads I was wearing. Only he had a red cross on his chest. And suddenly he didn't look anywhere as old and unshaven as he had when I first met him. He was now a young blond guy with twinkling eyes and apple cheeks.

Don't you just hate apple cheeks, Bitsy? You can never trust a guy with apple cheeks, no matter how mythological he is.

And Bohort did the same, flanging away his shredded robe. The two dudes looked like brothers, all right. "Know you not our tales?" goes Bohort.

"Nuh-uh." I knew I was going to hear 'em, though. I glanced up at the giant, and he smiled at me. He was still in no particular rush.

"I am Joseph of Arimathea," goes Joe, "into whose keeping passed the Saint Graal, that I provided unto our Lord and Savior, and thencefrom carried it I unto the nations of Britain, in order that it should be made ready for the beginning of the noblest of all Questes."

"Wow," I go.

"And I was the companion of Sir Perceval, and we had the greatest and surpassing honor to be with Sir Galahad upon the moment of the completion of his Queste. We beheld the most puissant Saint Graal, and we beheld Sir Galahad's most holy and peaceful death, and the angels that bare his soul unto Heaven."

And I'm like, "Wow," again. "So the two of you are going to pitch in and help me with this tall dude?"

"No," goes Joseph of Arimathea, "we'll watch. This is your third and final Test, and we mayest not help thee."

"Really," I go. Now, of course giants are just another phallic symbol, so I wasn't totally haired out or anything. I just fell back on Mrs. Stickney's feminist disclosures. According to Hindu traditions, giants could live a thousand years because like their whole existence was what they called centered in the blood. And the blood, you should forgive me, Bitsy, was the menstrual blood of the Triple Goddess. Oh, don't go *ewww*. This is all true stuff. You know of course that in Greek mythology, the River Styx was really a river of blood. Guess whose?

Look, I can't tell you where it says that. I just *know* it, that's all.

So I like pointed all this out to the giant, and he mulled it over for a while, a heavy frown on his craggy features. At last he came to some decision, because he just stepped out of my way. I guess I dazzled him with my brilliance or something. Anyway, I thanked him kindly and started again on my Queste.

"A moment, good my lady," goes Joe. "Wot ye not that the giant is to be slain?"

"What for?" I go. "Seems to me I was just supposed to get by him, and I done did that."

Joe looked at Bohort, and Bohort looked at Joe. "The giant is supposed to be dead," goes Bohort.

I shrugged. "A dead giant is a useless giant, and this giant looks pretty useless to me, so he might as well be dead. Come on if you're coming."

They hesitated a few seconds, and then they followed me all right. I have these sterling leadership qualities, you know.

Clue number three wasn't far away. It was just a note tacked to the last tree before a vast and peaceful meadow. The note said:

Seek thou, O fortunate pilgrim, seek thou the Castle of Seemly Joy in thine heart of hearts.

Good luck, and may God bless.

"In my heart of hearts," I go. What was I supposed to do, tap my heels together three times and wish? I had to think about this one. It wasn't, you know, like the most revelatory clue in the world.

"The Castle of Seemly Joy," I go. "Joy, huh? As in Joyous Gard? Where Guinevere split to with Lancelot? You know that's just another name for Venusberg which is another name for Mons Veneris. I don't have to spell that one out, do I? See, like I said, it's all sexual symbols, but the male-dominated terrified pathetic heterophobic Church co-opted them and changed them into castrated and powerless images. But we women know. We've been keeping notes."

"I wish you wouldn't say castrated," goes Bohort.

"Never mind," I go. "I know where the Castle is. 'Seemly Joy', my heroic ass. You *wish* it was Seemly. In your next life, dudes."

"Why . . . what do you mean?" goes Joe. He was turning into a real hairball right before my eyes. I mean, Bitsy, he was getting into F.D.F.M.N., you know? I don't *expect* you to get that one, sweetie, I just made it up. Feet Don't Fail Me Now. He was like freaked, huh.

"What I mean is the Castle is right . . . over . . . there!" And I spun to my left and pointed into the butterfly and songbird-filled meadow.

"Where?" goes Bohort. "I see nothing."

"There," I go, and sure enough, there was the Castle of Seemly Joy. A woman's power had created it, and it was too much for my buddies. When I looked back to see the expressions on their wheezy faces, they had disappeared. No great loss.

See, it was all so figurative around there that I wasn't letting anything surprise me. I had my key ready, and lo and behold! it exactly fitted the golden lock on the Castle's front door. I opened it and went in, feeling sort of like Goldilocks, like you know? "Hellooo!" I called, but I guess nobody was home. Nobody with lungs, anyway.

And there it was, the crystal Saint Nappie, just as I'd been told. It was sitting on like this comfy-looking satin pillow. I reached out slowly, expecting like these horrible last-second Indiana Jones kind of traps to spring loose all around me. My hand touched the berry bowl and I felt, like, glass, huh? I picked up the bowl, and in that very instant the pillow, the table it was resting on, the parlor, and the whole goddamn Castle of Seemly Joy disappeared. I was standing in the Pearly Path again. Even the nice meadow had gone with the wind.

It was just me and the Saint Nappie. I looked at it, you know, close up, and I saw these letters of fire along the rim. I peered even closer until I could read them. They said:

HAZEL-ATLAS GLASS COMPANY, WHEELING, WEST VIRGINIA

Suddenly I had a terrible headache. I mean, like I had to wonder if all the derring-do had been worth it. Was this the very berry bowl used by Jesus at the Last Supper? Who could tell? The ways of the unreal and symbolic can be inexplicable, even to such a nimble and resourceful mind like mine.

I took a deep breath, let it out, and muttered. "Son of a—"

And then like uh-oh I whooshed right here to your car. And you know the most bizarre thing? I don't even have the Saint Nappie to show you! How's that for irony, huh?

Typical. Just too goddamn typical. I dropped Muffy off at Penn Station because she said she wanted to visit her mother, who had recently remarried. Before she left, she asked about Malachi Bret and how was I doing with a little rugrat to take care of. Muffy is not, you should know this, the maternal type. I told her I was doing just fine, that Josh was a great help with the baby, and that under no circumstances did I ever want any old Greenberg School chum to become Aunt Muffy. If I could work it, I'd make it so Malachi Bret never even heard the name Maureen Danielle Birnbaum.

Not that I really disliked Muffy, I guess I don't. I just think Malachi Bret ought to learn to handle a Louisville Slugger before he gets his hand on a full-tilt, bloodied and ready-to-party broadsword.

Still, can you feature the expression on his first-grade teacher's face if he brought Old Betsy to school for show-and-tell? In Muffy's elegant words, "Wow, huh?"

Seven Drops of Blood

————————— ✝ —————————

Robert Weinberg

"I want you to locate," said the man in dark glasses, his voice intent, "the Holy Grail."

Not exactly sure how to reply, Sidney Taine, known throughout Chicago as the "New Age detective," stretched back in his chair and stared across the desk at his client. The speaker was a short, stocky man, impeccably dressed in a grey pin-stripe suit and charcoal tie. His sharp, almost angular features appeared cut from solid rock. A full black beard covered most of his jaw.

Heavy dark eyebrows flowed together above his glasses, giving his features a sinister turn. His wide nose jutted out from the center of his face like the sharp beak of some massive bird of prey. He looked and sounded like a man accustomed to getting his own way.

Ashmedai was the name he used, not indicating whether it was first or last or both. His smooth, confident motions entering Taine's office made it quite clear that the eyes behind the black lenses were not those of a blind man. What secret those glasses actually hid, the detective was not sure he wanted to learn. According to ancient Hebrew tradition, Ashmedai reigned as king of demons.

"I'm not King Arthur," said Taine slowly, measuring his reply. "Nor am I a member of the Round Table."

"I dislike fairy tales," replied the bearded man, a slight smile crossing his lips. "The Grail I seek is real, not folklore. And, it is presently lost somewhere in Chicago."

"In Chicago?" repeated Taine, rising from behind the desk. He felt uncomfortable staring at those dark lenses. Ashmedai's face remained a mystery. Taine firmly believed that the eyes reflected a man's soul. Ashmedai kept his hidden for a reason. The detective looked out the windows of his office onto Lake Michigan. He was a tall, muscular man, built like a linebacker on a football team, his every move reflecting the dangerous grace of a stalking cat. Clients who spoke in riddles annoyed him. Dark, threatening clouds hovered over the placid waters. Jagged streaks of lightning flared in the late afternoon sky, reflecting the disquiet Taine felt addressing Ashmedai.

"You are aware of the theory," said Taine, "that claims the Holy Grail is not the Cup of the Last Supper. That instead, it is the container that held the burial wrappings of Christ. Which, the same scholars who advocate this position, identify as the Shroud of Turin."

Ashmedai shrugged. "I've read *The Shroud and the Grail* by Noel Currer-Briggs. He raises some interesting points. But, much of his book is filled with idle speculation. Too often, he manipulates the translations of early legends to fit his hypothesis. Worse, he shows no understanding of the true purpose behind Joseph of Arimathea's actions during and after the Crucifixion."

"Which is?" asked Taine, when Ashmedai hesitated. The stranger spoke with convincing authority about the most mysterious of all occult traditions.

"Currer-Briggs dismissed as utter nonsense the legend that Joseph used the Grail to catch drops of Jesus' blood from the wound made in his side by the Spear of Vengeance," replied Ashmedai. "He let his modern sensibilities overcome his scholarly curiosity. Instead of searching for the reason behind Joseph's actions, the author shrugged off the entire episode as tasteless and revolting. Seeking another explanation for the stories linking the Grail and Christ's blood, Currer-Briggs fastened on the bloodstained burial wrappings used by Joseph and Nicodemus. The container containing those linens, marked with the same blood, he concluded was the true Grail. Extending his theory, he then identified the wrappings as the Shroud of Turin."

Ashmedai chuckled. "A wonderful mental exercise, but absolute nonsense. Joseph of Arimathea knew exactly what he was doing when he caught the Savior's blood in the Grail. For all of his facts, Currer-Briggs refused to acknowledge the reality of the occult."

Taine inhaled sharply, suddenly understanding what Ashmedai meant. "Black magic relies on blood," said the detective. "The blood of Christ . . ."

"Would work wonders," concluded Ashmedai. "Especially when linked with Seth's Chalice."

Taine's eyes narrowed. Few people knew of the existence of that fabled Cup. The detective had learned of it only after years of studying the darkest secrets of the supernatural. Again, he wondered exactly who was Ashmedai? And what were his sources of information?

"According to *The Lost Apocrypha*," said Taine, "when Seth, the third son of Adam and Eve, traveled to the Garden of Eden he was given a chalice by the Lord as a sign that God had not deserted humanity."

"I'm glad to see your reputation is well deserved," said Ashmedai. "It's hard to believe a mere detective would know of such things."

"I'm not an ordinary detective," said Taine.

"If you were, I wouldn't be here," replied Ashmedai, chuckling softly. "A talisman of incalculable power, the Cup passed down through the ages, from generation to generation, held by only the greatest of mages. Until it was given as a gift to Jesus by one of his disciples. And became known ever after as the Holy Grail."

"Which you claim is now in Chicago?" said Taine, a hint of skepticism creeping into his voice.

"I *know* it is," said Ashmedai. The bearded man reached inside his jacket pocket. His hand emerged with a wad of money, held tightly together by a rubber band. Casually, he dropped the cash on Taine's desk.

"I'll pay you five thousand dollars to find the Chalice. It belongs to me and I want it back. No questions. If you need more money, just let me know."

Taine looked down at the cash, then up at Ashmedai. Down and up again, not saying a word.

"Nothing to worry about," said Ashmedai. "It's honest money. Over the years, I've invested in a number of long-term securities. They pay a handsome return. Money serves me merely as a means to an end."

Still, Taine made no move to pick up the package. Though he was not above bending the law for his clients when necessary, he held himself to a strict code of ethics which he refused to compromise. The notion of dealing in stolen religious artifacts crossed over that boundary.

"I need a few more details before I'll take the case," said Taine. "You state the Grail belongs to you. What's your claim to it? And how was it stolen?"

"Suspicious, Mr. Taine?" asked Ashmedai, a touch of amusement in his voice. "I assure you, *my right to the Chalice is more legitimate than most.*"

The bearded man hesitated, as if considering what to say next. "Details of what happened to the Cup after the Crucifixion are shrouded in mystery. Arthurian legend has Joseph traveling to England, taking the Grail with him. Several occult references place the Chalice in the hands of Simon the Magician. I've even read an account of the vessel surfacing in the court of Charles the Great, Charlemagne." Ashmedai shook his head, almost in dismay. "No one really knows the truth. Though I suspect it is much less colorful than any of those fables.

"The Grail and Joseph of Arimathea disappeared shortly after Christ's burial. They vanished into the murkiness of ancient history. In time, both became enshrined in legend. In 1907, archaeologists at a dig outside of Damascus, Syria, uncovered a spectacular silver chalice, decorated in great detail with images of the Last Supper. Comparison to like pieces dated the Cup as belonging to the 5th century A.D.

"After making discreet financial arrangements with certain government officials, the discoverers of the Chalice of Damascus offered it for sale to the highest bidder. A Syrian antique dealer, acting as agent for an American millionaire, bought the rarity for $700,000. Like hundreds of other pieces, it disappeared into the reclusive publisher's vast California estate."

"The Chalice of Damascus and the Holy Grail ...?" began Taine.

"Were one and the same," finished Ashmedai. "Some enterprising smith concealed Seth's Cup beneath a sheath of finely crafted metal, both protecting and concealing the relic. The truth emerged only after exhaustive scientific testing performed at the millionaire's estate. Hidden under a silver lining was the Cup of the Last Supper. I tried for decades, without success, to purchase the Grail. The new owner refused to let it go. The more I offered, the more obstinate he became. After his death, his estate maintained the same position. Finally, this year, facing a huge tax increase and declining revenues due to unwise investments, they relented. It cost me a king's ransom, but the Grail belonged to me."

"Only to be stolen," said Taine.

"I never even saw the Cup," said Ashmedai bitterly. "Last night, two security guards flew in to O'Hare Airport, with the Grail in their possession. They departed the terminal shortly after nine in the evening, in a hired limo, bound for my estate in northern Illinois. That was the last anyone saw of them."

"The police?" asked Taine.

"They're waiting for a ransom note," said Ashmedai. "The fools are treating the disappearance as an art theft."

"And you don't?"

"The Grail is the most coveted magical talisman in the world," replied Ashmedai. "I thought no one other than myself knew its location. Obviously, I believed wrong. Someone stole the Chalice and intends using it for his own ends. What that purpose might be, I have no idea. But, knowing the power inherent in the Grail, I shudder at the thought."

Taine nodded. There was no mistaking the worry in Ashmedai's voice. Still, he had his doubts about the man. "And your plans for the Grail?"

"If I thought to use the Chalice for evil intent, I would have stolen it years ago," said Ashmedai. "Instead, I waited, biding my time, and acquired the treasure honestly. My intent was never criminal." He paused. "My collection of occult rarities is the greatest in the world. I am assembling it for a purpose that need not concern you. The Grail belongs there, well-guarded and protected, away from the schemes of little men." His voice grew icy cold. "I am not a man easily crossed, Mr. Taine. Whoever stole the Grail will pay—pay *severely*."

Taine considered that Ashmedai seemed not to care about the fate of the two bodyguards. All the bearded man wanted was the Grail. Nothing else mattered.

"I have a few ideas," said Taine, dropping back into his chair. "Some people to call." He slid a pad of paper and a pen across the desk. "Give me a number where I can reach you."

"Call me day or night," said Ashmedai, scribbling a phone number on the paper. He passed it over to Taine. "Let me know the instant you locate the Cup. I'll come at once."

"If it can be found," said Taine, "I'll find it."

"So I have heard," said Ashmedai. "That is why I hired you. Good luck."

Somehow, Taine had a feeling he'd need it.

Seven hours later, the detective wearily pushed open the door to the Spiderweb Lounge on Chicago's northwest side. None of his usual sources had provided a clue to the missing relic. Nor had his own investigations at the airport turned up anything the least bit useful. Much as Taine disliked the notion, the only remaining option was to enter the Spiderweb. And deal with its owner, Sal "The Spider" Albanese.

According to crime insiders, Albanese's nickname came from his involvement in every sort of illegal activity in Chicago. Stolen property, guns, prostitution, drugs, and murder were all part of his everyday business. Like a giant spider, the crime boss spun his deadly web across the Windy City.

Others assumed that the moniker derived from Albanese's appearance. An immensely fat man who favored dark clothing, the elderly gangster bore an uncanny resemblance to a gigantic arachnid. Sal's unwavering gaze and jet-black eyes did nothing to dispel that image.

Only a select group knew of Albanese's youthful encounter with the outer darkness. They had actually seen the incredible scars across the fat man's back and understood the full significance of the title, "The Spider." Sidney Taine, occult investigator, was one such man.

While not an admirer of the gangster, Taine belonged to a certain occult fraternity that included Albanese as well. Which was why he was admitted to the crime chief's office without any hassle.

"Taine," grunted Albanese, waving one huge hand at the detective. In his other, the Spider held a foot-long meatball sandwich. Albanese was always eating, feeding his bloated three-hundred-pound body. "Long time no see. Join me for a late snack?"

"No thanks," replied Taine, nodding to Tony Bracco and Leo Scaglia, Albanese's ever-present bodyguards. Tony, short but built like a fireplug, crinkled his eyes in recognition. Leo, tall and thin, who handled a knife with the skill of a surgeon, grinned and nodded. He worked out at the same gym as Taine, and he and the detective had boxed more than a few rounds in the sparring ring.

Albanese made short work of the sandwich. Reaching for the tray on his desk, he guzzled down a stein filled with beer, then raised a second meatball hero to his lips. The mobster ate three or four sandwiches at a time.

They chatted for a few minutes, discussing the Bulls, the Bears and the Cubs. Albanese followed all sports closely. Making book helped pay the bills. Finally, the gangster got down to business.

"Whatcha here for?" asked Albanese, biting deep into his third sandwich. Carefully, he wiped little drops of meat sauce off his shirt. "From your call I take it this ain't no social call. You working for the Brotherhood?"

"Not tonight," said Taine. "I'm investigating a robbery. My client is willing to pay quite a bundle for the return of some stolen property. No questions asked. With *your* contacts, I thought you might be able to help."

"Always glad to help a frien'," said Albanese, taking another bite. "Whatcha missing?"

"A silver cup," said Taine. "A religious artifact known as the Chalice of Damascus."

Sal Albanese froze in mid-bite, his jaws gaping wide open. Seconds passed, and then, very carefully, he put his sandwich down on the desk. "Too messy," he declared, not very convincingly.

"About the Chalice . . . ?" said Taine.

"Don't know nothing about no chalice," declared Albanese curtly. "None of my people had anything to do with robbing relics, Taine. That ain't my style."

The big gangster sounded angry. Black eyes glared at Taine defiantly, as if challenging the detective to say otherwise. However, behind the bluster, Taine sensed something else. Fear.

"Are you positive . . .?" Taine tried one more time.

"You doubting my word, Taine?" asked Albanese, his huge hands clenching into fists. "I don't like being called a liar."

"No offense, Sal," said Taine. It made no sense to antagonize the crime boss without good reason. "I just assumed that with all your connections you would have all the details about this theft."

"I ain't heard," said Albanese, unconvincingly. "Now clear out, Taine. I got business to discuss with the boys. Don't got any more time for idle chit-chat."

Taine turned to leave. In the corner of an eye, he caught a furtive gesture made by Leo Scaglia. The tall bodyguard, half-turned so that only Taine could see the signal, moved one hand as if to indicate, "later." The detective dipped his head acknowledgingly, then departed.

An hour later, back at his office, Taine picked up his phone on the first ring. Scaglia, his voice muffled and barely distinguishable, was on the other end.

"You wanted information on the Chalice?" asked the bodyguard, straight off, without any word of greeting. "I know where it is."

"Sal has it?" asked Taine, uncertain what to believe.

"Nah. He won't touch no religious stuff. You know him. But ain't nothing goin' on that Sal don't hear about. He was just too scared to say anything to you at the Club. Sal suspects that somebody's passing on all our secrets to those crazy Jamaicans. Bracco's been acting pretty odd lately, flashing a lot of money and making big talk. So the boss had me make this call, private like.

Sal thought you'd want to know the truth. That lunatic, King Wedo, stole your precious chalice."

"King Wedo?" repeated Taine, taken by surprise. Though he had never met the mysterious Jamaican crime lord, he had heard quite a bit about him. In Chicago for less than a year, the gang leader had earned a reputation as a merciless, violent killer with a taste for the bizarre.

"Sal's frightened and with good reason," continued Scaglia. "Those Jamaican bozos working for King Wedo are crazy. They'd just as soon rip out your guts as look at you. Life is cheap, don't mean a thing to them. Bastards take a dislike to somebody, he's dead meat."

A note of fear crept into Scaglia's voice. "Joey Ventura made the mistake of crossing King Wedo. Got greedy during a coke delivery and swiped some goods he didn't pay for. Stupid idea. The Jamaicans pulled Joey right out of a restaurant at lunchtime. Shot down three bystanders dumb enough to interfere. Like I said, life don't mean nothin' to them devils."

Scaglia's voice dropped to a whisper. "King Wedo planned a special finish for Joey. Called it a demonstration. The maniac cut off Joey's fingers and toes, one joint at a time, and forced him to swallow the pieces. It took the poor slob three days to die. Now you understand why Sal is cautious."

"Perfectly," said Taine. "Any clue to why King Wedo clipped the Chalice? Ransom perhaps?"

"Nothing definite. But King Wedo don't need no money, not with the dough he's raking in from the drug trade. Word on the street is that the Jamaican is heavy into black magic. Maybe he figures this chalice of yours will give him some sort of mystical powers. Who the hell knows with these crazy bastards."

"Sure," answered Taine, his mind racing. King Wedo and the Holy Grail added up to a dangerous mix. He had to retrieve the Chalice. "Maybe I should talk to the King about returning the Cup. You have any idea where he holds court?"

"You're nuts, man. One wrong word to that geek and he'll carve out your heart. With his fingernails."

"Let me worry about that," said Taine. "Where's his main base?"

"On the near south side," replied Scaglia. "Around Twenty-sixth and the railroad tracks." The bodyguard hesitated for a moment, then cursed. "The Jamaicans might let you enter their hideout, but they sure the hell won't let you leave. No chance you'll change your mind?"

"Can't," said Taine. "It's my job."

"Well, you'll need some backup," said Scaglia. "And I guess that means me. I'll meet you there in an hour. Corner of Twenty-sixth and Rand. Don't be late, 'cause if you are, I might just lose my nerve."

"I'll be there," said Taine and hung up the phone.

Taine arrived at the designated location a few minutes after midnight. Amber-colored street lights cast an eerie glow on the otherwise deserted avenue. Huge old warehouses lined both sides of the street, towering into the night sky like ancient tombs. Soundlessly, Leo Scaglia beckoned from the doorway of a nearby building. After a quick check of the surroundings, Taine slipped out of his car and joined the mobster.

"What's the story?" whispered Taine.

"We're in luck," replied Scaglia, grinning. "King Wedo and his thugs are out celebrating. One of Sal's contacts spotted them a half-hour ago at the Kozy Klub. We should have no problem finding that chalice and making off with it before the Jamaican returns. Damned SOB is so sure of himself, I doubt he bothered leaving anybody on guard."

"Sounds too easy," said Taine, staring at Scaglia suspiciously. "Why are you so eager to help, Leo? I never knew you to take any unnecessary risks."

"Back off, Taine," said Scaglia, glancing around the deserted street. "Sal's pushing for King Wedo to take a fall. Wants me to lend you a hand. Anything that makes King Wedo look bad, makes Sal look good. I'm following the Capo's orders. Besides, we're friends."

Leo pushed open the door to the warehouse. "Follow me and

don't make a sound. There might be a guard inside. King Wedo's office is in the rear of the building. That's probably where he's keeping the Chalice."

The two men crept silently. Taine moved with surprising grace for a man his size. Leo Scaglia slithered through the darkness like some giant snake, intent on its prey. Past rows and rows of massive crates filled with unknown goods they slipped, only the soft sound of their breathing breaking the stillness of the stale air. Finally, they reached the rear of the building.

"That's the place," Leo whispered softly in Taine's ear, pointing to the foreman's office located at the junction of two walls. "No lights on. Looks deserted."

Both men pulled out their guns. "You go first," said Scaglia. "You know what to look for. I'll cover you."

Carefully, Taine twisted the knob. It turned effortlessly, not locked. Taking his time, the detective inched open the door. It was as dark inside the office as without. Slowly, ever so slowly, he slipped inside.

And found himself staring at a slender black man, sitting behind a wide desk. King Wedo. Waiting with him, standing at his side, were two powerfully built Jamaicans. Both men held Skorpion machine gun pistols aimed at Taine's stomach.

"Mr. Taine," said King Wedo, with a faint smile. "How nice of you to drop by."

Behind Taine, the door swung open. "Sorry, buddy," he heard Leo Scaglia say, "but orders is orders." Then something hard and unyielding crashed down on his skull and he heard nothing else.

When Taine regained consciousness, he found himself securely bound to a heavy wood chair. He was in the same room, now brightly illuminated. King Wedo faced him on the other side of the wide desk. The two massive bodyguards stood behind their boss's chair. Leo Scaglia, arms folded across his chest, lolled against a large metal filing cabinet.

"*You're* the informer in Albanese's organization?" said Taine, disgusted by his own stupidity. "Not Bracco?"

"So what else is new?" said Scaglia, chuckling. "When I called the King and told him you were fishing for the Chalice, he ordered me to reel you in. Easiest assignment I ever had. You didn't suspect nothin'."

"I'm too naive for my own good," said Taine. Whoever had tied him to the chair had taken his gun as well as the knife sheathed to his ankle. However, they had missed the razor blade concealed in his shirt sleeve. Cautiously, he started sawing at the ropes binding his wrists. "For some reason, I still trust my fellow man."

"A bad habit, Mr. Taine, especially for a private investigator," said King Wedo. The Jamaican spoke softly but distinctly, with the barest trace of an English accent. "But, of course, you are no ordinary detective. That is why I instructed Leo to bring you here. You are going to prove very useful to me, Mr. Taine. Very, very useful."

Reaching into a drawer of the desk, King Wedo pulled out a plain wooden goblet. Though Taine knew the Chalice's origin dated back thousands of years, there was not a scratch on it. "The Holy Grail," said King Wedo, to no one in particular. "Stripped of that foolish silver decoration, it appears incredibly ordinary. But, as we all well know, looks can be deceiving."

King Wedo rose from his chair, casually balancing the Cup in one hand. A short, slender man with pleasant, even features, only his narrow, mad eyes betrayed the cruelty lurking within. "Consider me, for example," he continued, circling the desk so that he stood only a few feet away from Taine. "I am notorious as a crazy gangster. An image I work hard to cultivate. Fear serves me well, Mr. Taine. Still, none of my enemies, or my friends for that matter, suspect that I am also a master of black magic. Only a select few even realize that sorcery exists."

King Wedo chuckled. "In my youth, I attended school in England. My father, a wealthy plantation owner, had dreams of me continuing and expanding the family business. Even then, I had other plans.

"You can imagine my surprise when I discovered, quite by accident, that my history professor was a practicing black magician. Delivering a paper to his home, I stumbled on him placing a curse on one of his faculty rivals. Immediately sensing my interest in the

dark art, he offered me the opportunity to become his apprentice."
The Jamaican's eyes narrowed. "For a price, of course."

Taine grimaced. Sorcerers always demanded payment for their
services. A fee paid in blood.

"I learned a great deal from Professor Harvey during the three
years I studied with him. He taught me some rather unusual business methods. Tactics for success I have employed well. Still, the
Professor and I parted on good terms nearly a decade ago. Never
once during the intervening years did I hear from him."

Taine remained silent, busily sawing his razor blade into the
ropes. Gangsters loved to brag about their accomplishments. King
Wedo was consumed by a desire to display his brilliance. Surrounded by thugs and assorted lowlifes, the Jamaican reveled in the
chance to show off for Taine. Which made it quite clear to the detective that the gangster planned murdering him afterwards. Dead
men never betrayed secrets.

"That was why I was surprised, a week ago, to suddenly receive a call from him. No sentimentalist, Harvey's contact was
strictly business. The old man told me of the Holy Grail and how
it was being shipped to Chicago. The Professor requested my aid
in stealing the relic, promising me fabulous riches for my cooperation. I agreed to help. But, my arrangements benefited only me.

"Using information supplied by Harvey, my men intercepted
the Grail messengers, killed them both, and made off with the
Chalice. Instead of turning it over to the Professor, I kept the Cup
for myself. The old fool should have known better than to trust
someone like me. I have plans for the Grail. Plans that concern
you, Mr. Taine."

A cold chill swept through Taine. He did not like the sound of
that remark.

"Why me?" asked the detective. Anything to stall for a little
more time. Cutting the ropes was proving difficult. "What makes
me special?"

"Sidney Taine, the psychic detective," replied King Wedo, his
lips curling in a slow grin. "I know all about you, Mr. Taine. Those
who practice the black arts like to keep close tabs on their adver-

saries. And, I believe that description fits you very well. *Adversary.*"

Gently, King Wedo placed Seth's Cup on his desk. Crossing his arms across his chest, he shook his head in mock dismay. "If I am an evil soul, my friend, then by definition, are you not a good one? A righteous one?"

Taine shuddered. King Wedo's words struck a chord deep within his being. He finally understood what the Jamaican planned—an ancient rite of dark magic, of blood sorcery. Evidently the concern showed in his face. The gang leader chuckled.

"Seven drops of blood from a righteous soul," he recited, using words of frightening power, "if the Cup of Purity is thy goal."

King Wedo strolled back around the desk and dropped back in his chair. Smiling, he reached into a desk drawer and pulled out a plastic bag filled with white powder. "Coke," said King Wedo, confirming Taine's immediate suspicions.

"Good stuff," continued the Jamaican, "but not perfect. Not pure." The gang leader leaned forward, his gaze fastened on his prisoner. "The purer the dope, the better the hit. That's the story on cocaine. Even the dumbest crackhead knows it. Problem is that no system filters out all the impurities. No matter how fine you make it, the stuff ain't perfect. It's never totally pure."

"You don't intend . . ." began Taine, shocked by the Jamaican's plan.

"Ah, but I do, Mr. Taine," said King Wedo, nodding. "I do. According to all of the medieval legends, *the Holy Grail purifies whatever it touches.* The mere contact with the Cup changes water into wine, poor man's bread into cake. Well, we're going to see if those stories are true."

The Jamaican opened the bag holding the cocaine. "Think of the rush, Mr. Taine. Imagine the purest cocaine in the world—available only from me. I'll be able to name my price."

King Wedo beckoned Scaglia closer. "You got your knife handy, Leo?" he asked.

"Of course," said Scaglia, pulling out a six-inch switchblade. With a bare whisper of sound, the metal blade glittered in the harsh light. "Never go anywhere without it."

"Take the Cup," King Wedo commanded. "And christen it with seven drops of Mr. Taine's blood."

"Whatever you say," said Scaglia, delicately balancing the switchblade in one hand, the wooden Cup in the other. "You want me to cut his throat?"

"Leo, Leo, Leo," said King Wedo, sounding properly shocked. "How wasteful. The formula calls for the blood of a righteous man each time we perform the ceremony. We don't have an endless supply of righteous men in Chicago." The Jamaican's voice turned grim. "We must make Mr. Taine last a long, long time."

"You're the boss," replied Scaglia, shrugging his shoulders. Nonchalantly, he slipped the cold steel beneath the first button of Taine's shirt. With a flick of the wrist, the hood slashed through the thin material up to the detective's neck.

"Tough break, buddy," he muttered, bending close with the Cup of Seth. "But orders is orders."

Another slash of the knife. A thin red ribbon blossomed across Taine's chest. Carefully, Scaglia collected his bounty. "Seven drops," warned King Wedo. "No more, no less."

"Got 'em," said Scaglia. He straightened, holding the Cup before him. "Now what?"

The gang leader opened the plastic bag holding the cocaine. Using his pinky, he casually stirred the white powder. "From what I've read, the blood activates the magical properties of the Cup instantly. Let's see what it does with the coke."

Scaglia growled—a beast-like sound rising from deep within his chest. A mad noise that caught all of them by surprise. Taine's eyes blinked in shock as the Grail-bearer's features twisted with sudden fury.

"You dirty son-of-a-bitch!" Scaglia shouted, and grabbed for his gun.

Weapons exploded and the room filled with the sound and smell of gunfire. Scaglia's body erupted in blood. Like a grotesque, drunken marionette, he staggered back and forth, driven by the fury of the bullets slamming into his torso.

"Be careful of the Cup!" shrieked King Wedo, standing, only his voice betraying any sign of panic. "Try not to hit it."

Hot blood gushing from a dozen wounds, Scaglia should have been dead, but wasn't. Only his burning will kept him alive. Somehow, some way, he pulled his gun free and returned fire. Taine, not sure he understood what was taking place, wrenched hard on the last few strands of cord imprisoning his hands. The rope snapped, and the detective dropped to the floor. Unarmed, he was not crazy enough to attack either Scaglia or Wedo's cronies.

The shooting stopped as abruptly as it began. Silence echoed through the small office. Both bodyguards were down—one shot through the heart, the second man's nose a red ruin where a bullet crashed up and through to his brain.

Scaglia lay sprawled across King Wedo's desk, the Grail clutched tightly in one hand. Amazingly, a spark of life still flickered in his eyes.

"I don't like traitors, Leo," said King Wedo, rising up from the floor on the other side of his desk, a stiletto tightly gripped in one hand. He spoke calmly, without the least trace of malice. "You took my money to betray your boss. But, evidently, he paid you even more to double cross me." King Wedo shook his head. "Bad choice, Leo."

Scaglia raised his head. "You scum," he gasped out, his mad eyes burning with hatred. "No one paid . . ."

"Enough lies," said King Wedo. With a savage twist of the knife, he ripped the blade across Leo's throat. The gangster's body arched in agony as his lifeblood poured out onto the wood desk. One last gasp and he was dead.

"Don't try anything, Mr. Taine," continued King Wedo, a .45 automatic appearing in his hand as if by magic. He never even glanced at the dead man. "Please rise very slowly from the floor. And, keep both of your hands in plain sight."

Taine stood up. At this range, King Wedo couldn't miss. The Jamaican seemed unruffled by the violence that had taken place during the past few minutes.

"I never panic," said King Wedo, as if reading Taine's mind. Careful never to shift his eyes from Taine, the gang leader reached down for the Holy Grail. "That's why I always come out on top. That's why I'm the king."

Wrapping his fingers around the edge of the wood goblet, King Wedo pulled the Grail free of Scaglia's grip. "I thought I could trust Leo, but I guess not. No matter."

The muzzle of the automatic never wavered. "Two can keep a secret if one of them is dead, Mr. Taine," said King Wedo. "Goodbye."

Desperately, the detective flung himself to the side. One of the dead bodyguards still held a gun. It was a forlorn hope, but Taine's only chance. He scrambled for the weapon, expecting any second to hear the roar of King Wedo's automatic and feel the impact of a slug in his back. Surprisingly, nothing happened. Taine whirled, the dead man's weapon in hand. Then came to a sudden stop, caught completely by surprise.

King Wedo stood frozen in place. Sweat glistened on his forehead. Madness twisted his face in a grimace of incredible pain. The .45 automatic no longer threatened Taine. Instead, its muzzle touched right against the gangster's forehead. Wild eyes met Taine's in a silent plea for help. But there was no time left. King Wedo's finger's jerked hard against the trigger. The gun roared once, then fell silent.

"An interesting, if not surprising tale," said the man called Ashmedai. "Many legends refer to the Grail as the Cup of Treachery." He paused, and shook his head, as if in disappointment. "A title it has well earned. Too many men have been betrayed. I wonder if this King Wedo ever grasped the truth?"

"I think he did," said Taine, staring at the Holy Grail resting on the desktop between them. "In that last instant, I believe he realized the trap into which he had fallen. But, by then, holding the Cup, there was nothing he could do. In a way, it was a grim sort of justice."

Ashmedai shrugged and reached for the Cup. "The fools never understand that the Grail turns *all* that come in contact with it pure. Including those men foolish enough to hold it."

Taine nodded, his gaze fixed on the Chalice. "The conflict in their souls destroyed them both. Repentance was not enough. Scaglia could no longer serve evil, so he tried to destroy it. And

King Wedo, overwhelmed by his monstrous crimes, resorted to suicide."

The detective paused. "Do you dare risk taking it? I carried it here in a box I discovered in King Wedo's office. I never touched it myself."

"The spell wears off quickly," said Ashmedai confidently, lifting the Grail. "Joseph was no fool when he covered the Cup in silver. No ordinary mortal could touch the Chalice and live with himself afterwards. No man is that pure."

The bearded man examined the Cup carefully, a wistful smile playing across his lips. "So many years—so many years."

"Now that you have it . . ." began Taine.

"The Grail goes into my collection," replied Ashmedai, his gaze still fixed on the Cup. "Where it will remain out of the sight of man until needed."

"You called it the Cup of Treachery?" said Taine, puzzled. In all of his studies of the occult, he had never encountered the phrase before.

Ashmedai lowered the Chalice to the desk. Unseen eyes stared at Taine from behind dark lenses.

"The Chalice was a gift to Christ from one of his disciples," said the bearded man. His voice sounded weary, terribly so. "One who doubted and thought to use the Grail as a final test. And thus began a tale of treachery—and eternal damnation."

Ashmedai sighed. "Now do you understand?"

"Yes," answered Taine, no longer curious to see the eyes behind those glasses.

The Yellow Clay Bowl

✛

Robert Sampson

Perhaps time passed.

Then he was rising from a deep place through a tumble of softly roaring shapes. Now I am becoming conscious, Chalfel thought. Against his cheek pressed the harsh surface of the table-cloth, each thread a minute ridge against his skin. Close beside him a woman shrieked. Sight returned. He found himself observing an upset glass and a plate of food sitting incongruously at eye level. This seemed strange.

Fingers touched his shoulder.

The woman's voice, fear at the edge of her words, "He's dead. Fell over."

Chalfel said, "I'm all right," in a voice that, even to his uncritical ears, sounded blurred.

Now he realized that he did not know where to find the yellow clay bowl. Fright, like a kind of vivid current, darted through him. The feeble, desperate things that were his fingers groped across the table.

Finding nothing, he began to sit up, with great attention to doing it right.

The woman yelped.

Arms straightened him in the chair. A man and woman bent to peer into his face, concern in the attitudes of their bodies. Behind them stretched the dimness of the restaurant, filled with empty tables.

Consecutive memories trailed across his mind: it was night,

late; he had arrived at the restaurant only minutes before the kitchen closed.

Then his mind jumped. The bowl is at home, he thought, hidden deep in its box, white tissue over pale yellow clay. His fright ebbed. To be instantly replaced by more familiar anguish, as his responsibilities rushed back into memory and their weight again plunged down on him.

The bowl was at home, safe until he died.

And after that?

The man bending over him asked, "You want a doctor?"

With a profound shock, he recognized the face so close to his own. "Tom Ketteridge," he cried. "Well! Tom!"

Faint surprise came into Ketteridge's eyes, but not recognition. "It's Chalfel," he said. "Grant Chalfel. Remember?"

What seemed a kind of controlled horror moved into Ketteridge's face. He was a blondish man, with a wide, pale forehead and a tightness around the mouth suggesting restrained indignation.

"It's me," Chalfel said. He was careful to form each word before speaking. "I've changed some."

"Let's get you out of here," Ketteridge said.

"Pay the girl, please," Chalfel said. He felt himself lifted from the chair and his body, so light, so unstable, threatening to float sideways at every step, was supported across that terrible hollow between the table and the door. Outside the dark air smelled warm and leafy. Against distorted clouds glowed the lights of Atlanta.

"You!" Chalfel whispered. "After all these years. Providential."

"Do you have a car?"

Chalfel explained in a slow, exact voice that he had walked to the restaurant, that his apartment was in the next block. He found himself escorted to a large silver car and carefully placed onto a dark-blue velvet seat. Rich green and gold light spilled from the dashboard. He had never ridden in such an expensive machine or seen such light.

Head lolling against the blue velvet, he said, "You really must see the bowl. A formidable responsibility. Crushing."

"We better find a doctor," Ketteridge said.

"No need," Chalfel said in a distantly amused voice. "Nothing doctor can do. Body's determined to die. Circulation rotten. Heart rotten. Remember me now?"

"Oh, yes," said Ketteridge. "Not likely to forget you."

"I suppose not," Chalfel said.

They fell silent, the residue of old memories bitter between them.

The car turned corners, slowed, slipped between brick walls up a narrow drive past the bulk of a magnolia whose dark skirt of limbs spread grandly across the grass. Untended bushes strained toward the clouds. Ahead sprawled a large brick house, unlighted and somber in the night.

Dismay probed Chalfel's chest. "Lucina's waiting," he thought. "Listening. Watching for me."

As earlier that evening she had been listening, watching, waiting for him, a hunting creature crouched.

He stepped diffidently into the big front room that smelled of dusty upholstery and old wallpaper and the terrible corroding breath of time. By the double window sat his cousin, Lucina Wynn, malignantly obese, slowly sorting piles of photographs with her bulging fingers.

Not looking up, she asked, "Are you packed?"

"I'm not going to leave."

"You'll leave when I want you to leave." Her voice was slow and old and shook a little from the tension in her.

He said, "I'll not go off to die in a furnished room."

"You'll not die in my house," she said fiercely. "You will not. We've had too much dying here. Mother, right upstairs. And Brother, and Grandmother. I nursed Daddy. Even when he was disgusting I nursed him. Even then. I can't stand any more dying, Grant. You get yourself packed up."

The silence became a terrible waiting thing. Turning without speaking, he walked away from her into the shielding darkness of the hall.

She shouted after him, "Can't you be merciful to me?"

* * *

"Merciful," Chalfel repeated, twisting his head on the blue velvet. From his throat jerked a succession of hard syllables that could have been laughter.

Glancing curiously at him, Ketteridge slowed the car to a stop. He helped Chalfel into the warm night. They shuffled along a walk treacherous with uneven brick and entered a small annex joined to the rear of the main house.

Chalfel snapped on the lights, closed the door. For a moment he braced himself against the wall, dazed with the unchecked plunging of his heart.

"You OK?" Ketteridge asked.

"Fine."

He saw Ketteridge's eyes pass across the pleasantly worn room, the wall ranked with photographs of young faces grinning an indecipherable message from past to future. In a cabinet the lean spines of long-playing records stood closely packed.

From high on the wall, a small bell rang twice, a bitter silver sound.

Chalfel ignored the bell. In his mind images of the yellow clay bowl and Ketteridge rushed together, and in that fusion, he felt the lightness of hope.

He said, "Tom, I want to show you something wonderful. You've never seen anything like it."

"I can't stay," Ketteridge said.

"It won't take a minute."

Ketteridge said in a low, casual voice, "I never intended to speak to you again. Not to look at you, not think about you. Let's leave it at that."

How many times had his imagination created this scene? Chalfel wondered. How often had he struggled to word an explanation? From his sense of proprieties outraged, he had worked out what must be said to Ketteridge. It was a speech composed over God knows how many years, through God knows how many nights, while anger and embarrassment hacked at him with rodent teeth. But he had never expected the blond man to be so formal and rigid, so terribly remote, giving him no chance to speak.

His mind clutched for the familiar words, only to feel them

slither out of memory, like greased stones. Panic got at him, for he knew that he must speak, must persuade.

In a tearing voice, Chalfel cried, "I was young. I thought I could say anything and be amusing. That was all I wanted—to introduce you to the best people of Atlanta. To be witty and amusing."

"Witty," Ketteridge said. "Amusing."

The bell rang sharply three times, thrusting nails of sound through Chalfel's body.

"Hell came out of me," he said. These were not the words he had planned, but he had no others. "I can't explain. Twenty-five years, I still don't know why."

Derision got into Ketteridge's face.

"I envied you, Tom. I admired you. I was proud to introduce you. But when I opened my mouth. . . . Dear God, I know what I said about you. How I said it. I never meant that."

In the mirror by the door, he saw the twisting face of his reflection, a starveling old man with skin like dirty wax, bloodless and impure-looking.

He said to Ketteridge, "Yes, I hurt you then. I know that. To my shame."

"Words are easy," Ketteridge said.

"All I have left is words." The bell rang again and, in gusting fury, he shouted at the silver sound, "Damn you! Wait!"

To Ketteridge, he said, "What's past can't be fixed. But I can do this for you. I can show you the most wonderful thing in the world and you can look at it and touch it and not two living men in this entire world can say they've done that. That I can do. Repayment. Not much. But something."

The bell rang a half dozen rapid strokes, imperious and irritable.

"That," Chalfel said, quietly savage, "is my cousin, Lucina. This is her house. She allows me use of these rooms."

The silence between them became a painful tissue. The two men stood without moving, facing each other, lashed together by bonds of anger and regret.

Then Ketteridge wrenched away from the door. His hand

slashed a complex symbol of anger across the air. "Better see what she wants."

He threw himself ice-faced into a cane-bottomed chair, not removing his coat.

Chalfel muttered thanks. Unlocking a door, he hurried into the main house, crossed an unlighted room smelling coldly of dust, and walked with hard, quick steps along an uncarpeted corridor. Huge pieces of furniture bulked in the darkness. At the front of the house, he turned right into the enormous hollow of the living room. A table lamp spilled light across the carpet. At the fringe of the light waited Lucina, shapeless in a dark dress, her pale eyes eating at him.

"You brought home a woman, didn't you?" she asked.

"A friend. He drove me back from the restaurant."

"A friend? I thought you said you had no friends."

Chalfel said nothing, contemptuously staring until her eyes fell.

"Is your friend helping you move?"

"No," he said. "No. He is not."

"God will punish you terribly," she whispered.

He said, "God took everything from me but your charity. Will you take that away, too?"

"Please," she said, looking down at the photographs. "See how I beg you, Grant. Please leave. Do I have to take these hands and move you, myself?"

"Good night, Lucy."

"You disgust me, Grant. Go back to your woman. Tell her you disgust me."

He returned slowly through the darkness, feeling the deep despairing tremble of his body. He knew no one who might accept the burden of the bowl. Through all the years of loneliness, concealing himself from the memory and pity of others, he had completely lost touch. Now he could think of no other person but Ketteridge. How strange that matters would work out in this way.

He entered his lighted room. Ketteridge sat rigidly erect, studying the line of Indian pottery across the bookshelves.

Chalfel closed the door against the darkness on the other side.

Walking carefully to the davenport, he sat carefully down, feeling winter growing in him like a white plant.

His voice diffidently broke the silence. "Are you here visiting in Atlanta?"

"For a few days. On family business."

"Things work out so curiously," Chalfel said. "You plan. You make arrangements. But nothing ever goes the way you expect it. Tonight—when I went to the restaurant—it seemed I could sense a kind of inevitable flow, things coming together. Have you ever felt that?"

Ketteridge said, "I am not particularly intuitive."

"I felt it tonight," Chalfel told him, "only not knowing how it would work out. You never quite grasp the mechanism of how."

Ketteridge said, with faint mockery, "According to my great-aunt, that restaurant serves the only reliable food in Atlanta."

"Things dovetail," Chalfel said vaguely, feeling winter edge delicately into his chest. He rose. "I won't delay you longer. Let me show you . . ."

In the next room, by the bed, he knelt before a dark brown cedar chest, icy with polish, about the size of a small coffin. Hinges creaked as he thrust back the lid. Wadded masses of white tissue paper filled the interior.

"Some associated pieces came down with the bowl," he said. "A nicely preserved wine jug. The platter for the Passover lamb—but that's badly broken. A sauce bowl. All of them smoothed, baked clay. Da Vinci showed them using metal goblets, which is quite incorrect. Only the wealthy used metal."

Plunging both arms into the wadded tissue paper, he lifted out a foot-wide wooden box and placed it on the bed.

"You forget how impoverished they were. Itinerant preachers, after all, depending on charity. Use of the room at Jerusalem was a gift. The food was donated. Even the dishes were borrowed."

He removed the top of the box.

"In celebrating *Pesach,* the Passover, they used special dishes. These were always stored separately from dishes for everyday use. Likely why these few items survived to begin with."

Ketteridge, listening in astonishment, said, "I don't understand what you're telling me."

Chalfel said, "Oh! Excuse me. I was only sketching in the background."

Removing a layer of tissue paper, he lifted from the box a small bowl of pale, fired clay. It was no larger than two hands closely cupped together and perhaps two inches deep. The faintly yellowish sides, smoothly and simply molded, were circled by a pair of incised lines.

"This," Chalfel said, "is what I wanted to show you."

He turned it slowly in the light.

"This," he said, "is the Holy Grail."

Ketteridge's eyes moved from the bowl to Chalfel's face. His own face became infused with a curious expression of regret and pity.

"You can touch it," Chalfel said. "It isn't particularly fragile."

Ketteridge's fingers glided obediently down the pale yellow curve of the bowl.

Chalfel said, "How it got here to Georgia is a fascinating story, rather complicated. More gaps than story. What really happened I doubt we'll ever know. Didn't someone once say that history is a series of agreed-upon lies? My great-grandfather wrote down what he could find out. But honestly it isn't much. Roughly the story seems to be this: the dishes used for the Last Supper were carried from Jerusalem, probably with other household effects, about 70 A.D. That was about when Rome crushed the great Jewish insurrection. Refugees carried the Grail west along the African coast to Fez, a city in Idrisid. That's now Morocco. There the dishes remained for nearly a thousand years, handed through the generations. Not as divine artifacts, of course, but as vessels used by a prophet and therefore treasures. Around the fifteenth century repeated massacres of the Fez Jews drove them to Spain. The Grail was first carried to Seville—we know this for a fact—and later, into France. During the French Revolution, the Grail was moved again, this time across the Atlantic to New York City. During that voyage, its caretakers died. Their possessions ended up in a warehouse owned by my family. So we acquired them by default. No claimant ever appeared. Not that any serious effort was made to locate one. Eventually the boxes were opened. Packed in with the relics was a sealed roll of historical notes, rather fragmentary, mainly in Spanish. Also scraps of Latin scroll and an inventory list in Hebrew. All too fragile to handle now, I'm afraid. My great-great-grandfather, a notable scholar, eventually translated that formidable mixture of languages. Immediately he recognized the bowl as the Grail. Imagine his delight. The legendary thing in his hands, and his hands only.

"At that time, my branch of the family left New York. They settled on newly opened Indian lands in Georgia. Here's where the Grail has remained—through Indian War, Civil War, World War, Depression. Passed from son to son. Each generation continues the responsibility that began accidentally, centuries ago, in Jerusalem. Until now. Until me."

He paused, lifting his eyes from the floor, sharply observing Ketteridge's face.

Ketteridge asked, "Don't you have a son?"

Chalfel shook his head. "No. Myself only. The last."

"Then turn it over to a museum. The Smithsonian. The Louvre."

"I can't do that. I'm not free to do that. How many generations in two thousand years? One hundred? For nearly a hundred generations, the Grail has been a private responsibility."

"Long enough," Ketteridge said, looking at the bowl. "End it."

Chalfel said ruefully, "How can I flaunt the will of a hundred generations?"

Reaching out, Ketteridge took possession of the Grail, weighed it in his fingers, tested the smooth side with his thumb.

Chalfel bent forward, his breath shallow and his cold fingers locked together. As always the Grail filled him with unsettling emotion, of pleasure mixed unpleasantly with awe and dread. And, always he felt the terrible corrosion of responsibility for this wonderful thing.

He said, "For this simple piece of clay the Crusaders turned the Near East into bloody shambles."

"Maybe so," Ketteridge said.

He handed back the bowl and watched Chalfel lower it gently into the box.

"Quite a fancy story," Ketteridge said. "I wonder what the truth of it is."

One single pulse of blood burnt across Chalfel's face. In a stifled voice, he said, "I'm responsible for passing it on. I hoped I might pass it on to you."

Across the blond man's mouth grew a smile like the glint along the edge of a blade. "No, no," he said instantly. "Not to me."

"This is the Grail—the Messiah's cup."

"Is it? But you can't really know that, can you?"

Without warning, a terrible deep disturbance began in Chalfel, a huge coming that swelled and rose and lifted him, giddy and light, into an intolerably brilliant place.

He said forcefully, "One hundred generations, Tom."

Ketteridge shrugged. "One hundred generations can be flat wrong."

"You don't understand," Chalfel said urgently. "There's death in me. I have to do something with it now."

"Do whatever you want," Ketteridge told him. "Throw it against the wall. Step on the pieces."

He turned away and Chalfel, grown tall and fearfully powerful, swept the box from the bed and, with a feeling of intense surprise, drove it against Ketteridge's head.

A thick animal sound tore from Ketteridge's mouth. The box lid flew off, spewing tissue paper into the air. Ketteridge's legs collapsed. He tumbled sideways. His head struck the edge of the cedar chest with a single intense sound.

Past Chalfel's eyes fell the pale yellow blur of the Grail. As if watching from a far distance, he saw it bounce across Ketteridge's body and hop away over the carpet. It came spinning to a stop in the doorway.

Face down by the chest lay Ketteridge, legs jerking, fingers opening and closing.

In a soft voice, Chalfel whispered, "This is so unfortunate."

He looked down at Ketteridge's body and understood that it was not unfortunate. That it was right and desirable. He found in himself hatred for the blond man so pervading and elaborately structured that it did not seem possible his body could contain it all. He felt sheathed in black pearl. All these years the hatred hid in him, grew in him. He had never allowed himself to acknowledge these terrible depths. For no gentleman permitted himself the luxury of ungovernable emotions.

He should have known. The terrible failure of his introduction of Ketteridge to Atlanta society should have informed him at once. Even then, he had not understood what was clear to Ketteridge. As doubtless to others.

Hatred, hatred. Envy and hatred.

He lifted his head, a crushing weight, and strained his wet eyes to focus.

The Grail seemed entirely unharmed. Tentatively he stepped toward it. And discovered that he could not feel his legs. He looked down in confusion, saw nothing, and in that moment felt emptiness glide through his body, moving upward, extinguishing all sensation. He toppled backward onto the bed, head and shoulders against the pillow. His legs dangled over the side of the bed. One foot may have rested on Ketteridge's body.

He detected no pain. Fear, apprehension, or regret did not disturb him. Pale blue haze fell over his thoughts. In sleepy indifference, he sprawled on the bed, eyes turned to the Grail, an immeasurable distance across the beige rug.

He might have slept.

Quite suddenly, sunlight from the bedroom windows was angling across the bowl. Its pale yellow sides glowed so warmly that it seemed the clay had softened to ripeness, become saturated with rich juice.

In the bedroom doorway stood Lucina, looking down at the Grail. Curiosity and anger channeled the thick stuff of her face.

He felt dim resentment that she should trespass into his private area. Then equally faint amusement touched him. She had come to pack his possessions with her own hands and see him go.

So late, Lucina. So very much too late.

As he watched, her cumbersome body slowly bent, and the thick whiteness of her hand angled down through the sunlight to grip the bowl. With an effort she panted erect. Head thrown back, anger in her movement, she took a single challenging step into the bedroom.

Then her eyes touched his.

The outraged strength slipped from her face. Her mouth became loose, showing small teeth. Her eyes stared and darted and jerked down, inch by harsh inch, toward the floor and Ketteridge's body. Both hands gripped the Grail against the mass of her.

Taking tiny steps, she inched toward the bed, stood swaying and gasping, looking down at Chalfel.

He did not look at her. His attention was elsewhere. The bedroom walls, he observed, were gradually distorting, folding sluggishly in on themselves. As part of that creeping slow complex motion, the room itself seemed to be stretching out, slowly drifting away from him. He could see the movement clearly.

These engrossing changes were interrupted by the appearance of Lucina's face, huge above him.

She shouted, "Can you hear me? Are you dying?"

"Of course," he said patiently.

Behind her head, the bedroom ceiling flowed as smoothly as a thick white liquid.

"I'm going to help you pack."

"Give me the bowl, Lucina."

She held out the bowl. Fear and anger rutted her face. "Grant, get up now. Please."

With a great effort he received the bowl's familiar weight and smoothness into his hand. By an enormous effort he levered up his weightless body. With an even greater effort he willed the trembling column of his right arm to lift the Grail. Its sheer brute weight was appalling. Finally the exertion became intolerable. He thrust blindly. The Grail, weakly thrown, fell against the polished brown chest with a sharp, explosive noise.

Fragments chattered across the floor.

Chalfel fell back. Decidedly the room was sliding from him. Lucina's face slurred into blurred whiteness.

"Please, Grant!"

The intelligence that was all remaining of Chalfel looked into the whiteness. In a fragile voice, the voice of a ghost, he whispered:

"Step on the pieces."

Elvisland

—✠—

John Farris

I was wrapping up another long day when the crisis line in my office rang. I was tempted not to answer. Then I chided myself for having become a little lazy of late. Also, I have to admit, I was afraid it might be Oral Roberts again.

"God speaking," I said.

"It's Elvis, Lord."

"Oh, hello, Elvis. I was wondering if I'd hear from you. How long have you been out of Limbo?"

"Couple days. Uh, they gave me a week, but I, uh—"

"Don't know where to begin?" I prompted.

"That's it. I just, uh, can't seem to get started. It's bigger than I thought. But, Lord—" I didn't miss the note of desperation in his voice—"if I can't pull it off, it means I'll be stuck in Limbo forever. Never get to see Mama, or Daddy, again! What I'm tryin' to say is, Lord, I need your help real bad."

I should have been strict with him. If I meddled in committee decisions, there'd be no harmony in Heaven. And the half-angels who were in charge of Dispensations down there in Limbo were a prickly lot. I was surprised they'd let Elvis out. But the situation on earth was beginning to smell, even where I was.

"I suppose I could come down," I told him. "But no fireworks, Elvis. No hands-on miracles. You've got to find the answers yourself. There's a heavy debt against you in this jurisdiction."

"I know it. But Lord, I swear, I never meant to kill myself! It was an accident."

"We won't debate that now. Give me a few minutes to close up here."

"Thank you, Lord! I'm at—"

"I know where you are," I said. "What's the weather like?"

"Clear."

"Not for long," I said. *"Ciao,* Elvis."

I rang for one of my assistants.

"Taking a little trip, Apricot," I said. "Nothing too pressing, is there?"

"It's been quiet around here since the new Pope was elected."

"Hold all prayer petitions, then, until I—"

Apricot snapped her fingers. "Almost forgot. Billy Graham's opening at Wembley Stadium tonight, and he'll probably want a little something personal from you."

"Let Number Two deal with it. Give Billy a jolt of white light behind the eyes, turn his knees to jelly, the usual thing. Tell wardrobe I need something appropriate for the Mississippi delta on a hot June night, and, let's see, a '63 Cadillac convertible with wire wheel covers. Puce or heliotrope, I'm not fussy. Then get me a thunderstorm. The last time I descended from a clear blue sky, I started a cult in Chile that's lasted for 163 years."

"If I might ask, Lord—"

"I've got some business with Elvis."

"Elvis? Wow!"

"I'll tell him you said hello."

The sudden arrival of a thundercloud with flashes of lightning over Elvisland didn't do much to diminish the enthusiasm of the crowds along Elvis Presley Boulevard. Since I was driving top-down and wearing an ice cream suit with a a string tie, I moved the rain out over the Mississippi River.

Elvis was standing on the curb in front of one of the fringe souvenir shops on the Boulevard, the kind of shop that specializes in toenail clippings from his bathroom and scarves stained with his sweat, displayed in shatterproof glass cases like the Shroud of Turin. He was wearing a white leather suit of unborn pony hide, the tight-fitting jacket open to the waist, and purple boots with three inches of heel. He looked good—not more than thirty, in his prime—but his eyes were old, and frightened. Nobody paid any attention to him, because there were at least a dozen Elvis impersonators, in equally elaborate getups, on the sidewalk behind him, and probably a thousand more inside the six-story gates of Elvisland.

I sounded the musical horn twice—it played the first bars of "Love Me Tender"—before he looked my way. Traffic piled up behind the Cadillac. A cop started over from the other side of the street. I gestured to Elvis.

"I'm waitin' for somebody," he said.

"It's me," I said.

"Colonel," the cop said in my ear, "want to move on? Everybody's trying to get to Elvisland tonight."

"Why?" I asked, like a dumb tourist.

"Because this is the night it's *happening*. Two blocks down and hang a right, there's underground parking."

"Thank you, suh." Elvis slid into the seat beside me, staring at my face. The white goatee might have been too much.

"You two have a fun evening," the cop said, with a hint of a smirk, and gave the Cadillac a slap to move us on.

"Lord?" Elvis said, in a subdued voice.

I drove with one hand and slipped the dark glasses down the bridge of my nose. He blanched, and closed his own eyes, and trembled. Then he clasped his hands together and mumbled, "Lord, I humbly apologize for not knowin' you right away, but I thought you were that old guy who sold chicken."

"Let me get rid of this Cadillac, then we'll talk."

Elvis bit his lip and looked at the searchlights crisscrossing the sky, the souvenir shops and hotels chock-a-block for more than a mile. His music blared from loudspeakers—"You Ain't Nothin' But a Hound Dog" competing with "Blue Hawaii" and "Return to Sender." Traffic cops in orange vests kept the cars and tour buses moving toward the ultimate destination: Elvisland.

He put his face in his hands, unable to look anymore.

"I never meant for this to happen," he said. "I just wanted to cut a record for Mama's birthday. I swear that's all I was thinkin' about."

"You can't blame yourself because it got out of hand."

"But *why,* Lord? It's been fifteen years. Why can't they just let go?" He gestured hopelessly toward the crowds, the faces of Elvis impersonators strutting their borrowed stuff. "It's a blasphemy. It's like they think they can bring me back, bigger than life, just by wishin' it."

"*Demanding* it," I said. "And that's the big mistake. It's the wrong kind of power they're generating with their idolatry. Question is, son, what can you do to stop them?"

On a hill overlooking the boulevard the lights of Graceland were visible through huge oak and magnolia trees. The original estate, now dwarfed by an assemblage of amusements and Elvis-themed attractions as large as Disney World. Teenagers in shorts and sneakers wore rubber Elvis masks. Older people carried palm-sized portable TVs tuned to the Elvis cable network, in order not to miss a minute of one of his thirty movies or filmed concerts in endless reruns. Harmless obsessions, perhaps, but the marriage of obsession with delusion is not so harmless. Over Elvisland twin blimps floated lazily, displaying electronic messages. *Over the Top with Elvis!* And, *Tonight's the Night! Thirty Million for Elvis!*

We left the car and joined the crowd.

"How're Mama and Daddy?" Elvis asked me.

"Half-angels already. Vernon's learned woodworking and Gladys is completing her degree in Archival Science. They live in a nice little clapboard cottage Vernon built for them."

"Say what, Lord?"

"Surprised? You thought Heaven was a free vacation that goes on forever? Kind of loll around on fleecy pink clouds listening to spiritual music? The only thing that goes on forever, son, is the immortal soul. And the education of the soul is never-ending. Look around you. Human beings in all shapes and sizes. Everybody needs to be human from time to time, it's part of the educational process. But the soul drowns in flesh, all the hazards of desire that's part of the human condition. So the soul has to be fished out and dried off and shaped up, and that shaping-up takes place in what you call Heaven. Eternity. But Eternity is what you make of it. It's no place for the uncommitted, or—the unworthy. Not every soul makes it to Heaven, as we know."

There were tears on his cheeks. "Will I be there, Lord? Someday?"

"You know I can't answer that." People were stacked up forty-deep in front of the ticket windows and turnstiles. Two excited teenage girls with ponytails jostled against us.

"Do you think he'll *really* come tonight?"

"Don't you?"

"Oh, he *has* to! That's all there is to it, he has to!"

"Girls," Elvis said, looking at them with a profound sadness, "Don't you recognize me?"

They looked him up and down, speculatively. "Pretty good," one of the girls said. "Your hair's not long enough, though. Can you sing?"

"Elvis was *taller*," the other girl said scornfully. "My mother said so. And she went to *school* with Elvis."

They turned their backs on us. Elvis looked at me, helplessly.

"So now you know what you have to do," I said.

He grimaced. "My hair's not long enough. I'm not tall enough. I mean—I'm just not *good* enough for them anymore."

"Quite a dilemma, not being equal to your own legend. But you found that out a long time ago. Well, I don't think we have much time. Let's use the VIP gate."

"How do we get in?"

"With the gold lifetime Elvisland pass in your breast pocket."

He searched and came up with it, wonderingly. "How did you—?"

"That's not all," I said.

Elvis fished out another card. "What's this?"

"Your official entry in the finals of the Best-Ever Elvis Impersonator contest."

He didn't get it at first, then he nodded. "But even if I win, what does it mean? How will that put a stop to—" he looked up at the blimps circling overhead, aglow in hot blue shafts of light—"all this bull?"

"Your power is the truth; and the truth must overcome the power of the crowd's idolatry."

He looked around. "I could do it, once. I took all they gave me, just soaked it up and gave it back to them, and they loved me for it. They never knew me, but they loved me. Will they love me tonight? And if they do, what will I say to them?"

"Just tell them to go home, Elvis. And mean it. Then you can go home."

Inside the gates of Elvisland there were booths and another *Thirty Million for Elvis* sign. Thirty million petitioners. Elvis for President of the United States. They were getting the necessary signatures, but they didn't have the candidate. What they had was all the confidence in the world that tonight he would answer the call, the challenge, and appear before them. I could feel that kind of electricity in this crowd, a deeply communicated thrill that impressed me. And I'm not easily impressed.

Elvis was shaken, seemingly stricken dumb. I had to take him by the elbow and lead him backstage at the amphitheater, where ten thousand of his most fervent believers were gathered for the Best-Ever contest.

The stage manager took his entry card. "What's your name?"

"El—Elvis."

"Yeah, yeah, sure it is, but I mean your real name, bud."

Elvis looked at me.

"Joe," I said. "Humes." For the high school he'd attended.

"Okay, Joe Humes," the stage manager said, making a note of it on his clipboard. "You go on sixty-fourth, Joe."

"Why so late?" I asked him.

"Late? I just take 'em in the order they check in, and they been checking in since last night. Over there, stage right, the room with the green door. Where's your guitar?"

"I—I didn't bring one."

"You expect to win the Best-Ever contest, and you didn't bring no guitar? I'll bet you don't even play." He sighed. "Looks like a long night ahead. Next!"

We crossed to the green door, and Elvis opened it. In the dormitory-like room sixty-three other Elvises lounged, slept, fretted, gargled, thumbed their guitars, hummed to themselves. He shut the door, looking panic-stricken.

"I ain't goin' in there, Lord. I thought Limbo was bad, but that—that's purgatory."

"Let's walk around," I said. "Have a little confidence."

There was a walled garden behind the amphitheater. We had it to ourselves. The carnival sounds of roller-coaster and carousel were muted by the high walls. Elvis slumped on a stone bench by a fountain, hands knotted between his knees. The Best-Ever contest got under way. The crowd was not in a good mood. They booed several of the early contestants off the stage. Elvis breathed heavily through his mouth. His color wasn't good.

"I only wanted to make a record for Mama," he said, in a sad, lost voice.

"Make her proud of you tonight, Elvis."

It was all I had to offer by way of encouragement, but he responded. Little by little, as he thought of his beloved Gladys, heart and soul of his inspiration and worldly success, Elvis's courage came back. His determination. The killer instinct that had made him one of a kind on stage. The boos from the amphitheater for failed impersonators reverberated from the walls of the garden like sonic booms. His chin came up. He began to pace.

"We want Elvis!" they chanted. "We want Elvis!" And then, the boos for the next hapless entrant, the roars of derision. It was no longer a crowd, it was a mob feasting on the hapless, but hungering for more. Hungering for the event they inspired each other to believe was imminent, the return of Elvis Presley.

I had kept count of the entries, and at last it was time.

"Stay with me, Lord," he said, and then he walked out onto one of the biggest stages he'd ever seen and faced them. They were bored and noisy. But somehow he wasn't like the others, as he stood near the apron of the stage with his head slightly bowed, already perspiring, waiting, then lifting his eyes and staring, staring them into an uneasy, expectant silence.

He sang, a cappella, "Battle Hymn of the Republic." And the silence continued. He had their full attention.

Elvis was inspired. I'd never heard him in better voice. He

dominated the stage with power and sincerity. I saw tears in the audience. I thought, *He's got them. And now he can talk to them.* They'd waited for his return all these years. Their faith had built a billion-dollar-a-year business where he used to ride motorcycles in a pasture. And I wondered. Faith was a tricky proposition. A powder keg, really. There was a good reason why I hadn't sent Jesus back, although he'd been raring to go for centuries.

They didn't applaud when Elvis finished. Not that they were sitting on their hands out of disdain; we didn't hear any boos either. They were curious, perhaps a little in awe of him.

"Friends, I'm Elvis Presley. And I have to talk to you tonight."

Another few moments of silence. And then it went bad. A few titters, a catcall. "Sing!" somebody demanded.

"I can't. I can't sing anymore. Don't you see, that's over with. Me, I'm—not what I used to be. After I died—"

You could feel their animosity rolling toward that lone and lonely figure on stage. It was like a tidal wave. He had said the wrong thing. They weren't here to be reminded. They were here to propagate a miracle.

"Get off!"

They began to stamp their feet and cheer. The amphitheater shook with the force of their authority. They were one mind, one emotion. Delusion collided with truth and swept truth under, as it always does.

"Elvis! Elvis! Elvis! Elvis!"

Elvis withered in this blast. And then the spotlight swept away from him and focused on the sky above the cantilevered stage roof.

"Elvis!" they screamed. "Now! Elvis! Now!"

And the screaming grew louder as their wish was fulfilled.

On stage Elvis turned and looked up. Behind him, rising slowly into the black sky, was a monstrous head, a grinning replica of himself. Then the lean torso, the twitching legs. It looked like an oil-on-velvet painting, but, somehow, it lived. This Elvis had a guitar. This Elvis stood a hundred feet tall, and sang "You Ain't Nothing But a Hound Dog." And they loved it.

Elvis slumped beside me in the wings. He was sobbing. He

couldn't take his eyes off the monster that dominated Elvisland with its swagger and deafening voice.

"What *is* that thing? It ain't flesh and blood!"

"Doesn't need to be," I said. I was beginning to feel annoyed. "Just another version of the golden calf. If you ask me—and I'm the final judge in these matters—it's time for some old-style wrath and vengeance."

Elvis looked terrified. "No, Lord!" he pleaded. "Don't blame them. Blame me! I started it all! Cast me into a fiery pit if that's what it takes to spare their souls!"

"Do you really care about them? They don't do you honor." Even now the frenzied idolatry of the crowd was pumping more life into Elvisman, heightening the ghastly red of its plump lips, the coppery sheen of its gold-draped chest. I could imagine it being elected president in another fortnight, boosted into political orbit by all those write-in votes.

"Lord, get rid of it!" Elvis moaned. "I can't stand another second of this! Hell's got to be better. At least I'll sleep nights."

"Maybe," I said, "there's another way."

He stared at me, and wiped mascara-tinted tears from beneath one eye.

"You mean—I might not have to go to Hell to atone for this sacrilege?"

"No reason for you to go to Hell, if you never left Heaven."

"Never left—?" I could see he didn't get it.

"Don't turn around and look," I said. "Just listen."

Elvis steeled himself, as if he was afraid I was going to drop a load of bricks on his head. Then he shook his shoulders and pressed a hand against an ear. "I must be going deaf."

"You're not. You can hear me, can't you?"

"But—but the crowd—and—I don't hear that godawful singing."

"What do you hear?"

He drew a quick breath. His eyes squeezed shut. A last tear fell. "Crickets."

"What else?"

"Why—I—I think I hear Mama callin' me!" He trembled, and smiled. "Yeah. It *is* her!"

"Okay, Elvis. Now you can open your eyes."

The sound of crickets, and frogs in a nearby pond, were louder. He looked around. Twice. He nearly fell down when he realized that he was standing stark naked in a cow pasture. I was a little peeved at myself. But it was a spur-of-the-moment job, and sometimes you skimp on the details.

"What—happened?" he said. "Where did—where's everybody gone to?"

"What do you care? Time to get along, Elvis. Your mother's waiting on you, son."

He smiled incredulously, then looked up at the lights of Graceland on the hill. "She is?" he said. He started off through the high grass, giddy with excitement.

"Wrong way," I said. And he disappeared in front of me, with a small pop of light not much brighter than a firefly's butt. I thought I heard him say "ouch!" It probably stung a little.

I didn't go back to the office right away. If Death can take a holiday, so can the Chief. I'd been fond of that puce Cadillac. I made another out of a Chef Boyardee can I found by the side of the road and drove east on 78 out of Memphis, heading toward Tupelo. I don't like driving at night with all the eighteen-wheelers they have on the road these days, so in a couple of minutes the sun came up. I had the top down. I kept the morning temperature at a pleasant seventy-two degrees. Every truck on the highway was pulled off to the side with mechanical problems. It was a fine day. Quite a while since I had had the opportunity of looking over what I'd wrought when I had that burst of creative energy way back when. For the most part I was satisfied, but I thought that if I was going to do it again, next time I'd leave out kudzu.

I rolled into Tupelo about eleven o'clock, then drove slowly up one residential street and down another until I saw him on the stoop of a white frame house set well back from the street and shaded by some oversized magnolias. He was drinking a lemonade and gossiping with the lady of the house: middle-aged and dumpy in a flowery faded dress; but she could still appreciate a fine-looking young man with dark wavy hair. I pulled over to the curb and waited until he came whistling down the walk to resume his route.

"Hey, there," I said.

He stopped and smiled, shifting his shoulders a little to ease the weight of his mailbag.

"Yes, sir?"

"You remind me of somebody I used to know. Wouldn't be any kin to the Presleys hereabout?"

"Well, yes, sir, I would. You must be thinking of my daddy Vernon."

"That don't beat all! I'm not keeping you from your appointed rounds, am I?"

"Oh, that's okay, mail's light today. Tuesday I got to hustle a little faster, it's all them magazines and bulk-rate catalogs." He held out his hand. "I'm Jesse Garon Presley."

"Oh. Could've swore you was that other one, what's-his-name?"

He looked puzzled. "I don't have a brother. Well, I *did* have. Twin brother. He died at birth. Mama like to never got over it. She still talks about him. Little Elvis Aron. That was the name she had picked out for him."

"Oh, I see. Reckon I made a mistake. Say, how do you like working for the post office?"

"Can't complain. Good hours, all the benefits. It's important to have those benefits."

"Married?"

"Fixin' to be." He smiled again. "Well, reckon I'd better get on."

"Surely. Oh, by the way—with your looks, did you ever entertain the notion of getting into show business?"

"Shoot! Not me. I can't act, and I can't sing. Cut a record once for Mama's birthday—"

"You did?"

"I stunk out loud. Even Mama couldn't stand to listen to it more than once."

He waved to me and drove his red white and blue post office Jeep to the next stop. I heard him whistling again.

Maybe he couldn't sing, but he was a good whistler. And he seemed like a real happy guy.

When I got back to the office, Apricot was pouting, and not because she was overworked.

"Those are from you-know-who," she said, pointing to a mass of flowers on one side of my desk.

"Uh-huh." I read the attached thank-you note from Elvis. Another happy guy these days.

Apricot said, "I suppose you did what you had to do, but—"

"We aren't going to talk about it."

"The effect it had on the Beatles and the Rolling Stones! Not to mention—"

"Apricot!"

"My favorite song was—and always will be—'Loving You.' But it just isn't the same golden oldie. I mean, *Fabian?*"

"Can't you find something for me to do other than meddle in the music business?" It was a mild rebuke. After all, I thought, she did have a point.

To Leave if You Can

―――――――――― ✠ ――――――――――

Nancy Holder

Ay, mi corazón. Oh, my heart, my overflowing heart.

She heard him now:

"Gabriela? Gabi?" Her eyes burned, now with tears; back then, with exhaustion, and the stench of the backed-up toilets and the smoke of cooking oil.

"Are you asleep?" His voice was soft and deep. If it had been one of her brothers, she would have kept her eyes closed and snuggled under the covers. But for her father, her dear *papacito,* she opened them and smiled.

He towered over her in his plaid shirt and ragged jeans. The light bulb hung behind his head and his black hair shimmered like a halo of holy light. Warmth ran through her soul. Her *papa.* Her eyes shifted to the picture of Jesus on the bare wood wall. Same eyes, same sad smile, pulling back their outer selves to reveal their hearts. They could be brothers.

"*Ay,* I woke you," he said gently. The only daughter, she alone had any privacy; the tiny alcove she slept in was supposed to be a storage area. Her seven brothers slept in rows around the corner, some on the bed, others on the floor. They took turns.

Gabriela shook her head. "No, Papi, I was waiting for you to come home." She raised herself on her elbow. "You're so late."

The door pushed open. Gabriela's mother stood on the threshold, a shawl over her nightgown. One thick black braid trailed over her shoulder and curved over her huge belly. It was almost cold enough to see her breath.

"Laurio?" she said tensely. She took a step toward him and put her hand on his arm.

He turned to his wife and patted her hand. "It's okay, Elena. *Está bien.*"

They turned away as one being, her mother with her big belly, her father limping from the pain in his thigh that never went away. He had been cursed with it all his life, and though Gabriela's mother insisted that a doctor could cure it, there was no money. Of course not: it was 1958, and they were migrant farm workers.

Her father must be very tired; he had forgotten to turn off the light. She was to cold to get out of bed and do it herself, so she put her slender brown arm over her eyes.

Her stomach growled. They didn't have enough food for the eight children her mother had already had. They had no medicine for the sick little ones. Nobody had ever been to school.

But her father promised better days. He spoke often how they would have money, and medical treatment, and the growers would listen to them because they would raise one strong voice together.

"We are men, not animals," he would often say, "no matter that they treat us worse than dogs."

During the war, the United States had welcomed laborers from the south; there was no one else left to pick the grapes and lettuce. But then the war ended, and all the braceros were supposed to go home so poor Americans could work in the fields. But the Méxicanos were cheaper, bidding themselves down to starvation levels. The growers cut the hoe handles short—they looked like serving spoons—and said that only Mexicans would stoop so low for a dollar. And the Méxicanos answered, only a grower would stoop so low to save one.

"Papi," Gabriela whispered, and she was sure she felt his hand on her forehead still, and saw his smile through the dark, cold night.

And now, ten years later:

He was dead. Staring straight ahead as the tears welled, Gabriela put the receiver in the cradle. Numbness tingled through her; she stood naked in the spacious living room of her apartment.

Jack, her boyfriend, padded in. "Gabriela?" he asked, yawning. "Honey?"

Gabriela? Gabi?

"The bastard," Gabriela shouted. "I knew he'd find a way to make me go back!"

And then:

"Gabi? Gabriela?"

On the back porch of this week's hovel, Gabriela cradled her new baby brother in her arms. Pedro was his name. All he did was cry. Gabriela's mother was too sick to nurse him; she looked like an ancient crone, lying in her bed with her rosary. The sight of her frightened Gabriela, all the more so because José Luis Maldonaldo was hanging around a lot, and his jeans were tight and his smile was almost more beautiful than Gabriela's father's. It would be incredibly simple to marry him, and then they would begin a family of hungry, dirty children who lived in squalor, and who were spat upon by the *gringo* children.

"Gabi, look!" It was her father, still black-haired and handsome, and he carried a stack of magazines.

Gabriela, her arms aching, smiled up at him and said, "*Sí, Papi?*"

"*Mira, mira.* Look." He plopped down beside her and flicked open the first one.

A brightly colored picture of a man on horseback covered two pages. He wore splendid armor; he was a knight. In his iron fist, a banner with the heart of Jesus and a cross upon it unfurled in a fierce wind.

Gabriela stared at the letters below the picture. Her arms were so tired she was afraid she would drop Pedrito. *Ay,* to read those little squiggles! If you could do that, you could do anything.

"It's a contest, Gabi," he said. "We have to find the Holy Grail." He turned the pages.

"What?"

"These magazines, they're for kids." He shook his head and picked up the next one. "Every week, they print a story about the Knights of the Round Table. And in one of the pictures, they hide a little cup. You know, like the priest has for communion?" He touched Pedro's ruby face. "*Pobrecito.* Don't cry. Is he hungry, Gabi?"

"I don't know. Probably," she snapped, then caught herself. God forbid that she should add to her father's worries. "I think he just likes to cry." Shifting Pedro to her shoulder, she patted his bony back. "So in one of these magazines there's a picture of a communion cup?"

He picked up another one. "They come out every week. We don't have all of them yet. The son of El Flaco was throwing them out. I grabbed 'em." His eyes narrowed boyishly. El Flaco was the nickname of the man who owned the vineyard. "He's playing, too."

"Then it must not be in them," she said, vaguely disappointed, but not really surprised. Didn't things go like this, for Méxicanos? A flare of hope, and then the other shoe dropped, as they said.

Her father shrugged. "Who knows? He's not very observant, that little blond boy. Neither is his father." There was a strange note of satisfaction in his voice. Gabriela slid a glance at him. The crown of his head dipped toward her as he searched another magazine. She thought for a moment of raising her hand to bless him; Papi, oh, Holy Father, why must we suffer so?

"Do you know these stories?" he asked, raising his head. "Arturo, of England, and the knights?"

"How would I know such stories?" she retorted.

"*Ay,* Gabi. *Ay, hijita,* my little daughter." He pulled Pedro out of her arms and laid the baby down on a worn, stained blanket. It was so hard to keep things clean when the growers never fixed the plumbing.

He took Gabriela's hands in his own and rubbed her knuckles. "Gabi, it's not easy to live in the grape. I thought it would be better by now, but not all of us are like King Arthur. Some of us are like Don Quixote." His face was bitter.

Tears filled her throat. "Papa, I want to live like a *gringa,*" she burst out. "I want to have clothes, and go to the movies. I want to . . . to escape! We live like animals. You say we aren't, but that's how we live. Like animals!"

He swallowed very hard and pulled her against his chest. She heard his heart, his proud, untiring heart. He shifted his weight and straightened his limp leg. "I beg your pardon, beautiful woman," he murmured. "I beg your pardon."

Now, at his grave in the hard earth beside Gabriela's mother: Never.

Never would she forgive him.

Gabriela and five of her brothers, and their wives and children, and the many, many friends of Laurio Sanchez, stood in the cemetery of San Alonso, a small town in the San Joaquin valley, where her father had settled down after he could no longer work. The earth was hard as tarmac; the hazel sun hit mercilessly between her shoulders. On the casket, the flowers were shriveling.

People filed by, dropping roses onto the other dying blossoms. They shook hands with the family members, including Gabriela. She knew few of them, and she ignored their curious glances as she put on her sunglasses. She had been away ten years, and in that time she had learned to read, graduated from college, and now she made more in a day as a marketing assistant at a movie company than her father had made in a month.

After the crowds headed toward their noisy trucks and broken-down cars, her older brother, Roberto, took her hand and said, "He asked me to give you something."

"I want nothing from him."

She pulled away and walked toward her shiny white Volkswagen bug decorated with daisies. People had gathered around it, gawking, and she was ashamed, both of them, and of herself.

Whirling around, she shouted, "Nothing!"

In the distance, the thunder of horse hooves.

Back then, seventeen-year-old Gabriela lay on her back and watched for falling stars as her father said, "And Sir Galahad rode out to find the cup. There was a dragon, Gabi, longer than this field; its back was covered with spines that looked like grape vines. Its breath was as hot as the air tonight."

Perspiration trickled down her forehead and pooled in the hollow of her throat. The earth smelled dark and holy; back in the darkness, their bungalow reeked of garbage and shit. The women were calling and talking to each other, in the sing-song José Jimenez accent that marked them as low-class. Pots and pans banged and clattered; babies cried. Gabriela closed her eyes.

And saw her father on horseback, fighting the fierce dragon with the Grail on his shield. His earth-colored eyes, the halo of virtue a bright comet around his helmet.

How did he manage to get the magazines every week? He wouldn't tell her. Two months later, they were still playing the contest. She didn't know what they would do if they found the Grail first. The prize was a trip to Washington, D.C. Surely once the magazine people discovered Mexican farmworkers had won, they would take the prize away?

"And the dragon rose up into the air, high as an airplane. He dwarfed Sir Galahad. . . ."

She saw it all so clearly. After the sun went down, they would steal away together to stare at the pages, searching for the cup. And he would imagine what the pictures were about, and for hours, just the two of them, they were in a place called Inglaterra—England— and there were no pesticide rashes, no drunk and lonely old men, weeping for México; no hungry children. Instead, there were ladies in fine clothes, and castles, and men who won the day for justice.

"And then Sir Galahad met the Fisher King." He paused, "Gabi, are you listening?"

"*Sí, Papi.*" She was just so very tired. Now that Pedrito was bigger, she was back in the fields. Her hands stung from dozens of scratches; the small of her back throbbed. Her legs quivered. She was dirty, and wanted a shower. But as usual, there was no running water.

"His realm was a wasteland."

"Like this," Gabriela broke in, and began to cry silent tears. She turned her head, in case they sparkled in the moonlight.

"*Sí,*" her father said, momentarily silent as well. Then he said, "But Galahad freed the land, Gabriela. Galahad took over for the Fisher King. He was young, and strong. The Fisher King was old, and he could no longer care for his kingdom. He kept the holy relics of the Grail safe for the new king. All he wanted was a peaceful death, knowing the . . . the family was safe. He . . ."

She sat up and looked at him. "Papi, what are you saying? Are you saying that you're dying?"

Tears ran down her father's face. "I have made hard choices in my life, daughter. I have fought, and I haven't won."

"Fought?"

"Let's go back." He held out his hand. She got up first and helped him to his feet. These days his thigh hurt him more than ever; he could barely work. She flushed with fear, anger, shame. They lived on the land, in the grape.

In the wasteland.

They walked toward their shack. Her father took a deep breath and turned to her. He put his hands on her shoulders.

"Gabi, I—I must tell you something." Those sad, searching eyes. The moon beamed down on his head. She waited.

"*Ay, no.*" He turned away.

"Papi?"

"Come."

But Gabriela knew this was a moment that, once gone, would never return. He wanted to tell her something that would change everything. Fear wrapped itself around her heart, but she held firm.

"Papi."

And then it spilled out in a rush. As he spoke, he fell to his knees:

In Texas, he had been a schoolteacher. He was an educated man. He could read and write. He did not have to be here. None of them did. In the filth, and the poverty; he had exiled himself here; and imprisoned his family in ignorance and want. . . .

"Why? Why?" she demanded, sobbing.

"I thought I could save them." He waved at the fields, at the houses, in the darkness. "I was too proud, *hija*. I thought if we could organize—"

"What have you done to me! What have you done!" She leaped on him and hit him with her fists—his face, his shoulders, his chest. He made no move to protect himself. "*Bastardo!*"

"Please, Gabi, *por favor, por favor.*" Both of them were sobbing. "My daughter . . ."

She rose and kicked his sore thigh. With a cry, he doubled up, holding his leg. "No! I'm not your daughter!"

She ran to the house and gathered her pitiful possessions—two skirts, some second-hand patent leather shoes, her lipstick and earrings.

To her mother, lying in bed, she said, "Did you know we didn't have to be pigs?"

Her mother's eyes widened. She blinked hard. "There's money behind the statue of the Virgin," she whispered, gesturing to the plaster figure on top of an apple crate. "Run, Gabi! Run!"

" 'Berto, there is nothing of his that I want," Gabriela said now, in 1968, as her oldest brother caught up to her and put his hand on the door of the Volkswagen. Roberto was very handsome. He was dressed in good slacks and a sports jacket and tie, though all were out of date.

"Come back to the house. There's a reception. Please. For the memory of our mother, then, if not for his."

Gabriela hesitated. "She knew. All those years."

"The grape strike is working. The growers are begging for contracts from us." Roberto gestured toward the hard earth. "Papa dreamed of a farmworkers' union, but he didn't know how to gather the people together. Do you know they shot him?"

The wound in her father's thigh. She had figured that out long ago.

"'He had no right. Mama died because of his stupidity. And Nando and Pedro too." Little Pedro, her favorite, and Fernando, who could have been saved. Roberto had written her about their deaths.

"They revere his name in the movement. He sacrificed everything." Roberto touched her cheek. "Yes, including us."

"And that makes him a saint?"

"Come back to the house, *niña*. For me, then."

* * *

And now, they stood shoulder to shoulder in the two-room bungalow. A bare light hung from the rafter. The meager furnishings had been pushed to one side to make a place for the table sagging with food, and the guests. Gabriela supposed she should play hostess, but Amalia was bustling about, red-eyed and grim. Perhaps her father had taken Amalia to his heart to fill the space she, Gabriela, had vacated.

"*Venga.* Come here," Roberto whispered, drawing her into the smaller of the rooms, where a table and chairs took up the entire area.

Piled on the table was a stack of magazines.

"He saved them. He read them to his grandchildren." Roberto touched Gabriela's hair. "He found the Grail just after you left."

"And did he go to Washington?" she asked harshly, unwilling to look at him, or the magazines, concentrating instead on the plaster statue of the Virgin, where her mother had hidden their savings.

"No, but I'm going next month to testify before a Senate hearing," Roberto replied. "*Ay,* Gabi, is your heart so icy? Can't you forgive him?"

"Roberto, don't you remember?"

"He waited for you. He told me to tell you something if he died before you came back."

She took a breath and held it, raising her chin. "I don't want to hear it."

"That only Galahad could give the Fisher King a peaceful death. And then the land would become fruitful."

Her throat caught. She turned away from him and said, "That means nothing to me."

Roberto sighed. He bent down and kissed her forehead. Then he left the room and shut the door behind himself.

For a moment, she was seventeen, and it was very late; and her Papi was tiptoeing into the room. . . .

Ay, I woke you.

Moving stiffly, she sat in the chair and slumped forward, burying her head in her hands. It was hot and she was tired. Jack had wanted to come; she told him no. He said, "I can't ever get close to you. I mean really close." He wasn't the first man to say that to her.

She dropped her hands onto the table, on top of one of the magazines. She stared at the drawing on the cover: a big pink elephant, dancing with a dark-skinned boy. She remembered that picture; she had been washing clothes—quickly, in case the water ran out—and her back had ached. Her fingers had been bleeding.

"*Mira,* Gabi," her father had said, pulling the soapy clothes out of her hands and sitting her down on a low stone wall. "Maybe today we'll find it, eh?"

They had not, but he had told her the story of Lancelot and Guinevere. So romantic. But she had decided then and there not to marry José Luis.

Now Gabriela picked up another magazine. Aladdin's lamp gleamed back at her. She opened the magazine.

Ay, there was the castle, Camelot, with the banners and pennants flying. They had looked and looked. . . .

He had smelled of grapes and dirt, and her heart had filled with such love for him; and a childish exaltation as they searched for the Grail. They hadn't found it that day, but he had told her of the Lady in the Lake, and she had dreamed that night of pure, running water, as much as you wanted, with no stink and no pesticides.

And this one, with the cat on the cover: the story of Merlin, *brujo* of the caves and wind. And her thoughts had turned to a fine home, with real furniture and drapes all the same color.

And this one: a silly story about a giant boar, and Arthur's attempts to hunt it. "Like me and the growers," her father had said, rubbing his leg.

And this one, and this. The memories washed over her: Papi and she, dreaming; Papi, her Papi. . . .

And then, in a plastic bag at the bottom of the pile, an issue she had never seen.

Gabriela jerked her hands away. In the next room, someone was crying. A child asked shrilly, "Will Grandpa come home soon?"

Pipes shook as someone flushed a toilet.

And in the distance, horse hooves pounded the hard earth.

Gabriela pulled out the magazine. It was emblazoned with a king dressed in robes and a heavy gold crown. Arthur.

For a full minute, she stared at the king. Her heart galloped; her lips trembled. She opened the magazine and thumbed through it slowly. The pages were completely unfamiliar. Unconsciously she scanned the various articles and stories, the text once so arcane and unavailable, now a feat she took for granted.

The trumpet peal of a whinnying horse.

She raised her head. In the back of her mind, she had been waiting for the rider of the horse to show up at the reception. When there was no further sound, she bent her head.

The Grail contest story was the tale of Galahad and the Fisher King. Galahad was the only knight who could sit in the Siege Perilous, the Dangerous Chair. None could take his place.

"Papi," Gabriela whispered, and the tears burst out of her. She covered her face with her hands and let her heart break. She rocked back and forth, back and forth, with no one to comfort her. No memory of him to sustain her.

They had never seen this issue together. There was nothing to remember, so much to regret.

"*Ay,* my little one, did I wake you?"

Gabriela bolted upright.

Her father stood before her, clad in dazzling armor that gleamed so brightly she could barely look at him. The banner he held in his left gauntlet rippled in an unseen breeze, so that the eagle on it waved its squared-off wings. Around his helmet, a halo glowed.

"Papi?" She blinked rapidly at her tears. "Papi?"

"*Estoy aquí, mi amorcita.*" I'm here, my little love. The eagle on his banner was the symbol of the new farmworkers' union, Cesar Chavez's group. Roberto's group. She had seen it many times at the store, when people stood outside and begged other people to boycott, because there was non-union produce inside. She had never crossed the line.

But it was all that she had done.

He held out a hand. She hesitated. He stretched it out further, looking at her with his eyes of Jesus.

"*Por favor,* beautiful woman," he said gently.

His fingers were warm and solid, and smelled of dirt and grapes.

And he was her Papi again, in his plaid shirt and ragged jeans. A bow-backed, bony horse appeared beside him.

He mounted the horse and held his arms open. Gabriela found herself seated behind him, her hands clasped over his chest. She could hear his heart.

Ay, mi corazón.

"*Venga,* Rocinante," he said to the horse. It was the name of the mount of Don Quixote.

The creature rose into the air and cantered over the clouds. Gabriela and her father soared over green vineyards and scented orange groves, and rows and rows of lettuce. *Ay mi corazón,* my overflowing heart. They did this, God and the Virgin and the bow-backed Méxicanos; they made this into holy sustenance, they made this into life for the world.

The old horse dipped and pranced atop cool breezes and sparkling rivers and streams. Tanned, healthy children wearing shoes carried schoolbooks. From the doors of clean, new houses, mothers and fathers stood together, smiling, the sacred earth on their hands, in their blood.

"You see, Gabi? You see?"

"It's all wishes," Gabi said, her hands tight around him. His heart pounded against her palm. "All dreams."

"*Ay,* Gabi. God loves His dreamers best."

They said nothing more to each other. The horse flew back into the little room, and Gabriela's father helped her dismount.

"And I love *my* dreamer best," he said, looking down on her from the saddle.

On the table, the pages of the magazine flipped open. The picture of the Grail, hidden inside the cloak of Galahad, glittered like a diamond.

"Gabi, take the cup from me, *hijita.* Bless me. Forgive me."

"No! this is not my fight!" she cried. "You . . ."

"It is your fight. And *you* were *my* fight. I see that now." His smile made his face radiant. "And I have won, and made the wasteland rich."

"Rich? Nothing is different!"

"You are."

"Papi."

"You are, for your anger at me, Gabi. Because of that, you took me with you on your quest. You took my heart on your shield, and I knew you would return with it."

He made as if to stroke her cheek. "You are my best harvest, *mi amorcita*." The soft touch of his calloused fingers moved across her forehead. "Stay angry, *sí*, Gabi. But at the ones who really took it all away from you. From us."

She backed away. "You would like that I spend my life as you did, fighting for a hopeless cause?"

"It will be enough that we have fought, you and I. That we dreamed."

Though he remained some distance from her, the pressure of his hand weighted the crown of her head. Blessing her, forgiving her.

She shook her head. "No, *mi padre,* it won't be enough. It never was."

His voice was a whisper, an echo. "It was. It was, my Gala-had."

Then he was gone. She stared at the space where he had been. Her body shook from her feet to her soul.

The things he had shown her . . .

. . . could never be. Not for the Méxicanos, the Pedritos and Nandos and Mamas of this world. Better to escape the service of the earth, one by one, like those who snuck across the border and fled through the lines of cars and trucks that on occasion smashed the ones who ran too slowly.

Yes, better.

With trembling hands, she picked up the magazine with King Arthur on the cover. The room was small and hot, but it smelled of grapes and dirt; and the heat was the heat of her childhood. She could read every page if she wanted; there were a million things she could do. And why?

Gabriela swallowed. Her gaze traveled to the statue of the Virgin, who stood on top of a globe with her hands outspread in benediction. Blessed be the fruit . . .

The grapes, and the oranges, and the children.

The Grails Project:
Notes and Acknowledgments

———————— ✠ ————————

We each have the power to choose the form of the Grail we seek. Some forms are physical and some are spiritual. Some are literal and some are symbolic. Some are objects which bring the possessor great power, while others are those that bring the seeker great peace.

Grails: Visitations of the Night is the second of two volumes which Ed Kramer, Marty Greenberg, and I have edited about the Grail. (The first was *Grails: Quests of the Dawn.*) The contents for both were selected concurrently and planned as a single project. We found there were many more interesting stories than we had room to publish in one book, and thus the decision to expand the project into a two-volume set.

Containing over 300,000 words, this is perhaps the largest original anthology project to have been edited in one single process—if more than three years of work can be described as a single process. Nearly all of the stories were selected during the middle months of 1992 while we were preparing the Unnameable Press edition of this project. That one-volume hardcover, *Grails: Quests, Visitations and Other Occurrences,* contains about two-thirds of the stories you'll find in the completed project. There is a little, but not much, difference in the text of the stories from those you have read here. The primary reason you might find the shorter version of *Grails* of interest is that it is an absolutely gorgeous piece of bookcrafting, including a dust wrapper with cover art by Robert Gould. (It's also a bit more expensive.) For those of you who might wish to find a copy, your local bookstore can probably order it, or you can obtain the book via Ed Kramer at Box 148, Clarkston, GA 30021–0148.

I've been very, very fortunate to have had good publishers who care about the art of their craft. This trade paper edition you hold is a lovely piece of bookmaking in its own right. My particular thanks to Christopher Schelling and Greg Wilkin at Dutton Signet, who selected Tom Canty as the cover artist for this two-volume edition. Lots of authors go through a career without having their works illustrated by artists of the quality and stature of Tom Canty and Robert Gould.

We were also fortunate to have a great many outstanding authors participate in the *Grails* project. Andre Norton is the most senior, with a career that now spans seven decades. Connie Hirsch is the project's newest author—the story here is Connie's first professional sale. Lawrence Schimel is the youngest *Grails* author. He recently achieved his goal of making his twenty-first professional sale before his twenty-first birthday. Nearly half of the authors represented in these two volumes have won one or more major literary awards, and just about everyone has received some sort of award nomination. On behalf of Ed and Marty, our thanks to our contributors for helping to make this project a success.

On a much sadder note, Fritz Leiber and Robert Sampson died within weeks of each other, just before the publication of the hardcover late in 1992. Margo Skinner, Fritz's widow, passed away a few months after Fritz. Bob Sampson was a particularly close friend, and I knew Fritz and Margo from conventions. Ed, Marty, and I had already decided to dedicate this project to Fritz, about a year before he died. If I may exercise an editor's prerogative, I'd like to add a corollary dedication of this edition to Bob Sampson and Margo Skinner. May each of your rests be peaceful, and may your stories long be read.

And may each of you find your Grail, in whatever form you seek it.

—Richard Gilliam
Green Bay, Wisconsin